Knife Edge

Also by Simon Mayo

Mad Blood Stirring

Fiction for younger readers

Blame
Itchcraft
Itch Rocks
Itch

Knife Edge

Simon Mayo

BLACK SWAN

TRANSWORLD PUBLISHERS
Penguin Random House, One Embassy Gardens,
8 Viaduct Gardens, London SW11 7BW
www.penguin.co.uk

Transworld is part of the Penguin Random House group of companies
whose addresses can be found at global.penguinrandomhouse.com

First published in Great Britain in 2020 by Doubleday
an imprint of Transworld Publishers
Black Swan edition published 2021

A CIP catalogue record for this book
is available from the British Library.

ISBN
9781784164744

Typeset in Palatino LT Std by Jouve (UK), Milton Keynes.
Printed and bound in Great Britain by Clays Ltd, Elcograf S.p.A.

The authorized representative in the EEA is Penguin Random House Ireland,
Morrison Chambers, 32 Nassau Street, Dublin D02 YH68.

Dedicated to the memory of
Sophie Christopher (1991–2019)

A note on the text

The person who is 'slot' or 'in-slot' on the news editing desk receives all the incoming news from correspondents around the world, 'tastes' it to see if it's up to scratch, and hands each article to a sub-editor. They are also in charge of 'snapping' – sending out high-speed news flashes.

1

Tuesday, 22 May

MARY LAWSON WAS the first to die. Leaving Euston station shortly before 6.45 a.m, she made straight for her favourite breakfast stall. A sprawling market of food stands had blossomed outside the main entrance, the hiss and clatter of espresso machines fighting the traffic and the telephone chatter. She joined a queue for fresh pastries and coffee. It was her ritual. A routine to take the sting from the savagely early commute into London. Car, train, breakfast, tube, office. Her contactless card was ready in one hand, she scrolled her phone's news sites with the other.

A muggy May morning, the air still damp after an overnight deluge, she could hear the sound of screaming swifts that tore across the sky. She clicked her phone off, distracted by this stirring of early summer. Behind her, perched on a wet bench, a man enveloped in an oversized waterproof and grey baseball cap glanced up from his phone. His body suddenly tightened, his eyes flicking from the woman to his screen and back again. He lost the phone somewhere in the folds of his jacket and stood, slowly. He, too, looked to the skies.

She bought the food, smiled a few words to the vendor, then began to retrace her steps to the concourse. He was barely a metre away when she glanced at him, assuming he would be asking for spare change. He smiled. She only saw the knife as it pierced her chest. The man in the grey cap muttered three heavily accented, incomprehensible words and was still smiling as he held her close, withdrew the knife, then stabbed her again. Two inches lower this time. The only sound she made was a gasping, shuddering inhalation. By the time she fell, he was already running.

Two miles away, Harry Thomas had stopped for his first espresso of the day at the coffee cart in Kentish Town. He turned down the offer of a cut-price croissant, laughing and patting his stomach. He made it as far as the steps of the Underground when a jogger with a small rucksack slashed at his throat with a kitchen knife, pausing only to rebalance, mutter some words, then plunge it deep into his heart. The spilt blood and espresso pooled, then dripped down the steps.

At 6.55 Seth Hussain was crossing the road outside his Croydon flat when he was knifed by a man pushing a buggy. Sarah Thompson's throat was cut on the 259 bus from King's Cross; Brian Hall was stabbed then pushed in front of a tube train arriving at Pimlico. The last to die were Sathnam Stanley and Anita Cross – two more knives, two more punctured hearts.

It was 7.15. Seven murders in twenty-nine minutes.

2

FAMIE MADDEN PAUSED by her gate, adjusted her headphones, selected *The Magic Flute*. Pressed play. The overture played, oboes, clarinets, bassoons and horns pulling her away down the street. She knew there were endless numbers of news podcasts that she should be listening to, but she ignored them all. Famie was a journalist of two decades' standing but she had found she didn't much care for the news any more. Didn't want to read it, didn't want to watch it. Instead the intricate melodies from the eighteenth century seemed to work a spell over her every time; her face might be firmly pressed to a Piccadilly Line train window with a carriage full of commuters keeping her there, but the German wordplay in her ears acted as a portal to another, happier place.

At Green Park she changed lines, sighed and checked her overnight emails. An essay from her student daughter Charlie had arrived 'to check for spelling and all that stuff. Thanks Mum!'

Still useful then, she thought.

As the tube doors opened at Canary Wharf, she was too busy

correcting syntax to worry about the corporate restructuring which was due to dominate her day. Head down, she negotiated her place on the escalator by instinct; hedging, adjusting, sidestepping. The elaborate shuffle-dance of the London commuter. She felt the warmth of the day reaching into the tube exit and smiled. It had been a long winter and a cool spring. Some heat on her face at last. She fished out her aviator sunglasses, swapping them with her round wire-rim frames, and glanced up at the scrolling news ticker which ran across the length of the granite-and-glass Peterson-IPS building.

It was an old habit. In spite of the redundancies, in spite of her resentment, in spite of everything, a part of her was always grudgingly impressed by the urgency and glamour of the fast-moving golden words. Today they told her the French farmers were rioting and that the US President was in Berlin.

She took the marbled steps three at a time, flashed her pass at security and took the lift to the fourth floor. Through the security doors, and the clocks said 07.55 UK, 02.55 New York, 08.55 Paris. Five minutes early. Another habit. The vast, double football pitch-sized newsroom was library-quiet; of the hundreds of black computers barely a third were occupied. The eight o'clock shift change would alter that, the desks filling quickly as London took back control of the global news flow.

In the low-ceilinged, ferociously lit space, the air-con was working hard to deal with the night-shift aromas of sweat, stale perfume and cold, congealing Chinese take-out. Famie took it all in and breathed deeply. The newsroom had always been her home-from-home, her comfort zone. It didn't matter what battles had to be fought (and there were so many), here Famie knew what she was doing. She might have been a bad wife and poor mother, but this she could do. Here, Famie had always been at ease and in control.

Famie nodded at the EMEA editor, a smiling, tanned man in shorts called Ethan James who, in spite of his senior position – only the best got to be in charge of the Europe, Middle East and America desk – looked the same age as her daughter.

Time to go, old woman, she thought. It really is time to go.

Famie dressed young. Her look had barely changed since university: black bob, black T-shirt, khaki jacket, distressed jeans and black Converse. She had fiercely resisted her daughter's suggestion she might want to dress like other 'women of her age'. The thought filled her with horror. She had good skin, wore minimal make-up. Foundation and blusher maybe, lipstick never. A serious face, she was told. Wide, brown eyes. A silver hoop and a stud in each ear. Her running kept her trim and she knew she looked ten years younger than she was, but at forty-one and with a boss who looked twenty-one, Famie was becoming used to feeling ancient. Not to mention the lack of promotion, the salary tightening and the endless, joyless, fathomless restructuring.

'OK, who's Slot?' A balding man in front of two screens was stretching, looking around.

Famie raised her hand. 'Right here, Lucas.'

'Oh, hi Famie.' He raised his hand in salute. 'Pretty quiet overnight. There was a nasty-looking fire in Paisley but that was sorted. No deaths. That's it.' Lucas managed a weary smile. 'All yours.'

Famie slid into his chair.

'Horribly warm, Lucas.'

'The seat or the weather?'

'Mainly the seat.'

The man laughed as he picked up his bag and walked away.

Famie stared at the computer monitors in front of her: large, widescreen and in need of a serious clean. She used her glasses cloth to remove some of the more recent smears, then scanned the incoming, fast-moving type that rolled in front of her. She enjoyed being Slot more than she admitted. For a few hours she could forget her anger at the way she had been treated, forget her worries about the future, forget even that she missed her daughter. For this shift, the ship was hers. If she snapped a story, it had the International Press Service stamp. It had happened. It was official.

She wiped her glasses clean, tucked a few loose strands of hair behind her ears and waited. The TV screens on the wall showed CNN, Sky News, BBC and Al Jazeera (adverts, weather, weather and more adverts). A coffee appeared. She looked up. Sam Carter, another sub-editor, scrawny and dishevelled, waved a small bag of sugar at her, his eyebrows raised.

Famie shook her head. 'Get thee behind me, Satan.'

Carter shrugged and ripped the packet, pouring the granules slowly into his own cup. 'Suit yourself,' he said. Pale skin, white polo shirt, supermarket jeans, brown moccasins. A rugby player's nose. Rapidly receding hairline.

Famie smiled. 'I like to at least start the day feeling righteous, Sam. You know that.'

'I'll give you till eight thirty, tops,' he said. 'How are Charlie's exams going?'

Famie didn't reply. The Metropolitan Police had confirmed a stabbing at Euston station and she quickly sifted then snapped their statement.

BRITISH POLICE REPORT A FATAL STABBING
IN CENTRAL LONDON DURING MORNING
RUSH HOUR

'Euston is unusual, isn't it?' Sam's mouth was full of pastry but his words were clear enough.

'Hardly gang territory,' agreed Famie, 'unless you count the permanently furious commuters. They can be vicious.'

'Pictures!' called a voice, and Famie stood to see a screen running a Twitter video of a woman lying face down in a road. Black hair, red scarf, lots of blood.

'Do we know that's her?' she asked.

'We don't,' came the reply. 'Posted by an account called Birdie 99. It says, "This just happened. Sure she's dead. Guy ran off. I literally feel sick." That's it.'

Famie looked at the image, a feeling of disquiet settling on her. She wouldn't snap the picture, she needed it verified, but it looked right to her. She glanced up from her terminals – the UK bureau was now full; desks occupied, computers on. A hand went up by the wall. Tommi Dara glanced at Famie then back to his screen.

'More film, Famie. Another Twitter account, same shot but further away. It pans from the stalls, it's definitely Euston.'

That was two sources, but Famie wanted more.

'Can we get someone there? Police say a statement is possible.'

'On it,' called Tommi, his eyes narrowing behind large owl-round glasses. Black, late twenties, loose dark curls, undercut with neat, faded sides.

The Slot phone rang. Famie hooked the headset around her head.

'It's Famie Madden.'

'Famie, it's Serena, there's been a stabbing—'

Famie cut across her. 'We have it, thanks, Serena. Getting someone to Euston now.'

She was about to hang up when she caught her friend's tone: 'Didn't say Euston. This is Kentish Town. There's a body on the Underground steps.'

Famie's heart kicked up a notch. She raised her head, pulled the headset away from her mouth. 'Serena has another stabbing. Kentish Town.' Back to the headset. 'OK, talk to me, Serena.' She heard disembodied shouting and sirens from the phone, then Serena's voice. Measured but taut. Famie typed fast.

'There's a man, a white man, mid-thirties maybe, with his throat cut, lying at the bottom of the steps. The entrance to the tube is closed now but there's blood everywhere. I arrived shortly after it had happened, I think. A really nasty one, Fames – chest and neck injuries. Paramedics and police here now. One of the staff told me he'd seen a man running away, heading into town.'

'Stay there, Serena. Thanks.'

TWO PEOPLE STABBED TO DEATH IN SEPARATE ATTACKS IN LONDON, WITNESSES SAY

Two stabbings, separated by two miles. A coincidence probably, a busy morning certainly.

'More film from Euston!' It was Tommi again. 'Famie? You should see this.'

His voice sounded strangled and she looked up. He beckoned her over, pointing at the screen as she approached. This image of the dead woman was of better quality and taken from a different angle. Famie studied the bloodied clothing, the tangle of limbs and the slack-jawed face and, suddenly faint, realized she knew who it was.

3

'SWEET CHRIST, THAT'S Mary Lawson.' Famie held on to the desk. The woman in the Euston gutter was Mary Lawson, veteran IPS journalist and head of their Investigations Bureau. She wondered why she hadn't recognized her sooner – the blue cardigan and red silk scarf should have been all that was needed.

When Famie eventually tore herself away she found a small crowd behind her. The image had flashed across the floor, its progress flagged by the cries and gasps it triggered; many had instinctively graduated to the UK desk in sympathy and solidarity. Famie looked through a glass wall to Mary's desk barely ten metres away, a photo of two small children alongside her computer. Famie felt her sleeve being tugged.

'Slot? There's more.' Sam nodded to the double screens.

Famie didn't move, her head spinning. When her divorce was finalized it was Mary who had bought her a pizza. When her daughter passed her A-levels it was Mary who had high-fived her first. She was one of their finest, a tough, resourceful reporter who led her investigative team with élan.

'Famie. You're Slot.' Sam's words were kindly but firm.

'Her kids are eleven and thirteen, Sam.'

'I know. And it's awful. And we'll deal with it. But you're Slot, unless you want someone else to . . .'

Famie shook her head. 'No, no, I got it.'

She slumped back into her seat, wiped her eyes with her sleeve and scrolled back over the last two minutes of news copy. Famie felt her stomach lurch. The police were reporting three more stabbings, this time in Croydon, Hackney and Pimlico. Now the adrenalin kicked in. This was not a coincidence. On the wall, the TVs' 'Breaking News' scrolls were recording 'multiple attacks'.

Slot phone, Serena again, a scared voice. 'Jesus, Famie! I saw the man here. When they took him away. It's Harry. Harry Thomas from Investigations. Christ, I never saw such a mess.'

From somewhere Famie heard herself say, 'Was he dead, Serena, did they confirm that?'

'Yes. God. Dead. Very dead. Fuck.'

LONDON POLICE SAY MULTIPLE KNIFE ATTACKS ARE 'POSSIBLE TERRORIST ATTACK'

POLICE CONFIRM 2 PEOPLE KILLED, 3 WOUNDED IN 5 SEPARATE KNIFE ATTACKS ACROSS LONDON – STATEMENT

LONDON, May 22 (IPS) – London police said five separate knife attacks that occurred in the British capital were a 'possible terrorist attack'.

Two people were killed and three seriously wounded in separate locations across the capital, the Metropolitan Police said in a statement.

Famie blinked hard. 'Second eyes! I need second eyes on this!'

Ethan James, EMEA editor, the man in shorts, appeared at her shoulder, read the copy.

'And the dead man is Harry Thomas,' said Famie. 'Also from Investigations. Serena just confirmed it.'

'Jesus. She got that from the medics?' he said.

'No. But she and Harry are friends, Ethan. She knows.'

'It's good to go then.'

Famie snapped it. 'That's two of ours, Ethan. They sit next to each other. Just there.' She jerked her thumb at the glass. 'We need the bureau chief,' she said.

'Agreed. I'll call him. And I'll message the other bureaus to hold down non-essential copy.' The EMEA editor walked away, already dialling.

The ten faces in the bureau were all looking at her. They knew already, but Famie confirmed it. 'Kentish Town death is Harry Thomas.' Hands over mouths. Heads in hands.

Another phone began to ring, but this time heads turned. It was Mary Lawson's, a single red light flashing on her console, the shrill tone carrying through the glass. Then other identical tones began until it seemed all the phones in the Investigations cluster were ringing at once. Answerphones kicked in eventually, only for the ringing to start again. Tommi tried their door.

'Locked,' he said.

Seven phones ringing.

Sam Carter said it first. 'Do we have any ID on the other victims?' They didn't, Sam knew they didn't, but he'd asked the question anyway. The implication was clear. Holy shit, this was going to be a long morning.

Slot phone. 'Famie Madden here.' There was a beat's pause at the other end, then the sound of a deep breath being taken, enough time for dread to settle in Famie's gut. 'Famie Madden,' she repeated.

Heads around the bureau turned slowly.

'This is Dr Edmund Alexander from Croydon University Hospital.' He paused. Famie knew calls like this only led one way. 'Is this the news agency?'

'Yes,' she said. 'Can I help?'

'Do you know Seth Hussain?' he said.

'Yes, he's a colleague here. And a friend,' she added quickly. Her whole body tensed for what was coming next.

'Well I'm sorry to inform you that Mr Hussain died a few minutes ago. He had his work ID on him. It had this number on it. I wouldn't normally do this, of course, but we haven't got through to his family yet and under the circumstances . . .'

Famie's head was swimming. She made herself answer. 'Thank you, Dr Alexander. Can I, er, can I ask how he died?'

'Knife wounds to the stomach and chest. He never stood a chance. We did the best we could. I'm sorry it wasn't enough.'

Famie closed her eyes. 'Thank you,' she managed.

Seth Hussain. The most forensic, focused journalist she had ever come across. A quiet campaigner for human rights back in his native Egypt. And the last man she had slept with. It had been a terrible mistake, of course, but she had accepted his flattery and comfort when it had been offered. She didn't know who knew. Seth had been quiet, discreet and gentlemanly so it was quite possible that no one knew. Thirty-eight years old, charismatic, brilliant. And gone. She blinked away tears.

'Famie?' It was Sophie Arnold, the youngest in the bureau. 'Who was it, Famie?'

'I'm writing it!' she said, hands trembling.

DEATH TOLL IN LONDON KNIFE ATTACKS
RISES TO THREE – HOSPITAL SOURCE

'Seth Hussain,' she said, her voice catching, fading. 'It's Seth Hussain.'

For some reason, everyone stood up. As though to remain seated was somehow disrespectful. They stared at each other, at Famie, at the TV screens. Sophie put her hands in front of her face.

Ethan James appeared again. 'You OK, Famie?'

'Of course I'm fucking OK,' she snapped. 'I'll let you know when I'm too overcome with grief to continue.'

He recoiled, nodded and hurried away.

'Fucking cheek,' muttered Famie. A nod from Sam, another from Tommi. She knew she'd have to apologize for that some time but knew too that he would never have checked on a male colleague in that way. She took a breath. 'OK, so this is clearly a pattern. We need to find the rest of the investigators because—'

Tommi raised his hand. 'Just tried them, Famie. No reply from any, I'm afraid.'

She pressed her lips tightly together. The phones in the office behind them started ringing again.

All the news channels were now rolling with the London attacks; footage from Euston was now augmented with live pictures from Kentish Town.

'Sky have something,' shouted a voice.

The footage was of a crowd running away from a stationary double decker bus. There was around ten seconds of it which had been looped.

'That's King's Cross,' said Tommi, walking up close to the monitor. 'And they look shit-scared.'

The screen cut to a live shot from outside New Scotland Yard. 'Live statement!' called Famie. 'Sound, please.' She sat, fingers hovering above her keyboard. As an Assistant Commissioner began a prepared statement, Famie started typing.

'Today has seen another attack on the people of London.'

The AC, cap under one arm, glanced down the lens, then back at her notes. 'Between six forty-five this morning and seven fifteen, seven separate attacks were carried out in seven different parts of the city.'

Famie had hesitated over the second 'seven' and again on the third.

'Seven?' yelled Sam. 'Where did that come from?'

Famie switched to a headphone feed, carried on typing.

'We appeal for any witnesses to come forward as soon as possible and ask that no one share any images or footage of the attacks on social media. If you have any photos or video of the attacks, please send them to the police. We know the victims' identities and are contacting their families before any more details are announced.'

She knows, Famie thought. She knows they all work here.

When she was done, she snapped it, took off the headphones and heard a commotion. All her team were standing, staring over her shoulder. Spinning in her chair, Famie took in bureau chief Andrew Lewis and two armed policemen.

'Christ, this is bad,' she said.

4

ANDREW LEWIS HADN'T asked for silence but he had it anyway. TVs were muted, conversations halted, phones hung up. Stooped and gaunt, he cleared his throat.

'Erm. I, er . . .' He looked at his feet and swallowed hard. 'I have some very bad news, I'm afraid.' His voice was brittle. 'I've just had a conversation with Assistant Commissioner Creswell at the Met. They, er . . . know the identities of all seven victims. And . . . well . . .' He raised a shaking hand to wipe his forehead. He spoke slowly now, each word needing to be wrenched from him. 'They're all ours, my friends. Every one of them. All ours. Mary you know about. The others are . . .' He took a faltering breath. Famie felt her hand grabbed tightly. 'The others are Harry, Seth and Sarah, Anita, Sathnam and Brian.'

Each name was a hammer blow. Lewis's list brought groans and despair. Heads dropped. Seven was impossible. Famie spun back to check her screens, then back to the bureau chief.

'We have lost staff before, of course, killed doing their duty,' continued Lewis. 'The job they loved. But we've never had a day like this.' He paused, gathered himself. 'However, if you'll allow me . . . the grief will have to wait – we honestly don't know if we're done yet. It is possible there are other attacks we don't know about.' Behind Famie, someone vomited, then ran for the toilets. The stench and the retching triggered other rapid exits. 'Can all desk editors find their staff, please?' said Lewis, sounding exhausted. 'All of them. We need a full roll call, now. Any you can't account for within fifteen minutes, tell me. The building is in lockdown, I'm afraid it's not safe for any of us to leave. The police, as you can see, are here already.'

Famie had reported tragedies before, understood how they unfolded. The shock, anger and guilt that they triggered could be – should be – measured and recorded. She was aware that part of her was doing that even now; she read it in her colleagues' anguished silence or breathless sobbing, recognized the huddled groups giving physical support to each of the enveloped. But the rest of her was shut down. Too stunned to move. Too shocked to join in.

The seven dead were the Investigations team. Crime reporters, foreign affairs correspondents, technology specialists. All gone. Famie had sat next to them, joked with them, argued with them. For a long time she had wanted to be one of them. If she did a coffee run, she'd count them in. If she was working late, she could count on at least one of them offering her some of their cold pizza. Given the secretive nature of most of their work, they were a gregarious bunch and Famie enjoyed their company.

Had enjoyed their company.

She turned in her chair. The team had sat in two lines, three on one side of a long desk, four on the other. Each had a phone, a computer screen and a keyboard, two servers sitting under the desk. There were no drawers, no filing cabinets, no in-trays. There was barely any office detritus save for the photos where Mary had sat, a new pad of Post-it notes left by Sathnam and a large ball of Blu Tack somewhere between Anita and Sarah. It occurred to Famie that it didn't look like a used work station at all. It looked sterile. It looked wiped clean. In comparison with her desk – most desks – the Investigations team had set new standards of cleanliness.

'You know what the coppers will say.' It was Sam. She had forgotten he was there. He too was staring at the empty chairs.

Famie nodded. 'They'll say it looks like someone's tidied up,' she said. 'Cleared evidence away. Interfered.'

'That's because it does look like that.'

Famie managed a smile. 'Then we'll have to explain that they were always like this. It's what made them good.'

'And weird,' suggested Sam.

'And weird,' agreed Famie, and she felt her legs start to shake.

Her phone lit up. Four missed calls. Famie called her daughter back, and she picked up immediately.

'Mum?'

'Charlie, I . . .' A shriek then a burst of sobbing came from the other end. 'I'm OK, Charlie,' Famie said, pushing through the muffled tears and shielding her mouth from the cacophony around her. 'We might be here a while but I'm OK.'

Her daughter managed some words at last. 'Mum, thank God! They woke me in the flat, told me to ring and not look at the news. When I couldn't get you . . .'

Famie walked away from her desk. 'I'm sorry, Charlie, it kicked off as soon as I started the shift.' She took a breath. 'But how did you know . . .'

'It was a Facebook thing. Names were out there, Martha here saw it, put it together.'

'Really?' said Famie, momentarily annoyed at the protocol breach. 'Well it's bad here, I can't pretend otherwise.' She caught herself thinking how much she wished Charlie would be there when she got home; her daughter knew what the pause meant.

'I'll come home,' she said. 'I can be there by four.'

Famie's response was instinctive, urgent. 'Absolutely not, Charlie. We don't know when we'll be allowed home, there are armed police here. It's . . . not really safe.' Her voice was tight, her pitch high.

'Mum, you sound terrified.'

Famie felt the tears come again. 'Maybe. I hadn't realized till just now but I guess that's right. We lost seven today, maybe more. So "terrified" feels about right.'

'Seven?' Charlie's voice was more of a gasp.

Famie closed her eyes, shook her head. 'We just heard.'

'Who . . .' began Charlie, 'did you . . . know?'

Famie didn't think she could, or should, say it out loud. But it was her daughter and she wanted to tell her. 'It's the investigators,' she whispered. Famie caught the sudden intake of breath.

'Mum, I'm so sorry.'

Famie gripped the side of her chair. Said nothing. She had told Charlie when she'd applied to be on the Investigations team. Told her too how infuriated she'd been when she was turned down. There was a silence, and Famie knew what was coming. Knew it would be the first uttering of the question everyone would be asking.

'Who would do this, Mum?' Charlie whispered.

It was too soon for this, way too soon. 'I have no idea. Look, I have to go. I'll call you tonight.' Famie hung up.

Sam pushed a coffee in front of her. 'This one has sugar,' he said.

Famie forced a smile.

He nodded at the phone. 'And was that you being reassuring?'

'Yup, that was it,' she said, sipping from the plastic cup. 'Pretty impressive, huh?'

'You answered,' he said. 'You're alive. If I was Charlie, I'd be pretty damn happy about that.'

'Thanks for the coffee.'

'Second of many.'

Famie messaged her father, sister and ex-husband. She took a breath.

A seasoned reporter called Jane Hilton stood on her chair. Grey Agnès B. suit, long layered auburn hair. She shouted above the melee. Urgent, shrill. 'We need to tell this story, we need to get this out there!'

'Doing it!' yelled a voice.

Hilton nodded. 'It's the same as for *Charlie Hebdo* in 2015 and the *Capital Gazette* in '18,' she said. 'This is the same. Just the same. These are journalists killed for being journalists. We owe it to Mary and her team to tell the world what's happened.'

Famie found the word 'grandstanding' occurring to her. 'Getting the story out there?' she said. 'What the fuck does she think we've been doing?'

'And what is the story exactly?' muttered Sam.

Famie scrolled through her phone. 'Let's find everyone first,' she said. 'For now, that's the story.' She pulled a weathered sheet of A4 from a drawer. 'I'll call the top five, you call the bottom five. Then get our numbers in.'

Famie made the calls. She had five pick-ups out of five, Sam just three. 'No reply from Natalie or Meera. Both went to answerphone.'

'Christ.'

Famie took her numbers to Andrew Lewis. The bureau chief and his secretary, a bulldog of a woman, were ticking names on what looked like an old printout.

'We're missing Natalie Lloyd and Meera Elon.'

Bureau chief and bulldog both nodded, underlining and crossing out without looking up.

Famie hesitated. 'Andrew—'

'I don't know any more,' he said, cutting her off. He pushed his glasses to the top of his head, flattening his unkempt white hair. 'I've got a call with Peretti in ten minutes, maybe he'll know more. Though it's early hours in New York so it's just as likely he'll know less.'

'Need a quote, Andrew, I'm Slot.'

'I'll message it to you.' He flicked his glasses back to the bridge of his nose and she was dismissed.

Famie bustled her way back to her desk. If Carlo Peretti, the global head of news, was involved, their fear must be that the agency was being targeted worldwide.

Famie slumped at her desk. More missed calls. Berlin and Rome this time.

'Nothing like mass murder to bring old friends to life,' she said.

5

THE STORY OF 22 May was soon being told in a series of images that came to appal and fascinate the world. They followed in sequence. The first victim had fallen just short of Euston's main entrance. Three different Twitter accounts had posted their shock and outrage accompanied by graphic images of her blood-soaked clothes and twisted, tangled body. The Kentish Town 'coffee and blood' shot, with Thomas's body sprawled across several steps, became the front-page picture of that day's London *Evening Standard*. The Hussain video showed a slumped man on a zebra crossing and a livid, smeared blood trail marking his crawl to the kerb. The 259 bus pictures were considered the most disturbing – few news outlets ran the images of a woman who had been virtually decapitated – but within hours the video had been shared millions of times. There was grainy footage of running passengers at Pimlico followed closely by a man and woman bleeding into a grass verge. By eleven a.m., despite police appeals, it was possible to watch an edited online montage of London's bloodiest rush hour since 7/7.

Famie's shift was barely three hours old.

6

FAMIE WAS PERSUADED to relinquish the Slot chair at midday. She'd argued to complete the shift but her trembling hands had given her away. She'd snapped fifty-three stories, and all but one were about the IPS attacks. The link between the murders was established quickly and when armed police appeared outside the Peterson-IPS building the connection was confirmed. Andrew Lewis's statement, when it finally came, paid tribute to the astonishing bravery and professionalism of the journalists who had died. There was no mention of the Investigations team.

Lewis, his face candlewax-grey and beaded with sweat as he walked into the office, was the first to offer support. As Famie prised herself from the chair he held out his hand. 'A tour de force, Famie. Exemplary.'

She took his hand briefly. 'We played catch-up, Andrew. All morning. That's the truth. And I did what anyone else would've done. Just don't offer me any fucking counselling and I'll be fine.'

Lewis dredged up a grin. 'I wouldn't dream of it.'

She looked around the acre of newsroom, now packed with journalists, security and police. 'Always wondered how you report the news when you are the news.' She answered her own question before her boss could open his mouth. 'And the answer is, you just report the news.' She felt the beginnings of a headache nagging at the back of her skull. 'Being Slot was easy, Andrew. That's the truth of it. But now it's all real. Everything I snapped is real. It's all true. It feels like the worst fucking shit show of all time.'

Lewis bowed his head slightly. 'That's really what my statement was aiming to convey. You have, as ever, expressed it more . . . succinctly.'

His bulldog appeared and pointed at a policewoman four desks away, heavily braided cap again under her arm.

'Excuse me, Famie.' He raised an acknowledging hand at the Assistant Commissioner. 'And thank you again for this morning.'

She touched his arm, holding him back.

'Is it over?' she said. 'Is that it?' She knew it was a dumb question, embarrassed and surprised she'd even asked it. How could he possibly know? She let it hang between them anyway and Lewis seemed to deflate in front of her. For a moment she thought he was about to cry, but instead he mumbled 'I need to talk to the Assistant Commissioner' and walked away, the bulldog at his heels.

Famie joined Tommi, Sam and the crowd of end-of-shift workers by the large tinted windows. The plaza was empty. Canary Wharf tube station was still closed, the bike stalls and cafés deserted.

'They'll have to let us out soon,' said Sam. 'Whatever level of threat there is, we can't all stay here.'

'Smells bad enough already,' said Tommi.

Famie realized she'd been sweating profusely. '*I* smell bad enough already.'

'And we can hardly all be escorted home,' said Sam.

Their conversation was muted, one of many huddled discussions happening along the length of the windows.

'So maybe we have to sleep here.'

Famie's eyes closed and she pressed her forehead against the glass. Her guts churned.

'I know what you're thinking,' whispered Sam.

'I'm sure you do, Sherlock,' she whispered back, 'I'm sure you do.' She took a breath. He knew, but she was going to say it anyway. 'When I didn't get on that team, I was so pissed off . . .'

'We remember,' said Sam. 'Boy, do we remember.'

'I had everything they said they were after. I had Pakistan, I had Iraq, I had crime . . .'

'Well, whatever it was you didn't have,' said Sam, 'thank God you didn't have it.'

'I think I might, Sam. Every day.' Her breath briefly fogged up a few inches of window.

Famie thought of her daughter and the ten-year-old photo of her running through waves in Cornwall. The straw hat. The blue and white swimsuit Charlie loved so much. That was a good holiday. She thought of her parents – that hadn't happened for a while – how they'd wanted to come and help when Jim had walked out. And how she'd refused, determined to manage it herself.

What a selfish cow, she thought.

Then the Twitter and YouTube images of the seven dead played again and she saw Seth's blood smeared over the road. The white of the zebra crossing, the red of Seth Hussain. She fought the nausea, pressing her forehead against the cold glass.

Over the newsroom chatter, they heard Jane Hilton's clipped tones. Sam and Tommi turned to watch. Standing in front of a permanent, fixed camera she was answering questions from some unseen TV anchor.

'Shocked and devastated of course,' she said. 'The journalists we lost today were some of our finest.'

Famie snorted. 'Bet she couldn't name any of them,' she said to the window. 'Not one.'

Hilton was nodding at the interviewer's question. 'It's too early to speculate, of course. For the moment we just need to stand with our fallen colleagues.'

'Oh please spare us the bullshit,' said Famie. 'Say how sad you are and get the fuck off the screen.'

Tommi smiled. 'Just a little too loud, Fames. Heads are turning.'

'Think I'll cope,' she said.

Lewis and Assistant Commissioner Creswell returned then and Sam tapped Famie on the shoulder.

'Here we go.'

The bureau chief led Creswell to a point in the middle of the newsroom and again, within a few seconds, they had all the quiet they could need. All around the periphery people stood, a few even clambering on to chairs. Lincoln Jeffers, one of the newest subs and the current Slot, spun his chair, then stood too. The AC took a step forward. Mid-forties, short silver hair, broad shoulders. She did a three-sixty sweep of the room.

'Can I say first that these words are for you alone.' She projected just as much as she needed to. Measured, Home Counties. 'I'll be speaking to the press – the rest of them – when I leave here but you're entitled to know as much as I can tell you. Your seven colleagues were, we believe, targeted deliberately by seven different murderers, all working together. We don't as yet have any images of the attackers but we do have eye-witness reports and are working to get some e-fits published. We'll get some CCTV pictures I'm sure, possibly dash-cam and head-cam images too. Obviously the stories the investigators were working on will need to be examined as a matter of urgency. Please consider their office a crime scene. It has, as you will have noticed, been sealed.'

Most eyes flicked back to the investigators' office, now with yellow police tape running the length of the door jamb. Inside, nothing had been moved: photos, Post-it notes, computers, Blu Tack – a still-life in tragedy. Famie wondered what secrets those soon-to-be examined hard drives would reveal.

'Many of you,' continued the Assistant Commissioner, 'may have had conversations pertaining to what your colleagues were working on. Needless to say, if there is anything you can tell us, please come forward. That investigation has already begun. If you wish to speak in confidence, I'll leave some of my cards here. My phone and email are on them.'

Famie felt her insides churn again. She'd heard a thousand police statements before. They were routine, formulaic. By necessity, they were perfunctory, cold affairs; here's what we know, here's what we'd like to know, here's how you can help us. But hearing the events of the morning, the deaths of her friends, discussed in this way was deeply distressing. 'Hard-bitten' was a cliché often attached to journalists but Famie could tell she wasn't the only one struggling. Some were biting back tears, others questions. The AC began another three-sixty but there were so many veteran question-shouters present it was just a matter of time before the dam burst. The first of them, Jane Hilton, triggered the flood.

Are we safe here?

Are we safe going home?

Has the killing stopped?

Who do you believe is responsible?

Why did you confirm it as a terrorist attack?

Is the freedom of the press under attack?

Lewis tried to impose some kind of order but the Assistant Commissioner nodded her acceptance of the questions.

'OK, OK, in brief. I'll take some of them. Is the freedom of the press under attack? Yes, I think it is. Has the killing stopped? We think so, but we cannot be certain. And are you safe here or at home?' For the first time, Creswell hesitated before answering. 'My honest assessment is that I cannot say that you are. Until we know who carried out these attacks and why, no, you are not safe. Here or at home.'

7

'READY?'

'Of course we're ready, Tommi,' said Famie. 'Don't be so melodramatic.'

'Right then,' said Sam, 'let's be having you.' He hoisted a small rucksack over one shoulder.

The marbled entrance lobby of the IPS building – elegant, curving steps, angled reception desk, huge TV monitor – was teeming with staff. Around Famie, many were on their phones, huddled in muted, nervous conversations. There was no jostling, no rush for the exit, just a hundred and ninety-two journalists fearful of their journey home, waiting for the doors to be unlocked.

'Was she off-message?' said Sam as they all inched forward. 'You know, just a little?'

'Certainly not what anyone was expecting,' agreed Tommi. 'Coppers are always supposed to be reassuring.'

'Sure,' said Famie, 'if there's anything to be reassuring about.'

Famie and Tommi were shoulder to shoulder, Sam squeezing in behind them.

'We don't have to go,' Sam said. 'Lewis said they'd put us up somehow. Get bedding in and everything.'

Tommi shrugged. 'And I'm sure the dozen or so who took him up on his offer will have a fine old time. The rest of us seem to be taking our chances in the new Wild West.'

Through the revolving doors the police were preparing for the mass exodus. Those posted by the doors held semi-automatic carbines, one hand on the pistol grip, the other resting on the barrel.

'Well at least we won't die between here and the tube station,' muttered Sam. 'You sure about this, Famie?'

All staff had been offered cabs. Hundreds of London's black taxi drivers had volunteered to ferry IPS staff home. Currently the only traffic in South Colonnade was the largest cab rank London had ever seen.

'It is tempting, but what does it solve?' she said. 'We get home tonight, but tomorrow? And the next day? Transport Police are everywhere. The tube is open again, it'll be quicker, and you won't have to listen to some god-awful talk-radio-inspired shite theory about what's going on and what we should be doing about it.'

Sam laughed, briefly. 'You got a point there. Tube it is.'

The advice had been to take the cabs, stay behind or travel in groups. At Famie's suggestion the three of them, all north-east Londoners, would travel together. Sam and Tommi would escort Famie home, then Tommi said he'd stay at Sam's. She hadn't accepted an escort since college days but today she didn't argue.

'Lanyards off, IDs away!' someone near the doors shouted and the few remaining staff advertising their IPS employment hurriedly stowed the evidence. Famie's was already in a small shoulder bag, Tommi's in his back pocket.

The glass doors started to revolve and the crowd inched forward again. Outside, the police began to beckon them through. It was the theatre of it that quietened the crowd. Their workplace had been transformed from the mundane into the extraordinary. This was something they'd done hundreds, thousands of times without thinking; now it was covered live as 'breaking news', the giant screen in the lobby filling with shots of scurrying staff and departing taxis.

The throng of staff narrowed as it approached the exit, the doors now spinning at a constant speed, spitting out journalists. Tommi walked out first, then Famie and Sam. Two policemen waved them left. 'Taxis up on South Colonnade, quick as you can, please.'

Famie turned right. 'We're taking the tube, thanks.' She wasn't sure why she'd felt the need to explain to the officer. Maybe she was still rationalizing it to herself.

As it turned out there were plenty taking the tube option: she guessed maybe twenty others were opting for the steps down to the plaza. Six Transport Police officers stood at the entrance to the station. They nodded at Famie, Tommi and Sam as they walked past.

'I need a drink,' said Sam.

'You need to get home,' said Famie.

On the escalator, Tommi turned to face his colleagues. 'Honest question,' he said. 'Are you scared?' He glanced from Famie to Sam. 'Do you think we're in danger? Doing this?'

They both said 'Yes' together.

'A bit,' Famie added, 'but not much.'

'So . . . just a bit of danger?' queried Tommi.

They walked past another pair of Transport Police on to a sparsely populated platform. Everyone knew everyone else, and when an empty train pulled in all the IPS staff got in the same carriage.

'Enough danger for everyone to do this anyway,' Famie said, gesturing around at her colleagues.

Two policemen walked up to the carriage's doorway;

one nodded at a uniformed guard and the doors closed. The officers stood together at one end of the car, eyeing the passengers.

A woman opposite Famie cleared her throat. 'We're all IPS,' she said to the uniforms.

'We know,' said one of them. He pulled the ventilation window behind him shut. 'There was no one on this train till Canary Wharf. Special instructions.' He adjusted his cap. 'And we're sorry for your loss.'

Heads nodded in appreciation.

'How far are you riding?' called another voice.

'Till you all get off. Then we go back and do it again.'

'So how far are you all going?' asked the other officer. Most said Waterloo and Green Park, the furthest station being Baker Street. 'We stay on till Baker Street then,' he said.

The train pulled into Canada Water but the platform was deserted and the doors opened, then closed.

'What have you heard?' said Tommi. 'About today?'

Both policemen looked unsure of themselves, exchanging the swiftest of glances.

'Off the record,' added Tommi. 'No one will quote you.'

The older of the two, bearded and stocky, shrugged. 'They wouldn't tell us, we're too lowly. We're as much in the dark as you. Off the record.'

Now it was Tommi who shrugged. 'So none of us know jack shit then.'

The London Bridge platforms were busy. As they pulled in and the train slowed, Famie, along with most of her colleagues, stared at the waiting passengers – the usual crowd of commuters and tourists, maps, bags and coffees in hand, waiting for the train to stop. She held her breath as the doors opened. She thought about that taxi she had turned down. One of the police officers, the stocky one, walked to the middle of the carriage. Making a show, she reckoned, and she was glad of it.

Of the ten or so new travellers, most sat, a few choosing to stand, the closest just a few metres away. An exhausted-looking woman in her sixties, rucksack on her back, big headphones on her head, held on to the rail with both hands.

Sam was watching too. 'Why doesn't she sit down?' he whispered. 'There's plenty of seats.'

Famie smiled. 'Thanks,' she said. To his look of puzzlement she added, 'I thought it was just me. Being paranoid. "People behaving strangely on the tube" will turn out to be a big subject.'

Sam snorted, put his hand in front of his mouth in embarrassment, then joined in the laughter from his colleagues. The woman, oblivious, stared at the floor.

As they approached Green Park, Famie, Sam and Tommi stood, acknowledged their friends and waited by the doors. Famie caught her reflection in the glass, then looked away. How she looked was how she felt – devastated. Her glasses hid the shadows around her eyes but the tube lights found every line, every imperfection. 'This is no way to live,' she said.

They walked the connecting corridors and escalators in a grim silence. On the platform once again – 'next train one minute' – Famie thought she'd had enough. 'You guys don't need to do this. Go home.'

Sam and Tommi didn't move.

'Are you mad?' said Sam. 'We're sticking to the plan. We deliver you to your door.'

'Like you're a pizza,' added Tommi.

'Thanks,' she said. 'I'll be sure to tip you a few quid.'

The Piccadilly Line train was surprisingly quiet and they sat in adjacent seats. Sam looked around. The nearest passenger was at the other end of the carriage and, slumped over the arm rest, appeared to be asleep.

'So,' said Sam, his voice as quiet as he could make it, 'what were they working on? The investigators. Do we know?'

Tommi shook his head slowly. 'No idea. They never really spoke to me, to be honest.'

Both men looked at Famie. She chewed her lip.

'I've been trying to remember. Mary did talk vaguely about a big story she had. Said they'd dropped everything to see what they could do with it.' She looked at her friends. 'And that's it.' She shrugged. 'The whole point of being an investigator is that you don't talk about the investigation. So it's not surprising if no one knows about it.'

The sleeping man woke up and lurched upright. They all watched him until he slumped again.

'Wow we're suspicious,' said Tommi, 'even of him.'

'Especially of him,' said Sam. 'We have to be, don't we? Until we know who the killers are, don't we have to be suspicious of everyone?'

Famie put her head in her hands. 'What a life we have to look forward to,' she said.

Her headache was back and suddenly she couldn't wait to get home. 'Excuse me,' she said, 'I just need to do this.' She fished out her headphones, hit play on her phone. She knew Sam and Tommi would be raising eyebrows but she didn't care. Eyes closed, her *Magic Flute* had work to do. A few brief moments of peace, then she felt her sleeve being tugged. The train was slowing.

'Our stop, I think,' said Sam, loudly.

Famie nodded. 'I can hear you,' she said, 'but I can also hear Mozart. And he's winning.'

The doors opened and they walked to the steps.

'Fucking Mozart's not taking you home though, is he,' said Sam.

Famie, aware she was being annoying, removed the headphones. 'Sorry,' she said. 'A bad habit.'

'Feel better?' asked Sam.

'I don't know.'

'Did we miss something?' said Tommi, taking a left out of the station.

'You did,' said Famie. 'You missed everything. You should try it some time.'

'Will it make me as miserable as you?' asked Tommi.

'Quite likely.'

They walked to the park that led to Famie's flat. A pink and white ice cream van was by its entrance, the vendor ensconced behind a newspaper. Famie hurried them into the grounds.

'My God, I'm even worried about the ice cream seller,' she said. 'This is so bad . . .'

The green spaces of Arnos Park opened up in front of them, one tree-lined path snaking through the centre, a narrower, circuitous route forking left and right. With the exception of a few dog-walkers and a sleeping tramp on a bench, they had it to themselves.

'Surprisingly empty,' said Tommi, the note of suspicion unmissable.

'I'm not normally here in the early afternoon,' said Famie, 'but you're right. Pretty deserted.'

'In a bad way?' said Sam, unsure of what Famie was thinking. 'You want to re-route?'

The wide-open space should have been reassuring but Famie hesitated. Even with her friends, she felt vulnerable, exposed. She resisted the urge to put her headphones back on. Six dogs, four dog-walkers and a hobo was hardly *Mean Streets*.

'No, let's go,' she said. 'Gin and tonics in ten minutes.'

She set off down the central path at a brisk pace, eyes everywhere. The smell of newly cut grass, mixed with a ripe stench from the overly full rubbish bins. Banana skins, nappies, half-full coffee cups. The park sloped gently downhill, levelled out for the benches and picnic tables, then rose steeply to the ornate Victorian wrought-iron exit gates. Dog-walker one, retriever, was stooped, poop bag in hand. Dog-walker two, cockapoo, had stopped to talk to number three, wolfhound, the tramp was peeling an apple, and dog-walker four was striding around the far end of the outer perimeter, her three charges straining at their leads.

Something wrong. Famie pulled up short, heart exploding in her chest. Very wrong. She snapped back to the bench.

Sam had it too. 'What kind of tramp peels an apple?' he said, his words an urgent whisper.

'A tramp with a knife,' said Famie.

8

SHE GRIPPED SAM and Tommi's sleeves. 'Turn round?'

The man on the bench was now upright, carrier bag between his legs.

'What do you see?' said Sam.

Tommi held up his phone, started filming. 'I see a bearded white guy, forties, round-shouldered. Peeling an apple into a bag. Penknife maybe. Two-inch blade.'

They stood three abreast across the path.

'We can detour around him,' said Tommi. He sounded calm. 'I'll keep filming. There's three of us. And he might not be a tramp. He looks like he's just a guy having his lunch, that's all.'

Famie relaxed her grip slightly, reconsidered. Dog-walker one was throwing away the poop bag behind them, two and three were still chatting a few metres from the apple-peeling non-tramp, four was on her phone with the three dogs all sitting.

'OK,' she said. 'Let's do that detour.'

They resumed their walk, veering right, stepping on to the

grass and arcing around the bench-man. Twenty metres away now, he looked up. Tommi kept on filming.

'OK, he looks super annoyed,' he said.

Famie could see that for herself. The carrier bag and the apple had been stowed, the knife held loosely between his fingers.

'You stop filming me!' he shouted.

European, thought Famie, Central Europe at a guess. Poland maybe.

'You put the knife away!' replied Tommi, the three of them still walking.

The man seemed to consider that for a moment, before shaking his head then rising slowly from the bench. The knife was still in his hand, palm-up.

Famie inched closer to Sam. 'I'm calling the police.' She raised her phone.

Knifeman now pointed the blade at her, a stream of unidentifiable but clearly angry words pouring from him. Dog-walkers two and three had stopped their conversation and started walking towards them. Walker number one, over Famie's shoulder, was moving towards them too.

'Shit, it's a set-up!' she hissed.

Sam's head was darting everywhere. 'Keep filming, Tommi!' he yelled. 'Make the call, Famie!'

Walker four had tied up her dogs, all now barking madly, and was running towards the fray.

'Run first!' shouted Tommi, and they turned and sprinted back the way they'd come. They ran in a tight pack straight into dog-walker one, Sam's shoulder making contact with his midriff, Famie's boot with his shin.

'Police!' yelled Famie into her phone, then, on connection, 'Knife attack in Arnos Park. I'm Famie Madden. I work for IPS. We're running!' She left the phone connected as they made for their original entrance.

'Don't look back!' yelled Sam.

Tommi did anyway. Knifeman was running too.

'Go, go, go!' cried Tommi, his panicky voice telling them all they needed to know.

They slowed to negotiate the zigzag metal fences that formed the entrance, catching a glimpse of the closing Knifeman and, beyond him, a stooped walker attending to the man they'd just knocked over. They accelerated out of the park, instinctively heading back to the tube station – uniforms, barriers and order. Famie's breathing was heavy and her head was ringing but she heard the chatter of voices from her phone and some distant sirens. They raced along the street towards the T-junction, needing a gap in the traffic to reach the station.

'Come on, come on!' screamed Famie, but the enforced slowdown lost them their advantage. Knifeman was out of the park, running like a sprinter and gaining fast. The incessant traffic filled both lanes. No gaps. The tube entrance was unreachable.

We've got no choice, thought Famie, and stepped into the road. She ran in the gutter. Balls of her feet. She waved her arms. She caught the eye of the driver in a red Toyota. The woman jumped, startled, suddenly alert, her hands tightening on the wheel. For an instant Famie held her stare, then ran in front of her. She saw the panicked eyes and the steering-wheel lunge. The woman threw her car right as she braked, her wing ramming the rear door of an oncoming car. Both vehicles crunched to a halt then shuddered as they were hammered by a succession of cars hitting them from behind.

Famie danced around the wrecks, vaulted the station ticket barrier and leapt back down the stairs to the platform six at a time. A train was in, they had seconds.

She knew Tommi and Sam were behind her, she could hear their cursing. She didn't know if Knifeman was behind them and from somewhere she found one more burst of speed. Famie threw herself on to the train as the door alarm started its urgent, high-pitched closing routine, leaning back against the doors as they tried to close. Tommi and Sam leapt aboard together, Tommi sprawling to the floor. As the train pulled away they stared at the swiftly disappearing steps for any sign of Knifeman, but they were deserted.

Sweat-soaked and breathless, it was an age before any of them spoke.

'Christ alive, Famie,' was all Tommi managed.

They rode three stops to the end of the line, then hailed a cab. By the time they arrived at Famie's flat, there were six police cars waiting for them.

9

US PRESIDENT DESCRIBES LONDON KNIFE ATTACKS AS 'AN ASSAULT ON OUR VERY PRINCIPLES AND VALUES'

FRENCH PRESIDENT CALLS ON 'FREEDOM-LOVING COUNTRIES' TO UNITE AGAINST LONDON ATTACKS

GERMAN CHANCELLOR ASKS FOR CALM AFTER LONDON KNIFE ATTACKS

THE POLICE STAYED for three hours. They took statements from Famie, Tommi and Sam. They said they had the knifeman in custody and that the dog-walkers had disappeared. A police presence would be kept outside her flat 'for the time being'. Tommi and Sam only left when Famie tried to play them Mozart's *Requiem*. 'I've had quite enough death for today' were Sam's words, and she shooed them both out of the door.

'And yes, I've got food in,' she assured them. 'I'm not a fucking imbecile.'

As it turned out, she didn't have food in but couldn't face the thought of negotiating take-out with the police. So she made toast then raised the volume on the Dies Irae until she felt the drums and cellos vibrating in her bones. The treble – or was it quadruple? – gin was working its way rapidly through her shattered body and the crashing urgency of the music penetrated to her core. Sprawled on her sofa, waves of sadness overwhelmed her. Seth was dead. Mary was dead. They were all dead. She closed her eyes and in spite of the Mozart, in spite of the grief, fell asleep.

A fusillade of knocks on the door woke her with a start. Famie leapt to her feet, heart racing, head spinning. Images of knives, bloodied steps and zebra crossings faded quickly. She pushed back against the sofa, calves against its battered fabric, steadying herself. It was dark now. The streetlights provided the room's only illumination and there was just enough for her to get to the window without crashing into anything. She glanced down from her second-floor window. The police car was still there, its interior light on, an occupant talking into his or her radio. Did they know there was someone at her door? Her phone said 10.20 p.m. and sixteen missed calls. Christ. More spirited knocking, and she jumped again. Either it was one of her neighbours or someone had gained access to the block. No one in the block had ever visited before but then she'd never made the news before.

She drew the curtains in the lounge, then edged her way to the front door. She swallowed hard and was about to peer through the fish-eye security lens when a man's voice hailed her.

'Ms Madden, it's PC Grantley. We've been trying to ring. There's someone here says she's your daughter?'

Famie uttered the smallest of staccato gasps. She stooped to the fish-eye. Behind the uniform she could see a familiar head of curls and suddenly she couldn't get the door open quickly enough. The sight of her daughter, all angles and awkwardness, triggered a wave of emotion and Famie embraced her fiercely.

'I said don't come,' Famie said, once she had regained some composure.

'And I knew you didn't mean it,' said Charlie, extricating herself with difficulty.

They both nodded their thanks to the policeman, who disappeared down the stairs.

Famie steered her daughter inside and on to the sofa. 'I'll get you some tea,' she said. 'Or gin if you'd rather. Or both. I'll get both.'

Charlie stabbed a finger at the sofa cushion next to her. 'Just sit down and talk, Mum. I had a drink on the train anyway. Just talk.'

She tried a smile. It was what her grandmother would have called a brave face but Famie wasn't fooled. She wouldn't have noticed the smell of alcohol but she did notice the tobacco lingering in her daughter's hair, the trembling hands. The fear radiated off Charlie in waves.

They talked, arm in arm, until Famie's voice started to slur with exhaustion. Charlie put her mother to bed, then crashed in her old room, smiling briefly at the bed's familiar creaks. Both women were asleep in minutes.

10

Wednesday, 23 May, 6.05 a.m.

BRITISH PRIME MINISTER SAYS LONDON KNIFE ATTACKS 'BLATANT ATTACK ON OUR WAY OF LIFE'

BRITAIN IS 'COUNTRY UNITED AGAINST TERROR' – PM

'WE WILL SEEK JUSTICE AGAINST THE MURDERERS WHO COMMITTED THIS OUTRAGE'

LONDON, May 23 (IPS) – Britain is a 'country united against terror', the UK Prime Minister said in his latest comments on the multiple knife murders in London on Tuesday.

'When we have mourned, we will seek justice against the murderers who committed this outrage,' he told reporters outside his official residence.

The alcohol and the telephone woke Famie. She killed the phone, then went in search of painkillers. She pushed at the lounge door then recoiled from the savage brightness that enveloped her.

'Hey Mum.' Charlie appeared from out of the blaze, pulled her mother's T-shirt from out of her knickers. 'PC Grantley was here.'

Famie was rooted to the spot, hand over her eyes. 'Already? Only been asleep five minutes.'

Famie felt herself being steered into the kitchen, the door clicking shut behind them. She slumped on to the kitchen chair. Closed her eyes again.

'Paracetamol,' she mumbled, her mouth sticky with sleep. 'Nurofen. Aspirin. Whatever's in the tin above the microwave.'

She felt two tablets being pressed into one hand, a cup of water into the other.

'Christ you're good. Can I smell coffee?'

'By your right hand,' said Charlie, settling into the other chair. 'The police wanted to tell you the tramp guy with the knife was just a tramp guy with a knife. A penknife.'

'Is that right,' said Famie, her words blowing the steam from her mug.

'Apparently.'

'And the dog-walkers? Don't tell me . . .'

'Just dog-walkers. Well, two of them anyway. They contacted the police when they heard what had happened in the park.'

Famie sighed, sipped some coffee. 'Coppers must think I'm an idiot. Lost my marbles.' She felt the liquid scorch its way into her stomach.

'Actually they were very sympathetic.'

Famie shook her head slowly. 'To you, maybe. But trust me, they'll think I'm an idiot.' She sipped more coffee, peered at her daughter. 'You're dressed already?'

Charlie gave herself a cursory up-and-down. 'Slept like this. Needed to look my best for PC Grantley.'

Famie nodded. 'I'm sure he appreciated it. Crumpled university T-shirts will be just his thing.'

They both smiled, but Charlie's faded first. She leant forward on her chair, pushing loose curls from her forehead.

'You're not working today, are you?' she said, her words managing to be both a question and a request.

Famie felt the coffee buzz and wanted more. She reached for the pot, offering it first to Charlie, who declined.

'I'm full already. Mum, you've not answered the question.'

'Full already?' said Famie, pouring. 'How long have you been up?'

Charlie crossed her legs, irritated. 'Since five, which was when my phone started buzzing. Yours too by the way.' Famie reached for her phone, charging on the table next to her, but Charlie covered it with her hand. 'Tell me you're not going. Whatever those messages say. I haven't come home just to make you breakfast and then wave you off. Say it.'

Famie managed a smile. 'If I said it's supposed to be business as usual . . . that you can't let the terrorists win . . . life must go on . . .'

'I'd say you were talking bullshit and you know it. So tell me you're not going in.'

Famie gave in. 'OK, OK, I'm not going in. Life, it would seem, doesn't go on after all.'

Charlie released her phone. 'Right decision.' Mission accomplished, she popped bread into the toaster.

Famie read her messages. A text stream from Sam, then Tommi and most of her team. An invitation to join a WhatsApp group. Emails from IPS management and HR. The gist seemed to be that the offices would be open that day but staff were not required to attend.

'Correct,' said Famie out loud.

Charlie turned but said nothing.

Famie's phone vibrated again but she hesitated before reading the message, finishing her coffee. The cosy domesticity of a breakfast with her daughter was proving a welcome anaesthetic against the world. Famie didn't want it to finish.

'How's your course going?' she asked.

'Fine,' said Charlie, handing her buttered toast. 'Finish your messages.'

'Tough crowd,' muttered Famie, and read her text. It was from the EMEA editor Ethan James. She read it twice. It was succinct. It was heartbreaking. She folded her hands tightly around her phone, took a deep breath.

'You want to come to a funeral?'

Charlie was startled. 'Already?'

Famie closed her eyes, felt Charlie's hand on hers. 'It's Seth's. They prioritized the post-mortem.' She kept her eyes closed, realized how much she wanted Charlie to say yes. 'If you're not missing a lecture or anything,' she added weakly.

Charlie laughed. 'Do you ever stop your bloody parenting?' she said. 'Anyway, yes, I'll be missing a lecture and a tutorial.'

Famie opened her eyes and smiled. Shrugged.

'But you're coming anyway?'

Charlie nodded. 'But I'm coming anyway.'

Famie had been to six funerals before: her mother, three grandparents, an old school friend and a journalist colleague. Cancer (twice), dementia, heart attack, overdose and a land mine. They had all been unbearable, a time to rage against the injustice and indignity of life, and now, in a back row of the overflowing Palmers Green mosque, she raged again. The setting was different, her modest dress and head-covering were different, but the raw anger was the same. Eyes closed, she gripped hold of Charlie's hand for support.

Seth Hussain had managed to combine gentleness with a forensic toughness that had won people's admiration across IPS and throughout journalism – the turnout was testament to that. He had been a loyal friend then a devoted, if reticent, lover. He had been sweet and beautiful, and then some maniac with a knife had taken him away. She suspected the silent prayers were giving fulsome praise and thanks to a God Seth hadn't believed in, and she gripped her daughter's hand tighter.

Maybe funerals become an accumulation, thought Famie. It wasn't just Seth she was grieving for but all the others she'd lost. There was too much unfinished business here, too many people she missed. Whatever the truth of it, Famie could barely bring herself to look at the coffin. She had many wonderful images of Seth in her mind, she didn't need them sullied by his death.

Instead, she glanced along the rows of mourners. Most of her last shift were here. Tommi then Sam caught her eye and nodded. Young Sophie Arnold had overdone the head-covering and almost disappeared into a voluminous grey scarf. EMEA editor Ethan James sat nervously inspecting his fingernails, and next to the Met Assistant Commissioner, head bowed and hands shaking, sat Andrew Lewis. In twenty-four hours he seemed to have wasted away, his jaw slack, his cheeks sunken. He looked as though he could crumble at any minute, she thought.

She glanced towards the front. The first few rows were all men, some dressed in the traditional ghutra headscarf and robe. An ornate chair had been set closest to the coffin, occupied by a clearly uncomfortable man in his late thirties. Black suit, rounded shoulders, clean-shaven. Long black hair tied up in a bun. Although they didn't look similar, she was sure this was Seth's brother Amal. The brothers had barely spoken in recent years but Seth had had some old photos. The man in the chair fidgeted, glanced around. He nodded at some mourners on the front row. Famie looked at her feet. If Amal was checking who was attending his brother's funeral, she'd rather go unnoticed.

Famie felt Charlie lean closer. 'Life is pain, Highness,' she whispered. She paused, then added, 'Anyone who says differently—'

Famie finished the line for her: '. . . is selling something.' She smiled and nodded. Where would she be without Charlie? Their favourite, much-quoted line from the movie *The Princess Bride*. She nodded towards the imam in his finery and whispered back, 'And do you think he's selling something?'

'I do, Highness, yes,' she said. 'You want to go?'

Famie considered briefly whether it would be seen as disrespectful; whether she should stay for the burial, say a few words to Amal. Probably, she thought, but right now she didn't care. Famie nodded gratefully and they eased their way apologetically down the row.

'Pub,' she said as soon as they'd stepped outside the mosque. Famie breathed the air as though she'd been underwater.

'Taxi,' said Charlie, and they negotiated the cordon of police and press. Cameras pointed, flashlights flashed, and Charlie hailed a passing cab.

They bailed as soon as they thought they were far enough away from the mosque. The first café they passed sold wine and chips. 'Here,' said Famie. 'We'll finish the service in here.' They ordered Pinot Grigio, coffee, pizza, salad, fries, toast and cheesecake from a slightly nonplussed waiter and sat holding hands across the table. Famie poured two generous glasses of wine and raised her glass.

'This is how Seth would like to be remembered,' she said. 'With some shitty wine which has been made just about bearable – let's say sanctified – by great company.'

Charlie raised her glass, clinking it against Famie's. 'To Seth, then,' she said, holding her mother's gaze. 'You two did this a lot, didn't you?'

Famie nodded. 'We did.'

'He was special?'

Famie sighed, then smiled. 'He was special.'

'Mum, I'm so sorry.'

Famie smiled again. 'It was over a while back, but it was good while it lasted.'

'So you didn't want to stay at the funeral longer?' asked Charlie.

Famie took a bite out of a slice of pizza, gulped some more wine. 'I went. I sat. I wore the right clothes. I didn't complain about the patriarchy.'

Charlie laughed, and clinked her mother's glass again. 'Fair enough. Did you know his brother?'

Famie shook her head. 'Seth didn't talk about him much, said they were very different. I asked about him sometimes but it never went anywhere.' She shrugged. 'Anyway, I need to seriously pace myself.'

Charlie looked puzzled. 'Why so?'

'One down, six to go.'

Charlie's eyebrows shot up. 'You're going to all of them?'

'I am,' said Famie. 'I realized as we walked into the mosque. There's something at stake here, Charlie. If there's anything I believe in, it's journalists being able to be journalists without being intimidated. And if some murderous fuckers want to take us out then the very least I can do, the very least, is to stand with my kind. Stand with my people.' She dipped some chips in a small pot of ketchup, then waved them in front of her face for emphasis. 'I'm going to all of them.'

Charlie looked reassured then cast her eyes to the table, toying with the salad. 'Respect to you, Mum. Proud of you. But I'm really sorry, I do need to go back to uni. Tonight. If that's OK? I won't be able to come with you.'

Famie shook her head. 'Wouldn't expect you to. They weren't your colleagues.' She ate the last of the pizza slice. 'Anyway, I didn't sleep with any of the others. I'll be fine.'

11

A HUNDRED MILES away, north and west from Famie's café, the student sat hunched and sweaty over a portable typewriter. It was a 1966 Brother De Luxe with a pale blue cover, a threaded red and black ribbon and black on white keys. Functional, efficient, reliable. The O and I looked worn, and the S had almost disappeared, but the rest of the letters looked, if not exactly pristine, then certainly fit for purpose. His fingers were sweaty and he wiped them – again – on his shorts.

The attic was tiny, airless and overpoweringly hot. The fragile floor made movement of any kind extremely hazardous; one misstep and it would cave in, causing him to fall four metres to his bedroom floor below. It was, however, impressively soundproofed.

He shouldn't be there of course, there was no reason for anyone to be in the attic, but it was the only place in the house that was lagged and muffled enough to obscure his work.

The student held his breath, fingers poised above the keys,

and listened. The water tank hissed the way it always did and the joist he was sitting on creaked when he moved but, apart from that, the house was silent.

The attic door was shut. His bedroom door below was shut.

He began to type.

12

Wednesday, 6 June

ONCE THE OFFICIAL post-mortems and secondary, independent examinations had been concluded, Famie attended funerals in Brighton, Keswick, Penarth, Croydon and Hammersmith. They had been, she thought, Methodist, humanist, Catholic, Anglican, and one she wasn't sure about. She was aware of the continuing media outrage, had seen headlines and caught the occasional news bulletin, but as far as possible she kept her music playing. The endless speculation that followed an atrocity had always seemed to her one of the most demoralizing features of modern news reporting. In the absence of anything new to focus on, the screens and airwaves overflowed with a dizzying array of fools and liars. Famie resolved to avoid them all. Her 'Classical Chill' playlist, all forty-three hours of it, had become her panic room. She visited often.

The police had called once. Two detectives from the Met had asked her the most cursory of questions about the Investigations team and what they might have been working on. Famie found herself apologizing for being of so little help. One of them had left his card.

The final service, just over two weeks on from the attacks, was Mary Lawson's, and it was the one she was dreading the most. With the others, the grieving families were unknown to her, but Mary's was different. Famie had met her children, Freddie and Ella, at their house, bought them presents for their last birthdays. After writing them both letters about their mother, she had briefly considered asking Charlie back before calling Tommi and Sam instead.

Famie hauled on her 'uniform' one more time. Knee-length black shift dress, black beret. They travelled together to the Northamptonshire village of Ashby St Ledgers, 'population one hundred and seventy-three', declared Tommi, reading from his phone.

'Not today,' said Sam, eyes on the traffic jam they'd just joined. 'If we make it in time, it'll be many times that.'

'And all of them journalists,' said Famie. 'Lucky Ashby St Ledgers.'

They crawled through the village, along a twisty, narrow road lined with coach houses, thatched cottages and Land Rovers. One-way traffic all the way to the church. They were directed along a grassy track to an adjoining bone-dry and virtually grassless field. Billows of dust enveloped the queues of cars, directed into lines by a teenage boy in an orange beanie hat. Famie edged her Volvo X40 saloon up against a hedge.

'Apart from this god-awful knot in my stomach,' she said, 'for all the world this feels like we're going to Latitude.'

'Just without the designer beer tents,' said Tommi, opening his door.

Famie checked the dashboard thermometer. 'Thirty-four degrees. Christ, this is going to be tough.'

They joined the stream of mourners who were making their way to the church, shuffling back along the track. Low, ancient walls revealed a small graveyard. A few headstones were adorned with flowers. Most were bare.

The TV trucks had been lined up in a tight formation in front of the church's simple wooden gate. 'Open daily' said a sign. A short path cut through the graveyard to the porch, its ironstone walls glowing in the sunshine. Famie hesitated, the knot tightening. She took a deep breath and stepped inside. The cool air was a relief and carried with it the omnipresent church smells of damp wood and dusty books.

A solemn woman nodded at them. 'Out of service sheets, I'm afraid,' she stage-whispered. 'Last seats on the back pew.'

Tommi stood, Sam and Famie sat. No one spoke. The only sounds came from the fifteenth-century pews which creaked as their occupants tried and failed to find a comfortable position. Famie forced herself to face the front. Mary's coffin rested on trestles and was topped with a rose, lily and ivy wreath spelling 'MUM'. Freddie and Ella sat either side of their father, his arms draped around them both.

The vicar arrived. Another salesman. They sang, they prayed, they sang again. Mary's widower managed a few words of a eulogy which had to be completed by a friend.

So much crying, thought Famie. I've heard so much crying.

The committal was an old-fashioned burial at the back of the church, out of sight of the cameras. Famie held back, reluctant to encroach on the family's grief, but when eleven-year-old Ella, her face a study of stoicism, waved at her, she melted. Pulling Sam and Tommi with her, Famie forced herself to the graveside. It was a smaller party now, maybe thirty strong. Two weathered and worn old crosses stood nearby. Here, the grief was intense. It ran through every clenched hand, every tear-lined face. Famie was overwhelmed. The knot in her stomach finally unwound, and the tears flowed. She sobbed from the pit of her stomach. It was a convulsion. She felt Sam and Tommi support her, their hands hooking under her arms, lifting her gently. She steadied herself. Surely it would be over soon.

The priest read on. 'We brought nothing into this world, and it is certain we can carry nothing out. The Lord gave, and the Lord hath taken away; blessed be the name of the Lord.'

Famie opened her eyes.

'Lord, let me know mine end, and the number of my days: that I may be certified how long I have to live.'

Ella and Freddie were lined up by the graveside. The sight of them, faces now screwed up in grief, not wanting to throw their handful of earth on their mother's coffin, was, finally, more than Famie could take. She ran. She ran and sobbed, ran and raged, ran and cursed. Tommi and Sam caught up with her eventually but by then she was almost at the car park and they knew better than to talk to her. She slowed, they all slowed. They walked to the car in silence.

Sam noticed the envelope first. 'Someone's left a message,' he said.

A blue envelope had been tucked under the right windscreen wiper. They all peered at it. It had 'Famie Madden' typed on it.

'What the fuck . . .' she said, tugging it from under the rubber. Welcoming the distraction.

Sam and Tommi pushed closer as she opened the envelope. Inside, a single sheet of white paper, folded once. She pulled it out. Unfolded it. It contained two lines of double-spaced typewriter script.

Famie read out loud. 'You don't need a weatherman to know which way the wind blows.' She looked at Tommi, then Sam. 'Huh?' she said.

'Well at least it's not a parking ticket,' said Sam.

13

THE RETURN JOURNEY was a lighter affair. Three quarter-pounders and a pile of fries sorted their post-funeral hunger and when Famie offered Sam and Tommi drinks at her flat, they accepted. She found a new bottle of gin, some tins of tonic, and filled a bowl with some ice.

'Knock yourself out,' she said.

Famie opened the lounge windows wide to the early evening breeze and the stale, oppressive heat in the flat eased considerably. She sat on the sofa, grabbing her laptop as she propped herself up. From her pocket, she fished out the envelope.

'You don't need a weatherman to know which way the wind blows,' she read again. 'Any takers?' She looked up at Sam and Tommi, measuring tonic into three tumblers, her fingers poised above the keyboard.

'Sounds vaguely familiar,' muttered Sam. 'Line from a film maybe?' He handed Famie her drink.

'Probably someone advertising pizzas or something,' suggested Tommi, already pouring his second.

'OK, you're officially useless,' she said. 'Let's see what Dr Google has to say.' She typed and sent. Her screen filled with text and video links, and she hit the first one. 'There you go,' she said, spinning the screen to include Sam and Tommi. She hit play. A black and white video started to play. A young waistcoated Bob Dylan stood in a ramshackle street, white A3 cards held in his hands.

'What is it?' said Tommi.

Famie's jaw dropped theatrically. 'What is it?' she said. 'Really?'

Tommi shrugged.

'"It",' said Famie, 'is one of the most iconic videos of all time.'

'If you say so.'

'Remind me not to put you on any entertainment stories,' she said.

They watched as the singer held, then threw away the cards, each with key words and phrases from the song written on it in black marker.

'And that's Allen Ginsberg on the other side of the street,' she said. Tommi opened his mouth to speak but Famie ploughed on. 'And if you ask who Allen Ginsberg is, you're fired.' Tommi closed his mouth.

'I don't get it,' said Sam.

'Wait,' said Famie, 'I remember this now. My dad used to play this stuff all the time.'

Dylan was into the second verse, the words 'District Attorney' etched in black capitals on his card. There followed 'Look Out!', 'It Don't Matter', 'Tip Toes', 'No Dose', 'Those', 'Fire Hose', 'Clean Nose' and 'Plain Clothes'.

'I still don't get it.'

'Shut the fuck up, Tommi,' shouted Famie, pausing, rewinding slightly. 'Listen, for Chrissakes.'

She hit play. As Dylan dropped the 'Plain Clothes' card, he

sang the words they'd been looking for – 'You don't need a weatherman to know which way the wind blows' – while holding a card with 'Wind Blows' written on it.

There was silence in the room.

'OK, well, so what?' said Sam. 'It's a line from a Bob Dylan song.'

' "Subterranean Homesick Blues",' said Famie.

'OK, it's a line from "Subterranean Homesick Blues". And?'

Famie spread her arms wide. 'And . . . I have no idea. It means something. Rings a bell I think, but right now, I've not a clue. Neat video though. I'd forgotten how much I love his stuff.' She selected some tracks from a playlist on her laptop and the opening chords of 'Tangled Up In Blue' played from the speakers.

'Your brain has been addled by all that Mozart,' said Sam over the intro. 'Now this is music.' He raised his glass, clinked the ice.

They sat in silence, a companionable if mournful silence. Famie glanced at her friends; Sam with his eyes closed, Tommi leaning forward, eyes to the floor. She knew they were about to embark on an alcohol-driven, post-funeral reflection so she thought she would go first.

'Well today has been fucking awful,' she said. 'Much like yesterday and the day before that. But' – she waved her glass for emphasis – 'that burger and this gin taste wonderful. So I've decided to resign. Cheers.' She took her turn to raise her glass.

Tommi looked up. Sam furrowed his brow.

'Sorry, what?'

She smiled at her bemused colleagues. It wasn't what she had been planning to say, in fact she was surprised to hear herself say the words at all. But they sounded sweet so she said them again. 'The burger and the gin taste wonderful and I'm quitting.'

Tommi shook his head. 'You need second eyes on that

sentence, Fames. That's a non sequitur right there. The second half of the sentence doesn't fit with the first. Didn't you learn anything at journalism school?'

Famie dumped her laptop and spun herself to face them. 'This may sound stupid and I might message you in the morning taking it all back, but I'm serious. And no, Tommi, it all makes sense. To me anyway. I've had enough. Enough of the restructurings, the reorganizations and the improvements that *always* make things worse. Enough of the bullshit. I'd had enough before . . . before all of this.' She pointed at Sam and Tommi's funeral suits and her black dress. 'These are our work clothes now. This is what we wear. Every fucking day. Look at us! I never want to wear this again. In fact . . .' She stood up from the sofa, exiting the room as swiftly as the gin would let her. In her bedroom she pulled off the dress and grabbed some jeans and a T-shirt from the laundry bag. She reappeared in the lounge still zipping herself in. 'There. I've resigned. What do you think?' She paraded in front of them like a catwalk model.

'I think you're pissed,' said Tommi.

'Pissed but serious,' suggested Sam.

Famie pointed at him. 'In one, Sam, got it in one. There's voluntary redundancy on the table and I'm buggered if I want to spend one more second of my life feeling terrified. I have no idea what I'll do. But where I was just depressed about work before, now I'm depressed and scared, and that's just stupid. For any of us.' She felt surprisingly, delightfully exhilarated by her own words and wondered if she should call Charlie.

How swiftly our roles reverse, she thought, that I now need approval from my child.

'I know this isn't exactly the point here, Fames,' said Tommi, 'but where precisely does the burger and gin come into all of this?'

Famie sat cross-legged on the floor in front of him, glass in her lap. 'But it is the point, Tommi, it is precisely the point,' she said. 'After the funeral we were so hungry, so desperate for a drink that when we got both, they tasted amazing. That's what life should be like! That's what life is like for everyone else!'

Tommi looked sceptical. 'Burger and gin every day?'

Famie's shoulders slumped. 'It's a metaphor, Tommi, cut me some slack here. It's normal life I'm talking about and I'd like some. That's all.'

'You'd hate it,' said Sam. 'We'd all hate it.'

'Maybe,' said Famie, 'maybe. But right now I'd hate it a whole lot less than wondering if some psycho with a knife is waiting for me around every street corner.'

Many hours later, when Famie got up to close her windows and take some painkillers, she picked up the discarded windscreen note from the sofa. While she waited in the near dark of her lounge for the tablets to kick in, she played with it in her hands, wondering again why it had been left for her in the first place. No other cars had one. It wasn't a flyer. It wasn't mass-produced. It was just for her. In the silence of the night, it seemed a stranger, deeper puzzle than before. She fumbled for the light.

'Ouch,' she said, shielding her eyes with a hand. She took a few seconds.

When she could bear the brightness, she peered at the note. She held it up to the light. Looked on the reverse, then flipped it again. She felt the indent of the letters on the paper. Who used a typewriter these days?

'You don't need a weatherman to know which way the wind blows,' she said aloud.

The nagging bell was still ringing and she reached for her laptop. Repeating her earlier search, she ignored the videos and scrolled further. It didn't take long. Three more clicks and she was there. Famie read fast, her finger following, underlining each word.

> Terrorwatch International archive 1969. The WEATHERMEN. WEATHERMAN. WEATHER UNDERGROUND. Named after the line from Bob Dylan's 'Subterranean Homesick Blues' (1965) 'You don't need a weatherman to know which way the wind blows', this radical American left-wing terror group conducted a campaign of bombings through the mid-70s.

Famie's head cleared fast, her headache lost in the adrenalin rush. She sat on the edge of the sofa, all thoughts of returning to bed fading like the night. The lyric was also the name of this group's 1969 document which called for the destruction of US imperialism and the establishment of world communism. There were speeches to read, links to banned organizations to follow and whole histories to buy.

She stared out of the window to the already lightening sky; lines of grey cloud were flecked with egg-yellow sunlight, but Famie saw none of it. She looked back at the note.

Suddenly she was Slot again; assessing, judging, evaluating. She shook her head.

'Nah,' she said to the room. 'You have to say that seems unlikely.'

14

Thursday, 7 June

FAMIE FIXED A pot of coffee and set herself up at the kitchen table. She flexed her fingers, took a deep breath. Three cups later she had composed her letter of resignation. She knew it was too angry and forced herself to walk round the flat a number of times. 'Leave with grace,' she heard Charlie say. 'Why cause more trouble?' she heard her mother say. She drained the coffee.

'Fuck it,' she said, and hit send.

Her phone rang. The display said 'Andrew Lewis', then, in smaller letters, 'Be nice'.

She picked up. 'Christ that was quick,' she said.

'I'm sorry?'

'Hello, Andrew. Sorry. I've just this second copied you in on an email, and then you called. Anyway, I just quit.' There was silence. 'Sorry about that,' she added. She heard the depth of his sigh, its force rattling the phone's earpiece.

'OK,' he said. 'I was half expecting it. Listen, could you come in, Famie? Something's come up and I'd rather talk here if you don't mind.'

Famie shrugged. 'Sure. I was coming in anyway. Start saying goodbye to the troops, you know.'

She showered and dressed, feeling lighter than she had for weeks. In her best T-shirt and favourite jeans she caught the tube. Headphones on, she selected the brightest, jauntiest aria she could think of. She would not think of Harry who had died on the Kentish Town steps and she would not think of Brian who had ended up under the train at Pimlico. Instead she would focus on the tumbling melodies tripping through her head.

At the Green Park line change, forced to engage with her fellow travellers, she found the ordinariness of the rush hour upsetting. London was back to normal. The trains were on time, the carriages were full. It felt to Famie like a collective, city-wide shrug of the shoulders. Recent headlines had been all about keeping calm, carrying on and the spirit of the Blitz, but she was sure that most had concluded that this was, quite specifically, an attack on journalists. So, unless you were one, you didn't have to worry.

Ungrateful bastards, she thought.

However, in a month's time she wouldn't be one either. So what did that make her? Maybe the terrorists had won, maybe she was running away.

She had resigned to the head of Human Resources, Gibson Perks, a man she considered a patronizing fool. She knew he was sensitive about his name so Famie had always made a point of calling him Gibbo, even opening her resignation email with a brisk 'Hi Gibbo'. She looked forward to their imminent meeting. He would, she imagined, be sitting with bureau chief Andrew Lewis, and that conversation would be tougher. He was a man who cared about his staff, knew what it took to file a good story, and when the strikes were called last year he was the first one out. Famie knew he would be sad and disappointed in her. Might even try to talk her out of it. But her mind was made up.

At Canary Wharf she texted Sam and Tommi to let them know that she had quit as she had said she would, and was on her way into work to say her farewells. In the plaza she paused for the scrolling news ticker. 'London terror attacks: three further suspects sought. New statement from Home Secretary today. Victim's wife asks for calm.' Famie removed her headphones and reached for her pass. She glanced at her old ID photo encased under the plastic; a glasses-free, serious-looking, fatter-faced thirty-something stared back. She remembered that Charlie had been particularly difficult when the picture was taken – tantrums, bed wetting, even swearing at her teachers. Famie fancied she could see the stress in her laminated eyes. She'd be happy not to see it every day.

Famie bounded up the steps to the IPS building, rode the lift to the fourth. As she gazed out at the cavernous newsroom, the tables and computers fully loaded, her stomach tightened. This was what she was losing, this was what she was saying goodbye to. She reached for the typewritten windscreen note in her bag, pulled it out. Read it over.

'So be it,' she said, reassured. 'Let's do this.'

Across the floor, and as expected, Lewis was in his office with Gibbo hovering outside. Famie kept her head down and reached it without anyone noticing she was in. 'Hey Gibbo,' she said to Perks's back, then knocked and entered. A tidy office, glass on two sides, framed photos of family and certificates on the other two. The desk held only a computer screen, a phone and a bowl of sweets. Unlike many journalists of his generation, there were no trophies in Lewis's office. No photos of his reportage, no souvenirs of Berlin, Chechnya, Johannesburg or Rome. It was one of the reasons Famie liked him.

Andrew Lewis finished his call, beckoning her to the single chair on the other side of his desk. Perks had followed her in and had to stand.

'Mint?'

Lewis offered Famie the bowl. She shook her head. He unwrapped one, slipped it in his mouth.

'Well,' Lewis said, exhaling sharply. 'As I said, I can't say I'm surprised. Utterly miserable of course, but not surprised.'

She thought he looked slightly better than he had at Seth's funeral. There was at least some colour in his cheeks, but only just.

'How many?' asked Famie.

'You're the twelfth,' he said.

'Thirteenth,' corrected Perks, bowing slightly as he spoke, 'Brook Hitching. This morning too.'

Lewis ignored him. 'I suppose there's no point in arguing . . .'

'None at all,' said Famie.

'Thought not.'

She stared at her soon-to-be ex-boss wondering if he too was considering his position. The wrong side of sixty and clearly bruised by the forced reorganization, it wouldn't be a surprise.

'You could be the fourteenth, Andrew. You must have considered it,' Famie said.

Perks rustled his papers. 'Ah. I'm not entirely sure that is—'

'Oh do fuck off, Perks,' said Lewis, wafting his hand at him. 'Wait outside, there's a good management stooge.'

Famie snorted. Perks flushed, pursed his lips and slipped out.

'Class,' chortled Famie, 'particularly as you are management.'

'Maybe,' he said. 'That's certainly what it says on the door, though I seem to have a low tolerance for bullshitters like Perks these days.' He pushed his glasses up to his forehead. 'And, yes, of course I've thought about getting out. Mary certainly wants me to quit.' He leant back in his chair, stretching.

'But I've been selling the bright new streamlined future, Famie, I can hardly bail on it now.'

He pointed at the paper in her hand. 'What's with the note?'

She had almost forgotten she had it.

'Who do you think killed them, Andrew?' Famie said. 'Who did it? The papers speculate all the time but you've done crime stories all your life – what's your best theory?'

Lewis wheeled his chair forward, leant his elbows on the desk. 'The police seen you yet?'

'Just the once,' said Famie. 'I was seriously useless, I'm afraid. Couldn't recall a single conversation about what they were investigating. He seemed frustrated with our computers. Wanted to know where we store our work, keep the files. Sounded like they couldn't find much. Have they made any progress?'

He shook his head. 'No, I don't think so. Apparently all the investigators' work files stop on March the first. After that, everything went off book. That's what I'm told.'

'All of it?'

Lewis spread his arms. 'Emails are there, work files and contacts are not.'

'That must be a lot of paperwork somewhere,' said Famie.

Lewis shrugged. 'Presumably. But they wouldn't tell me anyway.'

He hesitated, and Famie took the opportunity to place her note on his table.

'It was on my windscreen at Mary's funeral.'

She watched while he read and reread the words.

'It's Bob Dylan,' she said.

'You don't say.' Lewis sounded offended. '"Subterranean Homesick Blues",' he said. 'I have the vinyl.' He flipped the paper, handed it back. 'And? Why are you showing me this?'

Famie could tell he was unimpressed.

'It's not just that it's Dylan,' she said. 'The words have been associated with the American Weathermen. They set off bombs in the seventies.'

Lewis rubbed his forehead. 'I know that too, Famie, but what has that to do with anything?'

She could feel the wind leaving her sails. Saying it out loud had sounded ludicrous. 'Just thought someone might be trying to tell me something, that's all. And the fact the words are associated with political violence is interesting. Isn't it?' She glared at Lewis with more defiance than she felt.

He reached for a box file, pushed it towards her. She guessed the contents.

'Green ink time?'

He nodded. 'And all the email equivalents. Every crazed conspiracy you've heard of and some you haven't. All with their personal "insights" and "evidence".' He mimed the quotation marks. 'Shall I add yours to the pile?' He offered her the note back.

Famie bridled. 'Oh come on, Andrew, that's unfair. And patronizing. It was addressed to me. Left for me. It means something. And so no, I won't add it to your crazy pile.' She stood up, snatching the paper back. She would have walked out too but, realizing this might be their last meeting, bit down on another retort.

Lewis was on his feet. He spread his arms. 'OK, I'm sorry if my tone was wrong. I do that quite a lot apparently. And . . .' He sighed again. 'There's something else you should know before you ride out on your high horse.'

Famie waited, eyebrows raised.

'It's what I wanted to talk to you about . . .'

'What is it, Andrew?'

'How well did you know Seth's brother?' he asked.

'Amal?' she said, surprised by the question. 'Saw him at the funeral. But didn't know him at all. They barely spoke. Why?'

In the second-long pause before Lewis gave her an answer, Famie guessed it wouldn't be good.

'Because,' said Lewis, 'he's EIJ. And he's disappeared.'

Christ. Famie sat down. Egyptian Islamic Jihad. No wonder Lewis had dismissed her windscreen note.

'Disappeared?'

'Syria probably. Iraq possibly. They're looking for him. It's their best guess.'

Famie felt the ground move underneath her. It would just be a matter of time before the police came back to her.

Lewis saved her the next question. 'And yes, they know about you and Seth.'

She nodded. 'Of course they do.' It was barely a whisper. 'And EIJ? Seriously? Seth was an atheist and . . . and a human rights campaigner, for Christ's sake. And he has an Islamist terrorist for a brother?'

They kept a brief silence.

'Left Stansted for Berlin the day after the funeral,' Lewis said. 'Then he disappears.'

Another silence.

Eventually Famie spoke. 'Well. You have to say it's a pretty strong lead,' she said.

Lewis nodded. 'Stronger than Bob Dylan anyway,' he said.

15

FAMIE WAITED FOR the police in Lewis's office. The detective who had left his card was, it turned out, already in the building, speaking to officers on the ground floor. DC John Milne had answered her call on the first ring. He'd be ten minutes. Andrew Lewis said they could use his office and left her to it. She watched him exchange words with Perks then smiled at the HR man's obvious irritation.

Famie paced the floor. Amal Hussain being EIJ was a big deal. It was going to mess up her life for sure, but she couldn't deny the logic of the story. It wasn't exactly a breakthrough, but when DC Milne came through the door, she knew it would be the first thing on his mind. There would be opening pleasantries of course, he'd pretend to be concerned for her welfare, ask after Charlie and so on. Then it would be the terrorist links of her former lover.

She took one of Lewis's mints.

John Milne was exactly ten minutes. She watched him stride across the newsroom floor, his eyes already on Lewis's office. In his wake, a diminutive woman hurried to keep up.

Famie resumed her pacing. She admired the police, had often needed the police, but that didn't mean she had to like dealing with them.

'Famie Madden?' The knock had been perfunctory, then a head was in the doorway.

She nodded, and Milne slid in. Six two, white, mid-fifties, safari suit, the khaki jacket worn thin and the trousers shapeless. The wardrobe of a man who cared little for presentation, Famie thought.

'DC Milne,' he said, wafting his ID. 'We met a couple of weeks back. And this is DC Hunter.' He gestured to the round-faced black woman, who nodded at Famie. Grey suit, white shirt, cropped hair. She too showed her ID. A polite smile.

'Well,' said Famie, looking around. 'Welcome to my office, make yourselves at home.'

She sat behind Lewis's desk, Milne folded himself into her recently vacated seat, Hunter leant against the door. Famie thought she'd get things started. Save the ballet.

'Shall we talk about Seth then or do you want to go straight for his brother? I'm happy with either.'

Milne opened his mouth to speak but Famie wasn't stopping.

'When I met you before, DC Milne, I had no idea that Amal was EIJ. I hadn't seen him before the funeral. Not once. Just pictures – you know, Seth had a few. Not many. He didn't speak about him much. Not at all really. I asked him about his brother every now and then but he just shrugged and said they had fallen out a while back . . .' Famie realized she was rambling, talking too fast and suddenly nervous. She took another mint.

Milne grasped the moment. 'If I may?' He ran a hand through his thinning sand-and-salt-coloured hair. 'And let me say at the outset that I apologize for the personal nature of these questions. It must be a very upsetting time for you and everyone here.'

Manchester, thought Famie, though softened by years down south in the Met.

'Thank you,' she said, slower now, 'and no need to apologize. I know how this works. What do you want to know?'

Milne pointed at his colleague. Her cue. DC Hunter pushed herself off the door.

'How long had you known Seth Hussain?'

'Tell you what,' said Famie. 'This might save you both some time. Here's all of it. We first met when he joined the Africa desk here about three years ago. We were an item for about six months. We split up February last year. It was mutual. There you go.' She folded her hands in her lap.

'Was it a sexual relationship?'

Famie snorted. 'Seriously?'

Blank faces from Milne and Hunter.

'Yes it was. Very much so.' Too much detail, she thought, think before you speak.

Hunter checked her notes. 'So you only began seeing each other after he'd joined the Investigations unit?'

Famie nodded. 'Actually it was at the party he held to celebrate his promotion to Investigations,' she said. 'To begin with I thought he was just being sympathetic because he'd got the job and not me – I'd applied too and was pretty devastated – then I realized he was hitting on me.' She smiled at the memory. 'I allowed myself to be consoled,' she added.

Milne frowned. He had a heavily lined, sun-damaged face, and it creased now. He leant forward. 'So this relationship only started after he'd become an investigator. Why do you think that was?'

Famie ignored his patronizing tone and just shrugged. Then a withering smile. 'I hadn't needed consolation before? Who knows?' She pointed back at him. 'How did you end up with Mrs Milne? Or Mr Milne? Or no one. But if you're suggesting, as I think you are, that he only targeted me because he was an investigator, then that is clearly nonsense.'

Milne let that settle, before adding, 'Actually that isn't what I was suggesting. Quite the opposite.'

Now it was Famie's face that frowned. 'Meaning?'

'Meaning,' said Milne, slowly, 'that *you* only targeted *him* once he became an investigator.'

Famie's face fell. She looked from Milne to Hunter and back. 'You think I did *what*?'

Milne cued Hunter again. She walked over to Lewis's desk. The two women stared at each other.

'Ms Madden.'

'Ms Hunter.'

Famie wondered what could possibly be coming.

'Ms Madden. Why don't we talk about your time in Pakistan?'

16

FAMIE'S JAW DROPPED.

'Pakistan,' repeated DC Hunter. 'You were stationed there for three years?'

Famie barely moved. Hunter's tone was light and conversational but there was no doubting the dangerous territory they were entering. She sat up straight, glaring at her interrogators.

'Really?' she said. 'You want to talk about my time in Pakistan?'

'If you wouldn't mind,' said Hunter.

'Not who killed my colleagues, then? Not what arrests you've made or have I remembered anything the investigators might have been investigating? Not that?' Famie felt her anger rising, knew her cheeks had flushed. The expressionless faces of the DCs in front of her merely inflamed her indignation.

'We will come back to that of course,' said Milne.

'Of course!' shouted Famie. 'But first Famie Madden in

fucking Pakistan.' She banged the desk with her fist, rattling the bowl of mints. 'Genius!' She was on her feet now, and DC Hunter stepped back against the door. Famie knew she had to get out before she made everything worse. She pointed at each police officer in turn. 'Everything there is to know – everything – about my years in Pakistan you can get from the records here. It's the usual mix of trials, elections, rallies, generals, Islamists and bombs. That's it. You want to talk about Seth Hussain any time soon, you come right back. Until then, I've got some job hunting to do.'

DC Hunter stepped aside and allowed Famie out. The door slammed, the glass walls shook.

Famie spun left, ignoring the turned heads, and made for her old team. Most of the UK desks were full; Sam was Slot, head down and typing. She slunk into an empty chair and threw a pencil at him. He looked up and smiled.

'Not being marched off the premises then?'

'Not yet. But I swear to God if I'd stayed in there another second I'd have been arrested for assaulting a police officer,' she said.

She took a few breaths, checked her phone, considered some Chopin. She craved a nocturne the way she used to crave nicotine. She fought the urge, put the phone away, and acknowledged the sad smiles from around the unit. They knew then.

'Look, guys,' she said, 'I'm sorry to go, gutted really, but, well, you know how it is. I need a break, I think.'

Sophie Arnold came over to embrace her, tears in her eyes. Held her for a few seconds. She shook hands with everyone else.

'Why the shouting?' asked Sam, gesturing back at Lewis's office.

Famie explained about Seth, Amal and the EIJ. Then their question about Pakistan. She could tell Sam was unimpressed with her. He was fidgeting, rearranging his crumpled shirt, breaking eye contact.

'Of course they're twats, Famie, but they're twats in uniform,' he said. 'And they are running this show now. So go right back in there, tell them about Pakistan, show them all your photos and bore them like you bored the rest of us. Then they can ask you about Seth. Then they can leave and go talk to some real criminals.'

She knew he was right, and so threw another pencil at him.

'When did you get to be quite so irritating?' she said.

Sam grinned. 'Joanna tells me it's a gift.'

Famie walked back towards the office. She remembered that Sam's police officer partner was the most understanding of women. She would have given a lot to have had someone in her life who was that tolerant but somehow it had never worked out.

Milne and Hunter hadn't moved; she was still by the door, he was still in the visitor's chair. Almost as though they were expecting her return. She perched back on Lewis's seat and smiled sweetly. In the silence, the hum of the air-conditioning unit sounded almost frantic.

'So,' Famie said, assuming they would ignore her brief absence, 'before we start on Pakistan, can I show you this?' She spread the weatherman note on the desk, explained how she had come by it and the significance of the words. Famie could tell they merely saw it as a diversion but humoured her anyway.

'Can I photograph it, please?' asked Hunter.

'Of course,' said Famie. 'Does it interest you at all?'

Hunter shrugged. 'We've plenty of theories to be going on with if I'm honest with you. This is certainly one of them.'

'What are the others?'

'Oh, let me see. The usual list. Jews, Masons, the Royal Family, immigrants, spacemen . . .'

'And now Weathermen from Ashby St Ledgers?'

'It fits a pattern, shall we say? But I've got a copy, thank you.'

'Don't mention it,' Famie sighed. 'So, you wanted to know about Pakistan?'

The cherubic DC Hunter picked up where she had left off. 'Seth Hussain's brother Amal was active in Egyptian Islamic Jihad, an affiliate of al-Qaeda. Al-Qaeda are very active in Pakistan – you must have had contact with them.'

'Why must I have had contact with them?'

'Isn't that what journalists do, Ms Madden, cultivate contacts to get stories, report what's happening?'

Famie stared at Hunter. Maybe it had been a mistake to return after all. She fought to keep it civil. 'We report the news, Ms Hunter. We aren't spies or MI6, we're journalists. Pakistan is a tough place to report from but I'm proud of the work we did and the stories we broke. If you don't talk to the hardliners, you're not doing your job.' Another deep breath. 'I was also delighted to come back home.'

DC Milne's turn. 'So in your three years there you never had any contact with al-Qaeda or any other terrorist organization?'

Famie hesitated. 'Not AQ directly, no,' she said, 'but other groups certainly. Affiliates. They don't wear a uniform, you know, or wear badges. You can't always tell who you're talking to; some army guys often seemed quite sympathetic to the Islamist cause. You never really trusted anyone. But if you're reporting from Pakistan, there are unsavoury men you have to speak to.'

Milne sat on the edge of his seat. 'So it's possible that some of your contacts were in sympathy with al-Qaeda?'

'That is what I've just said, yes. Some obviously, others less so. Like I said, they don't wear badges. You might be a Russian spy or a Chinese agent, DC Milne. I can't tell.'

Milne ignored the sarcasm. Both DCs wrote on their pads.

'And your colleagues?' he said. 'Might they have been Islamist sympathizers too?'

'We seem, Detective Constable, to be, if you don't mind me saying, a long way from the deaths of my friends.' The strain in Famie's voice was clearly audible.

Milne nodded. 'Maybe. Maybe,' he conceded. 'Unless Seth Hussain was, in spite of everything, actually in regular contact with his brother. And unless Amal had been demanding money from his brother. Quite a lot of money as it turns out.'

Famie felt a prickling sensation on her neck and scalp. A profound uncertainty took hold of her. Seth had always been adamant that he had no communication with his brother and that the silence between them had lasted several years. She had had no cause to doubt him. She had never given his honesty a second thought. He was the campaigning journalist and activist – of course he was telling the truth.

'How do you know this?' she said. Then added, 'Wait. Don't tell me. You found another phone in his flat.'

Milne made an expansive gesture with his hands. 'In one, Ms Madden.'

Christ.

Famie was aware of two sets of eyes watching and analysing her every expression. She tried not to show her embarrassment and anger but she was a poor actor. She was mad with herself, mad with Seth and mad with these bloody police officers who had just stolen her memories.

'Just one more question, if we may, and then we'll leave you in peace,' Hunter said. 'Did Seth ever ask you for money?'

The *coup de grâce.*

Famie put her hand in front of her mouth. Her eyes brimmed. She felt old certainties crumble. Yes, of course the answer was yes. It had been their running joke: he was always penniless, she always paid for him. She had lent him small amounts that he was always on the verge of paying back. She squeezed her eyes shut, propelling hot tears down her cheeks.

She nodded.

'We think most of it ended up with his brother,' said Hunter.

17

THE STUDENT HAULED himself back into the attic, pulled up the ladder and listened. Satisfied it was safe, he pulled the typewriter on to his knees.

In the silence before he typed, he recalled the woman from the funeral. He had noticed her in the coverage of all the previous funerals. Stylish. Black beret. Aviator shades. He'd assumed she would attend the seventh. Directing traffic in the field-turned-car park had been inspired. He had just rocked up and done it. No one had asked who he was and the orange beanie hat he wore had covered some of his face. And, he hoped, distracted from his brown skin. There weren't too many like him in Ashby St Ledgers.

When he saw the Madden woman arrive, it had been like an electric shock – he'd felt the adrenalin course through him. After the funeral she had read his note two, maybe three times before handing it to her colleagues. They had, in turn, studied his paper and envelope then handed it back. He hoped he had chosen wisely. She looked sharp, he thought, intelligent. Strong. The two men who accompanied her were deferential, letting her take the lead. In their conversations, it was they who seemed to be looking to her for the answers.

And now he knew where she lived. The unopened mail casually tossed on to the back seat of her car had told him everything he wanted. An unexpected bonus.

He threaded a blank sheet of paper into the rollers and began to type.

18

Friday, 8 June, 2.40 p.m.

FAMIE HAD BARELY slept, her mind racing. The heat was part of it – she had changed her T-shirt twice – but mainly it was the realization that she was in all kinds of trouble. She'd spent the previous afternoon and the morning tidying the flat and researching the EIJ, and a few hours ago had messaged Sam. She needed to talk and she needed to drink. Sam had told Ethan James he needed some time out, and was excused. Sam and Famie had met in a pub, then, with Sam getting hungry, they'd taken an Uber back to her flat. They both rode in the back. Their driver left his radio on, playing loud. Famie was miserable, Sam was reassuring.

'Seth borrowing money means he was terrible with money, that's it,' Sam said. 'Doesn't mean he funnelled every twenty-pound note to al-Qaeda.'

Famie groaned. 'This is so bad, Sam. I am so screwed.' Her words were only slightly slurred. She closed her eyes.

'I bought him a pizza once, you know,' said Sam. 'Spicy chicken I think it was. And he ate it all, Famie. Didn't give it to the nearest terrorist, didn't even try. Imagine that.'

She snorted. 'And the coleslaw?' she said. 'Did you see what happened to that too?'

'Good point, Fames. Maybe he posted it to Syria.'

Elton John was playing, and the driver turned the volume up even more.

Sam leant in closer to Famie. 'The police have to follow every lead, Famie, you know that. They're having hundreds of these conversations.'

Famie held up her hands. 'Enough consolation already. Appreciated and everything, but they seemed deadly serious to me. They think they're on to something, and who am I to say they're not?'

The car turned into Famie's road and Sam grabbed her arm. 'Shit,' he said, and leant forward far enough so that the driver could hear. 'Pull over, please. Soon as you can.' The driver checked the satnav on his phone and was about to protest, but Sam intercepted. 'Now! Pull in here!' The car swerved into the side of the road.

Famie sat up, suddenly alert. 'What is it, Sam?'

He pointed across the fifty metres to her front door. 'Visitors.'

Outside her block of flats, a small gathering. Six men and women were taking it in turns to buzz Famie's intercom. One had a small camera on her shoulder.

Famie slumped back into her seat. 'You have got to be kidding me,' she whispered. 'Oh my God. I know the police leak this stuff all the time but this really sucks.' She slipped lower in the seat. 'Fucking journalists.'

Sam leant forward again, gave the alarmed Uber driver a different address. 'And turn around, would you? Don't drive past that crowd.'

Famie looked up at him. 'Back to yours?'

'You got a better idea?'

'Nope.'

'Me neither.'

'Will Joanna mind? Bringing strange women home can go down badly, I've heard.'

Sam smiled. 'I'll text her now, let her know what's happening. I'm sure the food will stretch. And if you can keep the strangeness to a minimum, we'll be fine.'

'Wait,' said Famie. Then, to the driver, 'Hang on a second, please.' She turned to Sam, grimaced. 'Favour?'

'You mean as well as putting you up for the night?'

'Yes, as well as that. Please. I need my laptop. And a change of clothes.' She fished out her keys. 'Any chance?'

Sam sighed. 'Sure. I'll get the laptop but I'm not rummaging in your knicker drawer if that's OK. Then Jo really would kick off.'

Famie gave him the keys, the alarm code and details of where to find the computer. She watched him push his way past the waiting journalists and ignore their questions. She lowered herself down into the footwell behind the driver's seat. 'Go, Sam,' she muttered.

The driver craned round to look at her. 'You in trouble?' he asked.

'In a way, yeah,' she said. 'Sorry about this.'

He shrugged. 'Not a problem. You OK with the radio?'

She smiled. 'Yeah, I'm fine with the radio.'

'I'm Mazzie,' he said.

'Famie. And thanks for keeping these floor mats clean.'

He looked delighted.

Five minutes passed, then he turned again.

'Your friend is coming back.'

Thirty seconds later Sam opened the back door, his crumpled shirt pulled loose from his trousers. He handed a carrier bag to Famie.

'You are an angel,' she said. 'I'd kiss you if I didn't think that Joanna would somehow instinctively know about it.' She looked inside the bag. One laptop, some post and a hoodie.

'It's not exactly a change of outfit but it was on the floor in the lounge,' said Sam, slightly breathless. 'Might be useful.'

She pulled it on, tugging the hood over her head, then clambered back on to her seat.

'What were the journos asking?' she said. The Uber was moving again, the radio quieter than before.

'Oh,' said Sam, 'usual stuff. "Does Famie Madden live here? Do you know her? Have you seen her lately?" That kind of thing.'

'"Have you been through her underwear drawer?"' suggested Famie.

Sam laughed. 'Of course. The question on everyone's lips.'

She checked the charge on her laptop, then glanced at the post. Her heart started to race. She pulled a letter from the bag.

'Jesus, look at this.' It was the quietness of her voice that caught Sam as much as the tremor. She showed him an envelope with her name and address on it. Written with a typewriter. Sam blanched.

'He knows where I live, Sam,' she said.

There was silence between them.

'Could you drive a bit faster, Mazzie, please?' she said.

19

3.30 p.m.

FAMIE DECIDED NOT to open the envelope until they were at Sam's house. She'd been about to tear it open in the Uber but Sam had put his hand on hers and flicked his eyes towards the driver. 'Wait,' he'd mouthed. She had forced herself to drop the letter back into the carrier bag. The rest of the journey had passed in silence.

'Good luck,' called Mazzie as they got out.

Sam's front door opened as they arrived. They both stepped inside the tiny terraced house and Jo Carter first embraced her husband, then offered her open arms to Famie. She accepted. It was her first proper hug since Charlie left and it felt good. Five three, with shoulder-length black hair held back with a silver band, Jo was prettier than Famie remembered. Plain grey sweatshirt, faded jeans, broad smile. She moved swiftly, ushering them both through to the lounge. A sliding garden door was half open, and the room smelt of cut grass, fresh flowers and some kind of cooked chicken. Famie slumped on to their sofa, a saggy, wilted beast, livened up with the addition of half a dozen brightly coloured cushions. She clutched the carrier bag on her lap.

'Thanks, Jo, I'm sorry for the imposition.'

Jo cut her off. 'Please, no apology needed. Sam's told me what the deal is. Food is on the way, the spare room is made up whenever you need it. Oh, and Tommi said he'd be round in fifteen. Didn't want to miss the fun.'

Famie and Sam watched her leave the room.

'I did well, didn't I?' said Sam.

'You certainly did,' said Famie. 'You must have hidden depths, unknown to the rest of us. Is Jo South African? I forget.'

'Zimbabwe,' said Sam. 'Some South African in the mix, but mainly Zim.'

She took the deepest of breaths, then exhaled through pursed lips, as though controlling a sharp pain. 'So. Can't wait for Tommi. Let's see what our weatherman has to say for himself.' She tore open the envelope, removing a single sheet of folded paper. She unfolded it. In the middle of the sheet, just above the fold, was a row of typewritten numbers. She read them twice, three times. 'Huh?' she said, and held out the sheet for a clearly impatient Sam.

He frowned. '0800 272 4362. Is that it?'

Famie checked the envelope. 'That is most definitely it,' she said. 'I admit to some disappointment. I was hoping for another riddle, not the phone number of some dodgy helpline.'

'But it's an 0800 number,' said Sam. 'That's usually sales of some kind. I told you it was a pizza company.'

Jo returned with tea. 'Is that your mystery typist again?' she said.

Sam showed her the paper.

'Well you'd better dial it then,' she said. 'Use the house phone, we're ex-directory. Here.' She handed Famie a cordless handset. 'If it's a Busty Belinda-type number will you be relieved or disappointed?'

It was a good question. Famie paused, her finger hovering above the digits.

'Disappointed,' she said.

'Relieved,' said Sam.

'Right then,' Famie said.

Heart racing, she dialled the number, hit the speaker button. The phone rang twice, then a recorded message kicked in. No one breathed. Then a woman's voice: 'Thank you for calling the *Daily Telegraph* Classifieds. Here's how you can leave your message . . .'

Famie cut her off, dropped the phone on the sofa.

'Really?' she said, glancing from Sam to Jo. 'What the fuck does that mean?'

'Well either it's a scam or someone has left you a message,' said Sam. 'And no, we haven't got a *Daily Telegraph* to hand. The corner shop might still have one.'

Sam checked his pockets and ran from the room. 'Two minutes,' he shouted before the front door slammed.

Jo smiled at Famie. She oozed reassurance and comfort. No wonder Sam was so loyal. 'You OK?' she said. 'Been a crappy time, eh?'

'You could say that.' Famie tried to return a smile of equal warmth.

'Has Sam told you he's going to quit?' said Jo. Famie's startled look told her everything she needed to know. 'Oh, OK. Well.' She sat down opposite Famie. 'He's going to quit. Had enough. We both have. And when you bailed out, that was the final straw.'

Number fourteen, thought Famie.

Rapid and sustained use of the doorbell took Jo from the room. Seconds later Tommi appeared, jogging Lycra and sweatband competing for attention.

'How very 1985,' said Famie. 'For a moment I thought it was Huey Lewis and the News running in. How are you, Tommi?'

Tommi grunted a reply, snatched up the typed note, then grunted again. 'Is this it? Is this what I ran round for?'

Famie shrugged. 'You tell me.'

'A phone number?'

'The *Daily Telegraph* Classifieds number. And to save you asking, Sam's gone to get one.'

He slumped down next to Famie. He smelt ripe.

'Shower needed, by the way. Just saying.'

Tommi ignored her. 'Envelope?' She handed it to him. He inspected it. 'You should report this. Who knows who this crazy is, but in the space of a couple of days they've found out where you live. Maybe they followed us back from the funeral, who knows. But you should tell the office.'

'Don't have one,' said Famie.

'Oh yeah. Forgot.'

'Plus, Lewis couldn't have been more dismissive if he'd tried.'

'You showed him the note?'

Famie nodded. 'Said he'd put it in the crazy file.'

Tommi read the number again. 'There must be another message. I didn't even know the Classifieds were still a thing.'

The front door burst open and a breathless Sam appeared, throwing a newspaper to Famie. 'Their last one. I told them it was for research.'

Tommi laughed. 'It's not porn, you know, you don't need an excuse to buy it.'

Famie was turning the pages rapidly. 'Anyone know where the Classifieds actually are?' She found them a few pages from the back. Four columns of small messages. She guessed about a hundred. She ran her finger down the first column. Nothing. The second column. Nothing. The third and fourth, nothing. 'Huh,' she said, and repeated the search. 'Plenty of weirdos but not our weirdo.'

'Did we get the wrong day?' said Sam. 'Maybe it's tomorrow?'

'Or never, because he's just weird?' said Tommi.

'Why is this a "he" by the way?' said Sam. 'Plenty of weird women out there.'

Famie glanced again at the note with the number. 'Unless . . .' she said, then stopped. Her mind was racing.

'Unless what?' Sam and Tommi said together.

'Unless we're not supposed to be looking for an ad, we're supposed to be placing one.'

'I'm sorry?' said Tommi.

'Maybe our weatherman wants to talk. He, or she, wants *us* to place an ad.' She looked at three sceptical faces. Shrugged. 'Just a theory.'

Jo was reading the even smaller print. 'You have to place an ad by four p.m. We've got fifteen minutes if we're doing this.'

'We're doing this,' said Famie.

She retrieved her laptop from the carrier bag. She posted her ad with three minutes to spare.

20

5 p.m.

JANE HILTON SAT quietly in the corner of Andrew Lewis's office. Legs crossed, hands held together on her lap. She watched the bureau chief leaf through her report. Four pages, closely typed. He read the first page slowly then sped up as he got to the last page.

'Yeah yeah, got all that,' he said as he skimmed the last paragraph. As much to himself as Hilton. 'What's your point, Jane?' he added. 'As brief as you like. As blunt as you like.' He flipped his glasses to his forehead, sat back in his chair. His face twitched, then settled in neutral.

Hilton looked taken aback. She hooked a strand of hair behind each ear, brushed imaginary creases from her skirt. 'Well I'd have thought that was obvious, Andrew.' She leant in to make it more obvious, forearms resting on her knees, hands still together. 'Famie and I crossed over in Pakistan by nine months. Your high opinion of her is valid. But during that time she seemed to make a point of working with, and reporting on, the most extreme Islamists she could find.' She gestured at the sheets of A4 on his desk. 'I've outlined five cases where maybe what was seen at the time as bravery was, in my judgement, borderline reckless. The first is the 2006 attack on the Mumbai local trains. Seven bombs in eleven minutes. Two hundred and nine dead. An outrage, condemned across the world.'

Lewis raised both his hands, palms out. 'I remember, Jane,' he said, 'I remember. Please. You're not on air. Talk to me like I'm normal. See how that goes.'

Hilton regrouped. Pursed her lips, glanced at the floor. More hair, more creases. 'I think the right response would have been to have gone first to the mainstream parties. PTI, PAT, Pakistan Muslim League, for example. Ask them for comment. But Famie went straight to Lashkar-e-Taiba, the so-called "Army of the Righteous"—'

'Who carried out the attack,' interrupted Lewis. 'Again, I remember. Go on.'

Hilton took a beat. 'You incorporate the crazies in your reporting of course. You get to them. But if you ignore the mainstream then our audience get a skewed view of what's happening. The point I'm making is Famie goes to the extremes. Always has. She distorts and twists. Why talk to the moderates when there's a guy with a gun to talk to?'

Lewis flicked back to the report. 'And then the Mumbai attacks in 2008? The Taj Palace and so on.'

'Same again,' said Hilton. 'She was in Berlin by then but knew all the numbers to call. The quotes she got from Lashkar-e-Taiba were pretty inflammatory. They're just not the first call you make. If there's an outrage here, is the first person you call someone who'll justify that outrage? Or maybe you'd call the victims' families, the police and the ambulance service. I know how I would run it. I think I know how you would run it too, Andrew. When you were in Chechnya you knew who to speak to. You knew how to balance the horror without giving a justification for it.' She sat back, case made. Point proven.

'Fraternizing with the enemy?' said Lewis. 'Is that what you're suggesting?'

Hilton tipped her head one way then the other. Sifting the words. Panning for gold. 'Your choice of words, Andrew. But no, I wouldn't say that. She was on a story. Always on a story. Working her leads. That's what she does. Or did. It's just that her leads were always thugs.'

Lewis considered the point. 'You debated this with her? When you were both in Pakistan?'

Hilton nodded. 'Many times. But she was my senior back then, so . . . she carried on doing it her way.'

Lewis lowered his glasses, picked at the pages in front of him. Reread a few paragraphs. 'And did these . . . thugs, these extreme groups, ever contact her?' he said. 'As far as you know.' He studied her carefully. Hilton's face was impassive. Her camera face.

'I wouldn't be surprised if they did,' she said. 'That's often how it goes. But I don't know that for certain.'

'I see.' He let the silence run. Hilton shifted in her seat. 'And when she started dating Seth Hussain,' Lewis said, 'what was your reaction?'

She shrugged. 'I didn't have one really. He seemed a decent enough journalist. That's it really. They both thought it was some big secret of course. Played it like they were undercover for some reason. And no one knew about Amal then, so . . . that's it.' She shrugged again, this time accompanying it with open palms.

'And now you know about Amal,' prompted Lewis, 'that he is a wanted, known Islamist terrorist . . . what do you think?'

Hilton took a while to collect her thoughts. Eventually she said, 'I don't get surprised any more, Andrew. You said to be as blunt as I liked?'

Lewis gestured a 'carry on' to her.

'Did she date Amal too? Do we know?'

Lewis frowned, deep grooves running between his eyebrows. 'She never met him, apparently,' he said.

Hilton did the head tilt again. 'Oh. OK.'

Lewis recognized her tone. 'I take that to mean why shag a moderate when there's a guy with a gun you can shag instead,' he said.

Hilton folded her arms. 'I'm sure that isn't the case,' she said, her words weighted precisely to mean the opposite. 'But it's an interesting line of inquiry.'

Lewis took a mint, offered Hilton one. She shook her head.

21

6.10 p.m.

THE STUDENT LED that day's interrogation. 'Criticism and self-criticism' was the official term used, CSC for short. The Weathermen had called it a weatherfry. The leader's words were yelled endlessly, thrown in the face of a man who believed in them already.

Wade in filth. Embrace the butcher. Change the world.

There would, the student realized, be plenty of filth to wade in.

The main bedroom of the house was also the largest room in the house, so it doubled as a meeting room. Its windows and sagging, heavy curtains were closed, the temperature oppressive. Two spartan single beds had been pushed into a corner, four wooden kitchen chairs placed around a fifth, like a five of clubs. When the student entered, just behind the leader, a heavily perspiring man was already on a chair, sitting in the centre of the room. His shoulder-length sandy-brown hair was tied up in a messy ponytail, his small black eyes darting between them.

'Can we, maybe, get this done?' he said. 'I'm sure we all have more important things to do here.' He wore running shorts and a tired-looking yellow LA Lakers top with the number 23 stamped on it. One leg bounced nervously.

The student and the leader sat facing him.

'We need to begin.' The leader's voice was light, almost reedy, heavily accented. He wore black browline glasses on a sallow, thin face. A fresh buzz cut, clean-shaven. He placed a small grey box about the size of a remote control on the floor in front of him. Two buttons, one small meter under a clear plastic cover. The leader's own Geiger counter. To warn, he explained, of the inevitable security service attacks.

The man fidgeted some more. 'You tell us that these sessions work, yes? You say you learnt their importance back in Turkey and that they're in use in all citizen groups here.' He scratched his scalp vigorously with both hands. Now he glanced between the student and the leader. 'But aren't we just talking to ourselves? Who cares what I've thought in the past. We all know this country is available to us. All of the pillars that prop it up are hollow. If there's a war to be fought, let's get on and start it!'

The student held up both hands. 'We know, we agree. It's why we're here. But you know how we work.'

They all looked up as a woman entered the room, sliding into one of the remaining seats. 'Sorry I'm late,' she said. She was late twenties, tall, slightly stooped. A face of sharp features – pointed nose and chin, small ears. 'How was the exam?' she said to the student.

'This isn't a fucking social,' interrupted the leader. 'This is work. Hard work. The cell will only become stronger by purging itself. Begin.'

The student dragged his chair so he could sit facing the sweating man. Their knees were touching.

'How long were you a fascist?' asked the student.

The sweating man sighed. 'This shit again? You know it.' He took a breath. 'When I was at school I joined the British

Movement. There was this guy in the year above me and he seemed to know what was happening in the world. So I followed him for a while.'

'Answer the question,' said the student. 'How long were you a fascist?'

'About five years, give or take.'

'That's a long time to be working with criminals,' said the student. 'You must have made many good friends. Do they stay in touch?' He leant closer. 'Do you stay in touch?'

The sweating man shook his head. 'Stay in touch? Is this a joke? The rules – your rules – say no computers, no phones, no website, no online presence at all. We're off the grid. Invisible. Even if I wanted to stay in touch with the fash, I'd have to write them fucking letters!'

'And do you?' said the student, his tone still conversational.

The sweating man glanced around the room. 'What is the point of all this? Honestly? You know I don't. I spend all my fucking time here with you guys. We're all just waiting to be useful, to link up, to cause some damage. To bring the war home. It's what we're training for, isn't it?'

'When did you realize your crimes? Say it out loud.' The student placed a curled finger under the sweating man's dropped chin, pushed it back up again. 'Tell us.'

The man bristled, leant forward. He turned his head and spoke his words to the leader. 'My crime,' he said, speaking with a controlled emphasis, 'was not to see that globalization had made slaves of us all, that the corrupt oppressor class had control of the so-called left as well as the right, that human rights are an imperialist vanity and that elections don't mean shit.' He sat back.

The student leant in again. 'What doubts do you have about our project?'

'None. I have no doubts. This country is weak now. It is not how it was. Everyone knows this. Our analysis – your analysis – is the right one. It is ready for insurrection. The institutions are discredited, dysfunctional. All of them. Christ, even the ruling class attack their own Parliament and judges. The country is weak but our cells are strong. Some well-aimed blows and it all could crumble. So no, I have no doubts.'

The student kept his eyes on him. 'That's not quite right, is it?' he said.

The sweating man's eyes flashed with irritation. 'OK, sure, well I found the whole secrecy thing difficult for a while. That's not a secret. It's the twenty-first century. Using old tech seemed weird to me. But I get it now. The best way to avoid detection is to have no digital footprint. I honestly get it. Typewriters, letter drops, invisible ink, phone boxes, all of it.'

The leader removed his glasses. He was getting restless. The student had to go for it now.

'Are you a saboteur?' the student said.

The question caught the man off guard and he looked startled. 'Am I a what?'

'Are you a saboteur?' the student repeated, the words sticky in his mouth. 'A class traitor. An informant.'

The sweating man's face had changed from sneering aggression to extreme discomfort in a moment. His mouth fell open, his eyes darted between the student and the leader. 'Sweet Jesus, you're serious.'

The student punched him in the face. The leader took out a knife. Wooden handle, long blade.

Wade in filth. Embrace the butcher. Change the world.

22

Saturday, 9 June, 4.35 a.m.

THE STUDENT COULDN'T stop the leader's words rattling around his head. He might as well have 'embrace the butcher' tattooed on his eyelids. And yesterday they had all learnt the longer version. Just before the leader performed the cut. He had closed his eyes, as though making an ecstatic religious utterance. Said the words came from a play. His voice was controlled, soft, but his eyes had been wild. He had glowed with pleasure as he spoke.

If you could at last change the world, would you step up and do it? Wade in filth. Embrace the butcher. Change the world.

Then he had taken the sweating man's ear, stretching it out. The knife he rested on the top, the helix, its outer fold. He was ready to slice. He had addressed his words to the student and the woman. The jury.

'The operation is close. Very close. Soon, all the citizens will strike. We will get our chance to make our mark. To strike against the enfeebled imperialists that devastate the lives of so many. But the closer we get to the enemy, the more likely their attacks on us. We must be watchful. Always watchful.' He had stood on tiptoes. 'We too have a traitor. Yes? And who else than the fascist?'

The leader had cut. The sweating man had screamed.

Now the student lay on his bed, staring at the small red bulb of a smoke alarm high above his head. He had done his best with the salve and the bandages. The sweating man had slept, but his breathing was shallow, troubled.

The student thought about his sisters and took courage. As soon as the shops opened he would check the newspaper. If the IPS woman had replied, he'd buy a prepaid phone and send the next message. He ran through the words in his head, then muttered them under his breath.

They felt right. He swung out of bed and dressed quietly.

23

7.45 a.m.

THE CARTERS' SPARE room was tiny with barely enough space for the single bed and upturned wooden box that functioned as a bedside table. Famie hadn't slept much. She'd texted Charlie from bed, then got woken up by her reply at four a.m. That had been that. She'd lain awake with images of yesterday's journalist scrum at her front door running through her head.

A gentle knocking brought an already dressed Jo into her room. 'Sorry to disturb,' she whispered, 'but thought you'd like to see the paper.' She left a *Telegraph* on the end of the bed and exited.

Famie wiped sleep from her eyes and sat up. 'Thanks,' she called after Jo.

The paper had been folded at the Classifieds page. Her ad was nestled between an apocalyptic quote from the Book of Revelation and an advert for a new cat food.

Long-range forecasting is complicated.
Which way is the wind blowing?

Famie was pleased with it, given the haste of its composition. Her weatherman wouldn't miss it. If he, or she, was looking.

She swung out of bed and pulled her hoodie over Sam's old Def Leppard T-shirt that she'd ended up sleeping in. It came down to her thighs. Just about modest enough to eat breakfast in.

'So we're in then,' she said, flourishing the *Telegraph* as she entered the kitchen.

A radio by the sink played classical music. Sam stood by a coffee machine, frothing milk. He raised his hand in acknowledgement. Jo was eating a bowl of fruit at a small, round kitchen table, with more cut flowers displayed in a tin jug at its centre. Delightful, thought Famie, though trying too hard. Who had fresh flowers at breakfast? Sam handed out three coffees. He pointed at what he could see of his old T-shirt. A good twenty centimetres hung loose from beneath the hoodie.

'I looked for a Mozart but could only find Def Leppard,' he said. 'Suits you more than me anyway. Sorry it's not longer.'

Famie pulled her hoodie tight around her. Kept her knees together. 'It's hideous. But thank you anyway.'

'You can keep it if you like,' said Sam. 'If the media pile-on is still in position by your flat, you might need it again. You're welcome here any time.'

'You're too kind,' said Famie. 'But I reckon it'll be OK today.'

Sam and Jo exchanged glances.

'You're not just on page forty-five,' said Sam. 'You're on page one too.'

With a sinking feeling, Famie unfolded the paper. An old photo of Seth Hussain was topped with the words 'Slain man's brother linked to al-Qaeda'. Her trained eye scanned the text – her name was in the last paragraph: 'Detectives have been speaking to IPS journalist Famie Madden, 43, who is believed to have been in a relationship with Mr Hussain.'

She closed her eyes, sighed deeply. 'They got my age wrong,' she said. 'But obviously the rest is true. Did everyone know?' Sam and Jo both shook their heads. Then, another thought. A prickle down her spine. 'Not good,' she said. 'Not good to be even a small part of this story.'

'You think you might be a target now?' said Sam.

She tapped her fingernails against the mug, some indecipherable, long-buried rhythm. Charlie told her she did it when she was thinking and that it was very irritating. The tapping stopped. Famie shrugged, shook her head.

'No idea,' she said. 'Doesn't feel good though.'

Famie sipped and swallowed, relishing the first burn in her throat. The radio played some Mendelssohn. She knew this was just for her.

'Great service,' she said. 'I must come again.'

'Any time,' said Jo, 'especially if the press are after you.'

'Listen, before I go,' Famie said, 'can we just compare notes on this?' She indicated the ad in the paper. 'I'm assuming we never hear from whoever it is again. So, meantime, who killed our friends? Between us we should be able to cover the bases. Two journalists, or former journalists' – she raised her mug to Sam – 'and a copper. Best theories. Does everyone buy the al-Qaeda line?'

Sam shrugged. 'Speculation, all of it. And journalist speculation is the same as everyone else's. Islamist terrorists obviously are number one, some al-Qaeda affiliate presumably. Or the Russians. Their security services have been pretty incompetent recently but they are still capable of great brutality. I'd start there.'

Jo's turn. 'The drug cartels. So much of the knife crime in London is gang- and drug-related. Scores of deaths a year even without our friends joining the list. If your investigators were deep into organized crime, they would have rattled some pretty big cages. With some pretty big beasts in them.

I've had three stabbings this year in my patch. Just kids really, but no one really reports on this stuff any more. We have two rival gangs fighting for territory and selling rights. It's brutal stuff.'

Famie blew steam from her coffee. 'That makes some kind of sense,' she said. 'Seven stabbings in half an hour shows a level of sophistication but it isn't exactly flying a plane into a building. Anything else?'

Jo put a hand up. 'One thing. Again, speculative. The word we seem to be getting out of the Yard operation is that your investigators had nothing of interest on their hard drives. Not only that, but that nothing had been added for weeks. As though their computers had stopped working.'

'They were working,' said Famie. 'Andrew Lewis told me. Emails working. Just everything else is blank. No files, no reports, no contacts. Must be all offline.'

'On paper?' said Jo.

Famie shrugged. 'Their work must be somewhere. It must exist *somewhere*.'

No one answered.

'Anyway, that's it,' said Jo. 'All I have.'

Sam's phone buzzed. 'Tommi suggests a drive-past, to see if the good men and women of the Fourth Estate are still camping out at yours, Famie. He'll be outside in five.'

Famie gulped the rest of her coffee and was dressed and outside in four. Another hot day coming. She already regretted not showering. When Tommi's Peugeot 306 pulled up, she jumped in, retuned his radio. He tutted. She ignored him.

'Got a call from Sophie Arnold,' he said once they were moving. 'About four this morning. Why so early I have no idea. I answered because I always do these days. She says she wants to meet you, Famie. Says she only had your house number and you weren't picking up.'

'She has my email. Work haven't switched it off just yet.'

'I mentioned that. Said she didn't want to write anything down.'

'Was she drunk?'

Tommi thought about that. 'Could have been. But she was pretty coherent.'

Famie was puzzled. 'Maybe she's resignation number fifteen. Did she leave her number?'

'She did,' said Tommi, 'and said that she'd come to you.'

When the Peugeot turned into Famie's street, they'd gone only ten metres before they saw a couple of TV crews crossing the road.

'Maybe Sophie coming to mine's not such a wise move,' Famie said. 'I'll call her.'

As they drove past her flat, the scrum and their microphones, Famie, unseen, saluted them all with her middle finger.

24

AN HOUR LATER, Famie was on an already airless Tottenham High Road, two iced coffees in a cardboard tray, searching for 235 Flat B. She'd convinced a tired-sounding Sophie to stay where she was, that she would come to her. Famie assumed the coffee would be welcome.

Walking out from Seven Sisters tube station she had bought a baseball cap from a street vendor, pulled it low over her head until the peak touched her sunglasses. 'Paranoid already,' she told herself. As far as she could see there had been no photos of her published, just her name. The hat was a decent disguise. She caught her reflection in a twenty-four-hour supermarket shop window. The cheap blue hat looked ridiculous but at least she didn't look like Famie Madden.

235 Flat B was an apartment above a Chinese restaurant. The front door was shut, the blinds closed. Famie found a side door next to an overflowing rubbish bin. Foil take-out trays, congealed sauce and discarded ribs had spilled on to the pavement where they were beginning to heat up a second time. Famie held her breath.

The four buttons on the door's intercom were unlabelled. She pressed the second one in the row, hoping for the best. The door buzzed and she pushed her way in. She stepped over a pile of junk mail to reach the stairs. One flight took her to a landing and an adjacent door with a large A scrawled on it. Along a poorly lit corridor another door clicked open. Sophie Arnold leant out, waved her in.

'Hey,' said Sophie.

'Got you a cold brew,' said Famie.

'Thanks. Come in. And, er, sorry about the mess.'

'No worries. I'm not your mother.'

Famie stepped inside. It wasn't messy. One living room with a corner kitchen. A small sofa, an armchair, two wooden chairs, one holding a laptop charging. Two small framed prints were on the wall – old maps, Famie thought – and a family photo sat in a gilt frame above an electric fire. An open door led to a darkened bedroom. A clean sink, no plates or cups waiting to be washed up. The two small windows were open wide, the smell of the kitchens below already filling the flat.

'I hope you like Chinese food,' said Famie.

'I used to,' said Sophie.

She appeared agitated, preoccupied.

'Where's the mess?' said Famie, looking around. 'Looks pretty damn clean to me.'

'The bin is full,' she said, 'overflowing. And yesterday's clothes are behind the cushions. I just shoved them there.'

She was a young twenty-six, wild, curly blonde hair and a slender frame. Loose-fit cotton pyjamas billowed around her as she moved. They were right about the alcohol; Famie could still smell it on her breath.

'Hangover?'

Sophie grimaced. 'Just a small one.'

She sat on the armchair, Famie perched on the sofa.

'Tommi said you called him at four a.m.'

Sophie nodded, glanced down. 'Took me that long to get the balls to call. And the gin helped.'

'The gin always helps,' said Famie. 'But you didn't tell him anything.'

'I wanted to tell you.'

'What did you want to talk about?'

Sophie stared down at her cup, concentrated on drinking her coffee. Her hands began to shake. The ice in her coffee rattled. She cleared her throat.

'I'm scared, Famie.'

Famie waited for more but Sophie was drinking coffee again.

'We all are, Sophie,' she began, but Sophie shook her head.

'It's not that,' she said.

She was taking deep breaths. Pain control. Building up to something. Famie was getting anxious for the girl.

'Sophie?'

'I'm pregnant,' she blurted.

Famie, startled, kept her silence; Sophie's intonation suggested there was more to come. Another deep breath.

'I'm pregnant,' she repeated, 'and . . . and Seth is the father. Was the father.' She pulled her legs to her chest, wrapped her arms around them and started to cry.

Famie's head spun. Seth and Sophie. Seth and *Sophie*? My God. She clambered on to Sophie's chair and embraced her. She waited for the crying to subside. It bought her a few seconds. A few seconds without which she would have been cursing both Sophie and Seth as slut and manslut. A few seconds in which she then realized she had no right to feel angry, no right to be hurt.

'My God, you poor thing,' she whispered into Sophie's ear. 'I'm so sorry.'

Eventually Sophie calmed down enough to speak. 'I didn't

know who to talk to,' she said. 'I feel so alone, Famie. Then I read about you and Seth in the paper.' The tears came again. 'It'll be me next, I'm sure of it. And I don't know what to do.'

Famie held her hand. 'I saw you at the funeral,' she said. 'Christ, you must have found that difficult.' She felt her hand squeezed, a slight nod of the curls. 'I couldn't hang around. Had to leave.'

'I saw you go,' said Sophie. 'I so wanted to come with you. Didn't have the courage. And Amal would have noticed, I know he would. He kept looking at me . . .'

Famie pushed back far enough to see Sophie's tear-stained face.

'Wait. You knew Amal Hussain?'

Sophie's hands started to shake again. She gripped her cup tighter. 'Sure,' she said, 'we met quite a few times.'

Dread was beginning to sink deep into Famie's gut.

'Are you still working, Sophie?'

She nodded.

'So you know Amal is EIJ and has disappeared, right?'

Another small nod.

Famie sighed. 'So I'm guessing you haven't told the police and that's the other reason I'm here.'

Sophie hauled herself out of the armchair and walked to the kitchenette. Poured herself some water which she drank in three gulps. Famie studied her stomach. Nothing showing yet.

'I haven't told the police, no,' said Sophie. 'And there's one more reason I asked you to come.'

'Christ, there's more?' said Famie. 'I can't imagine what you've kept till last.'

Sophie pointed at the laptop on the kitchen chair. Famie glanced at it.

'It belongs to Seth,' Sophie said. 'And I know the password.'

Famie stared at the laptop. It had been between them all

this time but she had ignored it. It looked cheap; small, black, and with a manufacturer's logo she hadn't seen before. Not expensive at all. Classic Seth.

'What's on it?' said Famie, suddenly fearful. 'What have you found?'

'I wanted to wait for you,' Sophie said.

'I know that!' said Famie. 'But—'

'I wanted to wait for you, Famie, because there are pictures of you on it. That's why.'

25

FAMIE PACED THE cage. It was too early for a drink and she hadn't smoked since she'd got pregnant but she wanted both now. Sophie watched her as she circled the room.

'How many photos?' Famie asked.

'Eight,' said Sophie.

'How bad are they?'

'You want to see them?'

'Just tell me first! Then I'll look.'

'You're getting changed, I think. Taking off jeans, putting on a dress. Blue and white stripes. In his flat by the look of it.'

'You make them sound harmless.'

'You're naked in one, topless in three.'

'Christ, he was a shit.' She smacked the wall with her hand. 'He kept them. I remember him "deleting" them but he actually kept them all this time. Bastard.' She continued her laps.

Sophie knelt in front of the laptop, opened it, hit some keys.

'How come you know the password anyway?' said Famie.

'I've never shared mine with anyone. Don't know anyone who does.'

Sophie hit enter. 'Because I set it up for him. He suggested the first three words of his national anthem, so that's what it is.' She spun the screen to Famie. 'Here. You do this.'

Famie knelt next to Sophie, moved the cursor between the photos. Clicking. Enlarging. Cursing. Sophie's description had been clinically accurate. It wasn't exactly porn or anything near, but the nude shot was uncomfortably gynaecological. The rest she could live with.

'Are there any others?' she said.

'Not of you, no.'

'Of you?'

Sophie nodded. 'A few.'

'Did you know?'

'He said he was deleting them.'

'Jesus. Sounds familiar. Anyone else, dare I ask?'

It was clear from Sophie's face that there were.

'Three,' she replied. 'You'll be mostly interested in the last.'

She clicked and spun again. The photo on the screen showed a grinning woman in the process of showering. It was Mary Lawson.

Famie spluttered in disbelief. She stared at it for a long time, her fingers tapping on the side of the laptop. Eventually she looked away.

'And the other two?'

Sophie showed her the others. Both darker-skinned, both naked, both looking coy.

'We've got quite the charmer here,' said Sophie, her words almost a whisper. Famie felt her pain in every word.

'Well,' Famie said. 'First point, we're in some serious shit here, you and me. But second, if there's nothing other than smutty pictures, the police never need to see it. What else is there? Have you looked? Please tell me there's nothing about his terrorist brother.'

She spun the laptop back to Sophie who clicked and tapped.

'He seems to have used this as an overflow computer,' she said. 'There are sixteen documents that I can see, all containing articles he's written for our website. They all date from September last year to March this year. Then it all stops. So nothing for three months.'

'Dare I ask when the Mary shot was dated?' said Famie.

'February twenty-sixth last year,' said Sophie.

Another punch to the stomach. Famie's head dropped. 'We split on the twenty-seventh. It's my birthday so it's one of those break-ups you remember. I thought it was mutual but really it was because he was shagging his boss. He actually left me for an older woman.'

'What a total prick,' said Sophie. 'He must have transferred these pictures deliberately.'

'At least we were his favourites, then,' said Famie.

They both snorted.

'One more thing,' said Sophie. 'The last document was sent via Mary, and at the top of the email he wrote this.'

Another spin.

Famie read out loud. 'Hi M. Here's the piece on the President you asked for. The last before we all go quiet. You'll get the next one on parchment.' She looked up at Sophie. 'And this is the last document?'

'It is, yes.'

'No more pictures of old women in showers?'

Sophie's smile was a pained one. 'None.'

'No PS sorry for being a total dick?'

'No.'

'So it all goes quiet in March,' said Famie. 'By arrangement.'

Sophie shut the laptop. 'They must have started their new

investigation in March,' she said. 'One that needed electronic silence.' She unplugged the computer and placed it between them. 'So, what do we do with this? I wanted to delete the photos as soon as I saw them but got scared. What do you think?'

Famie said, 'I think delete. They're photos of us. We have every right.'

'And the Mary photo?' said Sophie.

'Stolen,' said Famie. A pause. 'OK. I know. Evidence, yes. But stolen evidence.' She felt suddenly exhausted. 'Do you have coffee? I need some drugs before we decide. Caffeine will do.'

Sophie produced a cafetière and a small bag with an elastic band around it.

'I'll make it, Sophie, you get dressed.'

'Are we going somewhere?' Sophie suddenly sounded very young indeed.

'I don't know,' replied Famie, 'but if we need to move, if the press or police do arrive, it might help if you're wearing proper clothes. Fetching as your pyjamas are. And please don't tell me Seth bought them for you.'

Sophie grimaced. 'Birthday present from my parents.'

She stepped into the bedroom, opened the blind.

Famie studied the couple in the family photo above the fire. Mid-sixties, smiling, the mother with curly hair also. 'And they know nothing of all this?'

'Correct,' called Sophie, who was undressing by the door. 'That's another conversation that'll take gin.'

Seeing her momentarily naked, Famie thought that maybe there was a slight bulge to be seen after all.

'How many weeks are you?' she called.

'Twelve.'

'Going to keep it?'

There was no reply.

Sophie dressed in ninety seconds. Denim dungaree-dress, blue T-shirt, trainers.

Famie smiled at her. 'We suddenly have a lot in common, you and me,' she said. 'And pretty soon the press will find us.' She put an arm around Sophie. 'So before that happens, we need to disappear.'

26

Sunday, 10 June, 12.30 p.m.
Warwick University, four miles from Coventry

THE ACADEMIC WAS five six, gangly, with an eager-to-please smile. A livid orange scarf was tied turban-style in her black curls. Dr Bathandwa Bambawani approached the accommodation block with a priest for company. The chaplain was an awkward six two, with the sunken face common in men who have lost too much weight. Reverend Don Hardin chatted easily with his friend, always happy to be helping with pastoral work. She had called in at the Chaplaincy as she passed. He had stopped his post-service tidying and taken a walk.

'Happy to pause the clear-up,' he'd said. 'I can always come back to finish off.'

'How was the service?'

He shrugged. 'I was lacklustre. They were forgiving. That's about the most of it.'

'Well I fancied some company, Don,' she said. 'And missing students are a nightmare. For everyone. Sometimes they don't want to be found. Sometimes they're not even missing. Sometimes they're actually in trouble. But finding out which is which . . . You're a pastor. I could do with some support.'

'And happy to help, BB.'

Bambawani nodded. 'Thank you. How's the little girl doing?'

Hardin's face clouded. They walked a few paces in silence. 'It's tough,' he said. A few more. Bambawani gave him the space he needed. 'She just looks jaundiced to me,' he said eventually, 'like all the time. And way too quiet for a four-week-old baby. But the midwife was reassuring. Said she was doing OK.'

'And is she a medically trained and qualified midwife?' asked Bambawani.

'Eh?'

'Does she, maybe, know more about medicine than you?'

'Oh,' said Hardin. 'Yeah. S'pose so.'

'Well then.'

There were six identical student blocks. Three facing three, the slight incline between them laid with wide paths and grassy banks. A semi-circle of women sat on one, books open, phones busy. Each block had four floors studded with scores of windows, almost all of them pushed wide open. A vain attempt to catch some non-existent breeze. Just one window was shut. The academic and the chaplain stood under block C, looking up.

'Guess which is his room,' Bambawani said.

Hardin squinted. 'Third floor, second along?'

'Correct.'

They were hesitating by the block's stairwell. By leaning against the brickwork they could stand in the shade.

'No one has seen him for a good few days,' Bambawani continued. 'Missed an exam, which is unlike him. I'm his personal tutor, Don, I should know what's happening. I need at least some idea before we go to his family and then the police. His scores have been impressive until the last few months.'

'You know him?' asked Hardin. 'You have loads of students.'

'I do. Well, I thought so anyway. I liked him. Earnest. Clear-eyed. Committed to the courses he was on. Courteous. Always asked me about South Africa. About Durban. He's the only student in five years who's asked me to teach him some words in Xhosa.'

The chaplain smiled. 'I like the sound of this guy. What words did you teach him?'

'He wanted to be able to greet his grandmother. She speaks Bengali, I think, but he thought he'd try Xhosa. Thought she'd like it. Said she considered herself a citizen of the world.'

Hardin waited. 'Well? How do you greet a grandmother in Xhosa?'

'Molo makhulu,' said Bambawani.

'Nice,' said Hardin. 'Very useful. I'll remember. Was our student religious at all?'

The academic pondered the question. 'Don't know. Hindu by culture certainly but seemed secular to me.'

Hardin laughed. 'Everyone seems secular to you, BB. When we find a copy of the Vedas on his desk you can buy me a drink. He might even have a bible somewhere, you never know.'

Bambawani removed a key from her jacket pocket. She turned to Hardin, eyebrows arched. 'If we find a bible in there, I'll come to Mass myself.'

The student's room was a furnace. Curtains wide open, the sun had super-heated the room. Hardin dived for the window lever, pushed down and flung the pane as wide as it would go. 'Good grief,' he muttered.

They scanned the room. A single bed, duvet, bed made. Twenty or so books on his shelves, some rotting apples on a plate on his desk; their sweet vinegary smell made Hardin wince. A laptop charger plugged into the wall, no laptop. A photo of two young smiling girls stuck on the back of the door.

Hardin peered under the bed. 'The laptop's under here,' he said.

'OK,' said Bambawani. 'Leave it there. We don't need to move anything.'

On the wall above the bed, a battered poster, peeling away from the wall at one corner. Bambawani reached out and stuck it back again. It showed a white hammer and sickle against a livid background. Beneath the sickle, in yellow type, the letters CPI-M. Then, in brackets, in case the reader was unsure, the words COMMUNIST PARTY OF INDIA (MARXIST). Bambawani and Hardin stared at it for some time.

Eventually Bambawani spoke. 'Like I said, Don, he seemed secular to me.'

A knock at the door, then it swung open. 'Hello?' A frowning white face, stubble, baggy shorts and stripy T-shirt. Possibly pyjamas, possibly day wear. 'Can I help you?' he said. 'I'm Paul. I live next door.' He jerked his thumb at the left-hand wall. 'I heard you . . . rattling around.' He sounded both suspicious and surprised.

Bambawani introduced herself and Hardin, explained their business.

Paul relaxed, stepped into the room. 'We haven't seen him much, to be honest with you.'

'Really?' said Hardin.

Paul found another frown which said 'Why should I trust you?' Then he noticed Hardin's dog collar and shrugged. 'He was always part of everything,' he said. 'Start of the year he was always here. Cooked his meals with us, you know. Then he started going to some weird meetings. He got all political. Saw him hanging out with an older woman. She was nice, like, don't get me wrong. But not a student. Not from here anyway. He went with her more and more. And with us less and less.'

'And in recent weeks?' said Bambawani.

'In recent weeks barely at all. Drifts in sometimes. Probably joined a cult or something. Got a job. No idea.'

'How did he seem?' asked Bambawani. 'When you did see him.'

'He seemed fine,' said Paul. 'Busy,' he added.

'How so?'

'Preoccupied.'

'Should the university be worried?'

Paul thought about that. 'Nope. Don't see why. Don't sweat the small stuff,' he said. He looked from priest to academic. 'Anyway. Shouldn't you guys know? Isn't that the kind of shit you're supposed to tell us?'

Hardin and Bambawani exchanged glances.

'Yes,' Bambawani replied, 'that's exactly the kind of shit we should know. But I'm not sure we do. Thank you for your help.'

Paul shrugged. 'Any time,' he said.

27

Monday, 11 June, 5.30 a.m.

WHEN FAMIE HAD said disappear, she meant a cheap hotel at the end of the Piccadilly Line. Sophie had packed clothes, toiletries and the laptop, Famie had borrowed some T-shirts. What Sophie couldn't lend, Famie had bought from a market trader on the High Road. It wasn't quite her smartest underwear but it would last until she got her flat back.

The hotel was a two-storey celebration of 1960s concrete and glass. Equally it could have been a school or police station. A blue and green painted board offered rooms and WiFi for £49.95.

Famie and Sophie's box room somehow managed to be twin-bedded, with beige and cream carpet, beige and cream walls, beige and cream curtains. A television was bolted to the wall; a kettle, cups, biscuits and tea bags sat on a brown plastic tray. Famie had taken the bed by the door, Sophie the bed by the window. The first-floor view showed a row of bins and an almost empty car park. They had spent the weekend lying low, drinking the tea and eating the biscuits. The TV had been on but unwatched – it masked their endless, looping conversations on Seth, Amal, Mary, and what to do with the photos.

Their second morning there dawned courtesy of an early bin lorry. They were both showered and dressed by six a.m.

At Famie's suggestion, Sophie had fired off an email to explain her absence from work. It said she was 'seeking support counselling' and asked for compassionate leave.

'How long till breakfast is served?' she asked.

'A whole hour,' said Famie. 'Which means it's time for more shortbread.'

She reached for the replenished tray and threw a wrapped biscuit at Sophie, keeping one for herself.

'So here we are,' she said, 'two journalists, one retired, one pregnant, on the run. Holed up in the glamorous Southgate Travelodge and eating the classic breakfast of the hungover traveller. I can't go home because reporters are stalking me. You've left home to avoid the same reporters stalking you. We are both victims of a bastard prick womanizer who happens to be dead. He is also the father of your baby.'

'If I choose to have it,' added Sophie.

'If you choose to have it,' repeated Famie. 'You met the bastard prick womanizer's terrorist brother a number of times but haven't told the police.'

'Let's try BPW for short,' said Sophie.

'OK,' said Famie. 'And neither of us has told the police about the BPW's laptop which has compromising photos of both of us.'

'And Mary.'

'And poor Mary. And the other women.'

'Which we might delete, even if they're evidence of some kind.'

'Yup. Apart from that, it's all good.'

Famie finished the shortbread.

'You missed out the *Telegraph*,' said Sophie.

'Ah, correct,' said Famie. 'We are waiting for a communication from a weirdo who leaves messages for me. Either on my car or in the post. Or maybe in the bloody *Daily Telegraph*.' She took a breath. 'Is that it?'

'That's it,' said Sophie. 'Let's go find a newsagent.'

They found a twenty-four-hour supermarket that sold them a paper and a greasy-spoon café that sold them breakfast. Two portable fans were already working hard blowing hot air, fine carbon particles and frying pan fumes over the handful of early customers. Famie and Sophie perched around a Formica-topped table with large plastic ketchup and mustard bottles. Seth Hussain's laptop was in a drawstring bag on a third chair. A small, tinny radio played a country song so loud it was unrecognizable. The clientele was all male. Two read a tabloid paper, the other three stared at their phone screens. None of them looked up.

Over fry-ups and stewed coffee, they found the Classifieds. There was no doubting which message was for Famie. This one was in capital letters. Famie shivered as she read it.

FREAKS ARE REVOLUTIONARIES
AND REVOLUTIONARIES ARE FREAKS.

She showed Sophie, who read it aloud. 'Another quote. Must be.' She tapped the keys on her phone. 'There.' Sophie held up the screen. Large green letters, italicized, low-res: 'A declaration of a state of war. Communiqué number one. From the Weather Underground.'

'Them again,' said Famie.

She took the phone. The document was dated 1971. There were thirty-four lines, the words and lines double-spaced. Three were italicized. The freaks line was one. 'Tens of thousands have found that protest and marches don't do it' was another. 'Within fourteen days, we will attack a symbol or institution of Amerikan injustice' was the last.

'America with a "k",' said Sophie. 'What's that about?'

Famie shrugged. 'It's radical, they're hippies, it's the seventies, who knows. The only thing that matters is this. I've been communicating with someone like we are still in the seventies. As though email and texting were never invented. So either this is all bullshit and I'm being trolled, in a very seventies way, or there's another story out there and no one is reporting it. Not even close.'

'Who've you told?'

'Well Sam and Tommi came to Mary's funeral with me, so they saw the first note. They know. And I told Andrew Lewis and the coppers. For all the good that did.'

Sophie got coffee refills. This time she was noticed. A large man in a stretched white football top looked up from his paper, his eyes following her to the counter and back. He clocked Famie staring at him and returned to his paper.

'What?' said Sophie.

'Nothing,' said Famie. 'Another BPW probably.'

They drank their coffee. Sophie winced. 'Shit coffee but it's working. I'm waking up.' She tapped the newspaper. 'So what's the other story then?' she said. 'What's the story no one is reporting?'

'That's just it,' said Famie, 'I don't know. But in the same way that generals always fight the last war not the new one, journalists often write the old story not the new one. When the Oklahoma bomb went off in '95, everyone assumed it was foreigners who were responsible. TV news channels were full of stories about investigators looking for men described as being Middle Eastern in appearance who had driven away from the building shortly before the blast. But it was a home-grown terrorist that did it. A white American guy. Here we're looking at Islamists and Russians and organized crime and maybe that's right, but maybe our freak, our revolutionary, is telling us something else.'

'Telling us what?' said Sophie. 'That they're going to attack a symbol of American injustice? That they've declared war?' Her tone suggested scepticism.

Famie chased the final crumbs of fried bread around her plate. 'Sure. Why not?' she said. 'A declaration of war can take any number of forms. This is one bat-shit crazy world we're in. Why shouldn't it get any crazier?'

28

6.34 a.m.

THE STUDENT LAY on his bed, facing the wall. There was enough sunlight through the gap in his curtains to throw a faint shadow of his torso against the pale green paint. He was still, but sleepless as usual. If he'd had the photo of his twin sisters with him he'd have stuck it on the wall, right in front of his eyes, right where a piece of plaster had crumbled. He wondered about retrieving it from the car but dismissed the idea as reckless. The last thing he needed was to remind the leader about his greatest vulnerability.

He knew he would do anything for them. Theirs was the only uncomplicated relationship in his life and he'd relished every moment of it. They always seemed so pleased to see him, always wanted to talk, always wanted to play. Everything seemed so unconditional. He suspected that that would change and he had, as a result, always dreaded them getting older. Now he dreaded never seeing them again.

He would manage without the photo.

On the other side of the room, the sweating man was silent. Still bandaged and sedated again, he had fallen asleep an hour ago. The student assumed he was the only one awake. The house was quiet. They talked late, got up late.

His mind still swam with the events of Friday evening. The self-crit. The leader's incredible assault. The damage had been less severe than the student had feared – the knife had 'only' taken the corner of an ear – but the effect on the group had been profound. The woman had produced the bandages, and he had leapt up to speak to the leader. 'We should throw him out? You want him out?' He had been amazed at himself; his instinct for self-preservation extended to undermining the sweating man even further. He could chastise himself later. If there was a later.

He was trapped. He could walk out, of course. The nearest police station was only ten minutes away. But the murders in London had shown how threats were dealt with. Violently. Ruthlessly. The images of the blood-stained zebra crossing came again and he shuddered. His sisters were vulnerable. His family was just too big and sprawling; they couldn't all just disappear into protective police custody. There were too many cells, too many citizens. He was the problem. Somehow he had to be the solution.

He pulled on some shorts and eased his way downstairs.

It was, as ever, immaculate. The house's exterior was in as much need of repair as the rest of the street – subsidence cracks, rotting window frames, peeling paint – but its interior was more or less pristine. The narrow hall was swept and clutter-free, there was no post or junk mail on the mat. The two day rooms were comfortably furnished, dusted and well lit. The sofas had cushions, the tables had books. In the kitchen, an old gas cooker was newly cleaned; plates and mugs had been either put away or arranged in neat rows on a small Victorian dresser. There was an order here that the student had, in his early days, found encouraging. Now he knew whose order it was, it just seemed sinister.

Beyond the back door was a small paved yard. It was warm already. The student poured himself a glass of cold water. Shoeless, he paced the slabs. It was his prison-style recreation. In the early sunshine he circled the square hundreds of times. There was a freshness to the early morning, a brief respite from the stale summer soup of smells, but lately he hadn't noticed. His mind was in turmoil. He knew his plan was too slow. He couldn't rely on the IPS woman piecing his life together – she might never do it anyway. There was a cliff-edge approaching and unless he did something drastic and soon, it would take him and his family to destruction.

The student had finished his water a while ago but still he held the glass, still he paced. As the yard continued to warm up in the first sunlight of the day, he recalled the leader's glittering certainty as he held the knife. There had been a different tone to his voice, a thrilled, almost ecstatic tightness to his words.

He suddenly stopped his pacing. His eyes were rooted on the freshly illuminated fence opposite him but he still saw nothing. He replayed the leader's words. What had he said? 'The closer we get to the enemy, the more likely their attacks on us.'

He raised a hand to his mouth. 'Oh. OK.' He looked around, as if noticing his surroundings for the first time. 'That might work,' he whispered to the yard. 'That might just work.'

On his next lap, he paused at the far corner. The high garden fence here sheltered two exhausted-looking rose bushes, and behind them two purple flowering plants barely half a metre high. He crouched down. Fighting the rose bushes for sunlight had stunted the foxgloves – he couldn't remember seeing them before. But he did remember the furious telling-off his mother had given him as a child when he had played with one. That they were poisonous. That he must never touch the velvety flowers. And that he should absolutely never put one in or even near his mouth.

He tried to remember the science. He thought three might kill him. One might do. With some leaves. He glanced back once. All curtains drawn, no one watching. He chose one of the tubular blooms, held it between his fingers, then used a fingernail to cut the stem. He placed it in his pocket, went inside the house and waited.

29

8.40 a.m.

FAMIE AND SOPHIE walked back to their room. The buildings alternated between suburbia and industrial trading estate. The roads were busy and the pedestrians hurried. No one looked at anyone else.

'Kind of easy to feel anonymous here,' said Sophie. 'I like it.'

'Welcome to Southgate,' said Famie.

They walked a couple of blocks. The morning heat was already beginning to sting. Famie could feel her shirt clinging to her back. She peeled it loose.

'I was thinking,' said Sophie. 'Don't you think we should go to the police? They don't need to know about the laptop but at some stage we need to talk to them.'

'Have they spoken to you at all?' asked Famie. 'I've told them about my note leaver, of course. It's filed with the extraterrestrials, I believe.'

'Well, at least show them the phone number and the *Telegraph* then,' said Sophie.

'OK, that Hunter woman gave me her card. We can set up

a meeting. But it's Amal they'll want to talk about. How many times did you meet him again?'

'Five, I think. I've counted them. Fairly certain it's five.'

'Tell me about them. Tell me about him.'

Sophie hooked an arm in Famie's. A row of canopied shops provided some brief shade.

'He's intense,' she began. 'Seth was so easy to talk to but Amal was cagey. Twitchy. Always suspicious. Guarded, I'd say, like he was considering every word before he said it.'

'Was that just with you or was he like that with Seth?'

'He was like that all the time. There was never any brotherly chat, no in-jokes, no family chat. Seth always seemed . . . on edge around him. And now I think about it, my arrival was usually the cue for Amal's departure.'

'And when he'd left, did Seth talk about him? How did he seem?'

'He never mentioned him. Changed the subject if I asked.'

'What a family,' said Famie. 'Did you speak at the funeral?'

'No. I had some words ready, but . . .' She broke off.

'But you never needed them,' suggested Famie.

Sophie nodded.

'And I assume he didn't know you were pregnant.'

'Correct. But I hadn't seen him for ages.'

Famie frowned. 'How long were you and Seth together?'

'Since January,' said Sophie. 'And all the times I saw Amal were in February and March. Nothing since.'

They walked a block in silence.

'The police will want to know if he mentioned Islamic Jihad or religion or any of that,' Famie said.

Sophie shook her head. 'Never.'

'They'll also ask if Seth ever asked you for money.'

Sophie turned her head, eyebrows raised. 'Yes! Did he do that with you too?'

Famie nodded. 'Yup.'

'I could never understand it,' said Sophie. 'He was twelve years older than me, earning much more than me and always on the scrounge. What was that about?'

'God knows,' said Famie. 'But on the list of things I'd like to ask him about, it's pretty low.'

'And top of the list?' asked Sophie.

'How did you become such a bastard prick womanizer, I think.'

'Fair enough,' said Sophie.

They waited at a crossroads.

'So is that a yes to the police meet?'

Famie pulled DC Hunter's card from her jeans. 'Sure. I'll call from our penthouse suite. But first I'd like to rope in Sam and Tommi. You OK with that? We don't need to tell them about the . . . about your condition.'

The lights changed, they crossed.

Sophie pushed her sunglasses to her forehead. She squinted at Famie. 'Yes please, leave my "condition" out of it. And the laptop? Do we tell them about the photos?'

'We tell them about them, yes. We don't need to show them. Their imagination can fill the gaps.'

Famie did most of the talking. Sam and Tommi's imaginations filled in the gaps. The women sat on Famie's bed, the men on Sophie's. The room's one window had been opened as far as the six-inch catch allowed. The air was stale, the temperature high.

'Is that the laptop?' Tommi was pointing at Sophie's drawstring bag. A black plastic corner protruded from the top of it.

Sophie nodded.

Sam's mouth gaped open. 'So . . . Seth and Mary? Really?' he said.

There was a silence before Famie said, 'I know. I'm thinking about her funeral too.'

'But it's like he was trying to humiliate all of us,' said Sam, 'like he was working his way through the team.'

'Oh thanks,' muttered Sophie.

'Choose your words, Sam, for Christ's sake,' said Famie.

'Sorry, Sophie, wasn't thinking.' Sam looked mortified.

Sophie acknowledged the apology.

'And you haven't deleted anything,' said Tommi.

'Not yet,' said Sophie.

'And there's no reference to Amal.'

'No.'

'You still need to tell the police.'

'We know,' said Sophie and Famie together. 'Tell us something we don't,' Famie added.

Sam fidgeted, then said, 'OK. Well. Look, tell me if I'm out of order here, but is it time to ask whether everything we knew, or thought we knew, about Seth is wrong? That the peace-loving, campaigning journalist thing was a front. That he was involved with EIJ like his brother. That he siphoned money from everywhere to fund them. And that the Egyptian government hated him, not because of his human rights work but because they knew what he was really up to.' He looked around the room. 'Just a thought,' he added.

'And then the Egyptians killed him?' asked Tommi, unconvinced. 'Along with his team? Doesn't make sense.'

Sam held up his hands. 'Agreed,' he said. 'You're right. I'm just saying that it's obvious we really didn't know Seth at all. And that all our assumptions might be wrong.'

Famie's head was reeling. 'Agree with that last sentence, Sam. But I'm struggling with the rest.' She massaged her temples. Might it be possible that she had been totally played? That when Seth had been attending protest meetings and rallies, he was actually working as some kind of spy? That the articles and blogs had been a front? She realized quite how unquestioning she had been. Seth had set out his narrative, told his story and told it well. She had lapped it up. Accepted it. Endorsed it. Even revelled in it. Christ, what an unholy mess this all was. Quite how much more of a shit was it possible to be?

Tommi pushed his glasses back up his nose, checked his watch. 'OK, we can do this then.' He took his phone from his pocket. 'I took a call from Dave Coolidge in the New York bureau over the weekend. He wanted to catch up on how everyone was. How the investigation was going.'

Famie leant into Sophie. 'He was based here a few years back. Good guy. Politics was his thing. American, British, European, wherever. He could probably tell you who the Belgian Foreign Minister is if you asked.'

'That's quite a party trick,' said Sophie.

'I told him about the weatherman stuff,' Tommi continued. 'He said he wanted to chip in. It's five a.m. in New York but he'll be at his desk.'

Tommi dialled a number, put it on speaker. The box room echoed to the single-note American ringing tone.

'He'll think I'm a dumbass for certain,' said Famie.

The call was picked up after four rings.

'Coolidge.'

'Hey Dave, it's Tommi again. Not too early?'

A rattling cough and laugh combined. 'Ha! Been at it for an hour already. Great to hear you, Tommi. Good morning from New York. You have the famous and fabulous Famie Madden there with you now?'

Famie rolled her eyes, smiled. It had been five years, but the image in her mind was still strong. Black, Chicago, mid-forties, probably still stick-thin, certainly still bald. 'Hey Dave,' she called out. 'How's tricks?'

'Hey, not bad at all, Fames, but listen, I just wanted to say first up how devastated we were and still are about your losses. You know the whole bureau here just stopped everything. Just so devastating. I remember working with Anita. And Seth of course. I'm so sorry.'

The four in the box room all glanced at each other.

'That's appreciated, Dave, thank you,' said Famie. 'I'm here with Sam Carter and Sophie Arnold who you never met but they're top people. And Tommi says you know about my weatherman correspondence?'

'He told me, yeah. Is this an official police line of inquiry, because that would be some story?'

'Oh. No. That's definitely a no,' said Famie. 'And not sure what it means myself just yet. We got a new message in the paper today. It said, "Freaks are revolutionaries and revolutionaries are freaks." That's it.'

There was a transatlantic pause, longer than just the satellite delay.

'OK,' said Coolidge, drawing out each syllable as far as it could go. 'Well that's certainly a Weatherman reference, but how it fits in with your story I have no idea.'

'Go on,' said Tommi.

'Well the Weathermen, or Weather Underground – they had a number of names – are an American story and a black American story at that. We're coming out of the sixties and into the seventies here. A pretty heavy time as you know. Vietnam. Black Panther. Riots. Nixon. All of that shit. Well the Weathermen were revolutionaries. They weren't just anti-war, they were anti-everything, anti the whole American way of life. They said they were against everything that was good and decent in honky America. I got the quote right here . . .' The rattle of a keyboard. 'Here we go. "We will burn and loot and destroy. We are the incubation of your mother's nightmare." Not bad, huh?'

Sam whistled. 'Good quote. And they did destroy, didn't they? They turned pretty violent.'

'Sure did,' said Coolidge. 'They set off bombs. Pretty small by today's standards but bombs none the less. But they never killed no one, apart from themselves when they messed up the explosives one time. In Greenwich Village that was.'

Famie knew all this. She'd even read the quote. It was good to hear from Coolidge again but she knew she wasn't getting anywhere.

'It's hard to see how that fits with what's happening here,' she said.

'Agreed,' said Dave. 'I don't think it does.'

Famie shrugged. 'So why are we doing this?'

The rattling cough again. 'Because, Ms Madden, you might not have a big hippy-led underground organization on your hands but it sounds like you do have someone who thinks he or she is a Weatherman. Or is with other Weathermen. And they're sending you notes. Someone who thinks the struggle – the violent struggle – against the West, against imperialism, needs to continue. Of course he or she could be a freak. But then . . .'

'He could be a revolutionary,' said Famie.

'Or both,' said Coolidge.

'Or both,' conceded Famie.

30

10.05 a.m.

THE STUDENT AND the woman were on the dead drop. Another cell had requested it, he didn't know which one. He didn't know how many other cells there were, but they had been told of a growing movement. The leader spoke of grand schemes, and the London attacks of 22 May had proved the citizens' potency. Their communication with other cells was deliberately, purposefully cumbersome, so each drop was significant, every message mattered.

There was an envelope to pick up. The leader had appeared agitated, wondering out loud if he should get it himself, before deciding at the last minute that the risks for him were too high. His fear of attacks 'from the forces of oppression' increased by the day. He had tested each room with his Geiger counter. Each random 'click' that came from its speaker made him jump.

The student had the car, the woman had been told where to go.

The leader had made much of her being a martial arts trainer and had insisted on them all learning karate punches, elbow and hand strikes. Today she wore a loose white polo shirt and blue joggers. Her black hair was now shaved on the sides almost as closely as the leader's. A homage maybe. The student wondered if they were sleeping together but had noticed no overt displays of affection. Today, she smelt of shampoo and cigarettes.

Sometimes the woman was friendly, other times not. Occasionally she appeared interested in his life, most of the time she didn't. His main contact with her was always the martial arts classes.

The sessions were brutal. She said she taught her own mix of fighting styles from around the world. They were taught the 'Four Pillars' from the Russian Systema Spetsnaz: breathing, relaxation, body position and movement. There were six 'levers': elbows, neck, knees, waist, ankles and shoulders; each one could incapacitate. From the American Marines she taught them hand-to-hand combat. Never staying head-on with your enemy, moving at forty-five-degree angles to either side to increase your chance of landing a blow. From tanto-jutsu in Japan she taught them to aim for the squishy parts of the body, where to cause maximum pain. Around the shoulder blades, kidneys, the sweet spot between the ribs.

The student was starting from scratch. He had never fought anyone before, never needed to, never felt the need.

She taught him the horse stance from Indonesian silat, mimicking the posture from stallion riding. He learnt joint-locks and chokeholds from Brazilian jiu-jitsu, then how to use side control, pinning the leader to the floor by lying across his chest. 'Use your levers!' she had shouted. The student had dug his elbows into the leader's hips until she had told him to stop. When the leader retired (hurt, presumably, thought the student) she had one more trick up her sleeve.

The woman was in jogging bottoms and a loose T-shirt, the student in running shorts and a football top. His 'games kit', she called it. Her hair was loose, her eyes wide and her smile broad. It made him nervous.

'You're about to enjoy yourself,' she said, taking the horse stance, crouching low.

She threw a white plastic knife to him. He caught it.

'Come at me,' she said. 'Stab me somewhere. Anywhere.'

He had tried to play it cute. He kept his off-hand close to his chest for defence, he kept swirling his bladed hand to keep her guessing. She was still smiling. Her stance remained casual; her arms were raised and her legs were firmly planted but she managed to make it look patronizing. He felt sweat dripping into his eyes. He tried to blink it away but his vision blurred. The student wiped his eyes with his sleeve, and that was that. She lunged. He felt her foot hook behind his, lift sharply, and he toppled to the ground. As his head hit the mat, she was on him. The woman sat astride his waist, then worked her way up his body till her knees were locked in his armpits. He felt paralysed, pain searing across his chest.

'Full mount,' she said.

'Submission,' he said.

Today the car radio was off – the woman said she preferred silence. The windows were closed – the woman said she found open windows distracting. The student was sweating copiously. The woman had her eyes shut. He took the inside lane of the M6 and stayed at seventy miles an hour until the service station signs appeared.

'We're here,' he said.

She opened her eyes, checked the buttons on her shirt. She picked at a thread, checked herself in the car mirror, retied the laces of her trainers.

She's as nervous as me, he thought. And she doesn't have poison in her pocket.

The slip road took them off the motorway and he swung the car into a space three lines of parking away from the main entrance. It was a wide space, but he made sure to park tight against a white van on his side, allowing the woman plenty of space to get out on hers. They both had clear lines of vision to the building's large sliding doors. He breathed deeply.

'Ready?' he said.

'Let's watch,' she said. 'We're early.'

He couldn't sit in the car another moment. 'I'll clean the windows,' he said.

He eased himself from the car, taking a cloth and a bottle of water from the driver's door as he stepped out. It was another day of oppressive heat but it was a relief to breathe whatever it was that passed for fresh air here. Diesel fumes and a Cornish pasty stall competed for dominance. He dripped some water on the back window and started to rub. His eyes jumped everywhere. An ancient Ford Cortina rattled past, a grey Volvo estate parked opposite, a shouty family with the remains of a burger breakfast in their hands wandered in front of him. He thought it unlikely they were the forces of oppression that the leader had warned them about. Or members of another cell. But he watched them closely anyway. A beggar approached him, a filthy coat wrapped around nothing much. He held up a hand-painted piece of cardboard: 'Very hungry. Homeless. God bless you.' The student waved him away.

The woman was staring straight ahead. The concrete rubbish bin a few metres from the entrance had been the drop point last time. He assumed they were sticking to the routine. The bin, they had established before, was emptied approximately every half hour. The emptying at 10.30 was the trigger. A deliberately messed-up envelope would be dropped inside the bin by one cell. Ninety seconds later it would be retrieved by another. His cell. The woman's cell. The leader's cell.

The back window was clean but the student continued to rub.

A red Mondeo, a black Mercedes, a black VW Golf. A

delivery man, a girl in a tracksuit, a wide woman in a business suit.

The student felt for the foxglove bloom. He wasn't sure how long it would take before the poison worked but figured if he swallowed it as the woman completed the dead drop, he should just make it back to the house. Nausea, sweating, fitting and heart tremors were all likely. He hoped the flower and leaves were small enough.

It was the delivery man. Twenty-something, average height, average build, white. Unremarkable in every way. Brown cap, brown jacket and invisible. He hesitated as he walked past the bin, then as if with an afterthought produced a brown envelope from an inside pocket and placed it in there. He then drained a can of drink, dropped that on top.

The student tapped the car roof. The door opened. The woman got out. For twenty metres she would have her back to him. He had to do it now. Heart racing, he palmed the foxglove. Ten metres. His hand to his mouth. The petals smelt of nothing in particular. Two metres. They tasted of nothing in particular either but stuck to the roof of his mouth. A swig of water and they were gone. He uttered a silent mantra and dropped back into the car.

The woman got in, holding the stained envelope in her hands. He glanced at it. Apart from the sauce marks and damp patches, it was blank. No writing of any kind. The dashboard clock said 10.40. They'd be home by 11.30, assuming he was still capable of driving.

He had never expected to be ill before. His speed dropped in anticipation of what he thought was coming. The woman noticed.

'Leader wants this as soon as possible.' She tapped the envelope. 'Speed it up.'

He felt fine.

31

THE STUDENT AND the woman arrived back at 11.35. She got out first, he glanced at himself in the mirror. He had messed up. Not enough leaves? The wrong leaves? He got out and walked to number 26 a few paces behind the woman. He had failed.

Boxer Street was narrow, shabby, unremarkable. The terraced houses were built in the 1930s; far enough from Coventry city centre to have avoided the Blitz of 1940 but close enough to the university to have been hit by students since 1968. Most of the entrances sported multiple doorbells. Bikes, overflowing bins and recycling tubs were scattered by front doors and along scrubby, broken paths. The smell of rotting vegetation was unmissable. Loud music pulsed from a high window opposite. Two women in denim shorts and sun tops smoked roll-ups on their front doorstep, an overflowing ashtray between them. They didn't look up.

Inside 26 the leader was waiting for them in the hallway. Khaki shirt, baggy black cotton trousers. He held out both hands, as if in supplication. The woman placed the envelope on his upturned palms. He seemed pleased. 'Today is a good day,' he said, then turned and walked to the kitchen. The student and the woman waited in the lounge. She took the two-seater sofa, he leant on the wall by the door. He still felt fine.

After a few minutes of silence the leader strode in, followed by the sweating man, his head ringed with bandages. The leader stood by the empty bookshelves, a sheet of lined paper in his hand. The student could make out the indents of five lines of type, twelve maybe fifteen words a line. A long message this time. The leader waited for the sweating man to ease his way on to the sofa, then smiled. 'A good day today, a better day tomorrow.'

Tomorrow? thought the student. *Tomorrow?*

He still felt fine.

The leader waved the paper. 'We are about to jump-start the revolution. We cannot leave it any longer and our citizen friends in the London cell have offered us the next target. We will strike at the bankers, priests and the Jews of the oppressor class. The other leftists who side with the bureaucrats and the status quo will be shamed. They have learnt nothing. Arguing with us is pointless. Negotiating is pointless. They will be reviled.'

The student had heard all this before, but his delivery was more urgent now, more desperate.

'When you marched against the war, did it stop? No. It stopped nothing. When you voted, in election after election, what did it change? Anything? No, it changed nothing. This is how we bring emancipation.' He produced his wooden-handled knife, pointed at his audience in turn. 'If you could at last change the world, would you step up and do it? Wade in filth. Embrace the butcher. Change the world.'

And in the space of a few seconds the student felt a sweat break, first on his forehead, then down his arms and legs, then throughout his body. His heart slowed. His eyes lost focus. As the leader folded his paper, the student slid his back down the wall.

Well this is it then, he thought.

The nausea enveloped him. He pushed himself on to his hands and knees. He knew it was coming. His insides turned to water. His body was expelling a poison. The last thing he heard before he passed out was the leader's shouts and a torrent of clicks from the Geiger counter.

32

THE STUDENT DRIFTED in and out of consciousness. He knew he was in an ambulance. His stomach was still on fire, his clothes soaked through. The lights were fierce, the suspension on the vehicle non-existent; every pothole and ramp sent spasms of pain through his body. He vomited continually. Careful latexed hands wiped him clean. Two voices, he thought, one male, one female. A conversation he couldn't reach. He thought he caught his name being repeated somewhere but through the fog of siren, engine and clatter he wasn't sure.

A crashing of doors, new raised voices. He screwed his eyes shut. He was strapped, jolted, and on a trolley. Propelled at speed, he found a handle to grab. Every bump, every turn made his head throb, his stomach heave. The light acquired shadows, the shouts gained echoes. He was inside. The acid burn in his throat and nose didn't stop the familiar sweet disinfectant smell filling his lungs. He'd made it to hospital but was weaker than he'd ever felt, sicker than he'd ever imagined. He needed to explain why he was here but not until he was safe. He tried to open his eyes, tried to form words, and failed at both. His eyelids were too heavy, his lips stuck together.

The leader had said tomorrow. It was getting darker.

The noise of the room elongated and twisted into a deep pulsing sound that throbbed around his head. It filled his chest. Voices, then whistling, then a crackling electric current.

Then it went black.

33

HE WAS SITTING at a large, crowded table. The noise was extraordinary. He knew everyone was family, it was just he couldn't name anyone. He would have to guess.

There was an old woman at the head of the table, her white hair drawn back in a black tie, gold wire-frame glasses over large, amused eyes, green and red embroidered sari. His grandmother, presumably.

Next to her was a white man reading a book. Black receding hair, hunched shoulders. The man held up the book for someone to see: *Bob Dylan Lyrics 1962–1985.* The man gave a thumbs-up and returned to its pages. He'd guess that was his father. The one who walked out when he was three and caused his mother a lifetime of doubt and low self-esteem. He remembered that.

Identical girls sat on either side, talking through him. As though he wasn't there. Straight black hair cut to a bob, red T-shirts with an embroidered elephant on each. Green and turquoise sequins down the trunks. He had twin sisters, these must be them. He tried to listen to what they were saying but their words were blurred. Out of focus. He tried to join in but they carried right on. As though he wasn't there. He tried to remember their names but nothing came.

Beyond the sister on his right were three women of similar ages – he guessed maybe fifty years old. Two were animated, one sat quietly, hooded eyes on her plate. The quiet one would be his mother.

Round the far side were men sharing a near-empty bottle of whisky, their shouting and name-calling suggesting they had consumed most of it. One flourished a book called *The Wrong Heaven*. Uncles? Brothers? Neighbours? He recognized none of them. He took a dislike to all of them. Empty clanging vessels.

Then came the two IPS women, the dead one and the new one. They were deep in conversation with each other, oblivious to the drunks on their left.

In the far corner, underneath a framed black and white photograph of an old man in a cream shirt and traditional white dhoti, sat a man he guessed was his grandfather who had died before he was born. He was dressed identically to the man in the photo. Maybe he was the man in the photo.

The student knew all of this was strange, wrong even, but felt he had to stay as long as he could. He was sure he would have to leave soon. It was the end of a meal, the plates contained only scraps; rice, chapatti, some fish curry. In the centre of the table, a large serving bowl had only a few spoonfuls of a yellow lentil dish left; an ornate stainless-steel platter contained what was left of the rice. He seemed to have no place setting.

His family, without him. His family, moved on.

The woman he assumed was his grandmother was on her feet, explaining something, and suddenly the room was quiet. All eyes were on the old woman, who held both hands in the air. The material of her sari had fallen back to reveal arms ringed with many gold bracelets, a dozen or so thin bands that had slid back to her elbow. Her forearms were deeply scarred; long, pale, jagged lines of pink skin ran like a maze from her wrist. When she spoke, everyone listened. So did he. These words he could hear.

'We will be jailed, you know. All of us.' Her voice trembled slightly. 'We are CPI-M.' She emphasized each letter, the M receiving the heaviest inflection. 'And they hate us. They are revisionists and class traitors so they will put us away. Cut us, yes, denounce us, yes, but we stay. The stinking Indian bourgeoisie in league with imperialists.'

And as though a spell had been broken, everyone in the room turned away from the old woman and resumed their conversations. The cacophony returned. His sisters talked through him. His father read his book. The whisky drinkers finished the bottle. His grandmother slumped to her seat.

It was getting darker.

The dead IPS woman pointed a finger at him.

Then it went black.

He was back at the station. The train arrived and the dead IPS woman with the red scarf stepped off. She said she didn't have long. She explained that she had kept his letter. That it had won her over. She didn't get many letters. He explained that it had been an act of drunken ambition. That he had wanted to be a journalist and thought she could make it happen. She said that she could.

He was nervous and anxious to please. She was effusive, engaging, and wanted coffee and cake. She suggested going somewhere nicer to talk but he said there wasn't anywhere, so they sat opposite each other in the station's ferociously lit café. Other shapeless, faceless people walked past; he didn't waste his time on them. He and the IPS woman were the story here.

Recently, she explained, she had been struggling with a story and realized she needed help. Remembering his neat, well-written, slightly desperate letter, she'd called his number. She had a startling proposition. She explained what she was looking for and how he might find it. She offered him a thousand pounds towards his university fees and an internship at IPS when he graduated. He accepted before the cake was finished.

Then it went black.

34

3.40 p.m.

MILLIE AND AMARA. His sisters were Millie and Amara. He knew that now. How shameful to have forgotten. Without effort he could recall their teasing, flashing eyes, their relentless, tuneless singing and their combined weight on his shoulders as he gave them rides around the garden. His mother was Misha, his father Sam, his grandmother Nyta, but his sisters were Millie and Amara. He had to keep them safe. He had to keep them all safe.

Very slowly he became aware that he had a visitor. Sounds first. The shuffling, the rustle of fabric, the plastic-on-lino sound of a chair being repositioned. The lights were coming back too. It was like a system reboot. Wherever he'd been, he was back. In hospital, with a visitor. He could hear the electrical buzz of the lights and the occasional beeps and clicks of whatever they had plugged him into. He could feel a needle in his left arm – a drip, presumably. His fever had gone, the nausea too. Only a soreness in his throat and pain in his stomach muscles remained. He remembered the poison, remembered why he had taken it. He hoped he was in an isolation ward. Except that he had a visitor.

He kept his eyes shut. The last image to fade was that of the two IPS women. Huddled together, deep in conversation. Had they known each other? Salvation past and present.

He heard the sound of a page turning. His visitor was reading. Someone who wasn't medical staff. Someone who was prepared to wait.

The page turning was regular, every two minutes he guessed. The pages sounded light and small. A book reader for certain. Only the student's cell knew he was here so his visitor's identity wasn't really a mystery. The systematic cracking of knuckles confirmed it. The man in the chair by his bed was the man he was trying to escape from. The leader.

The student's heart sank. The leaves had worked, the Geiger counter had worked. Yet here he was, in hospital with a crazed and angry revolutionary for company. If the leader had discovered that the Geiger's clicks had been generated by the hidden radioactive smoke alarm core in his pocket, the one that started life on his ceiling in Boxer Street, then retribution would have been swift. The wooden-handled blade would be in the leader's pocket for certain.

'Can you hear me, citizen?' The tone was urgent, conspiratorial.

The student decided that he couldn't hear him. He lay motionless. His breathing was steady. He would just wait until the leader got bored and left.

'Can you hear me, citizen?' A slight change in tone and emphasis. He sounded almost panicky. 'Your breathing has changed. I hope you're better.' His voice was closer now, the book cast to one side.

The student kept his eyes closed. Tried a few words. 'That

was close,' he said, his voice a painful rasp. His mouth felt stale and sticky. He licked his lips.

'Water?' offered the leader.

The student nodded. 'But not their water,' he whispered.

The sound of a plastic bottle being unscrewed.

'It's fresh. From the machine,' said the leader.

The student raised his head, smelt the tang of the plastic then sipped gratefully.

He slumped back to the pillow, eyes still closed.

'They say you are safe,' said the leader. 'I am not so sure.' He spoke quickly, softly. 'I believe you were poisoned on the drop. I spoke with her. She told me about the homeless man who approached you. It must have been him. You were sick. My Geiger counter speaks the truth. Now it says you're OK.'

The student cracked his eyes open. He was in a private room, one bed, two chairs; one chair next to him, the other by the closed door. A single window allowed bright sunshine into the room. The leader was a metre away, leaning forward in the chair. His glasses had slid down his nose, his face remained impassive. The student closed his eyes again.

'What time is it?'

'Quarter to four.'

I've been out a while, he thought.

'So I'm not radioactive?'

The leader found the Geiger counter, stuck it close to the student's face and pressed the trigger. Silence. A few clicks then more silence.

'You're not radioactive,' he said, 'but you were, you must have heard it.'

The student nodded. 'I did.'

'Must have been on your clothes.'

'Must have.' Or the smoke alarm core just fell out of my pocket, he thought. Either way, no clicks now. He chanced some more detail. 'Maybe it was a spray. Maybe I inhaled enough to make me sick but not enough to show up now.'

The leader nodded. 'The closer we get, the closer they get. This attack is proof.'

If this is what he wants to believe, thought the student, I'll see if I can help some more.

'Maybe it's a fascist group,' he said. 'Maybe they got a tip-off.'

The leader's head snapped back to the student. 'From within our cell?'

The student said nothing. Shrugged. Let the new poison take effect.

Eventually the leader muttered, 'We're too close to stop now.'

'How close?'

'Too close.'

Now was the moment to push. 'I'm a liability,' said the student. 'They know my face.'

'You're a hero.'

'I'm a liability. You should leave me behind.'

'Too late.'

'Not if I'm a liability. Not if I damage the operation.'

'You won't.'

'I will if the fash know me.'

The leader considered that. 'We can disguise you.'

Enough pushing for now. 'I just hope I'm out of here in time.'

'You will be. You're not safe here. We're going to take you out early. Then we have just over sixty hours.'

It's Monday afternoon. So it must be happening on Thursday now.

The student fought the tremble in his voice. 'How much filth?' he whispered.

The leader pushed his Browline glasses back up his nose. He smiled. Stood up. 'So much filth,' he said, and left.

The woman appeared then. One in, one out. She glanced around the room, hawklike, unsmiling.

'Where are your clothes?' she asked.

The student shrugged.

'I'll find some,' she said, and ducked out again.

He heard her shout at someone, then silence.

The student lay as still as his racing mind and heart would allow. Thursday. The leader had said just over sixty hours. Whatever they'd been recruited for, it was happening in three days' time.

A doctor came in and told him what he already knew: his sickness had probably been caused by a poison and they were waiting for toxicology reports.

Alone again in his room, he fought the urge to unplug the drip and run. The doctors wanted him to stay where he was. The leader wanted him out.

He sat up in bed, arranging the meagre pillows behind him. The smells of food mingled with floor disinfectant. The door to his room was ajar and he could see two beds in the main ward, one empty, the other occupied. An elderly man with a tube in his mouth slept heavily.

The woman wouldn't be long, all she had to do was find some clothes, but when she arrived he would be guarded again. She wasn't as twitchy as the leader, but she shared his obsessive, messianic determination. She had been his first link to Boxer Street. She had been the first to threaten his sisters. He found himself gripping his thin blue blanket with both hands and screwed his eyes shut. A headstart on his debt and a job after university had sounded like everything he'd ever wanted. He'd have made it. Made it in spite of his absentee father, in spite of his as-good-as-absent mother and in spite of his doubting friends. Then the killing started and his options vanished. The final throw of the dice – his plan to get the leader to leave him behind – had failed.

A woman with a green nylon uniform, pens in her breast pocket and a badge that said 'Gyongyi' brought him a tray. On it was a dinner plate with a metal cover on top, and a small bowl of ice cream. She smiled at him as she held it out, and for the briefest moment he wanted to tell her everything. It was a genuine smile. She seemed happy to bring him his food, and he wanted to talk. But 'Thanks' was all he said.

She lifted the lid. Some kind of fish, broccoli, potatoes.

'Would you like it now?' she said. 'I know you haven't eaten. It's what we have left.'

He wasn't hungry but he nodded. 'Sure, why not,' he said.

She placed the tray on the table over his bed. Metal cutlery, salt and pepper in paper sachets, a toothpick, a glass of water, a quarter lemon. The student stared.

'Excuse me,' he called out.

The woman with the Gyongyi name tag stepped back into the room.

'I'm sorry,' said the student, 'I don't mean to be difficult, I'm sure you're busy and everything, but might I have some more lemon?'

She looked surprised. 'Sure,' she said. 'Wait a minute.'

She ducked back out of the room and he heard the clatter of metal covers being lifted and dropped. She emerged with two more quarters.

'These were left over. Most people don't like them. You want both?'

He smiled his thanks. 'I've heard they're good for you,' he said. 'Vitamin C and all that. Thank you . . .'

He attempted her name, and she laughed.

'It's pronounced "Jon Gee",' she said.

He tried again and she smiled again.

'That was your friend just now?' She nodded her head towards the door.

He shrugged. 'Yeah, kind of.'

'She shouts a lot,' she said.

He nodded his agreement. 'Yeah, sorry about that. She's kind of on edge.'

Gyongyi turned, then hesitated, uncertain, caught between two thoughts.

'Does she treat you bad?' she said.

He shook his head. 'Oh it's not like that.'

She stared at him, unconvinced. 'OK,' she said, and left.

Thursday. Three days. He had to try something. When she had gone, he pushed the table away and swung his legs out. Carefully manoeuvring the IV bag, he retied his hospital gown, cursing his lack of clothing. He closed the door to the room then quickly drank his glass of water, wiping it dry on the sheet. Kneeling on the bed, and with as much precision as time and nerves allowed, he squeezed each quarter lemon into the glass. Breathing heavily, he caught the sharp, acid smell as he pressed the skin between his fingers. He kept pressing until he was sure there was nothing left. He removed the pips, then held up the glass and peered at what he had. A few millimetres of juice at best. It wouldn't be enough, he was sure of it. He would use small letters, few words. He had to try.

He pushed the plate, lid and cutlery off the tray and on to the blanket, replacing them with the glass and the toothpick. There were two 'hospital comments' cards on his bedside table. He reached for the first one, placed it on the tray. He dipped the red plastic toothpick in the lemon juice, then twisted it slowly between his fingers. He tapped the pick on the glass rim, then hovered above the card. It left spaces for name, address and a comment. He stroked a letter on the card, dipped again, stroked again. The letters shone briefly on the card before disappearing. He wrote in capitals.

The leader had given many talks. He loved to recall his revolutionary heroism in Turkey, Syria or wherever he had pitched up. He had reminded them that the old ways can be the best ways. That the dark web is patrolled by the security services, that computers are inherently vulnerable, and that if they couldn't afford encryption, to stay analogue. Stay dark. No website, no emails, no texts. Instead, letters, typewriters and invisible ink would keep them hidden. And it had worked.

It was, he said, the Russians who had brought back invisible ink. For at least the last ten years they had been using paper impregnated with chemicals to transfer secret messages on to real letters. The student's method was, of necessity, more primitive. He dipped and scraped more letters. Small, capitalized, as few as possible. They shone, they disappeared, absorbed by the paper. He wasn't sure whether any of it would be readable.

He was close to finishing when the door opened. With a start he grabbed the dinner plate, pulling it back on to the tray and over the card. He started to retch.

'I can see your arse. And I'd rather not.' The woman flung some clothes at him. 'What are you doing anyway?'

'Trying not to be sick,' he said, heart hammering in his chest.

The wrong thing to say. She grabbed the tray.

'You just ate what they brought you? Are you fucking mental? You've just been poisoned, remember? Who knows who could have got this to you.'

There was a crash as she dropped the tray by the door.

He shook his head. 'No, no. It's just the smell. I didn't eat any of it.' He looked at her, red-faced, then looked for the tray. The plate was still covering the card, the glass with the lemon juice was on its side, empty.

He slid back into bed. She paced the room.

'I can't believe you even thought of eating their food,' she said.

He closed his eyes. Wished Gyongyi had come back.

'Well I've taken their medicine,' he said. 'If they were going to get rid of me they'd have done it by now.'

The woman, clearly anxious, continued to pace. 'You need to get dressed.'

'I haven't been discharged,' he said.

'He wants you out. So you're discharged.'

'He's discharging me?'

'Yes.'

'What's the hurry?' he said. 'The toxicology tests aren't through yet.'

She stood at the head of his bed. 'We know what happened. You were poisoned. You were compromised. We need to get you out. Get dressed.' Before he knew it, she'd removed the drip from his arm and motioned at the assortment of clothes she had flung at him. Jeans, shirt and shoes.

'Where did you get them?' he asked.

'Someone died.'

He stared at the jumbled clothing. 'You stole them? From a dead guy?'

She sat awkwardly on the far corner of his bed. Her face was fixed. Her voice was raised. 'You need to get dressed. You need to be ready. It doesn't matter where the clothes come from.'

He held up the trousers and shirt. They looked too big for him but not by much.

'Underwear? Socks?' he said.

She shook her head. 'You'll cope. Get dressed.'

He thought he would try one last time. 'You should really leave me here. I told the leader. If I'm compromised, I'll ruin everything. I'll be fine.'

She slid up the bed. 'Yes, you're compromised. No, you're not staying here. It's not safe.' She glanced at the jeans. 'I'll step outside if you're suddenly feeling modest.'

He nodded and she left, clicking the door shut behind her. He had just swung out of bed when the door opened again.

'Woman here to collect the poison shit she brought you. Decent?'

His heart kicked up a notch. 'Yes, of course.'

Gyongyi appeared, face like stone.

He reasoned he had thirty seconds, maximum. As she bent to retrieve the tray, he rescued the comments card from under the plate. Placing a finger over his lips, he took a biro from her breast pocket. He scribbled furiously on the card and handed it to her. He leant in close and whispered fast. 'I'm in big trouble with her. She's not a good person. Please post this to the address I've written here. Please. Please.' He slid the card back under the plate.

She held the tray and stared back at him. Startled. Frightened.

He placed his hands over hers. 'Please, Gyongyi. Last post.'

She nodded, and left the room.

35

4.35 p.m.

THE MINICAB DROPPED the leader two blocks from 26 Boxer Street. He paid cash and said nothing to the driver. He didn't tip. A three-minute walk to the house. He paused on the doorstep, key in the door. Late afternoon, a heavy heat, the street was quiet. The house was quiet too. The woman had taken the next shift in the hospital. He had the space to do what he had to do.

He turned the key slowly and slipped inside. Standing still, head cocked, he felt a breeze from the backyard blow through the house. It brought with it the shuffling, slapping sound of a man in sandals. He felt the smoothness of the wooden-handled knife in his trouser pocket. His thumb traced the spine of the folded blade all the way to the butt. He rolled it around his fingers.

From the kitchen he could see him pacing the courtyard. The table had two half-drunk cups of black coffee on it and a used, unwashed plate. A dirty knife and fork had been discarded nearby.

The leader picked up both mugs, the plate and the cutlery, and put them in the sink. He wiped the table with a cloth, then rinsed, folded and placed it over the mixer tap.

'Oh hi,' said the sweating man, pushing sunglasses back on to his forehead as he entered. 'Thought I heard you back. How is he?' He wore a Clash T-shirt, cargo shorts, sandals. A large plaster covered his right ear.

It was clear the sweating man hadn't given a thought to his appearance.

'Dressed for the revolution, citizen?' said the leader.

He glanced down at his outfit as if seeing it for the first time. 'It's hot.' He shrugged. 'What should I be wearing?'

The leader stood with his arms folded. 'You know we're close to operations, yet you dress for the beach. It's a mindset. A lazy mindset. A counter-revolutionary mindset.'

The sweating man was uncomfortable now, shifting his weight from one leg to the other. In a glance he noticed the now-clean table.

'Look, I'm sorry,' he said. 'It doesn't mean anything, honest.' He retied his ponytail. 'I'm ready for anything, you know that.' He looked imploringly at the leader. 'Is there something you'd like me to do?'

The leader didn't move. 'Sit down,' he said. He pointed at the nearest kitchen chair, then drew out a second chair to sit opposite. He leant forward, elbows on his knees.

The sweating man sat down, eyes suddenly wide. 'We've done this before,' he muttered.

The leader ignored him. 'Our friend has been poisoned. You asked how he is. Well, he is poisoned. With radiation of some sort. He should recover. The dose he received was small, too small to cause permanent harm.'

'Well that's a relief—'

'Not a relief, no. He was betrayed. Someone knew where

he'd be, someone gave him away. A traitor.' A sheen had appeared on the leader's face, neck and scalp. 'Who do you think it might have been, citizen?'

Eyes still wide, hands gripping the sides of the chair, the sweating man's words deserted him. 'What? Well . . . you said . . . but that . . .'

'Who betrayed him?'

'I have no idea. Are you sure—'

'Of course we are sure.' The leader's hand was back in his pocket. His fingers slowly traced the metal rivets of the knife handle. 'You heard and saw the evidence. The dead drop was compromised. We have to look for someone who might be collaborating.' His glasses had slipped down the bridge of his nose; he pushed them back. 'Someone who has a history of contact with fascists.' His voice was getting quieter. 'Where would you start, citizen?'

The sweating man was silent. His eyes darted around the room, his head moving left and right. Appraising his options.

The leader knew it. 'Thinking of running?'

The sweating man shook his head. 'Thinking this is madness.'

'How so?' Almost a whisper. His left hand palmed the knife.

Finally, the sweating man had had enough. 'Because you're fucking deranged, that's why. You were raised to see conspiracy, so you always see bloody conspiracy. Well get this, smartass. There isn't one! There really isn't! There are no traitors here, just revolutionaries waiting to be told what to do.'

He stood abruptly, knocking the chair over. The leader stood too, arms at his side. His chair didn't move. The sweating man was eight inches taller than the leader, who looked surprised by the advantage.

The sweating man leant in, their faces just a few centimetres apart. 'But you never tell us anything,' he said. 'All we get is secrets and silence. You think I'm a collaborator, or a traitor or something ridiculous. You have no evidence, you just have your bullshit theories. So I'll take my chances, thank you very much.' He strode to the door, reached the foot of the stairs in two strides. He turned. 'I know you'll remind me about how you have my parents' address, how you know where they live, blah blah blah.' He wiped his face with his T-shirt. 'More bullshit.' He leapt up the stairs.

The leader stood still, listening to the sounds of a man packing, fast. The fingers of his left hand felt for the blade again, tugging it free. He tucked it in his waistband, covering the handle with his shirt. He wiped a handkerchief over his face, then moved to the foot of the stairs and waited.

The breeze had gone, the house was airless.

The packing didn't take long. The sweating man appeared with a rucksack inside two minutes. The sight of the leader leaning against the balustrade caused him to pause briefly on the top step.

'You know, this could have worked,' he said, climbing down. 'When you talked about how we had learnt from jihadists. How they had shown that small groups, organized, working together, could change history. We were listening to that.' He had one hand on the banister, one on his rucksack strap. 'How revolution could start with just a truck and a few knives. We got that. But nothing happened. We failed. It was all fucking noise and posturing.'

There was no eye contact. The leader had kicked off his shoes and was staring at the floor. The sweating man passed him and walked the four metres of the hall, not hearing the leader fall into step behind him. He reached for the latch. As the sweating man pulled at the door, the leader reached for his ponytail and yanked hard. There was a brief, strangled shout of alarm as his head snapped back. The point of the knife entered with the blade flat, cutting edge to the right.

With one left-to-right jerk he severed the larynx and most of the muscle groups. The leader stepped sideways, the man fell to the floor.

He studied his dying colleague, crouched by his side. The man's legs were in spasm, shaking violently. His face stared at the ceiling, life draining fast. The leader leant into his eye-line. He told him where and when the attack was planned.

'It'll be when we bring the war home,' he said. 'The day we ignite the fight against the fascists. And it started right here.' He wiped one side of the blade on the man's shorts. 'Embrace the butcher,' he whispered. He wiped the other side on the man's T-shirt. 'Embrace the butcher.'

36

Tuesday, 12 June, 7.35 a.m.

FAMIE'S PHONE WOKE them both. She pulled it from under the blanket. The screen said it was Sam. 'Yeah Sam,' she said, 'what have you got for me?'

'You sound like I just woke you.'

'That's because you just woke me. Me and Sophe, burning the midnight oil here. What's up?'

'I'm coming over. Thought you'd appreciate a ten-minute warning.'

Famie sat up fast. 'Ten minutes? Are you crazy? No one's ready in ten minutes.'

Sophie walked past her, waved, and disappeared into the shower.

'Most people anyway. Why are you coming over, Sam? Is everything OK?'

'The press have gone, Famie. Your flat is paparazzi-free. I just drove past.' He was on speakerphone and shouting. 'I can drive you over if you want anything, or to move back.'

The thought of her own bed and rooms with windows that

actually opened was tempting. 'OK, see you in at least twenty.' She hung up.

Twenty minutes later they met in the Travelodge car park, slung their bags into his boot.

'Did you check out?' he said.

'Not yet,' said Famie, 'but we have our stuff in case.'

'In case what?'

'Just in case.'

Famie rode in the front, Sophie behind Sam. The radio played news, turned down to a slight rumble. They all wore sunglasses, and Famie's baseball cap was back. Sam cracked the driver's window open.

'Do we smell or something?' said Sophie.

Sam laughed, Famie smiled.

'Course we do. It's the gin,' she said.

'It sure is,' said Sam. 'Seeping through every pore. It's the smell of some serious journalism happening. What time's your meeting with DC Hunter?'

'Eleven thirty. Hackney Police Station. We're going to them, thought it would be safer.'

The traffic had thinned out, the lights in their favour. They'd be at Famie's flat in ten minutes.

'What are you going to tell them?' said Sam, his eyes flicking between Sophie in the mirror and Famie next to him.

'That I met Amal,' said Sophie. 'That I went out with Seth.'

An exchange of glances between Sophie and Famie.

'And the laptop? The photos?' said Sam. He sounded surprised. 'That's evidence. You know it. You know you have to tell them, however embarrassing.'

Famie stared out of the window. 'Spare us the lecture, Sam. We'll decide what they see.'

She turned the radio up. There were reports of an American presidential hopeful, a prison reformer who'd gone to jail and the imminent end of the heatwave.

'Thank Christ for that,' muttered Sam.

'And thank Christ it's not about us for a change,' said Famie. 'Though give it a few hours . . .'

They swept past Famie's flat. All clear. Sam parked.

'Come up, Sam, I'll make coffee. You know you want to.' Sam looked unsure, Famie took his head between her hands. 'Sam, you can be late just this once. You've quit already. You have no one to impress. Come and have coffee with us.'

His shoulders slumped. 'OK, you've won me over. Do I get to wash up too like usual?'

The press had all gone but not without leaving their trade-mark coffee cups and paper bags in an overflowing bin. They stepped inside the hallway. Famie put her key in the door.

'Three iced lattes coming up,' she said.

She pushed the door over a few days of post. Two freesheet newspapers, four take-out menus, two utility bills and a plain white envelope with a handwritten address. Famie tossed them all on the sofa. Several days of heat and no ven-tilation demanded as many windows open as possible, as quickly as possible. Sam and Sophie slumped on the sofa, Famie walked through to the kitchen and switched on the coffee machine.

Sam appeared, handed her the handwritten envelope. 'You probably should,' he said. 'Another Coventry postmark.'

Sophie walked in. 'Another weatherman forecast maybe. Exciting.'

Sam grimaced.

'Sorry,' she said.

Famie took the envelope. The other letters had been typewritten, this was biro-written. Small, meticulous hand-writing. She peered at the stamp. 'Posted yesterday.' She dug her nail into the envelope, sliced it open. Inside was a printed card from a hospital and a folded sheet of paper tucked behind it. Famie unfolded the piece of paper. No address, no signature. Three lines of writing, the same neat script as the envelope. She scanned it quickly then read the message out loud.

'I work in the University Hospital, Coventry. A young man insisted I send this to you. He said he was in trouble with a woman. I think he's telling the truth. I hope you can help him.'

Famie handed the note to Sam then picked up the card. She flipped it in her hands. 'Huh,' she said. Her address had been scrawled in the top right corner. Similar biro to the envelope, different handwriting. Hurried. Messy. She flipped it again. It was a cheaply printed postcard requesting hospital users to write comments in the spaces provided. Around the edges, more handwriting. In clear black capitals it read 'SEE THAT MY GRAVE IS KEPT CLEAN'.

'What the fuck?' said Sophie.

'That's our guy,' said Famie.

'And definitely a guy,' said Sam. 'A guy in trouble with a woman.'

Famie made the coffees, thinking fast. 'Is he telling us he's about to die? Because that's a desperately sad note to pass on.'

'It can't be that, can it?' said Sam. 'Surely not. We don't know who he is or where he is.'

Sophie was on her phone. 'It's the main hospital in Coventry. New-build in 2006. Used to be the Walsgrave.' She showed them a Google map.

'So we know he's in Coventry,' said Famie, 'we know he's trying to message us, and we know he's having to go to these ridiculous lengths to send cryptic messages. Might still be a fruitcake.'

'Not another Dylan song, is it?' asked Sophie.

Famie grabbed her laptop, opened it on her lap, typed in the words. She gaped. 'Holy shit, he's done it again. It's not Dylan but it is another song.' She spun the screen.

'A Texas blues song by Blind Lemon Jefferson,' read Sam. He hit play and the kitchen filled with a scratchy guitar and vocal from, the screen said, 1928. 'Why is he sending this?'

'We got one music reference,' said Famie, 'so he's sending another. Read the lyrics.'

Sam scanned and summarized. 'Essentially it says there's one kind favour I'll ask of you, see that my grave is kept clean. Then it says, "Did you hear that coughing sound? Did you hear them church bells tone? Means another poor boy is dead and gone . . . see that my grave is kept clean."'

The kitchen was quiet. 'That's one heavy song,' said Sophie. 'Sounds like he's given up.'

'But why would he tell us that?' said Famie. 'Why tell some folk you don't know that you're about to die, or give up?'

'Unless that isn't what he's saying. What's the story no one is reporting?' said Sophie. 'Maybe he's saying something else. Anyone know anything about Blind Lemon Jefferson?'

Sam started a search.

Famie picked up the card again. Stared at it blankly. 'Is there anything new in the *Telegraph*? Has anyone checked?' She fanned herself with the card.

'Me,' said Sam, scrolling through music history websites. 'I checked. Nothing. Obviously I'd have told you . . .'

'We've never struggled to understand him before,' said Famie. 'One look, one Google search and we've had it. What are we missing?'

'Put it on again,' said Sam.

Famie hit play. An image of a bespectacled, squinting young African-American, guitar on his lap, appeared on the screen.

'He's blind. We're blind,' said Sam, scrolling. 'He was from Coutchman, Texas, considered the father of Texas blues. You want more?'

Famie downed her coffee. 'Wait,' she said. 'This needs to be obvious. It's either the song or it's him. Title and artist. You said we're blind. That's right, we are. So "blind" and "lemon" and "Jefferson" all come into play. Does that take it somewhere?'

'Sure there's nothing else on the card?' said Sam. 'All blank?'

Famie looked again, flipping the card in her hand. She held it up for them both to see.

Sam shrugged. 'Looks blank,' he said. 'So maybe "lemon" is the word. Maybe that's it! We used it as invisible ink when we were kids.'

Sophie laughed. 'Really? That's a thing?'

'Sure,' he said. 'You just heat it up.'

Famie stared at the card's blank boxes. That adrenalin rush again. She placed the card on the coffee machine's stainless-steel hot plate. Famie, Sam and Sophie stood to watch. Brown letters started to appear within seconds. Famie grabbed Sophie's hand. The writing was hurried but the words clear.

In the first box: MY NAME IS HARI ROY

In the second box: FROM 26 BOXER STREET

And in the third box: URGENT! TERROR ATTACK THURSDAY!

37

9.20 a.m.

THEY CLIMBED INTO a black cab, switched off the intercom, shut the connecting glass. The driver got the message, turned up a talk station. Famie and Sophie sat in the back seats, Sam in the fold-down facing them. Hackney Police Station was twenty minutes away. Famie's heart was still racing, her nerves jangling. She was wired. She had a name. The messages were coming from a real person and his name was Hari.

'Facebook photo.' Sophie held up her phone, used her fingers to enlarge it. It showed a cheery round face, clean-shaven, light brown skin, spiky black hair. A blue and white striped T-shirt, a can of beer held up to the camera. She flipped the phone, read from his profile. 'Hari Roy. Second-year student at Warwick University, studying Politics. British Indian, mother's family originally from Bengal. Nothing on his father. Twin sisters, can't see how old they are just yet. He's single.'

'Christ, you got that already?' Famie was impressed.

Sophie shrugged. 'Just standard,' she said.

'When did he post last?' said Sam.

'Hmm,' said Sophie. 'Nothing for a few weeks. He's not on Twitter or Instagram. Not as far as I can see anyway.'

They all looked at each other with 'what-happens-next' faces.

'I want to call the hospital,' said Sam, 'but I guess we should wait until we know what the police say. If journalists start making enquiries about a Hari Roy then who knows what that will trigger.'

'But he's asking us for help,' said Famie. 'If we assume our guy is telling the truth, that he's not mad and that there is a terror attack planned for Thursday, we either convince the police to act or we go to Coventry to follow up ourselves.'

Sam and Sophie looked unconvinced.

'This is our story,' she said. 'This might have been Mary's story. Now we have to stay on it.'

'You quit, remember?' said Sam. 'I've quit too. Sophie's still there. Tommi's hanging on. But we're out. We're hardly the new investigators.'

The three of them stared unseeing through different windows.

'And is Hari the story or is Amal the story?' said Sophie.

'And would Mary have known about Amal?' asked Sam. He looked between the women.

Famie closed her eyes. 'Christ, this is messy. I didn't think so. I thought they had nothing to do with each other, but Sophie knows better.' She held her hand out to Sophie, cueing her in.

'Seth and Amal certainly saw each other. I was with them both. It's quite possible Mary was too.'

'So,' said Sam, 'the first journalist to die may have been friends with—'

'Too strong,' interrupted Sophie. 'Wouldn't have happened.'

'May have known,' Sam corrected himself, 'an Islamist terrorist. The brother of her boyfriend. Or former boyfriend.

That makes Amal the story, doesn't it? That's what the police will say.'

They exited the cab at a modern office block, its ground floor painted blue. Blinds covered the windows, signs in many languages covered the double doors.

'Christ, is this it?' said Sam.

Famie paid the driver.

'Looks like a charity shop under siege,' said Sophie.

'It's just safer,' said Famie. 'It's why I suggested it.'

In her flat they had stared at the hospital comments card for a long time, wondering if it had any other secrets to reveal. After ten minutes they'd decided it had done its work and Famie had phoned DC Hunter. Said they'd be early. The DC had said she would be waiting for them, and within a few seconds of the receptionist placing a call she appeared through a plain wooden door. Same grey suit, white shirt, silver buttons. She nodded at Famie, unsmiling.

'All three of you?' she said.

Famie did the introductions.

'Follow me,' Hunter said, and held open the door. A stark, undecorated corridor led to 'Interview Room 2G'. Four chairs, two on either side of a solid wood table, a small fan on the floor and the penetrating smell of disinfectant.

Famie sat with Sophie, the laptop in a bag between them. Sam was opposite. The DC pulled her chair away from the table until she could set it against the wall. She produced a notepad as she sat, then leant down to switch on the fan. Hot, stale air blew around the room.

'So,' she said to Famie, 'you wanted to see me. It sounded important.'

'Yes,' said Famie, 'it is. You remember the note on my windscreen? You took a photo of it.'

'I do, yes.'

Hunter's face stayed neutral but Famie sensed her disappointment already.

'Well, we've been communicating with him.' Famie, in spite of herself, paused apologetically. 'Through the personal ads in the *Daily Telegraph*.' Hunter's raised eyebrows told Famie everything she needed to know. She rapidly explained the sequence of notes and messages, then produced today's post. 'And then this came.' She handed the hospital card and covering note to Hunter. 'The words around the edge are a song by Blind Lemon Jefferson. That was the clue. The words in the boxes were written in lemon juice. We heated the card.'

Hunter waited for more.

'It's a type of invisible ink.'

Hunter's eyebrows were working hard. 'I'm aware of that fact,' she said. 'Every kid knows that.'

Sophie handed Famie her phone.

'This is Hari Roy. I think he's in trouble. I think he's caught up in something and he wants help. Who knows why he's picked on me but this is a credible warning about a terror attack. We thought you should know.'

Hunter studied the image. 'Credible?' she said, her tone flat. 'Why do you think it's credible?'

Famie felt her neck redden. 'DC Hunter, we are all journalists at IPS. We report stories every day. We sift, analyse and judge. It's what we do. We don't know what's going on here but, in our consideration, this is worthy of your attention.'

'Would IPS report this?' Hunter asked.

'IPS would investigate it,' said Sophie. She leant into the table, placed both hands palm down. 'You've got a name, you've got an address, you've got a warning. Why wouldn't you take this seriously?'

Hunter considered that, then nodded. She wrote on her pad. 'Ms Madden. This is, as you know, a huge police operation. It's the largest I've seen. Bigger than 7/7. Its scope is huge. It's multi-force and it's international. Everyone involved has an opinion about who was responsible and who we should be targeting.' She took a breath. 'I've heard many different theories. But there are two things we all agree on. The first is that the e-fits are next to useless and that our gang knew how to hide from the CCTV. The second is that this was a sophisticated attack by a sophisticated terror group.' She looked from Famie, to Sam, to Sophie, then back to Famie. 'And so therefore *not* someone called Hari who writes in lemon juice.'

Famie made to speak but Hunter raised her hand.

'And actually I have another point, since you're here.'

Famie braced herself.

Hunter looked to the ceiling, as though searching for words. 'What would you say to those who might criticize your work? That you have, in the past, after a terrorist attack, not pursued the most reliable of sources?'

Famie felt Sam's restraining hand. She brushed it away. 'What would I say, DC Hunter? Christ, really?' Famie forced herself to stay calm. Held her hands together, palm to palm, against her chin. Took a deep breath. 'In any big organization, DC Hunter, you find feuds. Rivalries. Jealousies. This place must be the same. You might loathe DC Milne, for example. His superiors might find him an insufferable prick.' She looked at Hunter for affirmation, got nothing back. 'IPS is the same. No difference. It's the professional and the personal. You've obviously been speaking to Jane Hilton, who has hated me, undermined me, since Pakistan. She was wrong then and she's wrong now. A bitch then and a bitch now.' She stared at Hunter. 'That's it really.'

The DC waited for more. 'I see,' she said, when there was silence.

Sam leant forward. 'Look,' he said. 'Famie might have followed a more . . . idiosyncratic path than Jane Hilton. But in

Pakistan? You should know that she was right. Her reporting was impeccable.'

'I see,' Hunter said again, clearly uncertain. She checked her notes.

'So,' said Famie. 'Boxer Street.'

'Very well,' said Hunter. 'I'll make some enquiries.'

'Which means what?' Sam asked.

'Which means, Mr Carter, that I'll make some enquiries.' She put her pen down and looked up at Sam. 'OK with you?'

'My God, you people are insufferable,' said Sam. 'We didn't need to come here, as you know, we just thought you'd be interested in a potential terror attack, that's all. Well, trust me, DC Hunter, this feels like a story to us and we shall be investigating it accordingly. We shan't mention you by name, obviously.'

He made to get up.

'Was that a threat, Mr Carter?' Hunter's voice was still flat.

'If doing my job is a threat—'

The DC raised her hands. 'OK, point taken,' she said. 'I could have put that better. We'll look at twenty-six Boxer Street, we'll look at Hari Roy.' She glanced back at Sam. 'I'll get on to the West Midlands force. But you must understand this. When there are COBRA meetings happening, intelligence briefings and international coordinated police operations, we're right at the fringes here.'

'Maybe,' he said. 'Maybe. But Hari could be in an extremely dangerous position, if what he's told us is right—'

'I do believe you're telling us how to do our job, Mr Carter,' said Hunter, interrupting.

Sam paused. The briefest of nods. 'I do believe I was. Apologies. But just "looking at Hari Roy" hardly sounds very urgent.'

'Communicating via the ads in the *Telegraph* doesn't sound that urgent either,' said Hunter.

'Unless it's the only safe way you have,' suggested Famie.

Hunter drew a line across her pad. 'Agreed. Give me a moment.' She left the room, closing the door behind her.

Famie, Sophie and Sam stared at each other.

'Do you think she's actually requesting a check on Boxer Street?' said Sam.

'Or having a piss,' said Famie. 'One of the two.'

Sam glanced in the direction of Sophie's bag. 'Laptop,' he said. 'What's the plan?'

'No plan,' said Sophie.

Sam began to protest, Famie put her hand on top of his.

'And no lectures, Sam.'

'It wasn't going to be a lecture,' he protested. 'Just a reminder of—'

'And no reminders either. No advice. Nothing.'

Sam sat back, beaten.

Hunter bustled back in, resumed her seat. 'I've passed on your information, thank you. I've spoken to a colleague in the West Midlands force. So. There was something else you wanted to say. The note wasn't the reason you asked for a meeting.'

Sam and Famie both turned to look at Sophie.

'Oh, right. This is my turn,' she said, fidgeting with a twisted leather bracelet. 'I don't think it's a big deal or anything but I also went out with Seth Hussain. And during that time I met Amal.'

Now she had the DC's attention. Hunter sat bolt upright.

'You met Amal Hussain?' she said, incredulous. 'How many times?'

'Five. I think.'

'Wait here.'

Hunter was gone again. She left the door open.

38

HUNTER RETURNED WITH a jacketless and flushed DC Milne. He took Hunter's seat, she leant against the back wall.

'Tell me about Amal Hussain,' he said, wiping his face with a handkerchief.

Sophie placed her hands in her lap. 'Well,' she began, 'there's not much to say really. I only met him when I was at Seth's flat. He usually didn't stay long after I arrived. We'd exchange a few words – just general greetings, you know – then he'd be gone.'

Milne and Hunter waited for more.

'That's about it,' she said.

'How did he seem, Ms Arnold?' said Milne. 'When you were there. How was he?'

Sophie shrugged. 'Quiet. Cagey.'

'Nervous?' suggested Milne.

Sophie nodded. 'Possibly, yes.'

'And how was Seth when you were all there together? The three of you.'

'A bit tense maybe. When Amal left, he seemed happy to see the back of him, I think. He relaxed a bit anyway.'

'Did he talk about him when he'd gone?'

'No, never.'

Milne swivelled. 'And you, Ms Madden, you say you never met Amal, that he was never round when you were there.'

Famie nodded.

'And, forgive me, this was before Ms Arnold here began her relationship with Seth Hussain?'

I know it's just a question, thought Famie, but you know you made it sound like we're sluts. She bit her lip, nodded again.

'I see. Ms Arnold, did Seth ever discuss politics with you?' said Milne.

'Yes, of course,' said Sophie. 'All the time. He was always campaigning. Human rights and civil liberties in Egypt were his passion. He kept up with a lot of contacts there.'

'Hmm,' said Milne. 'Odd, isn't it. That one brother is a peacenik, the other a terrorist?'

Sophie recoiled. 'Peacenik? What kind of a shitty thing to say is that? Campaigning for democracy in a country like Egypt is not being a "peacenik". It's not some weak hippy crap. It's not peaceful in any way. It's dangerous work that could get you jailed. Or shot.'

'Or stabbed?' said Hunter.

'It had occurred to me, yes,' said Sophie. 'He embarrassed the Egyptian government many times. I'm sure they won't be mourning his death.'

'Might they have actively sought it?' asked Milne.

'They may well have,' said Sophie.

Milne shifted his weight on the seat, mopped his face again. 'Excuse the question, Ms Arnold, but what was the status of your relationship?'

'I'm sorry?'

'When he was killed,' clarified Milne. 'Were you still seeing each other?'

Sophie nodded.

'I'm sorry, you must be devastated,' said Milne.

'Of course,' said Sophie.

A moment of silence.

'Forgive me,' said Milne, 'but you really don't sound it.'

Sophie glared at him. 'We don't all break down in tears, Detective. Even under tactless questioning.'

'Of course, of course.' Milne waved his hands. Moving on. 'Did he ever borrow money from you?'

Sophie nodded. 'He did.'

'Do you know what he spent it on?'

She shook her head. 'I honestly have no idea.'

'Maybe he gave it to his brother?'

'Maybe. Maybe he spent it on pizza. Like I said . . .'

'Might his support for human rights have been a sham, Ms Arnold? A front?'

'OK, I've had enough,' said Sophie, standing. Her right hand held the table, her left hand protected her stomach. Famie noticed, and she saw Hunter notice it too.

Milne tried again. 'I'm sorry, Ms Arnold, I realize this is all upsetting for you but one more question, if I may.'

Sophie sat down again.

'Was there anyone else at IPS that Seth had been . . . "seeing"?' The quote marks were audible. 'It would be natural of course. And we do desperately need to find out more about Amal.'

Famie felt the ground shifting again. The sense that everything was about to get worse. It was a fair question. It needed a fair answer. In the ensuing silence, she was aware that Sophie and Sam were both deferring to her on this one. Hunter and Milne were waiting for her too.

'As it turns out, yes,' she said. 'We think he had been in a relationship with Mary. Mary Lawson.'

It electrified the room the way Famie thought it would.

'Mary Lawson?' said Milne, not hiding his surprise. 'Happily married, mother of two beautiful children – that Mary Lawson?'

'Fuck off,' said Famie. 'Spare us your moralizing. It's a weakness of yours, in case no one has told you before. Which I doubt.'

Milne reddened.

'But yes,' she continued, 'that Mary Lawson.'

Hunter pushed off the wall. 'You think they had a relationship?'

'They had a relationship,' said Famie.

'How do you know?' Hunter asked. 'Did she tell you? Did Seth tell you?'

Famie knew the laptop was a few centimetres from her right foot. She knew it was evidence, she knew she should tell them. If it had been just the Hunter woman there then maybe she would have said something but the thought of this creep leering over the photos of her and Sophie was too much. She glanced at Sophie, who shrugged, then looked to the floor.

'We just know.'

'You just know,' repeated Milne. 'I see. So when we interview her widower and ask him about this relationship and he asks for evidence, we'll say that Ms Madden and Ms Arnold just know. Would that be right?'

Famie avoided looking at Sam. She knew what he would be thinking because most of her was thinking it too: that they knew Mary had been 'seeing' Seth because he had naked pictures of her, that Seth was a serial womanizer and pervert, and that it was quite possible Mary had met EIJ-supporting Amal Hussain. But the photos added nothing and took away everything. One more indignity. One final embarrassment.

'That would be right,' she said.

Hunter stood next to Milne. 'Ms Madden . . .'

'Ms Hunter.'

The DC looked exasperated. 'You wanted me to take you seriously,' she said, 'to take action on the suggestion that a terror attack is imminent. I did that. Thank you for bringing it to our attention. But you have to take us seriously. If your colleague Mary Lawson was in or had been in a relationship with one of the victims, we need to know. And as that victim was the brother of an Islamist extremist, we really need to know.'

'I'm sure you do,' Sophie said, 'and how long before the press get to hear of it? How long before one of your esteemed colleagues sells the information to the papers? I'd give it a couple of days. Probably less.'

Milne, redder than ever, was about to object when Hunter cut across him.

'Ms Arnold.' She fixed Sophie with a wide-eyed stare, her eyebrows raised. 'You might be feeling particularly . . . emotional at the moment. Vulnerable even.' Her words were delivered with a knowing sensitivity.

Famie saw Sophie flush with realization. Hunter saw it too.

'I understand that. You came here to tell us about Hari Roy and about how you think he is warning us of something terrible that is about to happen. If you have anything, anything at all, that might help us prevent that, please help us.'

Sophie looked at Famie. Famie understood.

'We'd like DC Milne to leave the room, please,' Famie said. 'We came voluntarily, we are not under investigation. And we'd like him to leave.'

Milne shot a furious glance at Hunter, then got up and walked out of the room. He slammed the door behind him.

'What you tell me now, I have to share with my colleagues,' said Hunter. 'Just so you know. Just so we're clear.'

Sophie nodded. She reached into her bag and placed the laptop on the table.

39

1.45 p.m.
Marseille

ALWAYS THE SAME. The jug of iced water and bottle of orange juice. The table under the blue and white Olympique de Marseille flag. The Café Montelu, rue d'Endoume, Marseille. Always the same. Sometimes he was there, usually he wasn't, but he paid well, so the proprietor made sure the routine was set in stone. If that was how his wealthiest client wished to proceed, that was fine with him. Today he was there, and he was early.

Amal Hussain poured the water into a worn glass tumbler, and drank it in three swallows. He wiped his mouth on a paper napkin, then the condensation from his fingers. He folded the napkin as small as it would go, then dropped it into a plastic bin at his feet.

He was a squat man, round-shouldered and brooding. He sat hunched over the table as though protecting it from prying eyes. He wore his black hair long, tied in a bun. Some strands had fallen loose, framing a wide, doughy face. Beneath his trousers, a fixed-blade boot knife was strapped to his ankle.

The café was empty save for an elderly couple by the door.

They were already well into their second bottle of rosé. Hussain ignored them. There were nine empty wooden tables, each set with cutlery, large salt and pepper grinders and olive oil. Two large floor-standing black fans pushed the smells of pine shrubs and fried fish around, without any noticeable cooling. The glass front door and all the windows were open. Football memorabilia hung on the whitewashed walls – photos of teams and players mixed with blue and white pennants, scarves and shirts.

Amal Hussain had no interest in football, couldn't name a single Marseille player, even the ones whose faces stared down at his corner table. The café was no distraction for him, which was why he liked the place. There were usually no women, the only music came from the kitchen's small, ancient radio, and the talk was rarely of politics or religion. He didn't trouble them and they didn't trouble him.

Hussain checked his watch, poured the orange juice. He had no phone, tablet or laptop, just a copy of *Libération* folded at his side. No computers, no emails, no texts. His rules. Any messages he received were typed or handwritten and he burned them all. No money changed hands. He was invisible and untraceable. He waited for his visitor.

The corner table gave its occupant a clear view out of the café and up the chaotic, claustrophobic street outside. Early afternoon was quiet, less traffic, fewer shoppers. Hussain preferred it that way. So when a man in khaki shorts, pale blue linen shirt, sunglasses and a white beanie hat appeared from the market square, strolling affably along the road, buying fruit then a pastry from a street vendor, Hussain was the only one who took any notice.

He poured more water and waited. Eventually the visitor ambled into the café, glanced around at the empty tables, removed his hat and earbuds, then pulled up a chair opposite. He tossed the earbuds into his hat, then placed a copy of

Le Monde on the table in front of him. Folded, it fitted perfectly within the place setting.

The proprietor appeared from the kitchen, glanced at Hussain, who shook his head. The proprietor ducked back again. Hussain poured his visitor a tumbler of water, then clinked his own against it.

'Salut, salut. Ça va?' His accent was recognizably English-educated Egyptian.

The visitor shrugged. 'Ça va,' he said. He was unshaven, with a flushed, serious face. The rim of his collar was dark with sweat.

Hussain pointed at his paper. 'Your *Le Monde* for my *Libération*, yes?' he said.

'It's a good swap.'

Hussain handed the man what he had come for. 'I wouldn't be so sure,' he said. 'They're both full of shit.'

The visitor shrugged.

They exchanged newspapers. Hussain unfolded *Le Monde*, dislodging a brown rectangular envelope which he pocketed.

'For tonight?' he asked.

'For tonight,' said his visitor, 'as you requested. The last flight. An unfortunate business.'

Now Hussain shrugged. 'Family business. But business none the less,' he said. 'And I will finish it this time. It is a blasphemy, Leo, you understand that.'

'Of course.' The visitor spread his arms magnanimously. Forgiving. 'You must act as you see fit. Of course. My friends are grateful for your commitment.'

Business concluded, he picked up his hat, recovered the earbuds and stood. 'I hope to see you again soon.' He bowed slightly.

Amal nodded. 'You will hear from me on Thursday, after our work has been concluded.'

40

3.40 p.m.

DON HARDIN HAD engineered a tea in the University's Social Studies building. The small ground-floor canteen was packed, each of its square orange tables surrounded by six or seven students. Some were still studying, open reference books propped up against ketchup bottles, but most were talking or sharing video clips on their screens. A despairing handwritten sign behind the counter read, 'We don't need to hear your music. It's why headphones were invented.'

Just one table had a lone occupant. Hardin had made a beeline for his friend, explained his plan.

'You're actually demonstrating?' Bathandwa Bambawani had interrupted her cake-eating, the sponge halfway between the plate and her open mouth. 'Shouting, marching, placards? All of that?'

Hardin looked sheepish. 'I'm still a priest in the Church of England, BB,' he said. 'I don't know how I'll respond. But yes, I'm going. I'm not sure I'll be shouting. I won't have a placard. But I will march.'

'But you've always said you're not a flag waver,' said Bambawani. 'That you find zealots deeply troubling.'

'Still do,' said Hardin. 'Imagine being so certain about anything! So certain you want to shout at people! I've never been able to do that. But the more I thought about it, the more certain I got. If you can't join an anti-fascist march, there's not much point in any of the gospel really. We try to be one religious community in the Chaplaincy. Of course I should be there. All the chaplains should be there.'

'You know that some of the Antifa groups have quite a reputation, don't you? Direct action. Property damage. Physical violence sometimes. That kind of thing. Tends to be as much anti-capitalist as anti-fascist. Quite a mixed crowd, to put it mildly.'

Hardin nodded, his brow furrowed. 'I know that. I've done my homework.' He appreciated her concern and smiled, briefly.

'Could be a baptism of fire, Don!'

'I can handle baptisms, BB.'

'Dog collar?'

'Yes, obviously.'

'Robes?'

'I should think so. Some of them.'

'It would certainly get you noticed.'

'That's the point, BB. I need to stand for something. And be seen to be standing for something.'

Bambawani raised her eyebrows, curious. 'What else is going on here, Don?' She smiled.

'How do you mean?' he said.

'Well,' she said. 'I think your new daughter has, in her very few weeks on this earth, turned your head.' Bambawani's smile got bigger. 'I'm not surprised of course. It's amazing what we women can do.'

Hardin laughed ruefully. 'Amen to all of that,' he said.

'The bishop will find out of course,' she said.

Hardin nodded. 'Almost certainly. Well, so be it.'

She ate a mouthful of the cake and smiled again as she swallowed. 'Respect to you then, Don. Respect. And I thought you had a gig with the bishop on Thursday. That's why you'd said you'd be elsewhere.'

'I do,' said Hardin. 'Though assisting at a mass for peace is hardly a "gig".'

Bambawani gave a 'whatever' shrug. 'You're all dressed up,' she said. 'Waving your arms. Performing the magic. Sounds like a gig to me.'

She offered him her last piece of cake. He took it. She raised her cup to him.

'Well, here's to you, Reverend,' she said. 'And when you're done radicalizing the students, I have to call my missing student's family. Then the police. If we haven't heard anything by then.'

'All the chaplains are praying for him now. I know you think that's of no consequence but there you are. It's what we do.' He folded his arms, stared at the table.

'You seem troubled,' said Bambawani.

Hardin raised an eyebrow. 'Maybe. You know me too well.'

'You're not exactly hiding it,' she said.

Hardin managed half a smile. 'Maybe,' he said again. He sighed. 'Do you know what the number one reason for dropping into the Chaplaincy is?'

'You've told me before, Don. Free food, isn't it?'

He smiled fully now. Nodded once more. 'We do interfaith work, we do pastoral work. We try to be relevant. But it's actually only pizza that works every time.'

'Why is that troubling you? I'd be the same.' Bambawani offered reassuringly. 'Free pizza delivers a crowd. A life lesson, right there.'

Hardin shook his head slowly. 'Because I think we've

failed, BB. The kid with the Indian communist poster is clearly in trouble but he still didn't come to us. We have all faiths looked after, but it wasn't enough. He went elsewhere. I'm proud of the work we do. We've built up good faith communities, we cooperate on mental health initiatives, food banks. The counselling is first rate. But if we don't add pepperoni, no one cares.'

'Well we both failed then,' she said. 'He didn't come to me either.' She chased some crumbs around the plastic plate. 'Plan of action?'

'I'll carry on praying for him,' said Hardin. 'You want me to help in any way?'

'No,' said Bambawani. 'You pray. Then, if the Almighty stays quiet, we call the family after the protest.'

'Amen to that,' said Hardin.

41

8.20 p.m.

FAMIE, SOPHIE AND Sam were holed up in Famie's flat. Tommi had joined them, bringing pizzas, the boxes strewn across the floor. The lounge and kitchen windows were all open, each trying to catch a non-existent breeze. Phones and laptops were plugged in and charging. Famie's was displaying a map with Boxer Street, Coventry at its centre and playing a Mozart piano concerto through its speakers. Sophie was on the sofa, Tommi and Sam were sitting on the floor. Famie was in the kitchen filling a jug with ice. A sheet of reusable whiteboard had been stuck to the wall, the names of the seven dead and their partners' contact numbers written on it in black marker. Another sheet had the Facebook photo of Hari Roy stuck to it. The rest of it was blank.

'We must be the only people in the whole of London working inside,' said Tommi, hanging up on a call.

'You wanna do this in the park?' said Sam.

'Not really,' Tommi conceded. 'That was Anita's husband. Didn't really welcome the call, to be honest.'

'I can imagine. What did you tell him?'

'That it was likely that the police would be contacting him. That Seth's personal life had become an issue in their investigation. That he had had relationships with a number of staff at IPS and that they would be asking if Anita was one of them.'

'And?'

'He thanked me for the warning and that was that. Can't blame him.'

Famie walked in with the ice. 'I got that from Sarah's husband,' she said. 'Didn't push it. And anyway, if there weren't photos of them on his laptop, they're probably in the clear. Unless there's another laptop somewhere.'

'Wouldn't put it past him,' said Sophie. 'BPW.'

'BPW indeed,' said Famie. Then to Sam, 'Don't ask.'

He shrugged. 'Wouldn't dream of it.'

Tommi was standing now, staring at the photo of Hari. 'And he fits this how?'

Famie stood alongside him. 'Whatever the investigating team were looking at, EIJ, ISIS, whatever, he's trapped in it somehow and he's trying to get out. And if his instinct is to tell a journalist at IPS, he must have had some contact with us in the past. Some family connections maybe.'

'And does he?'

Sophie put her hand up. 'Can't find any yet, still looking.'

'So, best guess,' said Famie. 'He's a guy on the inside, recruited for a cause he thought he believed in. Now he's changed his mind. Maybe when the seven were killed. He needs an out.'

Sam clambered to his feet, iPad in hand. 'Found his family. Mother, grandmother and sisters live in Leamington.' He wrote the address on the whiteboard. 'If Hari's in danger, so are they.'

'Do we let the police go there first?' said Sam. 'It's the same as the hospital. Can we make enquiries without putting them at risk?'

'We might have to,' said Famie.

'Discreetly and unofficially,' said Sam.

'It's all I have,' she said.

Tommi was updating the whiteboard, writing 'husband spoken to' alongside Anita's name. 'We're stuck, aren't we?' he said. 'Seven dead, a number of killers, one dissident. Or whatever we're calling Hari. We need to loosen this up a bit.'

'What aren't we asking?' called Sophie. 'Be wild.'

'Is Hari one person?' said Sam. 'Might the messages have come from more than one person?'

Sophie took a deep breath. 'OK. I'll say it as the police have already asked me. Might Seth have been involved in some way? Perpetrator and then victim? Just putting it out there.'

There were nods of appreciation.

'Sounds unlikely to me,' Sophie added, 'but we need to consider it.'

'It would need us to ditch everything we knew about Seth,' said Sam.

'Some of us have done that already,' said Famie. 'Better get with the programme. We know he was duplicitous. We know he was capable of lying, regularly and with astonishing ease. We know he had money issues, that he borrowed from everyone, and that his brother is a member of an Islamist terror organization. We've given the police his laptop. Apart from the porn, we don't think there's anything of interest.'

Sam, visibly uncomfortable, tried a question. He fidgeted with his hands as he spoke. 'Listen, this is bad, I know, and you would be quite within your rights to say no, but you said there were other women on the laptop?'

'Two others,' said Sophie.

'Who were they?' he asked.

She shrugged. 'No idea.' She glanced at Famie, who nodded consent. 'I copied all the contents of the laptop,' she said. 'Sent it to Famie's Dropbox.'

'You still have the photos?' said Sam.

Famie nodded.

'Look, we need to identify the other women. We should see the photos. It kind of matters who they are.'

Both women nodded.

'Agreed,' said Famie, pulling her laptop close. 'But you don't get Sophie and me into the bargain.'

'Listen, Famie—' Sam began.

'I'm joking,' said Famie. 'Relax, Sam, honestly.'

He smiled awkwardly but didn't relax.

Famie hit the keys, copied and dragged the photos till they were on one page, then spun the screen. Two women were shown in adjacent pictures. On the left a naked woman, mid-thirties, was shown in profile – light brown skin, slim build, black hair to her shoulders, hands covering her face, either in embarrassment or possibly applying face cream. On the right, a shot of a younger woman stepping out of the shower and reaching for a towel. Her skin was darker, her smile enigmatic. Embarrassed too, possibly.

Famie zoomed in on her face. 'So. The other woman is too obscured, lucky her, let's focus on this one.' She was late twenties, brown hair, brown eyes, plucked and shaped eyebrows, a wide, surprised face. A small scar across the bridge of her nose.

'Don't think she's IPS,' said Sam.

'Don't recognize her,' agreed Famie, 'but she may work elsewhere in the building. We need to check that fast.'

Tommi had his hand up, the other stabbing away at his keyboard, his eyes on the screen. He noticed the silence and looked up. 'Sophie said what aren't we asking. It's always a good question. So I've just accessed the crime reports for May twenty-two, the day of the murders. And if the question is how many murders, the answer isn't seven. It's eight.'

It was as though all the air had been sucked from the room

and they were all operating in a vacuum. The silence was sudden and complete.

Tommi looked around the room. 'We stopped counting when Anita died. Seven in half an hour. We told that story. And we got it right. No more IPS staffers died after that. But this guy' – he tapped his screen – 'Toby Howells disappeared on the same day, the twenty-second. His body was found three days later. Stabbed, then hidden around the reservoir in Edgbaston. It's not a million miles from Coventry. He was black, a student, twenty-one. He had a tube of crack on him so it was put down to drugs, gangs, the knife crime epidemic and so on.'

'So why isn't it just that?' asked Sam.

'It might be,' conceded Tommi, 'but the messages on his Facebook page say things like "RIP Toby, gutted. Loved your writing, man." And this: "Gonna miss you all the way. Was convinced you'd be the next Reggie Yates." Three of the posts link to articles he'd written online for the local paper.'

Sam looked up. 'So this kid was a wannabe journalist and he was knifed on the same day as Mary, Seth, Anita and the others. It might be a coincidence of course . . .'

The room was silent.

'Honestly, Tommi, it might be,' said Sophie. 'That's quite a jump from seven IPS investigators to a kid at uni.'

Famie did a quick online search. It took five seconds. She scanned the pages in front of her. Her tell-tale adrenalin kick told her everything. 'Unless,' she said, her voice tight with excitement, 'our Hari was exactly the same. Look.' Her screen showed pages of the *Warwick Boar* website, 'Creating Conversation Since 1973'. 'It's the student paper,' she explained, 'and look who's been writing for them. Hari Roy! He's been linked in three articles. Guys, Hari is a wannabe journalist too. Toby Howells and Hari Roy have a link.'

Tommi was on his feet, hooking his bag around his neck.

'And he was recently in hospital,' he said. 'And definitely in danger.' He shoved his laptop into the bag.

'Are you off?' said Famie, surprised.

'I need to check the Toby Howells case,' he said. 'Carol's at Canary Wharf till eleven. Easier to trawl this on her computers.'

Famie followed him from the room and down the stairs to the front door.

'You wanna come?' he said, intrigued.

'I'm good,' she said, 'but thanks.'

He nodded, waiting for whatever it was she wanted to say. She wasn't sure either.

Eventually she said, 'Carol Leven worth the trip?'

Tommi grinned. 'Always,' he said. 'Best crime reporter out there.'

Famie nodded her agreement. 'Tommi,' she said, 'if there is a link between Hari Roy and Toby Howells, and if that link is anything to do with May twenty-two, we are in seriously dangerous territory here. All of us. This isn't a game or just another story, this is actually pretty scary stuff.'

Tommi smiled. 'Are you telling me to be careful?'

Famie smiled back. 'Fuck off, Tommi.'

'That's much better,' he said. 'Far more familiar ground. I'll keep in touch.' He nodded, stepped outside and clicked the door shut.

A buzz from Famie's phone. Her daughter's face on its screen, a quick smile. She sat on the bottom step.

'Hey you,' she said. 'How's things?' The sounds of traffic and rapid breathing.

'Things are not especially great.' Charlie was walking quickly, running even. 'I'm coming home. On whatever train I can get.'

Alarm bells started going off in Famie's head. 'You're what? Why?' She looked at her watch. Eight forty.

'Because I'm shit scared, Mum, that's why.' Definitely running.

'Keep talking, Charlie. Tell me what's happened.'

The distorted rattle of heavy breaths. 'A girl got stabbed in Exeter today. Coming out of the Vue cinema.'

'In Exeter? Jesus Christ.' Slamming door, quieter acoustic. 'You're on the train now?'

'Yes, and without a ticket. Gonna be expensive.' Charlie's voice was a breathless whisper.

'I'll pay it,' said Famie. 'What happened to the girl?' The rustle of fabric crackled down the phone.

'Mum, listen.' Charlie was making her voice as small as she could. 'I was at the cinema too. It happened just before I got out. We got delayed because Emily needed a piss. When we got out people were screaming and this girl was just lying there, holding her stomach. Blood everywhere. But, Mum . . .' A deep breath. 'She looked like me. She had crazy hair and the same rucksack. I noticed her going in. Emily pointed her out and we laughed. From behind we looked the same.'

Famie closed her eyes. She fought to keep her voice calm, to keep the bile from rising in her throat. 'When was this, Charlie?'

'About an hour ago. We stayed until the police and ambulance came and she was still alive then. Her friends were with her. We didn't see the attack so we didn't say anything. But, Mum, she looked like me!'

'Where's Emily? Is she with you?'

'She's got an exam tomorrow. Last one. At least I'm done.'

'When does the train leave?'

'Two minutes.'

'Find the busiest coach,' said Famie. 'Sit with people. Talk to them. Make friends. All the way. I'll meet you at Paddington.'

'Can we keep talking till the train leaves, please?' said Charlie.

She sounds like she's ten years old again, thought Famie.

'Sure,' she said. 'And you do know that this is probably a coincidence, don't you. That no one really looks like you. That it was probably a gang thing. Or a mugging. Or a domestic.'

There was a long pause from the train.

'OK,' said Charlie. 'Let's stick with that one. But you don't believe it, Mum, and neither do I. I'll go and make friends.'

42

9 p.m.

THE LAST OF the day's sun at 26 Boxer Street. Hari Roy, Abi Binici and Sara Collins were in the courtyard. The student, the leader and the woman. Three chairs, three cups, one pot of tea. Despite the heat, Hari sat with a blanket over his legs. His eyes were closed as he listened to the to and fro between the leader and the woman. Binici was explaining again why he thought Zak had run away and why they now had to be extra vigilant. But Hari knew what had happened, had seen the blood stains under the rearranged matting in the hall. Zak was dead, Binici had killed him, and he, Hari, was responsible. He knew that. He had deflected suspicion, sown doubt, and Zak had paid the price. His body could well be still in the house. In the heat and under the blanket, Hari felt his flesh creep.

Wade in filth . . .

And now he was in terrible danger. He had tried to get 'left behind', to convince the leader he was a liability, yet here he was, back on the front line. He'd passed the note to the woman Gyongyi but had no way of knowing if she'd done anything with it. He had to assume she hadn't. That he was on his own.

It was another airless evening. The street's open windows and doors made for a backdrop of constant cacophony: music, voices and barbecue clatter that drifted in from all sides. It gave a surprising cover of privacy to the conversation at number 26. Binici was talking – lecturing – about Britain as a failed state, its moral collapse and the self-evident virtue of violent rebellion. The woman, Collins, made the occasional comment but this was not a discussion. It was never a discussion.

'In 1913 Lenin told his wife that revolution wouldn't happen in his lifetime,' said Binici. 'That they were nowhere. That the Czarist secret police were too strong and the opposition too weak. But! But! It turned out that Russia was *hollow.* A clanging, empty vessel. And when the revolution came it was a spontaneous, disorganized, chaotic uprising. Well.' Hari heard him sip tea, put his cup on the ground. 'This so-called United Kingdom is decaying fast,' he continued. 'The people know they are run by a failed class of the hyper-rich, the neoliberal elite who care nothing for their homes, their jobs or their families. Their votes are irrelevant, their marches are irrelevant. They see that now. Even the so-called left are millionaires and children of the establishment. When the people see what a few committed revolutionaries can achieve, they will welcome us.' Binici spread his arms wide. 'Imagine it! Lenin said one of the chief symptoms of every revolution is the sudden increase in ordinary people taking an active interest in politics. Well? Isn't that now?'

Embrace the butcher . . .

'Tomorrow we greet five more citizens. Thursday we strike.'

There was a pause.

'Strike what?' said Collins.

So she didn't know either.

'If we're making this great leap forward, citizen,' Collins continued, 'it would help if we knew where we are going.'

Hari opened his eyes. Binici, fully in the house's shadow, was smiling and shaking his head. White collarless shirt, black baggy trousers. Collins, sitting in the last corner of the yard with sunshine, wore large-framed shades, a loose-fitting grey T-shirt and denim shorts.

'Tomorrow, Sara, tomorrow. When the others get here. Then we can plan. Then your training will be for the benefit of all the cells. They are all watching, you know. Every citizen is waiting for us. As we waited for May twenty-two, they wait for us. When we move, they move. Hearts on fire, brains on ice.'

Hari stirred and they turned. He pulled the blanket higher. In truth, his throat and stomach were largely recovered but the blanket gave him some cover, a shield between him and the madness in front of him.

'What sort of work is it?' he croaked out.

'Noble work,' said Binici. 'Historic work.'

'Suicidal work?' Under the blanket, Hari held his breath.

Binici removed his glasses, wiped them with a cloth, replaced them and blinked twice. 'We are the vanguard. Our duty is to lead, not to conform. There are always dangers associated with storming the palaces of the ruling class. Of course there are. But we are smarter. We are prepared. This is progress, citizen, and progress can have a price.'

So yes, then, Hari thought.

Change the world . . .

From somewhere not far away, a screech of brakes and the percussive thumps of metal-on-metal collisions. Hari jumped, then instinctively turned his head to the street.

'That's close,' he said.

Binici and Collins were on their feet. They waited. Suspicious.

'Too close,' said Collins.

They ran inside. From the hall they heard shouting – two, maybe three male voices – then screaming. From the bay window of the upstairs room they could see a white van had crashed into a number of parked cars and then stopped, blocking the road. The van door was open. A crowd was gathering, some had hands in front of their faces, others were making calls.

'Someone's under the wheels,' she said.

'Doesn't involve us,' said Binici.

Hari was silent. He could see that his car was one of those hit by the van. The rear passenger door had caved, its window smashed. The van had then buried itself in the Ford Galaxy beyond. He strained to see what was happening. Might this be a police operation? A rescue? Had the woman in the hospital passed on the note after all? Or was it just an accident, of no significance to anyone other than the injured and the owners of the damaged cars?

Collins, at his shoulder, realized what they were looking at.

'That's your car, Hari,' she said.

'I just realized that,' he said.

Binici stiffened. 'You're parked up there?'

Hari nodded. 'Left it there after the drop.'

'That's too much of a coincidence,' he said. 'Stay inside. We all stay inside.' The wail of multiple sirens, approaching fast, stoked the leader's nerves. 'It'll be ambulance, then police. This street will be full of them. Shut the windows. Close the curtains. The house must look empty. We are not here.'

As the emergency services arrived in Boxer Street, Hari, Collins and Binici sat in silence and near-darkness. The kitchen table held three glasses of water, which they sipped regularly. The door to the yard was locked, the blinds lowered. The air was heavy, the temperature unbearable. Hari wiped his face with his already-damp shirt. They listened to the engines, the hissing of brakes, the slamming of doors, the running, heavy steps, the squawking of the radios.

Hari glanced at the faces opposite him. Binici and Collins were interpreting and reacting to every sound from the street. Hari thought of a submarine film he'd seen, its crew terrified of the patrolling enemy ships and their depth charges. Eyes everywhere, twitching faces, danger in every reverberation.

For Binici and Collins, everything was a threat.

'We are not here,' Binici repeated in a whisper, 'we make no sound.'

No talking on the bridge, thought Hari. He was sweating like the others but his hands, folded, out of sight, were trembling too. He was as terrified as he'd ever been. He was sure this was some kind of operation – Binici was right. It was just too much of a coincidence. Was he supposed to rush out, to run away and turn everyone in? Did they expect him to react first? He screwed his eyes tight. Find what you need. Know that I am here, he thought. Understand the danger.

Thirty minutes after the crash, the tangle of noise that was the accident's aftermath subsided. In the quiet, Hari picked out new sounds. Doorbells. Door knocks. Door-to-door enquiries. Getting closer.

Binici emptied his glass, replaced it, wiped his mouth. He folded and unfolded his arms, pulled at his shirt where it was sticking to him. 'We don't answer,' he whispered.

'Then they'll come back,' said Collins.

'We'll be gone by then.'

She leant closer to Binici, hands flat on the table. 'And what if they come back in two hours? Or tomorrow morning? What then? Let's give them what they want, then they'll move on. Leave us alone.'

Binici was silent, uncertain.

'They'll want to know if we saw anything,' said Hari. 'If we know anything. And when the answer is no, they'll go away.'

Binici had a neck muscle twitching and felt a sudden need to rub his scalp.

The body is still here, thought Hari. Somewhere. No wonder you're scared.

Their two-tone doorbell rang.

And now the police are at the door.

43

'I'LL GO,' SAID Collins.

Binici grabbed her arm. 'You'll stay.'

She pulled away. 'I'm white. I'll go.'

He hesitated. The doorbell rang again.

Collins persisted: 'I'm the only white British here.'

'OK,' he said. 'Be the only one here, period. Quick as you can. Get rid.'

She nodded.

'Coming!' she shouted in a voice Hari hadn't heard before – higher-pitched, overtly feminine. She ruffled up her hair, rearranged her T-shirt, then switched the hall lights on.

Binici pulled Hari from his chair, unlocked the door into the yard and they stepped outside. The air was fresher, cooler now, but Hari barely noticed. The leader pulled the door shut as the front door opened. Both men pressed their ears against the glass.

'Oh! Sorry, I was asleep. Shit. Is everything OK? What's happened?' Collins sounded surprised, flustered.

The police officers identified themselves.

'There's been a road traffic accident outside number seventy-eight. A woman has been knocked down and four vehicles are involved.'

Not a local accent, more like Yorkshire, thought Hari. Mid-thirties. Maybe older.

'Did you hear or see anything?'

'Sorry,' said Collins, 'I took a sleeping pill. I was crashed out upstairs. I only just heard you ringing the bell. Who was hurt?'

'A young woman has gone to hospital. Mid-twenties, white, black hair. She doesn't live here then?'

'No.'

'Does anyone else live here?'

Binici tensed.

'No, just me.'

Spoken with conviction, Hari thought.

'Really?' said the other officer. Hari assumed he was now checking some notes. 'We have a Tom Jarrod listed here.' Local accent, a friendly enquiry. Very dangerous.

'We had an argument. He moved out.'

'How long ago?'

'It'll be six weeks now,' said Collins. 'Looking for new lodgers if you're interested. Trying to avoid students. Bloody unreliable they are.'

'So there's no one else living here.' Copper number one getting to the heart of it.

'Just one person paying double rent,' said Collins. 'That's me. Fucking nightmare, if you'll pardon my French.'

There was a pause in the conversation. Hari imagined two sceptical officers peering past Collins into the hall. Binici's spartan aesthetic would guarantee they'd see no shoes, no coats, no post. No embarrassing give-aways. But they weren't leaving.

'Three parked cars were damaged,' said the local copper.

He read their number plates. 'They belong to . . .' His voice dropped away slightly: Hari assumed he was reading. 'Alfred Graham, Asmira La and Hari Roy.' He left the names hanging.

In the yard, neither man breathed. Hari felt fresh sweat run down his back.

'Do those names mean anything to you? We're trying to locate them – their cars are pretty messed up.'

Hari didn't know what he wanted Collins to say. When she spoke, it was with an audible shrug.

'Hmm,' she said. 'Asmira I know – she's OK, right? It's not her in hospital?'

'Is she white?'

'No. Of course. Sorry.' A small embarrassed laugh. 'And Hari I know, I think. Did a class at the university once. I'm a martial arts instructor there. He was terrible. The other guy you mentioned – Alfred someone? – I can't help you with, I'm sorry. I wish I could be more use.'

'So this Hari Roy is parked in the road, he was a client, but you haven't seen him?'

'Correct. There's lots of student accommodation in these streets. Any uni kid will know people around here. I'll look out for him though.'

Thanks and farewells. The door closed. Hari exhaled deeply, Binici touched his arm, mouthed 'wait'. Collins went back upstairs. Hari stood motionless, still listening. She'd be watching from the bay window again, tracking where the police went next. If it was next door, he and Binici would hear them from the yard. It was no more than twenty metres away. Sure enough the rattle of the door knocker at number 24 was answered and the same questions asked of their neighbour. Binici's shoulders relaxed. He opened the back door and they slipped back inside. The kitchen was still dark.

'She did well,' said Hari.

'Your car is a problem,' said Binici.

'It is,' agreed Hari. 'We need to go.'

'We can't. The citizens arrive at eight tomorrow morning.'

'Shit.' Hari stared at Binici. 'And what if the police are still outside?'

Binici didn't reply.

Collins returned, switched the lights on. She glanced between Binici and Hari. 'I think it's a straight-up accident – they're knocking up the whole street – but we've got a whole load of heat at exactly the wrong time. Our new arrivals won't like it.'

'Agreed,' said Binici. 'The fash will have to be moved.'

Hari frowned. 'And how is that going to happen?'

'I'm sure Sara can manage something,' Binici said.

His tone was flat, but Collins bridled.

'Meaning?'

'Meaning you'll think of something,' said Binici. 'You were getting on fine with the fash who just called. You can do that whole flirty dumb routine you did again.'

Hari could see the anger in Collins' face. She moved to stand face to face with Binici, shifting her balance from foot to foot as she talked. 'You're the leader, Abi, we know that. We're on operations, we know that, and we have a job to do. We know all of that.' She leant closer. There was barely a centimetre between them now. 'But if you talk like you're my fucking pimp again, I swear I'll kick your bollocks so hard you'll be limping till Christmas.' She waited a beat then stepped back.

Hari held his breath. Collins' words hung between all three of them. Behind the browline glasses, eyebrows raised, Binici's eyes didn't blink. When his left hand slipped into his trouser pocket, Hari tensed. He knew what that meant. The leader was wired. Every muscle was stretched, every vein was pumping. His authority had been challenged, violence had been threatened. He couldn't let that stand.

But she had stepped away. The challenge was over. His hand came out of his pocket, empty. He folded his arms.

'I misspoke,' he said.

Collins nodded.

'I'll make some tea,' said Hari.

44

10.20 p.m.

IPS AT NIGHT was a quieter, more sedate place, but in the opinion of many old hands somehow at its most potent. Freed from any UK-centric news cycle, the rest of the world took centre stage. Europe may well be sleeping but the Americas were wide awake, buying, selling, consuming. Soon Tokyo, Mumbai and Beijing would join them and set their agendas for the day. Where they led, the rest of the world would follow.

On the way into Canary Wharf, grabbing the WiFi at successive stations, Tommi had messaged some thoughts to Sam, Sophie and Famie.

'There's not much time. We need to be on the same page. Questions for Leven. What do we know about Toby Howells? Might the crack have been a plant? Do we know the murder weapon? Was he in a gang or associated at all with gang activity? What journalist contacts did he have (if any?), what do the cops really think? Did he know Hari Roy? Will post replies here.'

Carol Leven had joined IPS at the same time as Tommi

but instead of diversifying into economics, politics and the EU as he had done, she had stuck with crime. All of it. Domestic, violent, international, cyber, organized. If you needed trends, stats or leaky police officers, Carol Leven was a one-stop shop.

Tommi hailed her from across the newsroom, walked briskly to her desk.

'I got your message,' she said. 'Why the interest in Howells?' She was unsmiling, perfunctory. Five six, pale, unlined skin. Her eyes hadn't left her screen.

'Just a tip-off. Maybe the drugs were a plant,' he said.

'Meaning?'

He shrugged. 'Meaning maybe he wasn't killed for the usual shitty old reasons. Territory. Trade. Pride. Family. That kind of thing. And if I knew any more, Carol, I wouldn't be here, talking to you.'

He stared at her, she stared at the screen.

'These are the crime scene photos I've seen,' she said. She clicked on two images, one showing a close-up of a bruised black face with cuts above both closed eyes and a broken nose. The other, with a wider angle, a lacerated neck and a knife-wound to the heart.

'That's very dead,' Tommi muttered. 'Weapon?'

'A heavy knife. Not found, but the blade is maybe three centimetres wide.'

Tommi typed at speed.

'And the crack?'

'Small bag. Eighty, ninety pounds' worth maybe.'

'If he was trading, or just out of bounds, wouldn't they have taken that? Why leave it?'

Carol shrugged. 'Small fry. Not worth bothering with. Possibly.'

'Or planted,' said Tommi.

'Agreed,' said Carol, 'or planted. Howells hasn't had any

gang contact that I can find. I've spoken to three contacts who know this patch, they each said they knew nothing about any hit and had never heard of Howells. He wasn't on the police's radar either.'

'Anything else?'

'Ambitious. Decent marks at his college, hard worker. Not a bad writer, read a couple of his pieces. I'll send them to you.' She hit some keys, looked up at Tommi for the first time. 'It's an odd one certainly. I hadn't really focused on it till you messaged me. His girlfriend said he'd been away a lot recently. Said he had a commission. That he'd been excited. Had had a bit of money. And then he was dead. She'd explained it all to the police but they had the drugs angle to work on, so for them he was just another dead black druggie.'

'You spoke to her?'

'Just now.'

Tommi smiled. 'You're good.'

She returned to her screen, said nothing. He typed, then sent.

'A commission,' he said. 'And they paid. That's gotta be unusual. Who commissions a kid to write anything?'

'No idea.'

'Might the girlfriend know?'

'I'll send you her number. You can do the work.'

Tommi knew when he was dismissed. He began to put away his laptop. 'Interested?' he said.

'Interesting,' she said. 'Not the same. It's not neat and tidy if that's what you mean.'

'Is anything you do neat and tidy?'

'Sometimes,' she said. 'But not often. Whisky?'

'Sorry?'

'Whisky,' she repeated. She opened a drawer, inside which sat a square box of miniatures. Room for twelve, there were three missing. 'For the journey home, Tommi. Benefits of the late shift. Take what you want, I'm trying to cut down. Why are you interested in Howells anyway? It's not your beat.'

Tommi picked out a couple of the small bottles. 'Tell you some time. It's complicated.' He pocketed the whisky. 'While you're logged in,' he said, 'any chance you could search for Howells in our system, just to see if anyone else has been interested in him?'

A clatter of keys. A 'no results' sign appeared.

'Nah,' she said, 'no results' showing again in its own window. 'Bye, Tommi.'

He took the lift to the ground floor, pausing by the glass doors to make sure he'd sent everything that Carol Leven had given him. Files sent, answers sent, he checked the last tube times then walked the short distance to the station. He hesitated at the top of the escalator and messaged Howells' girlfriend, introducing himself, apologizing for the direct contact and asking for a conversation in the morning. Then he walked swiftly down the escalator.

A fifty-minute journey, he spent the time getting his notes in order and drinking the whisky. Its battery running low, he stowed his laptop in his rucksack at King's Cross, alighting twelve stops later at Cockfosters. The guards nodded their goodnights as he exited the ticket barrier, and Tommi was out. His walk home was a brisk ten minutes, past the BP garage and Trent Park cemetery. Aware of his computer bag and solitude, Tommi's pace was brisk. The street was wide, well lit and, for nearly midnight, busy. Instinctively he walked close to the road.

Two cars at the garage, one driver filling up, one driver paying. Tommi made the briefest eye contact with the one by the pump before the man returned to checking the dials. Tommi considered buying some late-night chocolate but instead opted for haste and health. He marched on. On the other side of the road, heading south, an old camper van trundled past, windows down, the driver and his passenger singing loudly. A black cab then an Uber driver with a single passenger followed close behind. It wasn't until they had all passed, and their engines had faded to nothing, that Tommi heard the footsteps.

A smiling man with ginger hair under a black cap was hurrying to catch him up. Twenty metres away. White, five six, stocky, khaki cargo shorts, red T-shirt.

'Hey, wait up!' he said, lengthening his stride.

Tommi hesitated.

'Saw you back at the petrol station,' said the man. 'You don't have a light, do you?' He waved a crumpled pack of cigarettes in his hand.

Ten metres.

Tommi shook his head, resumed his walk, brisker now. 'Don't smoke!' he shouted, too loudly.

'Please,' said the man, 'maybe some money for matches?' Accented English. Eastern European.

Five metres.

'Fuck off!' yelled Tommi, reaching for his phone. He was approaching a junction, a postbox marking a sharp right turn.

'Please!' said the man. 'Fifty pence would help.'

Two metres.

Tommi started dialling. He only looked up as he completed the 999, and the knife stuck him in the ribs, pinning him to the postbox. He dropped his phone, the man caught it one-handed, cancelled the call, posted it in the slot. The two men stared at each other, Tommi's wide, panicking eyes and his assailant's sparkling, smiling ones. He made a feeble attempt at a struggle, a kick, a punch, but his life was already draining out on to the grass. The man covered Tommi's mouth with his free hand, then pushed the knife till it hit metal. Gave it a quarter-turn. Tommi howled into the man's palm, blood and spittle forcing their way through his fingers. The man checked his watch, glanced up the road. He smiled, then leant in close, as though he might be overheard.

'We are waiting for the bus, you and me,' he whispered.

Tommi spluttered more blood against the man's hand.

'Shush now,' said the man. 'Not long.'

With what remained of his senses, Tommi heard the night bus approaching. He felt the man pull the knife out, then balance himself. He was grabbed, held tightly in two arms, positioned. Tommi closed his eyes.

The last words he heard were 'embrace the butcher'.

The night bus hit him at thirty-five miles an hour.

45

Wednesday, 13 June, 12.21 a.m.

FAMIE HAD RUNG Charlie every five minutes. From the flat, from Sam's car, then finally from the concourse at Paddington station. Her words, somehow measured and calming, had had to be wrestled from somewhere beyond the seething panic threatening to overwhelm her. Charlie had said she was with a family of Germans who had bought her wine but they had got off at Swindon. Soon after that, her phone had gone dead.

'She said her battery was low,' Sam reasoned. 'If it was low and she came without her charger, then of course it's dead now.'

'I know all this,' said Famie. 'You told me before. And I know it's a big, well-lit train with plenty of passengers and crew. But I'm her mother, so all of that counts for jack shit.' She looked at her watch. 'How can it still be two minutes away? I thought you said it was on time?'

'It is on time, Fames. Twelve twenty-three it's due, and that's two minutes away.'

They were arm in arm by the entrance to platform two,

fending off the drunks, the beggars and the miscellaneous lost. Each approach caused Famie to grip Sam's arm tighter. She looked at each one not as an unfortunate in need of charity but as an assailant with a hidden knife.

'I swear my heart rate is running at a thousand beats a minute,' she said. 'And if that cleaner comes any closer with his trolley it'll probably explode.'

The station was still busy even if most of the vendors had closed up for the night. A chemist, a fried-chicken shop and a coffee cart were all that was left of the traders of Paddington. Everyone else was running for last trains, tubes and buses, or waiting, like them, for the arrival of the eight forty-five from Exeter.

Famie scrutinized everyone within twenty metres. 'Talk me through our closest company,' she said to Sam.

He swung through a hundred and eighty degrees. A dozen or so people stood watching the departure and arrival boards.

'OK, we have two students,' he said, now back to back with Famie. She felt his shoulder bag press against her. He spoke slowly, analysing those closest to them. 'Both male, both drunk.. A middle-aged woman with grey hair, a stoner with a skateboard. Some Dutch or Scandinavians on holiday looking confused and an oldish couple maybe waiting for a child. Or grandchild. Then a man in a suit and a bored, bearded hipster. That's it.'

'Keep watching,' she said. 'It's hard not to feel exposed here. Christ, this is scary. Did Tommi get home OK?'

'Didn't say. He sent all his results through but he's not answering now. I've tried a few times, just ringing till the answerphone kicks in.'

'Hmm,' said Famie. 'Let's hope he's in a beery haze and in his own bed. Passed out. Any new board-watchers to report?'

'None. Same crowd. Any trains to report?'

'None. And it's twelve twenty-three. Fuck.'

Platforms two and three were empty. Their shared polished brown tiles and white pillars ran under the arched glass and metal roof between them and the west London night. The tannoy system echoed news of an imminent departure, accompanied by the rat-a-tat of slamming doors. Some drunken rugby fans sang and staggered down the escalator. Then Famie saw the lights.

'It's here! She's here!'

She was about to take off down the platform but Sam's hand pulled her back.

'Wait. What carriage did she say?'

'Coach J. If she stayed put.'

'Can be at the front. Worth waiting.'

Famie, agitated, pulled away from Sam. She ran forward a few metres, through an open barrier, till she was alongside the incoming engine. The driver and the train's enormous logo slipped past. She stepped back to widen her field of vision and saw a J on the first carriage, then a face against the first door's window. It was Charlic.

Famie pressed both hands to her face, waved, then pressed them back again. Charlie flew from the carriage and Famie felt her daughter's sinewy arms wrap tightly around her. She smelt the wine, the sweat and her daughter's hair. She inhaled deeply.

Famie managed the hoarsest of whispers. 'Oh my God, I'm so happy to see you!'

'Mum, it was terrible,' blurted Charlie, pulling away. Her eyes were bloodshot, her cheeks blotchy. She'd pushed most of her hair under a red baseball cap. 'It was so terrible. I'm sorry if I panicked you but she—'

Famie put a finger on her lips. 'No apologies and no time. Tell me in the car. Sam's parked just outside.'

Sam nodded, smiled broadly. 'Hi Charlie. We're kinda

pleased to see you. But we need to move. Now.' He turned and ran towards the exit.

Famie grabbed her daughter's hand and they sprinted till they could tuck in behind him. Two minutes later, they all tumbled into Sam's Fiat and he pulled into the late-night traffic.

46

1.30 a.m.

CHARLIE ASKED FOR the hottest bath ever. The night temperature had barely dropped but she said she felt like being 'cleansed'. The attack, the three-and-a-half-hour train journey, the terror of not knowing who to trust, had left every muscle in pain. Famie added bubbles, then poured the Jack Daniel's. A typical small London bathroom, engineered to make the most of every centimetre, it didn't take much steam to turn it misty. Famie opened the top window but still the condensation ran from the tumblers, the window and the mirrors.

When Charlie appeared, swathed in towels, Famie made to leave. 'No, stay,' said Charlie. 'Really. There's too much to talk about.'

'Hang on then,' said Famie.

The briefest of trips to the freezer and she reappeared with a tub of ice cream and two spoons. Charlie, neck deep in the water already, managed a smile.

'Perfect,' she said. 'Classic Mum. Half one in the morning and we're eating salted caramel.'

Famie sat on the floor, her back to the bath. She scooped up some ice cream then handed the tub and a spoon to Charlie. 'You eat, I'll talk,' she said.

Famie told Charlie everything. About Sophie, her baby, the laptop, the photos ('how incredible that at your great age you can be such an idiot') and about Hari Roy. She showed her a photo.

'So he's the guy sending you messages?'

'Yes, it seems so. And he's scared too. The DC we spoke to – Hunter – said she was going to check him out. Whatever that means.' Her phone buzzed. 'Sam's home,' she said. She sent a thumbs-up emoji and texted 'Thanks'.

Then it was Charlie's turn. She explained about the movie, the lookalike, the ocean of blood and the run for the train. 'I spent the first twenty minutes under a table,' she said. 'The Germans got on at Tiverton. I listened to them mucking about and realized they had to be safe. There were four of them. I told them I was worried about my sick mother and asked to join them. They were just great. We drank a lot of wine.'

'Still want the JD?'

'I'm not old like you,' Charlie said. 'Course I do.'

Famie handed her a tumbler. Charlie took a mouthful.

'Should I have told the police?' she said. 'Back at the cinema? I don't know.' Her hair was piled high and tied with a band, her face red and running with sweat.

'But you didn't see anything,' said Famie. 'What could you have said? That you look like the girl who had been attacked? That it was intended for you? Don't think that would have been taken very seriously.'

Charlie found a submerged flannel, rinsed it and placed it over her face. Famie drank from her tumbler, allowing the fumes to fill her senses. She swallowed slowly, relishing the ice and the burn.

Her phone buzzed again. She wiped the screen then read the text.

'Oh sweet Jesus,' she whispered.

Charlie peeled the flannel away. 'What is it?'

When Famie read the message again, Charlie understood. 'She's dead, isn't she.'

'Yes,' said Famie. 'It's from Sam, he just read it online.'

Charlie's face crumpled in an instant. Tears flowed with the sweat, and her shoulders shook. Famie turned, reached over and wrapped her arms around her daughter. Charlie hung on to her as though she were drowning. Famie felt the soap and hot water seeping through her T-shirt.

'I don't know what to say, Charlie. I know I'm supposed to have all this sorted but I really haven't. It might have been coincidence but you're not going to believe that. And neither am I. But you know what? They failed. The fuckers failed and some poor kid died instead of you. I'll call the DC tomorrow. All we can do is tell her what happened.'

Still Charlie clung on.

'What do they want, Mum?' she said. 'I don't understand what they want. Why try to attack me?' She slowly untangled her arms from her mother's neck, slipped back into the water.

'When the bombs started going off in Pakistan,' said Famie, 'everyone knew why. Knew what it was for. It was for jihad mainly, then maybe it was political rivalry, then it was business disputes. It was messy. Christ, it was messy.' She sipped some more of the liquor. 'But there was always a point, an argument at the heart of it. And there'll be one at the heart of this too. Politics, religion, money, race. Pick one. Pick all of them. But this? Tonight? This is about power. About intimidation. My name is in the paper. It's out there. I was once with Seth. Maybe they came looking for me, but you were an easier find.'

'Maybe this Hari told them. Maybe he's part of it.'

Famie sighed. 'Maybe. Who knows?'

Charlie wiped her face. 'I called Dad,' she said.

Famie froze. 'OK,' she said, flatly.

'When I got here,' said Charlie. 'When you were saying goodbye to Sam. He didn't pick up though.'

'Well. I'm sure he'll call you back.'

'Are you?'

'Not really.'

'Just thought he should know,' said Charlie.

'Of course.'

'And, Mum. Look at me. Why wait for the morning? Seriously. If the copper gave you her card, use it. Tell her now. A girl in Exeter died instead of me. That doesn't wait till morning.'

Famie's head swam with whiskey and emotion but she knew her daughter was right. If someone had tried to kill Charlie, what was she waiting for?

'I'll get the number,' she said.

She retrieved the card from her bedroom. When she returned, Charlie was out of the bath and wrapping the towels around her again.

'What's her name again?' said Charlie. 'This policewoman you're calling.' Famie held the card up. 'Detective Constable Channing Hunter,' read Charlie. 'OK, let's do it.'

Lid down, Famie sat on the toilet. From the street, the sound of a car engine and a muted door closing. Charlie tensed. Famie stepped into her bedroom, peered through the curtain.

'Black cab,' she called. 'I doubt it's ISIS.'

Charlie joined her. She had wrapped a towel around her hair, turban-style. Her face, red and glowing, was still etched with worry. 'Who is it then?'

'Couldn't see.'

In the bathroom, Famie's phone rang. She stepped back in to retrieve it. 'Huh,' she said. 'Really?' The screen display read 'Andrew Lewis. Be nice.'

'Who is it, Mum?' Charlie's voice was suddenly fearful again.

'It's my boss. My ex-boss. This won't be good.' She answered. 'Andrew? It's nearly two a.m., for Christ's sake. What's up?'

A deep intake of breath from the phone. 'What's up is that I'm outside your house,' said Lewis. 'I saw the light was on. I checked. I'm sorry, Famie, but I need to come in.'

47

THERE WERE FIFTEEN stairs to the front door, then two locks and a security chain. In the time it took to descend those steps and unlock, Famie had imagined every possible disaster. What could possibly have triggered a home visit from the bureau chief? She flung the door open.

'Andrew. What the fuck?'

Lewis looked wrecked. Shirtsleeves, suit trousers, stains on both. He'd lost the tie. Behind his glasses, his eyes were bloodshot. His hair was at all angles. He smelt of alcohol.

'Like I said, I need to come in. The taxi will wait.'

'Sure.'

Famie stepped aside, let him climb the stairs first. He grasped the wooden banister, hauled himself up. Fumes drifted in his wake.

'My daughter Charlie is here too,' Famie said to his back. 'We . . . have just been talking.'

Lewis reached the top of the stairs.

'Straight on, Andrew.'

Famie followed him in. He was standing with a steadying

hand on a table. He flipped his glasses to the top of his head and she realized he had been crying. 'Andrew, what is it?' She stepped towards him but he held up both hands.

'It's Tommi,' he said, his voice a croaked whisper. 'I got a call. He was in a crash.'

That gut-flip again. Followed by the crushing realization. She swallowed hard. 'You wouldn't be here if he'd made it.'

Lewis shook his head slowly. 'He didn't. Dead at the scene.' He wiped his face with his hand. 'Bus driver said he'd appeared from nowhere. Said he didn't even have time to brake.'

Famie slumped on the sofa. Numb. Regretting the Jack Daniel's.

'But he'd just gone in to talk to Carol Leven,' she said. 'He sent us all the information from his chat. He . . .' She checked herself. 'He was following a lead.'

Lewis stood with both hands on the table, fingers splayed. 'I spoke to Carol. She said she offered him whisky. He took a couple of small bottles with him when he went.'

Famie frowned. 'Meaning?'

'Meaning he'd been drinking.'

'That's bollocks and you know it. He could drink that ten times over and he still wouldn't walk in front of a bus by mistake.'

She stood up, paced the room, the enormity of what had happened still sinking in.

'That's number eight, Andrew,' she said, a tremor in her voice. 'You know it. IPS journalist number eight. It's an assassination.'

Lewis looked uncomfortable. 'We can't say that, Famie. It could be, I grant you. It was my first thought too. Many will make the link as we have.' He wiped his face again. 'But the bus driver stopped. He reported that Tommi fell in front of his bus. And we know he'd been on the whisky. They're the facts.'

'They're some facts,' said Famie. 'You've missed a few. First, he wasn't "on the whisky", he'd drunk some whisky. Big difference. Second, IPS journalists are under attack and being killed. That's the big one. And fact number three? Tommi was following a hunch that there were other deaths on the twenty second. He makes an enquiry, he falls in front of a bus. Don't tell me that doesn't sound fucking suspicious.'

Famie could feel the colour in her cheeks, knew she was getting loud. Charlie clearly thought so too – she appeared in the doorway fully dressed, hair almost dried. Famie recognized the look she gave her: she was taking control.

'Oh hi. I'm Charlie. Think we met some years back.' Composed. Apparently clear-headed. Famie took a moment to be impressed.

Andrew straightened, stuck out his hand. Preposterously formal. 'Er yes, I'm sure that's right.'

'Charlie,' said Famie. She pressed her lips together, dropped her head. 'Tommi got run over. Killed by a bus.' She felt the tears now, the act of saying the words out loud making them real. 'The driver says he fell in front of him. Apparently.' She wiped her eyes.

Charlie nodded her understanding, took her mother's arm. She was listening, thought Famie.

'When was this?' said Charlie.

'Just a couple of hours ago,' said Lewis.

Famie stirred. 'Who rang you, Andrew?' she said. 'Who called? There barely seems time for the identification process to have concluded. Next of kin located. Death message delivered. This is fast.'

He cleared his throat. 'It's certainly accelerated. It was the Met Assistant Commissioner. She rang me.'

Famie's eyes widened. 'So she's made the connection too then! Like I said—'

Lewis held up his hands. 'My caution is her caution. I'm merely reporting to you what she reported to me. I'm sure she'd be interested in what Tommi was working on.'

'OK, I'll tell her,' said Famie. 'Give me her out-of-hours number and I'll call her now.'

'You know I can't do that.'

'Tell her I want to talk to her.'

'Yes, I can do that.'

'When?'

'First thing tomorrow.'

'So today then,' said Famie. 'In a few hours.'

Lewis nodded. 'Right. So. Yes. I'd best be going. Taxi's waiting. Charlie. Famie.' He nodded at them both.

Famie followed him down the stairs.

'Have you spoken to his mother?' she asked.

'Not yet. As soon as the police have visited. Which will also be in a few hours. Goodnight, Famie. I'm sorry for your troubles. I'm sorry for our troubles.'

She watched him climb into the taxi, locked and chained the door, then slumped on to the bottom step. Head in her hands, she burst into tears. Yet more grief. None of this was over. She wiped her eyes with her shirtsleeve. 'Oh Tommi. You poor bastard. I'm so sorry. So sorry.'

Charlie appeared, put her arm around her. They sat without speaking. Eventually Famie noticed the rucksack in her daughter's arm.

'Going somewhere?' she asked.

'We both are,' said Charlie. 'We have to leave. I'm packing you a bag.'

'OK, wait up,' said Famie, pushing past her. 'If we're not going to bed, I need coffee.'

Kettle on, they sat at the table. Famie put her head in her hands. 'Christ Almighty, what a terrible, terrifying, god-awful fucking shit show this is.'

Charlie tapped her on the shoulder. 'Tell me what you didn't tell Lewis. I'll make the coffee, then we go.'

Famie looked puzzled. 'What do you mean?'

'Tommi was following a hunch – you said it, I heard it. Then, when you were getting mad, you said more people might have died on the twenty-second. I thought you needed to shut up a bit, like you were overstepping your own lines, so I walked in. To change the subject.'

'You should be a cop,' said Famie.

'Or a journalist,' said Charlie.

'No, absolutely not. I forbid it,' said Famie with a rueful smile. 'Yes, Tommi's idea was that more people might have died on the twenty-second. Turns out a student called Toby Howells was killed then as well. And that he was a wannabe reporter, same as Hari. Tommi copied us in on all his ideas and the conversation he had with Carol Leven, the IPS crime reporter.'

'Then he was killed,' said Charlie.

'Then he was killed,' said Famie.

Charlie put her hand over her mother's. 'So we need to leave, Mum. Tommi is dead, someone who looks like me is dead. This is getting way too close. Here's the truth. We're not safe here. Not any more. I don't know what we're still doing here. Do you think this is anything like the end of it? Because if you don't, we need to go.'

The kettle boiled, and Famie got up to make the coffees. She needed to think straight. How many scoops to cancel half a bottle of Jack? She went back to the packet, spooned in some more grains.

'Mum, focus, please! Follow the logic. Are we safe here?'

Charlie had upped the volume. Famie felt a headache coming.

'I am focusing, Charlie,' she said. 'I am following the logic. If "they", whoever "they" are, have targeted you, and you're here, then no, we are not safe.'

'You want me to go?'

'Wait! No! Obviously not.' Famie sighed. 'So. If they targeted Tommi because of his questioning about the facts of May twenty-two and Sam and I have been on the same investigation, then again, no, we are not safe.'

She plunged and poured.

'So?' said Charlie.

'So,' said Famie. 'We are not safe. But we are also drunk.'

'Speak for yourself.'

'Charlie, we demolished half a bottle of JD. And you had wine on the train. At the very least we're over the limit.'

Charlie leant across the table. 'This is risk management, Mum. We need to disappear. Or at least not make it easy for whoever is out there. Anywhere else is better than here where two of their targets are waiting for them.'

Famie swallowed some coffee and winced from the burning in her throat. Charlie's relentless logic was sobering her up faster than the caffeine.

'We were about to call the DC. Hunter. I should talk to her.'

'Sure,' said Charlie. 'When we're not here. We move, then call.'

'Where would we go?'

'Anywhere,' said Charlie. 'Anywhere that isn't here.'

'What about Sam? He must be in danger too.'

'Can you trust him?'

Famie was aghast. 'Sam? Of course I trust him.' She stared at Charlie. 'You're serious, aren't you?'

'Of course I'm bloody serious!' said Charlie. 'It must be what nearly getting killed does to you. He's married, isn't he?'

'Yes, to Jo.'

'Trust her?'

'Yes! I . . . I suppose so.' Famie's headache was strengthening. She downed more coffee. 'She's a copper. Christ, I don't know, Charlie! She's always been lovely to me. She's from Zimbabwe.'

'Is that relevant?'

'Who knows, Charlie? Probably not.'

'Fine, well, you should tell Sam then.'

'And Sophie. And, yes, I trust her too.'

Charlie poured the last centimetre of coffee. 'But that's it. Not Lewis. No one else.' She found the paracetamol in the table drawer, put two in Famie's hand. 'Take these, Mum. I'll finish packing the rucksack, you check I've got the right stuff, then we're gone.'

48

3.15 a.m.

THERE WAS NO phone signal till they arrived at the concourse, then Famie's phone went straight to five bars. Full strength. They had had the escalator to themselves but the station itself was humming. The Euston departure and arrival boards showed nothing for two hours but that hadn't stopped the vast shopping centre area being used as a thoroughfare. Late-night clubbers, early-morning shift workers and uniformed cleaners all stepped around the homeless and the destitute. Famie clocked the muted conversations, the exhausted faces, the grim determination. We fit in quite well, she thought.

Making the phone call here was Charlie's idea. They'd parked in a side road which Famie had thought was close enough. But Charlie had insisted, and as Charlie was less drunk than she was, Charlie had won. 'If we're calling the police, we need to be where we say we are,' she had said, and Famie wasn't going to argue.

'Here?' said Charlie, stepping a few metres from the escalator towards a shuttered cupcake stand.

Famie nodded, and dialled the number from the card. It rang four times. A fumbled, rattling pick-up.

'Hunter,' croaked a voice at the other end. Asleep certainly, but awake now.

'It's Famie Madden. I'm sorry to wake you.'

A rustle and a changed acoustic. A different room.

'OK, go ahead, Ms Madden. I'm listening.'

Famie glanced at Charlie, who nodded. 'Someone tried to kill my daughter tonight,' she said.

'What happened, Ms Madden? Is your daughter OK?'

'Terrified but, yes, OK. She's here now. Got the last train. She was in the Vue cinema in Exeter. Before the film she noticed a girl who looked like her, same height and hair. That kind of thing. When she left the cinema, it was this girl who had been stabbed. She died later. Your colleagues there are asking for witnesses. Charlie wasn't a witness. But we think she was the target.'

There was a silence from Hunter. Famie assumed she was note-taking.

'And there's another thing,' she said.

'Where are you, Ms Madden?'

'Wait,' said Famie. 'You might not know this yet but Tommi Dara was killed a few hours ago. Run down by a bus near Cockfosters tube station. He was working a lead in the May twenty-two story, then he was dead.'

'I didn't know that, Ms Madden,' said Hunter. 'I'm sorry for your loss. I'll get all the information I can and call you later. Maybe you could stop by the station again?'

Raised voices and a scream from somewhere made Charlie jump and grab Famie's arm.

'No, that won't be happening,' said Famie. 'We're off, DC Hunter. We're at Euston and we're disappearing. Someone is targeting IPS people and now they're targeting Charlie.

So. We're gonna hide up somewhere until we know what's happening.'

The comeback was swiftly, forcefully delivered. 'I'm not sure that's wise,' said Hunter. 'We need to know where you are. That's the best way to keep you safe.'

'Yeah, well,' said Famie, 'too fucking late for that, I'm afraid. If you know where we are, everyone else knows where we are too.'

'Hold on,' said Hunter, 'got something for you.'

Charlie frowned at her mother, made a winding-up sign. She was getting nervous again. Famie ran a three-sixty-degree check. A concourse of wasters and no-hopers maybe, she thought, but it's still probably safer than the flat. She held up one finger to Charlie. 'One minute,' she mouthed. Charlie nodded.

Hunter was back. 'I got a report back from the officers who went to Boxer Street,' she said.

Famie stood taller, adrenalin seeping into her tired body. 'And?' she said.

A beat.

'Ms Madden, I'll tell you this confidentially to show you how seriously we take your story and your security.'

'Understood,' said Famie, impatient. 'What does it say?'

'It says they conducted an operation. That there's a woman living at number twenty-six, on her own apparently. Said she knew Hari Roy, that he'd done one of her martial arts classes once.' Hunter was clearly subbing the story as she went – Famie recognized the audible sifting of words and phrases. 'It says his car is parked in the street but this woman said that didn't surprise her as there are so many student houses in the area.'

She had stopped.

'Is that it?' Famie felt herself deflating.

'They're still watching the house,' said Hunter.

'Did they go inside?'

'That's all I have, Ms Madden.'

'Hardly conclusive,' said Famie.

'Hardly surprising,' said Hunter.

'But that's it?'

'Like I said . . .'

'You got any better leads? Christ Almighty . . .'

Hunter realized that Famie was about to hang up. 'You might not believe me, Ms Madden, but I have been taking you seriously. And after what has happened tonight I'm sure others will too.'

Charlie was tugging Famie now. 'Too long,' she mouthed. 'Come on.' They stepped on to the escalator. Hunter was still asking where they were going when she put the phone down. Famie and Charlie walked the short distance back to the car.

'You're still definitely over the limit,' said Famie.

'It's a risk we'll have to take,' Charlie said, popping two extra strong mints. 'I'll be careful. Where are we going?'

She started the car.

'Coventry,' said Famie.

Charlie switched the engine off again.

'When I said anywhere was safer than your flat,' she protested, 'I obviously wasn't including Coventry.' She stared at her mother.

Famie stared ahead. Through the windscreen and down the quiet side street. She knew she was right. She let the silence run.

Eventually Charlie sighed, turned the ignition again. 'OK, you win,' she said. 'And God help us.'

49

3.30 a.m.

WHAT FEW POSSESSIONS Hari had taken into Boxer Street were in his rucksack. He was ready to run. He paced the upstairs room. Lights off, curtains drawn. Every few seconds he scanned the road through a carefully arranged gap in the curtains. And every few seconds he saw the same uniformed police in the same car.

As soon as the police moved, so would they. Hari fought back against a rising sense of panic. He had no escape plan, no idea how to keep his sisters safe and no idea how to contact the IPS woman again. He imagined walking from the house and letting himself into the coppers' car. Imagined telling them about Binici and Collins, the dead Zak hidden somewhere in the house, and about his imperilled family. He then imagined how long it would take the leader to order the execution of his sisters. No time at all was the answer.

He peered through the curtains again.

The house was silent. Occasionally Hari caught a whisper or the lightest of treads from Binici or Collins downstairs. The Geiger counter was back on too, its sporadic clicking sound telling Hari everything he needed to know about the leader's fevered state of mind. His obsession with radioactivity continued. If, Binici would reason, their enemies had used radiation poisoning once, they would certainly try it again. And he would be ready. Hari found the clicks an unexpected comfort. Each one was a reminder of Hari's only success – his fooling of Binici and Collins.

Click.

Fooled you.

Click.

Still fooling you.

Click.

I just have to fool you again.

And the clicks were getting louder. Binici and maybe Collins were on their way up. Hari hovered by the curtains. Two policemen, one patrol car, no movement. He stepped aside as Binici appeared at his shoulder. He smelt the leader's rosewater soap and wondered how he had managed to attend to his personal hygiene.

'No change,' muttered Hari. 'We have to assume they're not going anywhere soon.'

'Well we can't wait,' whispered Binici. Collins was at his shoulder. 'Either we leave or they do,' he said. 'All the cells are watching. The London Citizens will be on their way soon. They were told eight, they'll be here at eight. It's too late to change and we can't talk to them anyway.'

Click.

'In which case,' said Collins, 'I'll have to think of something.'

'That would be appreciated,' said Binici.

It was Hari's watch till four a.m., then Binici's. At five they were all back at the window, the sun about to emerge above the houses opposite. Motionless threads of orange-tinged clouds stretched high above them. Another airless, stifling day in prospect. Hari swept his eyes along the road again, right to left. His wrecked car, the incident tape. The nose-to-tail parking on both sides. The coppers. And at the far end of Boxer Street, a busy T-junction. Traffic swept past their road all day and night. This was where they expected the London cell to appear.

'Same fash, no change,' Binici said.

Collins had brought up coffee and fruit.

'How many citizens, again?' she asked.

'I'm told five.'

'I've cleared some space,' said Hari, 'but we're out of beds.'

'They won't be here for long,' said Binici, 'and there won't be any time for sleep.'

Two early joggers ran past the house. Hari watched the policeman in the driver's seat follow their progress. He was white, bearded and awake, his partner mostly obscured by the car's roof. Six cars drove past, three pulled away from their parking spaces. The police noted everything, photographed everything.

Hari picked up his coffee, left it black and strong. He said as little as possible, figuring that if he waited long enough, Collins would tell them what she was thinking. He knew better than to push it. Binici drifted away. When they could hear him in the kitchen downstairs, she sat on the floor, crossed her legs. She tugged at Hari's jeans. He glanced down.

'I've thought of something, just making him wait, that's all,' she said. She gesticulated downstairs. 'He's a genius, you know. His plan will be spectacular, and it'll work. It's just that he's also a total cunt. Maybe it goes with the territory.'

Tearing himself away from the window, Hari sat down next to her. 'What is the plan, do you know?' He tried to sound confident but it came out too breezy, as though they were planning a picnic.

Collins shook her head. 'I don't,' she said. 'Don't know about the other targets. Don't know our target. The shopping centre maybe? A cinema? A school? Christ, I hope it isn't a school.'

Hari's skin crawled. 'Four private schools nearby,' she said 'Wealthy kids. Children of bankers. Jews. Should be quite a haul, if you can cope with it.'

So this is it then. 'And can you cope with it?' he said.

She paused. 'If I have to. You?'

He shrugged. 'Don't know yet. I'll follow you.'

'OK.'

'Knives?' he said.

'Presumably,' she said, matter-of-factly. 'Maybe a lorry. Depends what London brings with them.'

Hari felt nauseous. He needed some air.

'Assuming we don't all get arrested when they get here,' he said.

Collins shuffled closer.

'So I was thinking,' she said. 'Your car is still up there, at the end of the road. I go out, start poking around in the wrecks. The fash won't be able to resist. As long as they both come down, I should be able to keep them there for long enough. If London are as punctual as Abi says they will be, both coppers will be with me when the citizens arrive. You and Abi let them in. That's it. That's the plan.'

It had some logic to it. It could work. As long as there were only two coppers.

'And the police know it's my car,' he said.

'They do. They said so.'

'They'll have gone to the campus looking for me. Home too. When they don't find me, they'll be back here for certain.'

'Why would they come back?' she said. 'They've been already.'

Said too much. Hari scrambled up to get a quick glance at

the road to cover his awkwardness. No change to report. 'You told them I'd been to your classes. And that I was terrible at them. Thanks for that by the way. They'll want to retrace their steps. It's what they do, isn't it?'

She shrugged, unconvinced. He moved the conversation on.

'Who did they think lived here with you?'

'Tom Jarrod. It's the name Binici wrote on the rental papers.'

'Time to tell him your plan?' Hari said.

She checked her watch. 'Almost. One other thing,' she said.

'Go on.'

She looked awkward. Hari hadn't seen that before.

'Tonight is dangerous for me,' she said. 'The night before an operation, men get . . . demanding. I don't know these new arrivals. And after what happened earlier, I don't know about Binici either. So. I need to say that I'll be with you tonight. And then actually stay with you.' She raised both hands, palms out. 'We're not screwing or anything but they don't know that.'

Hari was sure he was reddening. 'Me?' he said, surprised. 'But you can look after yourself, Sara.'

'I can,' said Collins. 'Trust me, I really can. But it's a numbers game, Hari. I've heard so many bad stories. It's just easier this way.' She stared at him. 'This isn't pretending any more, Hari. This is revolution. Bad things will happen. This' – she waved her arm around the room – 'has all just been pissing about. But it's about to get fucking scary, so if we can make life easier for ourselves we should. I trust you. So. You watch out for me, I'll watch out for you. Comprende?'

Hari nodded. 'Comprende,' he said.

50

7.57 a.m.

DRESSING GOWN PULLED tight and flip-flops slapping the pavement, Sara Collins exited number 26, turned right and headed for Hari's smashed-up car. She ignored the police; if she did her job correctly, they'd be following her anyway. She shuffled across the road just to make herself as obvious as she could, a red revolutionary rag for the fascist bull. Most houses in Boxer Street had their windows wide open already and a street's worth of breakfast routines spilled out into her path. Music, voices, television, radio, washing up, hoovers, the clatter of life.

Collins was twenty metres from the yellow police incident tape when she heard the slamming of car doors behind her. She smiled and picked up her pace to where the white van had smashed into a row of cars. The van was gone but Hari's car, the Ford Galaxy and a Fiat Punto were still there, doors, mirrors and windows caved in or missing altogether. The road had been perfunctorily swept to keep it open, but a carpet of glass and twisted metal lay underneath the vehicles.

The tape stretched around two lampposts, the pavement, the three damaged cars and two large orange bollards, one placed by the Punto, the other by Hari's VW. Collins ducked under the tape. The Ford Galaxy was the worst hit. Both right-side doors were gone, the windscreen and rear window shattered. The chassis had buckled on impact, with the metal floor ripped open and both front seats thrown forward on to the dashboard. Tiny squares of glass littered the interior. Collins peered into the wreck then crouched and picked up an empty Coke tin from the rubble.

'Are you looking for something?'

She looked up to see one of the policemen staring at her through the still intact passenger window. He was on his own. Late thirties, cap on, no jacket.

'What are you doing?'

'Is this Alfred Graham's car?' she said.

'Is it what?'

'Your colleague, the one who knocked, told me who these cars belonged to. I'm sure he said it was an Alfred Graham who owned this. Or Graham Alfred maybe, I'm not sure.' She put the can back.

'It's Sara Collins, isn't it?' said the policeman. He held up his ID. 'PC Jon Roberts, Coventry Police. You need to leave the car alone. Step behind the tape.'

Collins stayed in the crouch, checked her watch. Seven fifty-nine. She glanced down the street. The other policeman, the bearded driver, was out of his car and, one hand on its roof, was staring at her.

'It's just I remember him now. I'm sure I do,' she said. 'He's a tall man. Kind. Always helping others.' She pulled out some chocolate wrappers from behind the pedals, folded them together, then put them in the pocket of her dressing gown.

'What are you doing?' PC Roberts walked round the front

of the Galaxy, stood behind her. 'Ms Collins, step away from the car. Behind the tape.'

Collins kept rummaging. 'Needs a tidy, don't you think?' she said, reaching again into the car.

The constable stepped over the tape. 'Enough,' he said. 'Go back to your house.'

The sound of a radio news bulletin's opening headlines. Eight o'clock. Collins climbed into the car.

From the bay window, Hari switched his attention to the police car opposite. The bearded officer had stepped out of the car to watch his colleague's approach. He had stretched, radioed once, put his sunglasses on. He had seemed nothing more than curious initially, but now slammed his door shut and jogged to join his colleague. Binici, at Hari's shoulder, was muttering. Turkish, Hari assumed. It sounded like a chant, a prayer, an incantation.

'Now would be good,' said Hari, glancing left to the other end of the street.

'And now is good,' said Binici.

The prayer had worked. On the main road, a plain white van was approaching the turn into Boxer Street. Slowing, indicating left. It edged into view before stopping just shy of the corner. Two faces strained at the windscreen, peering, twisting. Looking for parking, looking for cops, looking for trouble.

'Stay here,' Binici said. He flew from the room, then took the stairs in a few jumps. 'Be ready on the door!' he called from the hall, then slipped noiselessly from the house.

He was alone. It would only be for seconds but for the first time in days, Hari wasn't being watched. Run. Hide. Last chance. Next stop the butcher's shop. But stage left was Binici and the London goons, stage right were the cops. The fash. If he hid with a neighbour, in a shed, in a cellar, he'd be too late to stop Binici's revenge. Same equation, same algorithm, same result.

Paralysed, Hari watched both dramas. Binici checked right then jogged left. Hugging the wall, he briefly disappeared from view before reappearing crossing the road at the T. He held up a hand. The men in the van didn't respond. Hari swept right. One policeman was bent over, hand on the car roof, the other stood face on to Collins. Both were concentrating on getting the mad woman out of the car. Hari swept left. The van and Binici had disappeared. Boxer Street was clear.

Three minutes past eight.

He looked right. Collins was still inside the car, both policemen were crouched.

He looked left. Still nothing.

Right. One policeman was climbing inside the car.

Left. Still nothing.

Right. Collins was coming out. He saw one bare leg, then the next – the bearded policeman was pulling her out. She stumbled and was caught, losing her flip-flops. She brushed glass from her dressing gown. She walked herself back into her flip-flops.

She's all out of stalling. Thirty seconds left of this pantomime. Maximum.

Four minutes past eight.

Left. A delivery van turned the corner, trundled past Hari at 26, pulled up at 39. Hazard lights flashing, the van sat squarely in the middle of the road, completely blocking Hari's view of Collins and the police. He saw a uniformed woman leap from the cab, music blaring, parcel in hand, and ring the bell.

'Be ready on the door,' Binici had said. That was now. Whatever was happening, with Binici or Collins, London 'citizens' or Coventry Police, he needed to be downstairs.

As he scrambled down the staircase he saw fast-moving,

darting shadows at the door. Ducking, pushing. Too many for Collins and the police. The lightest of knocks. Hari tugged the door open and five men ran in with Binici, breathless, sweating, wordless. They wore black tops with black trousers and grey caps. They were light of foot, wide-eyed and totally wired.

The London Citizens, the killers of May twenty-two, were in Boxer Street.

51

9 a.m.
London Ramada hotel, M1 junction 2

FAMIE SAT ON the scorched grass bank that framed the car park. The Volvo's front wheels were two metres away, a paper cup of black coffee steaming on its bonnet, another cradled in her hands. High cloud cover was keeping the temperature, for now, in the mid-twenties but she swallowed the hot drink in large gulps. When it was drained, she stood and reached for the second. This one would last longer.

Sunglasses and baseball cap, fresh blue T-shirt, same old headache. She'd taken the paracetamol Charlie had given her before crashing into bed at around four a.m., she took some more now. Behind her, the continuous rumble and roar of the M1, in front of her, the glass-and-tile low-rise that had given them all of three hours' sleep. Sam had rung at seven; devastated, inconsolable. He was on his way to them. He said he had to come and Famie hadn't argued. Her phone vibrated twice in quick succession. Charlie was on her way out with some snatched breakfast, Sam was in an Uber. She didn't reply to either.

Famie noticed a slight tremble in her hands as she raised

the new cup. She knew she was scared, but hadn't realized it showed. She held the coffee tighter. The shaking disappeared. Get a grip, woman. She had been shot at in Islamabad, car-jacked in Lahore and had witnessed two suicide bombings in Karachi. She had been felt up on a train, called an English whore and a Jewish bitch. It had been, some of it, perilous, stomach-churning work but she had accepted it as part of her assignment. She was a journalist in a war zone. It's what happened.

Yet here she was, hiding, fearful, trembling, in an English car park. Afraid for her daughter, afraid for a man she didn't even know and mourning another dead colleague. This was different. This was family. No wonder her hands shook.

Charlie brought pastries and fruit. Same denim shorts, a loose-fitting cream cotton shirt, shades and an olive army-style cap. 'We can get more but I didn't want to draw attention.' She perched the plates on the grass and sat down.

'We'll need more coffee,' said Famie. 'Sam's here in two. He just texted.'

'Is he coming with us?'

'Don't know. Probably.'

'I'll get the refills,' said Charlie. 'Then we should go.'

She stood, brushed the dried grass from her shorts, and disappeared beyond the car. Famie had tried to argue they should do everything together but had received short shrift.

'Too much?' she had said.

'Too much,' Charlie had replied. 'Pretty sure we're OK here. As far as we know anything.'

Famie had just finished the world's driest croissant when her phone buzzed. 'Here' it said. She stood to see a grey Prius looping slowly around the car park. She raised her hand, the car stopped, and Sam tumbled out. He ran to Famie like they were lost lovers. His legs buckled a few metres from her and she grabbed him. They embraced, and he buried his face on her shoulder. She felt his chest heaving and held him till he was cried out. When he pulled away they slumped to the grass.

Sam cleared his throat. 'They killed him, Fames. Killed Tommi, I'm sure of it. That's eight of us. Christ.' He turned to look at her, his eyes filling again. 'And now I don't know what we're doing.'

'I think we're hiding, Sam. That's the best I can do. Me and Charlie.'

Sam nodded. 'Hiding is good.'

'You joining us?'

'After what happened to Tommi, yes. I think I should.'

'We're hooking up with Sophie later too. What did Jo say?'

Sam's shoulders slumped. 'We argued. She's a copper. She trusts the system.'

'And you're a journalist who doesn't . . .'

'That's what it boiled down to. I told her to take leave and disappear but I don't think she will.'

'Coppers don't hide, I suppose.'

'Cops from Zim certainly don't. Tough breed.'

'Did you tell her about Charlie?'

'I did.' Sam wiped his eyes, produced some old sunglasses. 'She was shocked, you know. She gets it. And she said she'll liaise with Exeter and get what she can from Hackney.'

'She knows we're disappearing, right?'

'She's in no doubt about that.'

Charlie arrived with a cardboard tray of coffees, another paper bag of pastries perched on top.

'You with us?' she said to Sam.

'Thought I'd be useful,' he said.

'Always,' said Charlie. 'You, Mum and Tommi went through a lot.' She stood awkwardly by the car bonnet. 'I'm so sorry about what happened, Sam.'

'I know that, Charlie. Thanks anyway.'

'We should go, Mum.'

'Agreed,' said Famie, scrambling to her feet. 'Hard to think we'll find a more anonymous corner of Britain to hide in, but I'm all for trying.'

Famie drove, Charlie slept. The motorway traffic was heavy; Famie stayed at sixty, clinging to the inside lane. The fields of Northamptonshire rolled past without her noticing. The coffees and paracetamol were at last making inroads into her headache. Behind her, Sam had been texting but was now staring out of the passenger window.

'I spoke to DC Hunter, before we took off,' Famie said. 'Told her what was happening.'

'I'm sure she was thrilled.'

'Delighted to be woken up certainly. She said she had been taking me seriously. And that after what had happened, she was sure others would too. Which struck me as odd.'

Sam continued to stare out of the window. 'Suggests she's been fighting a losing battle. Maybe she's the only one who doesn't think you're a lunatic.'

'Maybe.'

A sudden clutch of road signs sporting familiar names. They both read them.

'I know what you're thinking,' she said. She saw him nod.

'Mary's funeral,' he said. 'You, me and Tommi.' He broke off. 'Christ this hurts,' he said.

Mary, Harry, Sarah, Anita, Sathnam, Seth, Brian and now Tommi. Beautiful, loyal and optimistic Tommi. Another death and another funeral to go to. Famie was overwhelmed with the certainty that the carnage wasn't over.

The next onrushing sign offered an exit at junction sixteen. 'Of course,' she said, and left the motorway.

52

10.42 a.m.

THE LAWSON HOUSE was two miles from the village of Ashby St Ledgers, set back from the single-track road and almost invisible to the casual, drive-by observer. The garden was bordered with silver birch trees and thick, dark green box hedges. Famie drove past, pulling on to the first verge she could find. She put her hazard warning lights on, turned the music off.

Charlie stirred. 'What's happening?' she slurred.

Famie handed her a bottle of water. 'Sam and I are going to see Martin Lawson. Mary's husband.' She corrected herself: 'Widower.'

'Why?' said Charlie, coming round quickly. 'You warning him or something?' She sat up, stared at Famie. 'You're going to tell him about Seth?' Her mouth stayed open, eyebrows raised.

'Maybe,' said Famie. 'Though we really don't want to screw his life up any more than it actually has been already. Maybe we can talk around Seth. We haven't got long anyway. I texted Martin and he needs to be gone in twenty minutes. Called him yesterday but he didn't pick up.'

'I'm not sitting out here by the way,' said Charlie. 'I'm not paranoid or anything but alone in a car near the first victim's house seems a bit freaky.'

'Of course,' said Famie. 'Come in with us.'

Famie U-turned and pulled into the Lawsons' short drive, her nerves jangling. The hedgerow and trees gave way to a newly renovated two-storey Georgian house with wide, shuttered windows and an open front door. As Famie pulled up behind a black Range Rover, Martin Lawson appeared and raised a hand in salute. He stood on the step waiting for them. Greying hair cut very short. Black suit trousers, white shirt and powder-blue tie. A businessman with a business meeting to go to. Mid-fifties, paunchy but stylish, he smiled as Famie walked towards him.

'My God, Famie, it's so good to see you!' He hugged her warmly.

She inhaled tea, toast and cologne. Creed Pure White probably. He's bearing up, she thought.

'Sorry to just drop in on you like this, Martin,' she started.

'Nonsense,' he said, 'just a shame it's for such a short time. Sam, good to see you. And this is Charlie?' He embraced Sam, shook hands with Charlie. 'There's tea and coffee, I'll bring it out. Ella and Fred are at school so we won't be overheard. The shade will last for a while yet.'

Sam shrugged. 'Anywhere is good. And don't worry about the teas and coffees. Water is fine.'

They moved to some lilac-painted wicker chairs and a rectangular glass-topped table. A computer tablet and some newspapers were arranged neatly in a pile.

'I'll get a jug and be right back,' said Martin, and disappeared inside.

Famie and Sam sat together, Charlie pulled her chair slightly away. 'I'll keep schtum, don't worry about me,' she said.

Famie glanced around. The house was set in the middle of

an acre of freshly cut lawn; the flowerbeds that traced the treeline border overflowed with hydrangea, peonies and phlox. Greens, pinks, blues and purples surrounded them, running riot across the garden.

'Wow,' whispered Charlie, 'someone's doing OK.' To Famie's frown, she added, 'I mean financially, obviously.'

Sam leant towards her. 'Just what I was thinking,' he stage-whispered.

Martin hurried out with a jug of iced water and four glasses. He set them down, poured, then perched on one of the wicker chairs opposite Famie. His eyes darted between them. 'So. I assume this is about Mary? I'm sure I never thanked you for coming to the funeral but—'

Famie held up her hands. 'Please, Martin, where else would we have been? She was one of the most talented journalists we had. And one of the kindest.'

'That's a great comfort, thank you. So.' He looked at Sam, at Charlie, then back to Famie. 'How can I help?' He smiled, almost.

A tiny alarm bell rang in Famie's head. His manner seemed wrong, forced somehow. He was like a doctor asking patients what was wrong with them.

'I know the police will have been through all this,' said Famie, treading carefully. 'I hope you don't mind the questions, but we're trying to work out what Mary and her team were working on. What the story was that got them killed.'

A small nod from Martin. 'I explained to the police that she never talked about her work,' he said, sipping at his water. 'I used to ask her what she was working on, but eventually you stop, you know?' His tone was flat, expressionless.

'Was she different these last few months at all?' asked Sam. 'Did she mention any different names, visit any new places? As far as you know?'

Martin stared at the ground. Famie wasn't sure if he was

concentrating or gathering himself. He seemed to be struggling. The silence became uncomfortable.

'We didn't keep tabs on each other,' he said eventually. 'I travel a lot, so did Mary. Lots of her life was a mystery to me. A closed book. She would probably have said the same about me.'

Famie was aware of the adrenalin running again. Sam was writing studiously.

'She was certainly working hard,' Martin added.

'Harder than usual?' said Sam.

'Yes, I think so. She was always on the phone. Like, *always* on the phone.'

'On her laptop?' asked Sam. 'Computer?'

Martin shook his head. 'Not so much. Not here anyway.' He looked at Famie. 'Is that odd?'

Famie shrugged. Possibly, she thought. 'Not necessarily,' she said. She paused, uncertain. 'Have the police looked at her computer? Her phone?'

'Yup. Don't think they found anything. Not that they told me anyway.'

'Did she keep a diary?' asked Sam. 'A journal of any kind?'

Martin looked apologetic. 'Not as far as I know. I'm sorry.'

'Did she ever mention a Hari Roy or a Toby Howells as far as you know?' asked Famie, but only because she felt she had to.

Again, an almost embarrassed shake of the head. This was going nowhere. Famie thought of the visit to Hackney Police Station and the contents of Seth's laptop. The police would be back here soon enough. She glanced at Charlie and Sam but they were impassive. This was her decision. She decided to tell.

'Martin, I feel as though I should warn you about something.'

Martin frowned. 'A warning? About what?'

Famie sighed deeply. She stared at the ground, then her hands, then, finally, Martin. Charlie and Sam were watching him too.

'The police might ask you about whether Mary was having an affair,' she said.

Martin tensed. His back straightened. His face coloured. 'I'm sorry?' he said. 'Really? Are you sure?'

'I'm sure they'll ask you, yes,' said Famie. 'And I think they're right. I think she was.'

Martin stood and walked away from the table, beyond the shade, his face in the sunshine. Hands in pockets.

'When was this?' His voice was quiet but steady.

'We're not sure, Martin,' said Famie.

Silence. Famie and Sam exchanged glances. Charlie was on her phone.

'And this is a police matter?' he said.

'Apparently,' said Famie.

A further silence. Famie's phone vibrated in her pocket, she stole a glance. An image from Charlie. She glanced up, frowning. Charlie, with urgency, stabbed a finger at her phone. Famie enlarged the screen shot she'd sent. It showed Charlie's screen with four phones indicated as being nearby. Grey circles, with small type underneath. Martin's phone, Sam's phone, Famie's phone, Amy's phone. Charlie had circled the last name. 'Who's Amy?' she'd written. Another quick glance at Charlie, who was pointing at the house.

Martin hadn't moved. She was going to let him ask the next question. Meantime, he appeared to have a woman inside called Amy. Way to go, Martin. That's some recovery.

Eventually he turned round, walked back to the table. 'How did they find out?' he said. His arms folded, his tone resigned. 'Does everyone know?' This question seemed to be directed at Sam.

'Not everyone,' he said. 'But quite a few.'

'You don't sound surprised,' said Famie.

Martin shook his head. 'I knew. Well, I found out.' He perched again. 'It's the Egyptian, yes?'

Sam and Famie nodded.

'And, Martin,' said Famie, her voice dropping a register. She paused. 'There are photos. Seth took photos. Of Mary.'

Martin closed his eyes, said nothing.

'We thought you'd prefer to hear it from us,' said Famie. 'I'm so sorry, Martin.'

He sighed. 'What sort of photos?'

'Naked shots,' said Famie. 'Not posed.' Hardly a comfort, she thought.

Martin didn't move. Then a deep breath. 'You knew this Seth Hussain, yes?'

'We did, yes,' said Famie. 'I did particularly.'

'And? You liked him?'

'I did, Martin. Great reporter. Just turns out to have been a dick. I'm sorry.'

Martin shook his head. 'Will this come out?' he said, then shrugged. 'Of course it will. Stupid question. It all comes out in the end. I'll need to tell the kids, I suppose.'

'How are they coping?' said Famie.

'They're coping,' said Martin. 'Just about. Ella better than Fred, I think. We'll get there, Famie.'

'If you need any help . . .'

'I got some, thanks.'

Hello Amy, thought Famie.

Martin looked at his watch, and they took the cue.

'We'll head off, Martin,' she said. 'I'm sorry about the whole shitty mess, really I am.'

They embraced briefly.

'Thanks for the heads-up,' he said. 'You're right. Hearing all that from the cops would have been a nightmare.'

Famie lingered over one of the newspapers, scanning the headlines. A May-twenty-two-free zone for a change.

'They're yesterday's,' said Martin.

'Could I have one for the car?' asked Famie. 'Conversation is getting a little dull.'

He waved expansively. 'Help yourself. Of course. Still the journalist then, Famie.'

She cringed, theatrically. They said their goodbyes.

As Famie spun the car out of the drive, she handed the newspaper to Charlie. 'I don't think I've ever stolen anything before,' she said. 'But it seemed like a good time to start.' From the folded pages of *The Times* slid a black tablet computer.

53

'MUM, YOU'VE GONE mad.'

'Just wait.'

'No, seriously. You've gone mad. And got me worried.'

Charlie was in the back, Famie in the driving seat, Sam in the front passenger seat. They were on the dirt track Famie had used to U-turn. They were parked up, facing the main road and shielded from view by a line of thick-trunked sycamore trees and wild, white-flowering hawthorn. The engine was off, the windows open. The honey and almond scent of the hedge filled the car. No one noticed.

'They're coming,' said Famie.

They could all hear the sound of a powerful car approaching, its low revs rumbling through the hedgerows.

'Range Rover,' muttered Sam, 'incoming.'

Martin Lawson's car swept sedately past in a matter of seconds, rolling past the track at around twenty miles an hour. His passenger – a woman, late twenties, short black hair, singlet and sunglasses – was in view for just enough time for Famie to say, 'He's gone for the younger model. What a surprise.'

'She could be the nanny,' suggested Sam.

'Probably is the nanny,' said Famie. 'How totally predictable.'

'And so what?' said Sam. 'Even if he is shagging the nanny, even if the Lawsons' marriage was a sham, what's it to us?'

He had a point, Famie knew that.

'And why have you stolen his tablet?' said Charlie, again.

Another good point. Maybe they had the same answer.

'There's something here,' said Famie, waving her arms. 'In the tablet, in the immaculate house, in the immaculate garden, in his demeanour, his manner. Now a beautiful young woman at his side. You notice he didn't invite us inside? Did he seem like a grieving husband to you?'

Charlie pushed herself forward, between the seats. 'Mum, why did you steal the tablet?'

'In case,' said Famie. 'In case there's something there. Chances are there's nothing and I can just take it back. Innocent mistake.'

Sam was uncomfortable, annoyed even. '"In case"?' he said. 'Really? That's not good enough, Fames, and you know it. The tablet isn't going to be Mary's, is it? It'll be Martin's, or one of the kids'. So a total waste of time. And what's your plan for the password?'

Charlie, from the back: 'You can barely remember your own, Mum, never mind finding someone else's.'

'OK,' Famie said. 'If my idea doesn't work, we'll just drive back in and I'll put it back. OK?'

'OK,' Charlie said after a short pause, and handed the thin screen to Famie.

She spun it over in her hands. On its polished base, Famie pointed to a small piece of adhesive plaster that had 'LawsonFam01' written in biro. 'Exhibit one,' she said, and typed the password into the on-screen box. 'Wouldn't have nicked it if I hadn't seen this.'

The next screen offered four accounts: Mary's was top left, Martin's top right, Freddie was bottom left, Ella bottom right. Each had a jokey, face-pulling selfie for its wallpaper. They all looked so happy. Famie swallowed hard, hesitated only briefly. She touched Mary's photo and another password box appeared. She tried 'LawsonFam01' again. Turned down, no entry, nothing doing. She folded her arms.

'That'll be the family code,' said Charlie. 'Ella or Freddie will have written it because one or both of their parents was incapable of remembering it. Imagine that. Now it's just the individual code word for Mary's account we have to guess.'

'I'm not guessing,' said Famie. 'That would be dumb.'

'You know Mary's password?' Sam was astonished, unbelieving.

'No. I know Sophie's password for the laptop. Seth gave it to her. It's just possible Seth gave Mary the same one.'

'Which is?' said Sam.

'First three words of the Egyptian national anthem.'

'Which are?' said Charlie.

'No idea,' said Famie.

Charlie Googled it first. 'It's "My country" three times,' she said, 'which in Arabic is "bilady" three times.'

She spelt it out, Famie typed it in the box.

'No numbers? No caps?' said Sam.

Famie hesitated, capitalized the first word, hit enter. Rejected.

'You might have only one guess left,' Sam said.

A small van shot past the end of their track, closely followed by another de luxe 4×4. Famie found herself holding her breath, expecting trouble, but the engines faded to nothing. For a brief moment the only sound in the car was the singing of blackbirds and thrushes.

'I'll call Sophie,' said Famie, once she was sure the birds were their only company.

She answered on the second ring.

'Sophie. The password for the laptop. Is it "bilady" three times?'

Somewhat surprised, Sophie came back with, 'Er, yes, that's right. Have you got the laptop back from the police?'

Famie ignored the question. 'Any capitals or numbers or fancy shit?'

'Just like it is on the page,' said Sophie. 'Capitals for all of them, commas after the first two.'

'Thanks. See you later.'

Famie hung up, then typed with precision. Pressed enter.

'Bingo,' she said.

'Bloody hell,' said Sam.

'Always knew you were a secret tech genius,' said Charlie. 'What happens now?'

Famie angled the screen so both Sam and Charlie could see. A generic blue wallpaper was scattered with icons, haphazardly spaced.

'Messy,' muttered Charlie.

Each icon was a newspaper app, the title of the paper typed in small letters below the logo. Famie scanned the familiar titles: *Times, Telegraph, Guardian, New York Times, Daily Jang, Times of India, Le Monde, Süddeutsche Zeitung, El País,* the *Australian, Washington Post*. The last badge was, on closer inspection, a black folder icon with 'locals' written underneath. She tapped the folder. A long list of web addresses appeared.

'Huh,' said Famie.

'That looks like every decent local paper in the country,' said Sam.

'And some not so decent,' said Famie. 'This tablet is a reference tool. It's all of her newspaper reading in one place.'

'Makes sense,' said Charlie.

'But no help for us,' said Famie.

'Depends what she's been reading,' said Sam. 'Browsing history?'

Charlie found it. The screen filled with links to articles and sites.

'We need to look at those,' said Famie. 'All of them. There must be something in Mary's reading which links her to what they were working on. We know her team were off-grid on this one but surely her reading material will show us something. Charlie, can you drive? I need to work on this.'

Charlie nodded, reached for her door. 'We're keeping the tablet?' she said.

'We're keeping the tablet,' Famie replied. 'Crime pays. It's my new slogan.'

54

STARTING AT THE top, Famie worked her way through Mary Lawson's reading list. Charlie was driving, her music playing. Sam and Famie sat together in the back, the screen between them. Some of the links were to newspaper websites, others to specific articles.

'They'll be in chronological order,' said Sam.

Famie tapped the first link. Her stomach flipped.

'Christ, it's May twenty-second,' she said. 'The last thing Mary read before she was killed.' The time and date of last viewing were displayed at the top of the page. 'Five twelve a.m. So she's reading this first thing, before leaving the house. The *Daily Jang*.'

'Where's that from?' said Charlie, glancing in the rearview mirror.

'Pakistan,' said Famie. 'Karachi. An English translation.' She scanned the story. 'It's a piece about some arrests of a terror cell near Jinnah International Airport. Joint operation between police and security forces. They arrested mainly

Uzbeks and some Europeans. Believed to be TTP again.' To Charlie, she added, 'That's the Taliban in Pakistan.'

No one spoke for a long time. Ariana Grande played on the speakers, the A425 traffic flowed easy, the parched fields of Northamptonshire radiated heat and dust.

Eventually Sam broke the silence. 'It doesn't necessarily mean anything,' he said, his words slow and uncertain. 'Not really. Just that she read the article before she left the house. Then when she got to London, she was killed. That's it.'

Charlie glanced at her mother in the mirror, ready to defer to her. Famie stayed quiet. She knew her daughter was about to disagree.

'True,' said Charlie. 'But doesn't it feel, I don't know, more significant than that? This is your world, not mine, but I'm just saying it shows what she was thinking just before she was killed.' Another quick look at Famie, then back to the road.

Famie sighed. 'It does,' she said. 'We all know it does. You're right, Sam, of course – technically it's a nothing. She could have been ordering wine, shoes or shirts, but one minute she's reading about a terror plot, the next she's killed in one. And she's been shagging the brother of an EIJ terrorist, for Christ's sake.'

'EIJ and the Taliban are—' began Sam.

'Not the same,' acknowledged Famie. 'Agreed. Obviously. Not the same.' She caught another look from Charlie. 'And I'd been shagging him too. Fair point.'

'I wasn't going to say.'

Famie smiled. 'Didn't need to. Maybe we should check the other articles. Look for a Waitrose delivery or something.'

Sam and Famie tapped and read. The next article was the *Times of India* on the same TTP story, adding the detail that Indian security forces were increasingly alarmed about the extent of Islamist collaboration. One of the arrested was a member of Lashkar-e-Jabbar, a fringe militant group from Srinagar.

'Heard of them?' asked Sam.

'Nope,' said Famie. 'But I never worked in India. I covered Lashkar-e-Jhangvi, the LeJ, out of Afghanistan, and the rest was all al-Qaeda. There were loads of fringe groups back then, breakaways, factions. I don't suppose much has changed.'

Charlie turned the music down. 'Is Mary reading this on the twenty-second too?' she asked.

Sam checked the screen. 'Yes. Just before the *Jang* story.' He tapped the screen again. 'She read the front pages of the big UK papers first, then the *Times of India*, then the *Jang* from Pakistan. Then left the house.'

Famie stared through her window. Petrol station, flower stall, dual carriageway, caravans. 'And waiting for her at Euston station, a man with a knife who wanted to stop her telling this bloody story she was writing,' she said.

'And he did,' said Sam. 'He succeeded. So now we need to tell it for her. And the other six.' A pause. 'Make that seven,' he said.

The rest of the links took Sam and Famie to a series of articles in a vast range of journals. Immigration statistics from Germany, education in Mexico, Cuban austerity, abortion clinics in the southern United States. They were precisely what Famie thought Mary would have been reading. And of absolutely no use to them.

'Mum, your phone's ringing,' said Charlie, passing it over her shoulder.

Famie took it, recognized the number.

'Hello, DC Hunter,' she said.

'Ms Madden. Where are you? Are you safe?' She sounded alarmed.

'I'm safe,' said Famie. 'Safe and hiding.'

'Ms Madden, I strongly urge you to report to the nearest

police station,' said Hunter. 'Hiding is not safe. Not a sensible option.'

'We're good,' said Famie. 'But thanks.' She could sense Hunter's exasperation.

'I'm afraid you're not "good". My colleagues in Exeter need to speak to your daughter urgently. It is a murder inquiry, Ms Madden, and if she has information—'

Famie cut across her. 'Sure. What's their number, we'll call them.' An audible sigh from Hackney.

'I'll text it to you, Ms Madden. But before you decide how safe you are, you should know there was an attempted break-in at your flat this morning.'

Famie felt the blood drain again. 'I'm sorry?' she said.

Sam heard the change of tone, put down the tablet. Charlie glared into the mirror.

'One of your neighbours disturbed two men outside your door. They ran off once they were discovered but there is no doubt that they were trying to force it open. The door jamb is splintered but the lock is sound.'

Famie's headache was back with a vengeance. 'You've been there?' she managed.

'I'm there now, Ms Madden. I'm outside your flat at the moment.'

'One minute,' she said, covered the phone. Famie cleared her throat. Spoke to the car. 'Two men tried to break into the flat. They ran off apparently.'

Charlie, wide-eyed, swerved slightly then pulled the car into a lay-by. She swivelled in the driver's seat, reached for her mother's hand. Sam, grim-faced, stepped outside.

'What time was this?' asked Famie.

'About six thirty,' said Hunter.

'And I seem to recall, DC Hunter, you advising me to stay put. Yes?' A brief silence. 'You wanted me to stay in the flat "for my own safety". And if we had followed your advice, my daughter and I might have been killed. That's about it, isn't it?'

'I can understand your concern,' said Hunter, recovering. 'It was, as it turned out, fortunate that your neighbour disturbed them.'

'And that we weren't there in the first place,' said Famie. She could feel the anger rising in her chest. 'Here's some wild speculation for you, DC Hunter. The man or men who killed Tommi Dara last night had more work to do. Me and Charlie were next on the list. As you say, fortunately they were interrupted, but even more fortunately we weren't there in the first place. You said stay, my daughter said go. Well. I think we'll stick with our own counsel, thank you. If you text me the Exeter number, Charlie will ring them. Meantime, we'll carry on hiding.'

She hung up, switched the phone off, then reached for Charlie's, turned hers off too. Sam followed suit.

'Thank you, Charlie,' whispered Famie. 'For getting us out of there.'

'They came for us?' said Charlie. The tremor in her voice had returned, unmistakable.

Famie nodded.

Two enormous trucks thundered past. The car shook. Sam continued his pacing.

'We're really not safe, are we?' said Charlie.

'We're really not,' said Famie.

She glanced around, looking at their surroundings for the first time. The Volvo was parked in the middle of a gravelly lay-by. A high, overgrown grassy bank ran the length of it, an overflowing rubbish bin stood at the exit. Two lanes of traffic her side of a metal barrier, two lanes the other side. And directly opposite, a mirror-image lay-by, complete with its own overflowing bin, was empty, save for an old sofa which had been dumped, then set on fire.

Famie felt suddenly exposed. A car that was stationary. A lay-by on a busy dual carriageway. Another friend murdered. A Charlie lookalike murdered. The killers trying to break into her flat.

'We should go,' she said. Famie opened her door to call Sam.

On the far side of the road, beyond the barrier, a grey BMW braked hard, changed lanes, then pulled into the opposite lay-by. It came to a stop a few centimetres short of the sofa.

'Sam!'

He'd seen it too, sensed the danger. He jumped in the front passenger seat and Charlie shot the car into the traffic. Horns and brakes accompanied her manoeuvre but they didn't care.

Famie knelt on the back seat, peering at the fast-disappearing BMW. 'Two men maybe,' she said. 'Could be one. Can't see. No idea. Could be nothing.' She slumped back into her seat. 'Good driving, Charlie.'

'Bad driving actually,' said Charlie, 'but effective. And it's two miles the other way before they can get off their side of the road. Assuming they want to.'

Sam twisted in his seat. 'We need to assume they want to. We need to assume everyone wants to. Let's get to the most anonymous hotel we can, meet up with Sophie, and hide the car.'

55

12.20 p.m.

THE TABLET SHOWED a map of Coventry and its surroundings. The white and green was rural, the dark grey was the city. The shading formed a dog's-head shape, with the hospital in the neck, Boxer Street in the jaw, the central ring road and cathedral at the base of the ears. Instructions were called out and Sam navigated them to the Coventry Travelrest, located on the neck-side of town. In a search for the most anonymous hotel he could find, this was the winner. Famie thought he had excelled himself. Its car park was a four-tier concrete multi-storey, the hotel the same. A matched pair.

They parked on the third floor in the space furthest from the lift and stairs. Behind a pillar. They traipsed to the stairwell, Sam followed by Charlie then Famie. They marvelled at the cold, dank air, miraculously untouched by the searing heat outside. Stepping over discarded nappies and needles, they swung open the fire door on the ground floor. Back to the inferno. A slabbed path took them across a piece of scorched grass towards the Travelrest. Box-like, with small windows and a khaki-and-brown colour scheme, Famie thought it was perfect. Hideous but perfect.

Sam pushed the revolving door. They took it in turns to step inside. The lobby was dark, swelteringly hot, and smelt of toilet disinfectant. Two lines of potted bamboos formed a path from the door to the front desk. Beyond the bamboo were a selection of uncomfortable-looking armchairs, a hot-drinks vending machine and a small bookcase with battered, abandoned paperbacks arranged horizontally. Old street maps had been hung on the walls. Light orchestral music played too loudly from invisible speakers. There were no other customers.

Sophie had booked adjoining rooms in a fake name, texting them confirmation of the numbers. Sam nodded at the young man behind the desk, then peered at his badge.

'Hello, Florin,' he said. 'We're staying with Miss Turner in 203 and 204.'

The boy frowned, then smiled. He offered a brown envelope which he shook to indicate it had keys inside. 'From Miss Turner,' he said. 'Nice lady. Have a good day.'

They avoided the lift. Two flights of stairs brought them to a low-ceilinged, right-angled corridor, carpet-tile floors, plain wooden doors. Same overpowering disinfectant. The lightest of knocks on 203, an audible shuffle behind the spy hole, and the door swung open. Sophie, in a printed fringe-line skirt and white T-shirt, stood aside to let them in then shut the door behind them. She hugged Famie and Sam, then, after an introduction, hugged Charlie too.

'Happy to see you guys. Like, seriously happy. This is a grim place to be on your own. The grimmest. Unless you want porn. Then it's a party.'

They all sat on the bed, Sophie and Famie against the headboard, Charlie and Sam at the foot. The room was clean, the bed comfy. There were two small bedside tables with old-fashioned angle-poise lamps, a threadbare brown carpet and an oversized flatscreen television next to a flimsy wooden door leading to 204. In the corner, a green plastic kitchen chair had been given a thin cushion. One small, sealed window looking on to the hotel's driveway was the inadequate source of the only natural light in the room. Above their heads, a single bulb with lampshade provided the rest.

Sophie was desperate for news of what had happened to Tommi. Many tears later she was up to speed on the murder, on Charlie, the visit from Lewis, the call from Hunter, the attack on the flat and Mary Lawson's tablet.

Sophie was astonished. 'You stole it?'

'Don't you start,' said Famie. 'I'll give it back. But we now know she was reading about a Pakistani terror op on the morning she was killed. We're still sifting the rest of the info.'

Sophie produced her laptop, spun the screen. 'So,' she said. 'According to Hari Roy, there's something planned for tomorrow. Whatever the attack is, Thursday is the day. We have to assume a geographic reason for being in Coventry. We're nineteen miles from Birmingham, twenty-four from Leicester.' She shrugged. 'Could be there, could be here. There's no obvious reason to attack Coventry but then there was no obvious reason to drive a truck through Nice either. But let's assume Hari is here for a reason.' She pointed at the street map she'd pulled up. 'There's a meeting at the synagogue on Barras Lane at three p.m., there's a controversial play at the Belgrade Theatre in town here called *Corpus Christi*, there's a prayer service at the cathedral.'

'Quite a mixed bag,' said Sam. 'What's the problem with the play?'

Sophie checked her screen. 'It features Jesus and his disciples as gay men living in Texas. The playwright got death threats, shows cancelled, you know how it goes. Some local churches are planning to protest.'

Famie looked doubtful. 'Sounds unlikely to be our thing. Unless they put the play on in the cathedral of course. That might be different. I think we're looking for something a whole lot grimier than protesting Methodists.'

'Agreed,' said Sophie. 'There's also this. Warwick University – Hari Roy's place of course – has an Islamic Society-organized anti-fascist demonstration. That's where the police presence will be.'

'You've spoken to them?' said Sam.

'Made an enquiry,' said Sophie. 'They said they were keeping "a watchful eye". Usual back-up available if needed. On standby.'

'That's the shortlist?' said Famie. She felt underwhelmed. It all seemed so trivial. Hardly the climax to, or the reason for, the murders of eight journalists. She had witnessed quite how mundane the worst terrorism could be, but this all seemed so particularly unremarkable.

'Yes, that's the shortlist,' said Sophie. 'If this was predictable, the police and security services would have it covered. Until then, this is what there is.'

Famie shrugged. A synagogue meeting, a play, a church service and a student demonstration. Or something else. Take your pick.

Charlie's hand was up. 'Excuse me.' She sounded annoyed, her face furrowed. 'You all sound like you're properly reporting on this. Like you all still work for IPS, which you don't. Apart from you, Sophie. Aren't we supposed to be hiding? We can't hide and expect to write anything. I don't for sure know if we're safe here, even if it is a shit hole. Maybe shit holes attract these guys. Maybe we should have gone to the Ritz Carlton instead. I don't know about you, maybe it's because

I'm not keeping busy like you are, but I'm still fucking terrified.' She flashed wide eyes to the room.

Famie briefly considered reaching a consoling arm towards her but quickly dismissed the idea.

'But I'm not writing anything,' said Sam, defensively, 'just trying to unravel a story. I think that if we can find out what Mary was investigating, we might find Hari Roy. That's the point.' Then, to Charlie, 'And I'm terrified too if that helps.'

'Me too,' said Sophie, one hand on her stomach, 'me too.' Then she added, 'Anyone checked the *Telegraph* today?'

'Christ, no,' said Famie, reaching for the tablet, tapping the icon. 'Should have got a copy this morning but what with one thing and another . . .'

'Friends getting killed, you mean,' said Sam.

'Yeah, that,' said Famie, scrolling fast for the personal ads. She found them, scanned at speed. 'Nothing,' she said. 'Bible verses, Viagra ads, lonely hearts. That's it. Great combo. Whatever Hari is doing, he's not posting any more.'

Sam slid off the bed, started his pacing.

'What?' said Sophie.

'So we should post again,' said Sam. 'When's the deadline?'

'Four p.m.,' said Famie. 'We've got plenty of time. Good call, Sam. Of course we should post. And we need to tell him we're here. Somehow.' She reached for her phone. 'Reckon I'm OK to switch on?'

'Depends how desperate the police are to find us,' said Sam, shrugging.

Famie shrugged too. She turned it on, tried to access her account.

'Huh,' she said.

'What?' said Sophie.

'No signal.' Famie hit some apps, tried to call Charlie. She looked at Sam. 'Phone's dead. No signal. Nothing.'

Sam reached for his phone, switched on, tapped the screen. He blanched. 'Me too.'

'Fuck,' said Famie. The dread had returned to her stomach.

'It's fine,' said Sophie. 'They're work phones. You quit your jobs. You don't get to use their phones any more. Mine's OK.'

'Mine too,' said Charlie. 'Panic over.'

Now Famie was up. She walked over to the tiny window that didn't open. 'Not really,' she said. She stared at the restricted view of the car park, the path and the brown grass. 'Maybe we need to lose the phones. All of them. Whether the police are desperate or not – and only Hunter seems at all interested – the fuckers can trace our phones. Maybe they're not safe. Maybe they were never safe.'

'And we don't even know which particular set of fuckers to be worried about,' said Sophie.

'All of them,' said Famie. 'Let's just stick with all of them.'

Sophie and Charlie exchanged glances. Then, with almost perfect timing, both removed the batteries and SIMs from their phones, throwing them on to the bed.

'Better?' said Sophie.

'Great,' said Sam, infuriated. 'Now we're operating totally blind. And deaf. How do we get our ad in the paper now? Ring it through the front desk? Trust Florin to get it right? Not sure that's entirely thought out.'

Her back to the bed, Famie missed Charlie reaching for the tablet.

'You were right, Mum,' she said, framing it between her hands.

'What?' said Famie, turning.

'Crime pays,' said Charlie.

56

Your favourite highway. Add 7,958,593,262. It's nearby.

THE MESSAGE SENT. One last message to Hari Roy before it was too late. Too late for who or what Famie wasn't sure, but too late anyway. The idea had occurred as soon as Charlie had found the way to access the tablet's phone number (touch apps, touch settings, scroll, touch status, scroll again).

Famie knew it was unlikely he would see her words. It seemed preposterous even to be sending them. But the personal ads had been his idea. It was worth another shot. And it was risk-free. She could do it from the room. She could do it from a number that couldn't be traced to her. Or any of them. She doubted Martin Lawson or his children knew the tablet's number. So if anyone called, it had to be Hari Roy.

She explained the message to Sophie. Charlie and Sam were there already.

'*Highway 61 Revisited*,' she said. 'Famous Dylan album. If he sees it, he'll understand. He adds the sixty-one to the seven billion figure and that's the tablet's number. He'll make the call. Whether he can do anything about it, that's something else altogether.' Famie glanced at the battery indicator which had just turned red. Nineteen per cent. 'Gonna need a charger,' she said.

'Surprised you didn't steal one of those too,' said Charlie.

'Next time,' said Famie. 'But we'll definitely need one. If Hari Roy has this number, we need the tablet charged. Always.'

'There's a shopping centre ten minutes away,' said Sophie, 'I'll go find one.'

Sam put his hand up. 'I'll come too. We'll buy some burner phones while we're at it.'

With Sophie and Sam gone, Charlie slept. Famie chained the door. Was room 203 of the Coventry Travelrest any safer than her flat? Yes, she thought. Probably. It depended on who was doing the looking. It depended on who was doing the killing. Her and Sam's phone disconnection was probably, as Sophie had said, the inevitable result of leaving IPS. No work, no work phone. Even so, it troubled her. Another trouble to go on top of the others. *I'm sorry for your troubles.* Isn't that what Andrew Lewis had said? Yeah, well. Not as fucking sorry as I am, she thought.

Famie eased her way back on to the bed, propped herself up next to her daughter. She stared at the tablet. How long would nineteen per cent last? Thirty minutes or three hours? She knew it would depend on the age of the tablet and how the battery had been charged but the overwhelming feeling of time running out won the day. She logged on again. Browsing history. Show all.

Eighteen per cent.

She wondered how much anyone's online reading really revealed about them. Famie took a deep breath. Maybe everything she read would be purely superficial and a waste of precious battery, but in the absence of any other clues, this was all she had. Fighting drowsiness, she hit the keys.

Articles from the world's press followed one after the other. The latest American presidential hopefuls. Climate campaigners in Canada. Declining law and order in South Africa. Useless, useless, useless, thought Famie. The future of the monarchy in Thailand, an oil scandal in Nigeria, a new chairman for the Bundesbank. All useless. Then three articles about the Real IRA and the Continuity IRA were followed by two on the Maoist Communist Party of Turkey. When that was followed by a CIA analysis of the People's Liberation Army of Manipur, Famie realized she wasn't sleepy any more. In all, Famie read fifteen articles about extreme far-left groups around the globe. Some of the organizations she knew, most she did not. The Thieves in Black, Anti State Justice and the Informal Anarchist Federation followed each other in a bloodcurdling parade of ideological ranting, guerrilla warfare and economic sabotage. This, Famie realized, was a thread. She checked the dates. Six weeks before her death, it was clear that Mary Lawson was extraordinarily interested in terror groups of the far left.

Eleven per cent.

With battery drainage seemingly accelerating, Famie was reading faster now. Racing the battery, racing the clock. She developed an eye for spotting the web addresses of the most promising articles. The Earth Liberation Front. The Communist Party of Turkey (Marxist-Leninist). Then came the Antifa movements, and Famie read with particular focus. If the university demonstration tomorrow was calling itself anti-fascist, surely this was the most likely target. All the articles shed light on organizations whose avowed aim was revolution and some of whose methods were violent. Bombs, kidnapping, extortion, torture, rape. All apparently excusable, defendable, desirable in the cause of revolution.

On and on Mary's reading went. A spate of recovered articles from the 1970s detailed the activities of the Red Army Faction, Baader-Meinhof and the Angry Brigade. Then it jumped to the present day and British police reports of the work of Red Action, Red Front and the Revolutionary Communist Party. People's wars, paramilitaries, vanguardism, insurrection, oppressors, uprisings, expulsions, assassinations.

Five per cent.

Then came the Islamists. These Famie did know. She skim-read insider accounts of life in every terror group in Pakistan, India, Afghanistan, Iran, Iraq, Egypt and Indonesia. There was a terrifying list of their links to radical preachers in the UK. Now the buzzwords were caliphate, pure religion, offensive jihad, kuffar, near enemy and far enemy. Videos of executions and drownings were offered, Famie declined.

Then, by accident, a train timetable. Famie was about to backtrack when she stopped short. Her hands recoiled, pulling back from the screen. 'You. Are. Joking,' she whispered. In place of the familiar newspaper fonts and photos, a poorly presented list of arrival and departure times lined up on the screen. She read aloud the words that were making her heart race. 'Your trains to Coventry,' she said.

She leant back against the bedstead.

Charlie stirred. 'What?' she said.

'Mary came to Coventry,' Famie said.

The next http address sealed it. Famie recognized it from their last team meeting in her flat. She clicked the link. The *Warwick Boar.* The student newspaper. 'Creating Conversation Since 1973'. And an article by Hari Roy.

'Mary came to Coventry, and she met Hari Roy,' Famie said, her voice an awed whisper.

Charlie sat up. 'What?' she said again.

'Mary came to Coventry,' said Famie, 'probably met Hari, maybe even hired him.'

'Hari Roy was working for Mary Lawson?' Charlie's voice managed to be scared and admiring in equal measure.

'Yes,' said Famie. 'That's what it looks like to me. How about that.'

She was sitting back, staring at the screen, when the tablet went black. Out of power. Out of time.

'Oh fuck,' said Famie.

57

1 p.m.

THE TRANSIT VAN had been parked for too long. Its occupants were hot, sweating heavily and restless. Six citizens sat in the back, two up front. The rear of the van was seatless, a large green rug and a brown blanket the only attempts to provide comfort. They sat three and three. Hari sat by a wheel arch, with Collins wedged next to him on one side, and a stocky man with a tuft of red hair on the other. On the other side sat two white men and one brown. Hari remembered the brown-skinned man was called Kamran but he'd forgotten the others. Kamran was lean, no more than twenty, clean-shaven, and looked as though he'd just stepped out of a college lecture. The white men were very white, one with an arm full of tattoos, the other with a mouth full of uncomfortably protruding teeth. The killers of 22 May. The only light came from two darkened windows at the rear of the van. Burger and chip wrappings were scattered everywhere, the smell of vinegar and grease working hard to obscure the stale sweat of the occupants. They knew they had to wait. They just didn't want to wait in a sauna.

Tattoos cracked the door an inch, and the slightest of breezes drifted inside.

Hari closed his eyes, sat on his hands. The men he was sharing the van with had executed seven between them. Maybe more. Slit throats, stabbed lungs and hearts. It's what they did. That and God knows what else besides. Hari wondered which of them had killed poor Mary. Teeth guy? Tattoos? Kamran? It didn't matter. Each of them could have done it and any of them could have been tasked to kill his sisters too. He'd known this moment was coming for weeks, but now it was here he wondered if he'd get by without vomiting. Wondered if he'd be able to stop his hands from shaking. Wondered whether he would make it out alive.

He could hear the muffled talk from the front. Driver and passenger. The lighter voice was Binici's, the heavier basso profundo was from a powerhouse of a man called Gregor. The London Citizens' obvious leader, he radiated menace. Mousey-blond beard, bald, with grey, darting, intelligent eyes. A boxer's nose, a boxer's biceps. To Hari, their words were indecipherable, reduced to a low rumble by the metal panel that divided them, but the raised voices, the to-and-fro, were unmistakable.

They had left the house in Boxer Street as soon as Binici had briefed the newly arrived London Citizens. All of his comments had been addressed to their leader. In front of him, Binici had become deferential, his whole manner transformed. He had poured them all water in the kitchen, then sat himself on the worktop. He had explained that the fash were out front. That there were door-to-door enquiries and that they may well return. The decision was obvious, but it was Gregor who had taken it. They had to leave, immediately.

Collins, Binici and Hari had each led the way in twos and threes. Hari had been teamed with Tattoos and Kamran. Binici went with Gregor and Teeth. Collins had taken Red Head.

Her route took them from the courtyard over three fences to a twisting alley. They had regrouped at adjoining cafés, staying in their 'teams' while Binici and Gregor retrieved the van from its parking space near Boxer Street. Teeth had stayed at a table by himself. No words were said. When the van drove past the cafés then parked in a side street, the 'teams' took it in turns to amble away, then climb inside.

That was three hours ago. Since then, the van appeared to have been driving in circles. City centre, cobbled streets, ring road, narrow lanes. And now not moving at all.

'Recce or accommodation?' said Hari.

It was a question intended for Collins but it was Kamran who answered.

'It's somewhere to stay,' he said. 'Your house is bad. You guys fucked it all up. Now we need somewhere.'

Hari clocked the accent.

'No one fucked up,' said Collins, her voice casual, controlled. 'There was an accident in our street. The police came to call. It was unfortunate. End of.'

Kamran looked unimpressed. He looked away. A slight shake of his head. 'This van, this stink, all of it, says you fucked up.'

OK, leave Sara alone, thought Hari, we can do this inside. Or not at all maybe.

'You from Karachi?' he asked.

Kamran blinked, surprised. 'Not any more,' he said.

Well that's that conversation shut down, Hari thought.

From the driver's seat, the sound of a phone ringing. Quickly answered. Hari exchanged glances with Collins. No phones, no computers, no technology. They were the rules. Simple, effective. And now broken. He strained to hear the half of the conversation that was leaking from the cab, then realized everyone was doing the same.

'Accommodation,' said Collins, finally answering Hari's

question. 'That's my guess. We need to be off the streets. We need to hide.'

'We need to rehearse,' said Kamran.

Hari's stomach flipped again.

The engine fired and Tattoos slammed the back door shut. The van spun round, Collins leaning into Hari, her head touching his. Then when the manoeuvre had been completed, she stayed there. Hari held his breath. They'd been butted up against each other anyway, legs and torsos pressed together, but that could be put down to the cramped conditions. Now she was sending the signal. Opposite, Kamran, Teeth and Tattoos all noticed. Collins straightened up.

Job done.

Sara Collins' guess had been correct. Accommodation had been found. When the doors opened again, the van had been backed on to a tarmac drive and Hari and the others eased themselves into the comparative cool of the afternoon. Hari stretched, prised his shirt from his skin, took a three-sixty. They were in the heart of an industrial estate studded with drab, functional sixties warehouses fronted with high roll-up garage doors. Large painted signs pointed the way to companies offering tyres and motor repairs, pharmaceutical packaging and furniture restoration. The network of roads was busy, vans and cars of all sizes ferrying goods and customers to the appropriate outlet. Across an enormous roundabout, the other side of what Hari imagined was the ring road, two ugly concrete boxes. One a hotel, the other its car park.

Binici and Gregor had scored two large rooms above a packaging company. They formed the first and second floors of the building, linked by a single wooden staircase. Both rooms were light and high-ceilinged. Both had a large steel-framed central window, metal divides running between smaller panes of glass. On the first floor, many had been smashed, keeping the temperature bearable, but the ancient glass on the second floor had, miraculously, stayed intact. Out of range maybe. As a result, it was an oven. All the floorboards were scuffed, deeply grooved, and in places covered by battered rugs and blankets. Hundreds of flies and a sharp, pungent smell suggested dead rats hidden beneath. Floor one had some stacked wooden tables and chairs, floor two had two piles of mattresses. There was no kitchen. The only toilet was off the stairwell.

Binici, as sweaty as Hari had ever seen him, clapped his hands. 'Citizens! Gather, please! We have history to make.'

Hari shuffled forward. Tattoos stood to his right, Kamran to his left. He smelt Collins behind him, felt her brush against his shoulder. Gregor leant against a wall. The rest of them gathered round Binici like he was some old street preacher handing out salvation.

Binici's eyes were glowing. 'Tomorrow we make history,' he said, making sure he made eye contact with each of them in turn. 'For the comrades, citizens, brothers and sisters who, through the long years of struggle, would have died for the opportunity we will be given, we will strike hard. The work is heroic. The work is ferocious. But the work is glorious.'

Stump speech, thought Hari. He watched his fellow citizens. Revolutionaries or mercenaries? he wondered.

Binici was into his stride. 'We have rejected the twin errors of sectarianism and opportunism. We are the vanguard,' he declared, 'a revolutionary base camp to collapse this nation and build a new one. Tomorrow we can jump-start the revolution.'

Kamran and Red Head applauded first, everyone else joined in.

'We embrace the butcher!' called Binici. 'We change the world!'

Applause from everyone now. Hari started his clapping on 'butcher' just to be sure he wasn't left behind.

Binici checked his watch. 'Finally. Three things now. Food and drink are on their way. Final training in an hour. And we need to move the van from outside. It advertises our whereabouts, obviously. There's a large multi-storey across the way.' He threw the keys at Hari. Hari caught them. 'You and Sara, please. Be quick but be careful. Park it away from the ramps. Watch for the fash.'

Hari drove the Transit, Collins rode in the passenger seat. She held on to the seatbelt strap as he swung the van around the roundabout. 'Steady as she goes, citizen. We don't have to be that quick.' Hari took it down some revs. He hadn't noticed his speed. He steered on to the service road that ran past the hotel, slowing as they passed its revolving front door. A striking woman with a head of blonde curls and a plain man in drab clothes were just leaving. He kept the van at five miles an hour all the way into the gloom of the multi-storey.

58

THE GROUND FLOOR was full. The first and second had a few spaces. Hari carried on up to the third. Just the one car was parked up, a black Volvo sat in the far corner. He went to the opposite end, tucked the van behind a pillar. Much like the Volvo had done. Hari killed the engine. Neither he nor Collins moved. They both stared at the concrete wall in front of them. This is it then, thought Hari. When I walk back into that warehouse, it's a killing party. He could hear Collins breathing heavily. He wondered if she was having second thoughts.

'It's going to be knives,' she said.

'Oh?'

'Binici told me. Gregor told him.'

'I see.' Hari felt sick.

'The day before is the worst,' she said, still staring out of the windscreen. 'Doubts. Nerves. Fear.'

'How do you know?'

A long pause. 'Zak told me.'

Dead Zak.

'So you . . . haven't done this before?'

'No. But this is my path, Hari. When I was seventeen I met Anna Mendelssohn. You know her?' Hari shook his head. 'Member of the Angry Brigade. Anarchist. Communist. Went to prison for trying to set off bombs in the early seventies. They targeted Cabinet ministers, judges, civil servants, police, prison officers, big property companies. These people are the enemy, Hari, and you can't get rid of them by voting. You get rid of them by fighting. She was clear-sighted. She knew what had to be done. She was consumed with a passion for revolution and was prepared to kill for it. I am too. Binici might be a prick but he's right about the butcher. The Angry Brigade knew that.'

Hari stayed silent.

Collins undid her shirt. Hari gripped the steering wheel. *What are you doing?*

Above her left breast was a tattoo of an automatic rifle clasped by two hands. The first hand was circled by the gender symbol for woman, the second hand by the gender symbol for man.

'It's the Angry Brigade logo,' she said.

'Oh,' said Hari.

'Seen it before?'

'No. Well, maybe in books. Not . . . in the flesh as it were. Sorry, I didn't mean—'

'You're fine. Don't worry.'

Collins left her shirt unbuttoned.

Hari couldn't believe what was happening. Collins had been consistently cold to him. Always belittling, occasionally cruel. He forced himself to look away. Back to the concrete. There were cracks running through it like a river delta. A meandering line of rust-coloured residue ran from top to bottom.

'Have you heard of terror sex?' she asked.

He hadn't. 'That's not a thing,' he said.

'Oh it is,' she said. 'Before and after. If you choose it, it's fine. If someone demands it, it isn't. It's biological, Hari. End of the world stuff.'

She turned to face him. He made himself turn to face her. She took off her shirt.

'Would you like me to show you?' she said.

Hari nodded.

59

IT TURNED OUT there was such a thing as terror sex. Loud, wild and brief. Very loud. Extravagantly wild. Incredibly brief. All the fear, rage and grief of the last eight weeks overwhelmed Hari.

Afterwards, he apologized. Collins told him it had been just fine by her. Full mount and submission. They had rearranged the rug and blanket so that no one would notice. Not that they thought anyone would be looking.

They walked back from the car park in silence. Hari and Collins were back in the warehouse within sixteen minutes.

60

2.45 p.m.

AFTER PIZZAS, AND with the room still smelling of cheese, garlic and steamed cardboard, Binici nodded to Collins. 'You're up,' he said.

She jumped to her feet, looked at the men. The large windows behind her faced south-east. Despite the decades of grime, there was a hazy intensity to the light. With the door shut and only the feeblest of breezes coming through the broken windows, everyone had chosen to sit in the shade.

Sat against a wall, Hari was between Teeth and Kamran. Then came Tattoos and Red Head. Collins, bouncing on her feet, was flanked by Binici and Gregor, who held a small holdall. She stood for a moment, hands on hips. A power stance. Grey shirt, denim shorts. She pulled her hair back into a short ponytail, snapped a rubber band around its base. Hari noticed she'd missed a button on her shirt. The second one up from her waist.

'I teach martial arts,' she said. 'Silat from Indonesia, Systema Spetsnaz from Russia, American Marine Corps martial arts and tantojutsu from Japan. I know you don't need to be told how to use knives but tomorrow will be intense. Gregor thought some close-quarter practice might be in order.'

She looked to Gregor, who unzipped the holdall.

'You each have a knife,' she said. 'Italian stilettos.' She held up a twelve-centimetre black handle finished with steel. The merest whisper of a click and the blade appeared, a nine-centimetre black-finished bayonet. 'These are AGA Campolin Zero Bayo Leverlock automatic knives. Carbon-fibre handles. Böhler N690 steel blade. It has rock-solid blade lock-up, and snappy automatic deployment. I don't know where we'll use them yet, we'll get told that soon enough. But get to know the knife. Feel the balance and weight. If you've brought your own, fine. But these will be better.'

Gregor dispensed the knives as though they were the Holy Eucharist. Slowly. Reverently. Personally. He even muttered each recipient's name as they took their gift. Binici first, then Red Head, Tattoos, Kamran, Hari and Teeth. Hari stared at his, weighed it, inspected it. It had a textured and shaped handle with stainless-steel bolsters at each end. A small lever snapped the blade into position. Hari thought it managed to be both the most beautiful and the most terrifying thing he'd ever held in his hand. Next to him, Teeth seemed impressed too. He whistled his admiration as he flicked the lever. Hari watched as the blade sprang from the handle then was reset and sprung again. Teeth ran his finger across the cutting edge of the open blade. Another whistle.

Collins had collected the pizza boxes and now lined them up, square face on, against the far wall. Hari counted ten in total. Some of the lids fell open, spilling crusts and used paper napkins to the floor. She closed them up again, removed the rubbish. 'Throwing practice,' she said. 'The Russians have each recruit trained to hit the target three consecutive times from four metres away. Help yourselves.'

Teeth, Red Head and Kamran jumped to their feet, blades

in hand. Hari had put his knife down when his hands started to shake. He closed his eyes. Folded his arms. Tried to make it look as though he was meditating before the rigours of the next twenty-four hours. But the reality was that he felt he was crashing. He couldn't stop the nightmare. He couldn't end it without risking the lives of Millie and Amara. If he walked, he disappeared; if he talked, a knifeman would pay a visit. Probably one of these knifemen in front of him now, with their new Böhler N690 steel blades. The sound of pizza boxes being ripped to shreds made him shudder.

And Collins had used him, he knew that. She had needed sex with someone, and he was the safest option. He had said yes, so it was his fault. And it had worked for her. She had smiled a lot since their return. But it hadn't worked for him. He felt drained, exploited. He re-ran her little foreplay speech about the Angry Brigade – it turned his stomach. When the moment came, she would be a butcher too.

And tonight they were supposed to be 'together'. To protect her from rape. Or gang rape. That was the logic of what she had said. Someone had warned her. She wasn't taking any chances.

Hari heard her exclaim and opened his eyes. Collins and Kamran were sparring. He was advancing, step by step, knife in his right hand. She was backing away, balls of her feet, biding her time. Smiling. Only one winner here, Hari thought. Kamran began an attack, turning, reducing his angle, but she had read his body language, spotted the feint. His move was telegraphed. She crashed a fist on his forearm and he dropped the knife. Then, for good measure, she tipped him off his feet. Full mount and submission. The room's floorboards shuddered and cracked. Hari closed his eyes again. She wouldn't be needing any help from him.

When the pizza boxes were shredded and Collins had fought most of the men, Gregor called everyone to the middle of the room. He had stacked enough of the chairs to reach a height of about one and a half metres. The holdall that had contained the knives was perched on the top. Zipped up. Hari stood behind Kamran and Teeth. They could spread out more now. The shaded section of the room had increased to around seventy per cent, the temperature had eased back a few notches.

When he had everyone's attention, Gregor unzipped the bag, produced a phone. Presumably, thought Hari, the one he was using in the van earlier. He turned it on, tapped the screen three times then propped it up against the back of the top chair. The screen was the size of a small book, the definition of the video he had paused was crystal clear. A ripple of excitement passed through the men. Hari felt faint. Gregor smiled. He relaxed. He knew what was coming. Everyone knew what was coming.

'A short film,' he said. He spoke slowly in measured, accented English. 'The camera work is shaky. But you will understand I think. You will "get the picture".' He smiled again, apparently pleased with his words.

Hari braced as Gregor hit play.

The film began with CCTV images of a shopping centre, a wide shot. The time code in the top left corner said it was from last July. Hari guessed it was Africa. Kenya maybe. Busy, prosperous. He recognized some big chain store names. Then there was a commotion, people running and falling, and the screen switched to a different angle. Three masked men were running amok, stabbing and slashing as they went. The attack was indiscriminate. An elderly man and woman at a café table both had their throats cut; the man falling forward on to the table, the woman collapsing backwards off her seat. A shopworker who ran to their aid was stabbed in the stomach. A different camera. Two boys in football tops lay on top of each other, blood pooling from their necks. A different camera. Two men fought back with cutlery they had grabbed from a nearby table; both were slashed from chest to navel. Each attack, each murder, was greeted with cheers and applause in the room. Hari clapped too – it was something to do with still-shaking hands.

Next on the screen, a different location. A western street. It looked to Hari like it could be France but the film was grainy and shaky. Shopfronts and market stalls, shoppers and tourists. A heavy truck appeared on the roundabout at the bottom of the picture. It orbited three times then, accelerating, careered off the road towards the crowds. Few had time to react, to move, to run. A bowling ball through skittles. The camera didn't see those who disappeared beneath the wheels, just those who were flung into the air. The camera operator could be heard cheering. In front of Hari, Kamran and Teeth cheered too.

When he was sure no one was looking at him, Hari shut his eyes. So he only heard the sounds of the last film. Only heard the screams of the synagogue congregation as they were attacked, the muffled cries, the shouts, the crying and finally the gunfire that finished it all. Hari felt his balance go, his legs start to give way. He knew he mustn't faint but also knew he was going to anyway. He opened his eyes as he started to fall, then two arms slipped around him. It was Collins. She made it look like they were embracing.

'Thanks,' he said as they both sat against the wall.

'We're quits,' she said.

Quits? he thought. We're trading now?

He turned to remonstrate but she had leapt to her feet. Binici, Gregor and most of the others had too. They had a visitor. A squat, round-shouldered man with his black hair in a bun stood by the door in the remaining pool of sunlight. Dark glasses. Doughy face. Black suit trousers and white shirt. Hari watched the London Citizens greet him, one by one shaking his hand or nodding an acknowledgement. One of them, he assumed. Probably their boss. Had other things to do – until now. Binici introduced him as Amal Hussain.

The man peered into the room, looking for those he didn't know. He ignored Collins. His eyes flicked between Binici and Hari.

'We have a traitor here,' he said.

61

HARI STUMBLED TO his feet, his guts churning and bile in his mouth. Hussain was patrolling, snarling. 'Red alert, my friends. We have a red alert. We must look for traitors everywhere.' He walked towards Hari, his eyes narrowing. 'And you're the one I don't know anything about.'

'I'm Hari Roy.'

'Well, Hari Roy,' said Hussain, stopping just a few centimetres away, 'I'm looking for journalists. I know the people in this room. I don't know you. So my guess is, it is you. You are the journalist.' He spat the word with contempt. 'A fucking IPS fucking journalist like that other fucking guy!'

Eyeball to eyeball. Hari's back was against the wall. Kamran was to his right, Gregor on his left. The others stood behind them.

Deny, deny, deny. Confession means death. You've got a knife.

Hari tried to speak but his mouth was too dry. His tongue was sandpaper.

Hussain had more. 'We found him, you know,' he continued.

'He was with us for quite a while. He was good, we thought. Committed, we thought. Howells, he said his name was. A citizen. A comrade. But mainly . . .' Hussain pushed his fist into Hari's chest, pinning him to the wall. 'Mainly he was a fucking traitor. Kamran here found him sending messages to that Lawson bitch. Kamran slit her and slit Howells. Now he can slit you.'

Kamran stepped up on cue, a satisfied smile on his face.

So, it was Kamran.

Hussain fished in his pocket, pulled out an old-fashioned Polaroid photo, held it in front of Hari's eyes. The shiny oblong of paper contained an image which caught Hari's breath. Caught within its white frame were the unsmiling faces of Millie and Amara Roy. Not posed, taken from distance. It was a photo he hadn't seen before. The twins' hair was shorter, styled differently. It was new.

'I decided to get to know you a little better. Your sisters,' he said. 'I stopped by.'

Hari closed his eyes, despair and fury welling from deep inside him. He forced himself to stay silent. He knew this man would talk more.

'Cute kids,' Hussain said.

Hari nodded, opened his eyes.

'Good,' said Hussain. 'We agree. So. You can tell me what you know about IPS and I'll get Kamran to deal with you. Just you. Or you can fight us. Deny everything. Then Kamran gets to visit your sisters too.' He held up the photo. 'Like I said. Cute kids.'

Hari forced some deep breaths. He recalled Binici's words from what seemed like years ago. *We don't deal. Arguing is pointless. Negotiating is pointless.*

So Hari found his voice. It sounded like a strangled roar. 'Wait! This is bullshit! I am not a journalist. I am not a traitor. I am Hari Roy, student, grandson of Indian revolutionaries and proud citizen.' He cast his eyes around the room – caught Binici's frown – but his words were for the thug in front of him. 'I have no idea who you are, sir. I am sure you have carried the struggle with pride but you are wrong. When the fash attacked our group, a radiation attack, it was me they went for. I was in hospital! I can tell you that right here and right now, you have the wrong man.'

Hussain held his gaze. Kept his fist in place too. 'I think I have the right man. Was it just a coincidence that you joined a few weeks after the Howells boy? It can only be you. Lawson hired you, didn't she?' He waved Kamran closer. 'Ear to ear,' he said, 'just like last time. There is nothing else to say.'

'Wait!' called Binici. He stepped forward a few paces.

Hussain glanced round. 'What is it?' He looked, and sounded, irritated. A man not used to being told to wait. 'You have something to say?' The threat was clear: Binici was in the dock too.

Binici looked nervous, adjusted his glasses, put both hands in his pockets. 'It was *us* who recruited him. Sara found him on campus. He wanted to join us. We did have a traitor. You are right to be suspicious. But I dealt with him. Two days back.'

Hussain turned to face Binici. 'Dealt with?'

'He's dead.'

'Who was he?'

'His name was Zachary Bourton-Jones. Zak BJ, he called himself.'

'How do you know it was him?' Hussain sounded unconvinced. 'Tell me. Make it fast.'

Binici took another step forward. 'He had a history of fascist sympathies. He kept his contacts. And he betrayed us. It is true that Hari was attacked with radiation. He only just survived. Zak was the traitor. No question.'

Hussain turned back to Hari. 'You look scared,' he said.

Hari nodded. 'I am scared, sir.'

'Scared of being found out?'

'No. But scared of you, sir, and scared about what we have to do tomorrow.'

'Convince me,' said Hussain. 'Because you may not look like Howells, but you do *smell* like Howells. If you see what I mean.'

Hari had no time to think. He ran to the stacked chairs, climbed on top. Kamran was at his heels but Hussain called him back, saying, 'Let him speak.'

A preacher in a pulpit. A sceptical congregation. And the only soul he had to save was his own. Hari took off his shirt. Took a breath.

'Tomorrow we have a job to do,' he said. 'We don't know what it is yet but we will follow the instructions to the letter. I am a citizen first. I am committed to our revolutionary path.' From his pocket, Hari produced his knife. His Böhler N690 steel stiletto. The blade was folded.

Kamran made to move forward but Hussain kept him back.

Hari held the knife to his chest. Right where he remembered Collins' tattoo was. 'We at Boxer Street were always reminded of the words from that play. Embrace the butcher. Because that's what we are doing. So . . .' Hari was flying, words spilling out of him. Out of control. He flicked the lever. The blade locked into position. He stuck the tip of the knife against his skin and pushed and pierced. Blood pooled, then ran down his chest. 'Embrace the butcher!' he yelled, and carved a deep horizontal line into his skin. The pain was blinding and immediate. He stuck the tip in again and cut two more lines, one below the other. It opened his skin like a zipper. Three parallel bloody lines, which he now joined with a vertical.

A capital E.

Next he carved a vertical with a horizontal on top.

A capital T.

Murmurs from the floor. They got it now.

The horizontals bled more than the verticals. They hurt just the same. Hari wobbled. Corrected his stance, restored his balance. His waistband was soaked. He could feel the blood running down his legs. His breaths were becoming deeper. His hands were steady.

One more vertical. Two more quick flourishes. A capital B. He had finished. He stood, ecstatic, agonized, chest heaving, blood running in three streams down his torso.

'ETB – embrace the butcher,' he said, his voice catching on the last word. He pointed the bloodied knife at his startled audience. He swung it left and down till it pointed at Kamran. 'Your turn.'

62

BLOOD WAS IN the air. Gregor's carnage film followed by Hari's self-mutilation produced a tidal wave of cutting. Everyone but Hussain and Binici removed their shirts and cut 'ETB' into their skin. A new knife. A new blooding. A new bonding. There were no showers, no bandages, no antiseptic creams. The blood dried where it had run. For thirty minutes, bellowing, whooping and chest-beating filled the warehouse, the fear of discovery blown away by testosterone, adrenalin and pain.

Hari was startled by what he had done, stunned at the reaction. Kamran had cut his own letters as soon as Hari had suggested it. The others had swiftly followed. It wasn't that they didn't want to be left behind, they had wanted to join in. A herd branding. His own knife work was precise, the scar would be neat, and he was off the hook. Gregor's was bigger, the letters longer. His 'B' was botched, looking like a childish, sideways M, but no one cared and certainly no one thought of pointing it out. Collins had cut her left forearm. She waved it at Hari, and mouthed a 'wow' from across the room. Hari could see that Binici, too, was thrilled. He wore a strange, teeth-filled, beatific smile.

Hussain, however, was torn. Hari could tell he liked the bonding, approved of the pre-battle psychology. The troop camaraderie. But throughout all the bizarre ceremonies his eyes kept coming back to Hari. He had barely moved. Around him his men were strutting and roaring, but there was a stillness about this new arrival that Hari found chilling. Kamran, Hari's new best friend, had whispered his name.

Shadow had claimed the whole room by the time Hussain, Gregor and Binici returned to speak to Hari. Red Head and Teeth had crashed on the mattresses upstairs, Tattoos and Kamran were perched against the wall, under the windows, arguing about something with Collins. Hari was about to stand when Hussain approached, but the Egyptian motioned him to stay where he was. Hussain sat in front of him, cross-legged. Binici and Gregor stayed standing.

'A neat trick,' said Hussain, nodding.

'It wasn't a trick,' said Hari.

Hussain tilted his head from side to side, as though weighing the evidence. Maybe yes, maybe no. Maybe a traitor, maybe not. 'So you say.'

'I've explained.'

'You have. And your heroics were impressive.'

'They weren't heroics.'

The head tilt again. Maybe yes, maybe no. 'We'll see.'

Hari felt Hussain's gaze as a physical weight. He had bought himself time but maybe that was all. Although Binici had spoken for him, his judgement was under scrutiny too.

Hussain produced the photo again. The white-framed Polaroid. Millie and Amara. Not smiling. He folded it in two, placed it in Hari's top pocket. 'You will be with us for tomorrow, Mr Roy. We are too close now for changes. The men want you there. They expect to embrace the butcher.

We can all embrace the butcher.' He patted the folded photo. 'But you should know that your sisters will be there too. I will see to it. An insurance policy for me. And I'll be right behind them myself.' He tried a smile. 'Just in case it was a trick,' he said.

63

AS THE LAST of Wednesday's light leaked from the warehouse, Amal Hussain told the Coventry and London Citizens where Thursday's attack would take place, when it would happen and who would be attending. He wished them a good night.

No one expected to sleep well.

64

10.34 p.m.

DON HARDIN CRADLED his baby daughter over his shoulder. He hummed her a tune as he did laps of his lounge. She snuffled and coughed a little but seemed settled. He inhaled what was left of her new baby smell. Wipes and nappy cream was some of it certainly, leftover amniotic fluid was, apparently, the rest. He'd looked it up. She was asleep for now, his wife too. Tomorrow was busy, he'd be out all day, so it was his turn. All night. The bottles were ready, the spare bed made up. His vestments were ironed and packed, his day clothes laid out. Tomorrow he'd wear the shorts and T-shirt for the walk to the cathedral, then stay in the cassock and alb for the service and the demonstration.

'Demonstration.' He said the word out loud. Trying it on for size. 'Protest,' he said. 'Protester.' The smallest of smiles. He whispered to his daughter. 'Your daddy is a "protester". How about that?' He stroked her few silky strands of black hair till they were flat. 'I know the bishop will quote St Paul to me. He loves that letter to the Romans.' A few more strokes. 'He'll say, "Let every person be subject to the authorities." Then he'll say,

"The person who resists such authority resists the ordinance of God."' Hardin sucked in his cheeks until he thought he looked like the bishop. 'What a pompous arse he is.'

The television lit the room, sound off, subtitles on. The local news carried a brief item about the university's precautions for Thursday's demonstrations. The vice-chancellor said he had confidence in the police and the good reputation of his students. Three men in hoods promised a day to remember.

Hardin kissed his daughter's head and, eyes still on the screen, muttered a blessing he remembered from college.

'May the nourishment of the earth be yours, may the clarity of light be yours, may the fluency of the ocean be yours, may the protection of the ancestors be yours.'

His daughter stirred. Soon she would be keening for a bottle. He held her a little tighter.

65

11.30 p.m.

FAMIE AND CHARLIE took the bed in 204, Sophie and Sam the bed in 203. Sam offered to sleep on the floor, Sophie told him not to be stupid. They lay with as much space between them as the barely-double mattress allowed. Sam gave a rueful laugh.

'What?' said Sophie, eyes closed already, hands over her stomach.

'If Jo knew I was in bed with Sophie Arnold,' he said, 'she'd melt the walls.'

Sophie turned, propped herself up on one elbow. Pushed hair from her eyes. 'Me in particular or just someone from work in general?'

Sam smiled. 'Oh, you in particular,' he said.

Sophie frowned. 'Really?'

'Yes, really.'

'I'm a threat?'

'Apparently.'

'Hmm,' said Sophie. 'Anyway, I think we're actually "sharing a bed" which is not technically the same as "in bed with".'

'I'll let you explain the difference to Jo,' Sam said. 'Assuming she hasn't walked out.'

The connecting door between 203 and 204 was shut, but it was made from the cheapest, thinnest plywood and in the silence they could occasionally hear Famie and Charlie's muted conversation. Only Sam had his bedside light on, its bulb struggling to illuminate anything other than its own shade. Underneath the curtained window, two new burner phones were plugged in and charging, their flashing green lights distractingly bright in the near-darkness.

'You don't really think Jo's gone, do you?' said Sophie, quieter now.

'She was pretty mad when I left,' said Sam. 'But I guess probably not. We should be OK.'

He switched the light off. The two phones blinked more brightly, in sequence like an aeroplane's wing. Sophie watched them for a while, swallowed twice, then spoke into the darkness.

'There's something you should probably know,' she said. 'Before whatever is going to kick off, kicks off.'

Sam turned over, the sheets tightening between them. Sophie's tone was serious, scared even. He waited.

'Go on,' he said.

'I'm pregnant,' she whispered. 'And Seth is the father. Was the father.'

Sam sat up, snapped the light back on. Mouth open, eyes wide. Sophie didn't move. She lay sarcophagus-style, hands folded above the sheet, eyes squeezed shut.

'The dark was fine,' she muttered.

Sam snapped the light off again. Lay back down. 'I don't know what to say, Sophie,' he said. 'Help me out here.' He stared at the ceiling. Floundering.

'You don't need to say anything,' she said. 'I just wanted you to know.'

'OK,' said Sam. 'Cos if the lights were on and there were other people here, I'd give you a hug. But under the circumstances . . .'

'A sympathy hug or congratulatory hug?'

'That's what I need help with.'

A long silence. A muffled Famie next door. Traffic on the ring road. Sam reached out, took one of Sophie's hands. She took it in both of hers. Three hands on her stomach. They were still there when Sophie fell asleep.

66

FAMIE HADN'T SHARED a bed with her daughter since Charlie was eight. A nearly empty bottle of supermarket Rioja sat on Famie's bedside table, half a portion of cold pad thai on Charlie's. A small plastic fan was perched on the windowsill, set to maximum. Propped up against the bedstead, Famie's head was turned to face the ineffectual breeze. In her hands she had the recharged tablet, Charlie had their two new burner phones. One in each hand.

'I'm putting our numbers in,' she said. 'It's failsafe. Three numbers only. Even you can use it, Mum.'

Famie missed the jibe, her eyes shut, sleep closing in fast. She knew Charlie was talking, just had no idea what she was saying. Famie made some sounds which she hoped were reassuring. Then she caught something about 'dad' and was hauled back to consciousness in an instant.

'What about him?' she said, surfacing quickly.

'I should add him to mine,' said Charlie. 'His phone number. To this.'

She waved the black flip phone in front of Famie, who sat

up, wiped her face with her hands and returned her daughter's gaze.

'Yes, you should,' she said. 'You certainly should.' She paused for a beat. 'He won't answer of course. Or call you back. But go for it. Why not.'

'Seriously?' said Charlie. 'Even now? Even here?' She was clearly exasperated. 'It's a security thing, for Christ's sake, Mum. Someone tried to kill me, someone did kill Tommi, then they tried to break into your flat. In case it all goes tits up tomorrow and Hari Roy turns out to be a mafia hitman, I thought I should put my father's number in my phone.'

'And I'm agreeing.'

'Sure you are.'

Famie closed her eyes again. Her husband had walked out two years ago, disappearing from her life for six months. When he had resurfaced, in New York, he had a publisher girlfriend and a son aged eighteen months. Famie was happiest either insulting him or forgetting him altogether. She knew she shouldn't begrudge her daughter contacting her father but she did anyway, and it hurt like hell.

'Just remember he's a prick,' she said. 'Tell him I said hi.'

Charlie stored her father's number, labelling it 'Emergency Dad'.

67

11.45 p.m.

ANDREW LEWIS ALLOWED himself the smallest extra whisky he had ever poured. Barely an inch, with an ice cube. He swirled the contents, inhaled the peat and spices, relished the clinking of ice on glass.

He had a deadline. He had promised the relatives of the victims of the 22 May attack that IPS would honour their memory and sacrifice in an appropriate way. He was due to meet them in a week's time and he needed a shortlist of suggestions. He also needed to go home. He checked his taxi app, watched a dozen or so tiny cars hovering nearby. They were all waiting for his custom. He gave himself five minutes.

He surveyed the ideas from staff, supporters, customers and the public. His PA had reduced them to one page of 'deliverable and desirable' outcomes. There was a plan for an annual award for investigative journalism – a cash prize for the most courageous reporting as judged by a panel of experts. Lewis gave it a tick. Swirled the whisky. There was a suggestion to build a peace garden in the square outside, an enclosed green space with a plaque to commemorate the dead. Lewis's pencil hovered for a second, then put down a cross.

He swirled the whisky again. He checked the app. Still the cars circled.

Two more suggestions. A travelling exhibition devoted to the art and practice of modern journalism. Lewis snorted. Another cross of the pencil, another swirl of the glass. And finally a proposal for a bursary to fund a reporter. A fund devoted to training one student a year. A placement with a local paper or website followed by a job at IPS. He smiled and raised his glass.

'Perfect,' he said.

The whisky disappeared in one swallow. He called the cab.

68

11.50 p.m.

THE WAREHOUSE WAS finally quiet. Gregor, Hussain and Binici sat on three chairs near the door, gesticulating, whispering. Binici rocked on his chair – it was his turn to talk. Hussain and Gregor folded their arms – their turn to listen.

Hari had decided he wouldn't sleep. He sat, shirtless, his chest still stinging, against the wall, legs pulled up in front of him. One leg bounced rapidly. Collins lay next to him, face into his side, her uncut arm flung across his waist. She was breathing deeply. He assumed she was asleep. He could smell her now. It was sharp and earthy. Sweat and sex. And maybe shampoo, or rose water. Maybe some of Binici after all. He didn't care. He looked straight ahead and up, through the warehouse window. The only light came from whatever size moon was behind the clouds and the seeping glow reflected from the streets of Coventry. The darkest hour. The quietest hour.

He had no prayers to offer, no meditations on Krishna he could recall. His mother would have had some but he had never listened to her or them. His father had left. Whatever strength he had was his own. Maybe his grandmother's. Whatever inspiration he needed came from his sisters and now, because of him, Millie and Amara would be there tomorrow. In his attempts to keep them safe he had only succeeded in putting them in the front line. Just in front of Amal Hussain. Just in front of his Böhler N690. And if the twins were there, then their grandmother would be there also.

Well done, Hari. A full house.

He thought of the IPS women. The last images. Mary Lawson, sprawled, bloodied, lifeless. Famie Madden, puzzled, elegant, in charge. Lawson had got him into this nightmare and he had hoped Madden would get him out. She had taken the bait certainly. He was convinced the police presence in Boxer Street had been down to her. But that seemed like weeks ago. He had told Madden that the attack was planned for Thursday but why would she take any notice of a student writing messages in lemon juice? Like he was a five-year-old playing at spies?

He adjusted his position, removed Collins' arm from his waist. He felt his wounds crack open. Felt the blood run again. He made no attempt to staunch the flow. The adrenalin had long gone and the pain was intense but the cutting had saved his life. He had no doubt about that. The longer his chest stayed a bloodied mess, the longer he stayed alive. It was a badge of honour. An insignia. The knife had been his saviour and in every possible future scenario that he could imagine, it would have to be again.

Under the window, Hussain, Binici and Gregor broke up their meeting. Hari saw Gregor glance at him, or maybe Collins, and walk over. He closed his eyes, his body tensed. He felt the knife under his thigh. Collins slept on. He heard heavy footfall, then felt the soft give of the wall as Gregor settled against it.

'Still bleeding,' said Gregor.

Hari opened his eyes. He had sat to Hari's left, propped up against the wall, legs straight in front, ankles crossed. He too was still shirtless. His bloodied torso was covered in tattoos.

'We both are,' said Hari, indicating Gregor's own cuts. His lettering looked like angry slashes in his chest, the blood running in stripes down his stomach.

'Strength. Discipline. Ferocity,' said Gregor. 'War is work, not mystery.'

Butcher and philosopher. What's not to love?

Where Gregor's skin was blood-free, Hari saw painted saints, angels, skulls, sailing ships and a black flag. All competing for space.

'Nice art,' Hari said.

Gregor smiled. 'They are stories, Hari Roy.'

'Your stories?'

'Of course. Travelling thief, murderer, anarchist.' He spoke without drama, pointing to the angels, skulls and the flag like an indifferent gallery guide. 'And now this!' He peered down at his chest. The newly cut, and still bleeding, left pectoral muscle. 'ETB! This will be my favourite because I did it myself.' He waved his arms in a circle. 'We all did it together.' Gregor turned to Hari. A twitch of a smile. 'But still Hussain isn't sure about you,' he said. 'I told him you were good but . . .'

'Thanks.'

Gregor shrugged. 'It's nothing. The men will fight with you, I said.'

'Thanks.'

A beat of a pause.

'Hussain wants your girlfriend.' He nodded at Collins.

So she was right after all.

'She's not available.'

'Everything is available.'

Hari stared through the window. There would be no

daylight for several hours, but the butcher was in the wings, waiting for his cue. It wouldn't be long now.

'I'm not her keeper,' said Hari eventually. 'I don't own her. If she wants to go with Hussain, she will. If she doesn't, she won't.'

'You should be careful,' said Gregor.

'Too late for that,' said Hari. 'We fight in nine hours. We are ready. Why would you upset that?'

Gregor nodded. 'I have said this.'

'Say it again if you need to.'

'I will. You speak well, Hari. We will be friends, you and me. After everything. After it all.'

That seemed unlikely, but Hari nodded, offered his hand. They shook, Gregor left.

It was two minutes before Hari noticed the small dark shape on the floor, half a metre to his left. Gregor's phone. Screen down, no lights. Switched off. A rush of blood rang in his ears. A rush of adrenalin killed the pain.

The thing I want more than anything has been gifted to me. And it's all too easy.

This was a trap sprung by Hussain, he was sure of it. Hussain was the doubter and Gregor was the tempter. Hari forced his eyes to close, his leg to calm. Collins stirred, her arm stretching back over his waist.

Make the call, Hari. Make a call. Make any call.

Tell someone.

69

Thursday, 14 June, 7.20 a.m.

FAMIE WOKE WHEN the fan died with a small pop. Breakfast in room 204 was instant coffee and painkillers. She woke Charlie, hauled on her jeans, knocked on the interconnecting door. Sophie was dressed, Sam was showering. The air in both rooms was fetid and unyielding. Famie opened the doors to the corridor. What passed for fresher air drifted in, a barely perceptible change.

She stood in the doorway for a moment, cradling a steaming mug. The coffee smelt sharp and chemical but it was freshly made, and its acidity was familiar and reassuring. She inhaled deeply. As she exhaled she noticed her tremor was back.

Famie leant her head against the door jamb. If she was right, somewhere nearby some men were in the final stages of planning an atrocity. The university, the synagogue, the cathedral, the theatre. One of them, all of them. Maybe none of them, maybe something else she hadn't thought of. And involved somewhere, and certainly more scared than she was right now, Hari Roy. A man she'd never met, never spoken to. A man who had got himself involved in something he couldn't control, couldn't escape from. The man in the stripy top, beer raised to the camera. Round face, spiky hair.

'Hey Famie.' Sam had emerged from the bathroom fully dressed in yesterday's clothes. Clean and not clean. Soap-scented steam billowed in behind him.

'Hey Sam,' she said, turning back into the room. 'We need to split up,' she said. 'Two and two. We can't cover everything.'

'Already?' he said. 'It's just gone seven, Fames. Where would we go?'

'Breakfast, please,' said Sophie. 'Anywhere with bacon rolls.'

'Not hungry,' said Famie.

'You're not pregnant,' said Sophie.

Famie, eyes wide, glanced at Sam, still rubbing his hair with a towel.

'She told me,' he said. 'Last night.'

'Seemed the right time,' said Sophie. 'Doesn't change anything.'

Famie didn't argue, what was the point? It did change everything and they all knew it.

She walked back into 204. Charlie was showering, the clattering of the pump uncomfortably loud in the cramped room. It was only when the water stopped and the shower pump was silenced that she realized there was another sound. What sounded like a glockenspiel played a ludicrously fast, urgent tune. Over and over.

A ring tone. Beneath the melody, a low, insistent vibrating sound. From somewhere close. The direction was not obvious, it seemed to be coming from everywhere at once.

'Whoever that is, I can't find the phone!' she called, loud enough for Charlie to hear. Loud enough for Sam and Sophie. 'Bloody stupid ring tone too,' she added. Famie reached the burner phones. Switched on. Charged. Silent. 'Huh?' she said.

The shower-room door burst open. 'It's the fucking tablet! Mum, it's the tablet!' Wrapping the towel as she ran, hair dripping, Charlie found it under the bedclothes, held it up. It was pulsing, the screen lit up. The calling number was displayed in a rectangular green box. It started with 07, Famie didn't recognize the rest. A mobile was calling the tablet. Below the numbers, a green phone icon and a red phone icon were offered. Accept or reject.

Sam and Sophie crashed in from 203.

'Is that the tablet? Is that him?' Sophie said.

Charlie held up the vibrating tablet.

'Shit, it is,' said Sophie. 'Well answer it then!'

Charlie handed it to Famie. Famie, hands shaking again, took three attempts to hit the green icon. For a moment she thought she should hold it to her ear, like a phone. Then she held it in front of her. She stared at the screen as though she was expecting visuals. It stayed black.

'Hello?' she said.

There was silence, a digital squelch, then the acoustic of an enclosed space. The noise from the tablet sounded indoors. Muffled. She heard movement, clothes brushing against a microphone. A satellite delay. Maybe the caller had missed her answer.

'Hello?' she said again, now closer to the tablet.

This time, an answer.

'Hello?' said the voice from the speakers. 'Is that Famie Madden?'

70

FAMIE FROWNED. 'YES it is,' she said. She knew the voice already. Not the one she wanted to hear.

'Ms Madden, it's DC Hunter.'

Famie deflated, her exasperation obvious and audible. 'Christ! We thought you were Hari.' She raised her eyes to the ceiling, nearly threw the tablet on the floor. 'What the fuck do you want,' she added. It wasn't really a question.

'Where are you, Ms Madden?' said Hunter. 'This really is urgent. It concerns the safety of you and your daughter. Threats have been made and we want to give you the protection you need.'

A moment's pause. Charlie hooked her arm through Famie's.

'What sort of threats?' said Famie.

'Real threats, Ms Madden. Believable threats. Sourced and credible.'

'Who from?'

'Both your names emerged in chatter on jihadi websites.'

'Which ones?'

A sigh. 'Really, Ms Madden?'

'Yes, really, Ms Hunter. Which jihadi websites?'

The exasperation now came from the police officer. 'When I see you, I can go through the details. I can show you the translated pages. But there is an urgency you don't seem to understand. You should assume that the people who tried to attack your daughter will try again. If she was my daughter, I know what I'd do.'

Famie glanced at Charlie, who shrugged. Sam and Sophie looked unsure, certainly unconvinced.

'My assumption is that you're in Coventry somewhere,' continued Hunter. 'Let me at least send a patrol car.'

'OK,' said Famie, 'wait up.' This was all the wrong way round. She was riled and she knew it. 'To start with,' she continued, 'what news of Hari Roy? Do you know any more about him? Surely you've found something.'

Hunter didn't even try. 'No, we haven't found him, no we don't know any more about your man. Ms Madden, this isn't a social call, this is an urgent request for you to get some protection.'

Famie spluttered with indignation. 'OK, so firstly he's not "my man", but that was very revealing about how you see this thing. And secondly, today's the day, Ms Hunter, you know that, right? Hari's attack is today. We've narrowed the list of possible attack sites to the university, the synagogue and the cathedral. Maybe a theatre. Presumably your guys have done this work too? You did listen to everything we told you?'

They were all staring at the screen. From the speakers, white noise and silence. The sound of nothing in particular seemed to Famie like something rather significant.

'We did listen. Which is why we're speaking now.'

'Huh,' said Famie. 'Right. The *Telegraph* and Bob Dylan. You listened to that bit.'

'We can add sixty-one to a number when we need to,' said Hunter. 'And you're in danger. An address for the patrol car?'

Famie ignored her. 'What plans are there for today's attacks?' she asked. 'Extra patrols? There must be something. First tell me that.'

More background noise. An enclosed space, tight, almost dead acoustics. A car maybe.

'The police here know of your concerns,' said Hunter, 'they followed up on Boxer Street. They will always respond robustly where they see evidence of criminal activity.'

'So nothing,' said Famie, disgusted. 'There are no plans for today and you're doing nothing. The only person you're interested in is me. So you know what you can do with that fucking patrol car.'

She hit the red phone icon, the screen went dark.

Famie held the tablet in both hands, Charlie, Sam and Sophie stood round her. Famie could smell the shampoo in Charlie's washed hair. She wondered what had just happened.

'What was that?' she said.

'That was the sound of us swinging in the wind,' said Sam. He took the tablet, plugged it to the charger. 'We're on our own.'

'No, it was more than that,' said Famie.

She'd spent the best part of two decades talking to coppers. Learning their moods, their methods. Understanding the nuances, interpreting the words they used. Eventually, like a parent learning to decode the language of their child's school report, she got it. The words might all sound fine but what wasn't being said? What was Hunter avoiding?

'I think that was a fishing call,' said Famie. 'She knew I'd say no to the protection. I've said no before.'

'Then she was checking the number, checking it was you,' said Sam.

'And she said the police "here" know our concerns,' said Charlie, tightening the towel around her. 'Which means she's in Coventry too.'

'She's tracking then,' said Sam. 'Tracking the signal. She knows where we are.'

Famie went to peer out of the sealed window. The ring road was still quiet. A row of three cars and a van waited for access to the roundabout, two slowly circulating lorries made them wait. Their sun visors were down, the early morning light already strong. She smacked the glass. Sam was right. Charlie was right.

'We need to go,' said Famie, the reality of their situation settling in her stomach. 'Before they get here. Grab your stuff.'

Sam and Sophie ran to their room. Charlie, her hair flattened, still dripping, used a corner of the towel to wipe her face.

'Are we running again?' she said. The tightness in her throat would have been missed by most.

'Looks like it,' said Famie, unplugging the new phones. 'I'm sorry, Charlie.'

'What about the tablet?' said Charlie. 'Remove the SIM?' Her hands hovered over the screen. 'Bring it with us? Hunter would know where we are but Hari could still call.'

Sam and Sophie reappeared. Ready to go. They both looked at Charlie, still in her towel.

'Tablet or no?' she asked them.

'Leave it,' said Sam. 'On balance he isn't going to call.'

Charlie tossed it on the bed.

Famie waved Sam and Sophie off. 'Like I said, two and two. We'll follow you out as soon as Charlie isn't basically naked.'

Sam and Sophie exited through the connecting door. Famie heard them lock it, then the door of 203, then push through to the fire exit door on to the fire escape. Charlie put on yesterday's clothes. She looked dishevelled, drawn and fearful but she was ready in sixty seconds.

'Let's go,' said Charlie, hands on hips. 'Wherever it is we are going.'

It was a display of false confidence that made Famie wince. For a moment Charlie was eleven again. Satchel on, fresh-out-of-the-box school uniform on, smiling through the terror.

Jesus, what have I got her into?

One last glance at the tablet. Black screen. No call. No message. Time to go.

Charlie put a hand on the door handle, then stopped. There was running in the corridor. Famie thought it was one person at first, then two. They stopped outside 204. Famie pulled Charlie away, peered through the spy hole.

'Fuck.'

'Hunter?'

'And her plus-one.'

Famie didn't wait for a knock. Or a boot. She unchained and opened the door.

71

7.35 a.m.

PC JON ROBERTS and his partner PC Glen Talbot, a rookie constable from London, had less than half an hour left on their shift. The atmosphere in the car was convivial, despite Talbot proving what Roberts had long suspected, that he didn't know one end of Warwickshire from the other. Confusing the rivers Avon and Stour was, as far as Roberts was concerned, a hanging offence. Talbot's turn to buy breakfast.

Coffee and pastries. A quiet night and a quiet morning. A reported break-in in Kenilworth turned out to be a false alarm, two drivers breathalysed, two drivers passed. And that had been it. The A429 into the city was tree-lined and free-flowing. Just one lane both ways, but with wide footpaths and cycle lanes. Talbot steered with his left hand, wiped crumbs from his beard and uniform with his right.

'Still annoyed?' he said.

'Of course.'

'Boxer Street?'

'Of course.'

'But the crazy woman's stories checked out.'

Roberts stared straight ahead at the undulating, gentle switchback of a road. Sky-high oaks, left and right, hid the expensive housing from all but the most curious. 'She knew so much more,' he said. 'The old man's car might have belonged to an Alfred Graham and the student with the messed-up VW might have friends nearby. But she knew what she was doing. The whole "barely dressed in the street" routine was the moment. We should have arrested her on the spot.' Roberts finished his coffee, wiped his finger around the inside rim.

Talbot grinned. 'I never noticed, I have to say,' he said.

Roberts glanced at him. 'Right,' he said. 'Sure.'

The road peaked by a red and black sign that read 'University of Warwick', a narrow lane falling away to the left, and a bus stop with a plastic shelter and bench. A brown and cream double decker stopped, disgorging a steady stream of passengers. Some had rucksacks and holdalls, a few held rolled-up banners over their shoulders, rifle-style. Talbot pulled over, watched them begin their downhill trudge to the campus. A few glanced back at the sudden police presence.

Roberts did a rough count. 'Sixty-four,' he said. 'That's high. Protest's not till noon. Why so early?'

'Breakfast?' said Talbot. 'Who knows.'

'You know what this place is called?' said Roberts.

Talbot said nothing. Another local knowledge trap.

'It's Gibbet Hill,' said Roberts, watching a group tying scarves around their faces. 'There used to be a scaffold here. For public hangings.'

Around a dozen masked protesters had hung back, allowing the others to disappear down the hill. They stood in a semi-circle, partially obscured by the bus stop advertising. Two were making calls. One was fixing an anti-pollution mask around her mouth and nose. They all had black canvas bags slung over their shoulders. Some had two bags, their straps criss-crossing the chest.

'You making this up?' said Talbot.

'They left the bodies up for years,' said Roberts. 'As a warning.'

Most of the semi-circle now donned bicycle crash helmets.

'Who did they hang?' said Talbot, checking the car's video recorder was working.

'Revolutionaries, agitators,' Roberts replied. 'Thieves, bandits and murderers too. Obviously. But mainly troublemakers.'

Talbot pointed at the nearest demonstrator, black hoodie and jeans, double satchels, who had started filming their car. 'You think this is trouble here?'

Roberts put his plastic cup in a brown paper bag by his feet, brushed his lap down. 'Twenty to eight is bloody early for a stand-off,' he said. 'So yes, I do. It's like we weren't supposed to see this. They're annoyed that we know they're here already.'

The police watched the protesters and the protesters watched the police.

'We should call this in,' said Roberts.

As he reached for the radio, the woman with the anti-pollution mask peeled away, walked down the hill. The rest of the group followed. The protester with the black hoodie carried on filming.

'Charlie Victor from Oscar 51.'

Control picked up.

'We're at Gibbet Hill bus stop, Kenilworth Road,' said Roberts. 'We've got at least sixty protesters heading for the university campus. A small group of around twelve have scarves and masks. All of them have bags or satchels. They look organized. They mean business. We're going to follow them to campus. Request back-up.'

Roberts nodded at Talbot, who turned the car down the hill. Five miles an hour.

The radio squawked back. 'Oscar 51 this is Charlie Victor. Wait please.'

Roberts and Talbot exchanged glances.

'Keep going,' Roberts said, pointing down the hill.

Five miles an hour.

He keyed the radio again. 'Wait for what?' he said.

A pause, then another squawk. 'Oscar 51, can you make a P1 – report of a disturbance at 26 Boxer Street.'

Talbot braked. Stopped the car. A P1. An emergency. 'What the fuck,' he muttered.

The radio again. 'You want that, Jon?'

'On it,' he said. 'Yes I bloody do!'

Talbot swung the car round and returned to the A429. Sirens and lights. Eighty miles an hour.

72

DC HUNTER HAD a new partner. Her ID said Jean Espie. White, uniformed PC, powerfully built. Just out of college was Famie's guess. At least she wasn't Milne. Both police officers were sweating and breathless.

'We were just going out,' said Famie. 'You can come if you want. You'd be useful, I'm sure.' She glared at Hunter. 'Unless, of course, you have details of those jihadi sites you were mentioning? We could always look at those.'

Hunter was impassive. 'We'd like to come in.' Same grey suit, different white shirt.

'Of course you would,' said Famie. 'And if you'd told us you were coming we could have adjusted our plans but sadly, as I said, we're going out.'

Hunter tried to smile. 'A few minutes of your time, please, Ms Madden.'

'No,' said Famie. 'No minutes, none of my time. We don't have any time. Hari is out of time. Now, if you'll excuse me . . .'

She made to step around Hunter. Espie blocked her path.

'What is this?' said Famie, spinning back to Hunter.

'This will be an arrest if you don't sit down.'

Charlie pulled her mother away, Espie shut the door. The four women stood facing each other. Famie and Charlie side by side, backs to the bed. Espie just behind Hunter, backs to the closed and locked connecting door. Two on two.

'You lied to me, Hunter,' said Famie, bristling. 'I don't trust you, but say what you have to say. Then fuck off. And quite what it is that could be more important than stopping a terror attack I'd love to hear.' She was aware that Espie's eyes were everywhere – looking for what, she had no idea – but Famie stuck on Hunter.

Hunter stuck on Famie. 'Can we possibly sit down?' she said.

There was a note of exhaustion in Hunter's tone. It was enough to make Famie pause.

'Sure.' She shrugged, then waved her to the plastic chair with the thin cushion.

Hunter sat, Espie leant against the connecting door, Famie and Charlie reversed on to the bed. Espie's radio spat into life – indecipherable words. She bent an ear, then turned its volume down. Hunter shifted on the cushion, shaping up for a speech.

'I'm sorry for . . . surprising you like this. I believe the misdirection was appropriate in the circumstances.' She alternated her gaze between Famie and Charlie but Famie got most of it. 'You're in danger, but you know that. Charlie is in danger, and you know that too. You say Hari Roy is in danger and the attacks are today. But here's my problem. There's another theory doing the rounds.'

'Meaning?' said Famie.

'There's another theory being discussed by colleagues,' said Hunter, 'which has you far closer to the original crime.' She paused. 'How would you describe your relationship with Mary Lawson?'

'What?' spluttered Famie. 'Why are we—'

'Answer the question, please.'

Famie felt Charlie's arm through hers. She knew what it meant. She breathed deeply. 'She was . . . was my friend. An inspiration. To me, to everyone.' Famie stopped there, anticipating the next question.

'Who stole your boyfriend.'

Charlie's arm tugged slightly.

'Yes,' said Famie, flatly. 'Who stole my boyfriend, if you want to put it like that. So what?'

Another inaudible burst from Espie's radio. Hunter gave a pained smile.

'This other theory I mentioned has you incensed, understandably, at Seth Hussain's and Mary Lawson's betrayal. And that your time in Pakistan gave you contacts with all kinds of fringe groups. Paramilitaries, criminals, terrorists.'

'Wait,' said Famie. 'You think I killed Seth and Mary? Because I was mad at them?' She gave a short, percussive laugh. 'And the rest of the team were what? Collateral damage? You must be out of your mind.' She stood up. 'Really this is pretty desperate stuff.'

Charlie tugged her down again. 'What do you think of this theory, DC Hunter?' she said.

Hunter nodded at Espie, who produced a thin grey cardboard file. She handed it to Hunter who removed a few sheets of A4.

'You invited us to go through your records of your time in Pakistan,' she said. 'You said that everything there is to know about your time there we could get from the IPS records.' She handed the papers to Famie. 'So we did. The first two sheets are a list of those meetings and, as far as we could ascertain, who was present. As you said, the usual mix of army and politicians with a few warlords here and there.'

Famie flicked through the sheets which had been fastened with a small metal clip. 'Someone has been busy,' she said. The last sheet was a photo of Seth and Amal Hussain together. Heads and shoulders, suits and ties. In this image, Seth was the happier of the two. His smile seemed warm and unforced, Amal was expressionless. Like he didn't know anyone was taking his picture. There were other people around them – Famie could see shoulders and hair at the edges of the picture – but the brothers were the focus. She turned it face down on the bed.

'Seen that before?' asked Hunter.

'No.'

'Recent?'

Famie looked again. 'I'd say so, yes.' She replaced it face down, returned to the other pages.

'The second sheet has only five names on it,' said Hunter, 'but each one you met in Pakistan and each one is, or has been in the last year, active in London. Three work in the embassy, one has a jihadi website, the other works for "community groups".' She mimed the quotes.

'You mean a gangster?' asked Famie.

'Pretty much.'

'And they all helped me execute my colleagues, did they?'

'One or more could have, yes. Like I said, that's the theory. You have links to the Hussain brothers, dead and alive.' She pointed to the photo. 'And they have links to the dark side, all the names on that list. It's all too much of a coincidence. You're the link, Ms Madden.'

'Except that I'm not,' said Famie. 'And Seth worked with human rights groups. All his life.'

'But was in huge debt,' said Hunter. 'And guess who was in the process of paying off those debts?'

Famie felt her energy drain. 'Our gangster slash community leader?' she said.

Hunter nodded.

One more sheet. Seth's bank statement. Crazy numbers in the credit column.

'You might not have wanted them all dead,' said Hunter, 'but you sure had reason for getting rid of Seth Hussain and Mary Lawson. You hated them and wanted revenge. You set the wheels in motion, your underworld connections took it from there.'

Charlie snorted with derision. 'Mum's "underworld connections"? Can you actually hear yourself? The same contacts who tried to kill me then break into our flat?'

Hunter tried to focus again on Famie. 'Ms Madden—'

'Wait,' interrupted Charlie, shouting now. 'Do you mean those contacts?'

'Charlie—'

'Those contacts? Yes or no?'

'It's possible.' Hunter didn't sound convinced.

'No it isn't. It isn't possible. And you know it.'

'You're a journalist,' said Hunter to Famie, 'you'd run the story.' She checked her watch.

'If I ran this story, I'd be sued for libel. I'm assuming it's Milne that's pushing this bullshit?' Hunter looked awkward and Famie nodded. 'Thought so. And I notice you didn't answer Charlie's question. What do you think of this "theory"?' More mimed quotes.

A beat, then Espie pushed herself off the door. Checked her watch. 'She thinks it's bullshit too,' she said. The sing-song rise and fall of a Birmingham accent.

'Bingo,' said Famie. 'So we are doing this because . . . ?' She looked between Hunter and Espie.

Hunter paused only briefly. 'Because we have our orders. Famie Madden, I'm arresting you for the murder of Mary Lawson, Seth Hussain, Harry Thomas, Sarah Thompson, Brian Hall, Sathnam Stanley and Anita Cross.'

Charlie was on her feet, screaming.

Famie started to laugh.

73

7.54 a.m.

TALBOT PULLED UP outside 26 Boxer Street. He'd killed the siren, kept the lights. Twenty metres ahead, a white delivery van had stopped in the middle of the road, hazard lights also flashing. A uniformed woman leapt from the cab. Brown skin, mid-thirties, hair tied high, sunglasses perched on her head. She approached the police car. Roberts and Talbot jumped out, pulled their caps on. She was talking already.

'Done this for three years,' she said. 'I know what I'm doing, I'm here all the time. I had a dead woman last January. She'd fallen in the kitchen and when I was pushing the note through the door you could smell that something wasn't right.' She pulled on a vape, vast clouds of sweet-scented smoke billowing between them. 'Straight out, like nothing I smelt before,' she said. 'Rotting meat and cheap perfume is what it was. Never smelt it again. Till just now.' She pointed at number 26. 'And that's what's coming from in there. No doubt about it. ''Swhy I called it in and 'swhy I'm smoking this shit.' More clouds. 'Doesn't shift the taste much, if I'm honest.'

Roberts glanced at the front door.

'You got all that just from the letterbox?'

She nodded. 'So will you,' she said, waving the vape in the direction of the front door of number 26. 'Weather like this, doesn't take long.'

Roberts and Talbot exchanged glances then looked again at the house. Terraced, bay windows top and bottom. Exactly the same as the rest of the street. Short-term renters and lazy, disinterested landlords had produced houses that were sagging and cracking under the weight of prolonged neglect. Number 26 wasn't the worst by any means – its front door was at least intact and not graffiti'd – but the front garden was scruffy and some of the weeds were a metre high. The downstairs curtains were drawn. All the downstairs windows were shut, one small upstairs bathroom window was a notch on its metal catch.

Roberts walked to the door, rang the bell, rattled the knocker, then bent to the letterbox. Talbot snapped at his heels. Roberts pushed the steel flap open, peered inside. He saw that the hall was clear. Saw that there was nothing of anything that could be seen anywhere. But the delivery woman was right. The stench hit you immediately, rolling through the small hole in the door like it was an open bi-fold. Roberts recoiled.

'Jesus that's bad.'

Talbot stepped in. Stooped, gagged, stepped away. The delivery woman, leaning against her van, called to them both.

'Can I go? Do I sign anything?'

'We have your details,' called Roberts. 'And thank you.' He raised a hand to his cap, waved her away.

The two men stepped back from the door. Roberts radioed that they were on the scene and that they were going in.

'You got an enforcer?' he said.

Talbot shook his head.

Roberts pulled at each of the downstairs windows, fingers around the frames. All locked. He put on his gloves, unclipped his baton, then smashed it through the bay window.

74

'WHERE'S MILNE?'

'Twenty minutes away.'

'He sent you ahead?'

'We were closer.'

'You know this is bullshit.'

'They weren't my words.'

'No, they were your partner's.'

Famie and Charlie were still on the bed, Hunter was on the plastic chair with the cushion, Espie stood behind her. Charlie's face was streaked with tears, roughly wiped away with the top of her T-shirt.

'Why isn't it Milne arresting me?' said Famie. 'I'm surprised he's letting women do his glamorous work for him.'

'He thought you'd run,' said Espie.

Famie had her head in her hands. 'You'd better pray that there are no attacks today because you can bet that every news agency, every paper, every website, every news channel in the world will have details of your incompetence. How you were told. And how you did nothing.'

The words hit home. It may have been Famie who was under arrest for seven murders but it was the policewomen who were on the defensive. She looked between Hunter and Espie, watched the body language. The upturned eyes, the flick of the head, the nods of encouragement. Then it clicked. She understood why Espie had seemed the bolder of the two women. A junior PC declaring a current police operation 'bullshit' was a woman confident of her position in the power dynamic of the room. These women weren't just partners, they were *partners*.

Famie thought she might have fifteen minutes.

'What does your instinct tell you, DC Hunter?' she said. 'Do you think you've got the right person arrested here? Did I also kill Tommi Dara? You missed him in your list. Maybe that was one of my "underworld connections".'

'I was ordered to arrest you. I arrested you.'

'Oh DC Hunter. Please. Fuck your orders! Just for once! I know I'm an annoying, cocky nightmare to deal with but for fifteen minutes, just indulge me. I'm under arrest, I know that. I'm not going anywhere. You've done your job. But let's park Milne's crappy theory for a second. Were there any more photos where this came from? Because if that's the most recent close-up photo of Amal I assume all your colleagues have it? At least the ones in Coventry?'

Hunter and Espie looked blank. 'That wouldn't be our job,' said Espie.

'Could it become your job?' said Famie. 'Just briefly?'

The PC sighed. 'I'm afraid not.'

'To answer your question,' said Hunter, 'we received the photo in the post.'

Famie frowned. 'You "received" it?'

'Milne got it. Passed it to me.'

'Anonymous?'

Hunter spread her hands. Shrugged her shoulders.

'That happen often?'

'Sometimes.'

'How cropped is it?' said Charlie. 'How many others in the original?'

'Four or five as I remember,' said Hunter. 'Some kind of family event maybe.'

'Do you have it?'

'No.'

'Can you get it?' More glances between Hunter and Espie. 'Please?' said Famie. 'Your boss will be here soon and it'll be too late. Make the call.'

Hunter made the call. Two minutes later her phone buzzed. She selected the image, handed the phone to Famie. Charlie leant over. She tilted the phone, spinning the picture to a wide setting.

An outdoor shot. Summer. Eight people in the frame, in three rough lines. The Hussain brothers were sitting in chairs, an older man and woman to their left and right. Two bored teenagers sat in front of them, one clutching his phone to his chest. Two women stood behind Amal, both with half-smiles as though sharing a joke. One rested a hand on his shoulder. Striking, mid-thirties, black hair to her shoulders. Next to her, a taller, younger woman turned her face to the camera. Her head lowered slightly, maybe to deliver the punch line.

Famie tightened her grip on the phone. She heard the thudding of her blood again. Her fingers reached for the younger woman's face, then enlarged it as far as it would go. A small scar was visible on the bridge of her nose.

'Jesus Christ,' she said.

'What?' said Charlie.

'Those women,' said Famie. 'Behind Amal. Let's say his wife. And his wife's friend. The one with the scar.'

Hunter finished the sentence. 'The women in the shower. The women on Seth's laptop.'

Famie briefly held one hand to her mouth. She spoke through her fingers: 'Seth was screwing Amal's wife. And whoever the scar-nose woman is.' The all-too-familiar feelings of loathing and revulsion flowed again. She stared at the image. The younger face, the smiling, amused eyes. 'Let's hope it's the nanny.'

They all stared at the screen. Espie straightened then stepped away. Hunter followed. Famie saw the glances between them.

'Now can we go?' she said.

75

AFTER DECIDING NOT to use Gregor's phone, Hari did sleep after all. He dreamt of his sisters, a bloodied Mary Lawson and a funeral procession where everyone was, for some reason he couldn't fathom, running. He woke with a start, drenched in sweat. Some had seeped into his chest wound, then oozed out again. Two lines, deep crimson, forked their way down and around his rib cage. He glanced to his left. The phone was gone. To his right, Collins knelt, facing the wall, eyes closed. The room was bright now. He squinted through the jagged shards of the broken windows. An electric-blue sky, no clouds. Framed in steel. The sun was up, the day was here.

Hari looked at the silent, intense preparations underway around him. He remembered an old documentary he had watched with his grandmother about the Indian cricket team. One section had featured the meticulous pre-match preparations of their star player Sachin Tendulkar. In the changing room he would unpack his kitbag, taking out his gloves, pads and shoes from polythene covers. He would check the photographs of his children, his flag of India. When he was settled, he would inspect the pitch, checking it intently for firmness and moisture. He would play a short football game. Play a few cover drives with his bat. When he was happy, he would retreat to the changing room. His grandmother had smiled broadly at him. 'You know what he is now, Hari?' She pointed at the figure of Tendulkar. 'He is ready for battle. That's what he is.'

In the warehouse, Gregor, Binici and Kamran were all going through their own preparation rituals. Getting ready for their battle. Gregor was inspecting, then polishing his knife. When he had covered every millimetre, he started again. Inspect, polish. Inspect, polish. Binici, naked, was anointing himself with oils. Different bottles for different parts of his body. He was paying particular attention to his thigh muscles, pressing his thumbs, then his knuckles, deep into the tissue. His skin shone. Inspect and polish. Kamran had a stretching programme. Flat on his back, he pulled each leg to his chest. He twisted, rolled, balanced. A makeshift bandage across his chest showed fresh bleeding, an oval of red spreading across the coarse cloth. He unwound the strip, dabbed then wiped the wound with a corner around the broken skin, then retied. Inspect and polish.

Hari didn't move. He had no routine, no ritual, no 'state of mind' to achieve. With shaking hands he drank water from a plastic bottle, then immediately vomited it all back up again. The acrid stench filled his lungs within seconds. He was about to apologize but no one else took any notice. Not even Collins, who was barely a metre away.

Part of my ritual, thought Hari.

He threw the rest of the water on the vomit, swilling it away as best he could, then sat back down. He reached for his shirt and eased it over his head, pulling and picking it away from his scabbing wounds. He felt the cotton settle against them. Sensed his racing heart. Wondered how much longer he had left.

Hari assumed he was the only one quite this scared, though Collins did look grey. He caught her eye, she looked away.

No one spoke.

Tattoos, Teeth and Red Head appeared from the upper room. Each was stripped to the waist, each had shirts over their right shoulder, each with their Böhler knives held in their right hand. Their appearance signalled the start of something. Kamran stopped the stretching, Binici got dressed and Gregor seemed to accept his knife wasn't going to get any cleaner. He pocketed it. Hari pocketed his too. Binici approached him, jangling the car keys.

'I'm getting the van,' he said.

'Third floor,' said Hari. 'Behind a pillar.'

Binici left with Gregor. Hari felt relieved it wasn't him and Collins again. He wondered if Binici knew what had happened with Collins. Or had guessed.

'Where's Hussain?' he whispered, as soon as Collins appeared open to the idea of conversation.

Her face was taut, her lips pressed tight. She wiped sweat from her nose with a thumb and forefinger. 'Left a while back,' she said. 'When you were asleep.' She looked away as though the act of speaking had been too much for her.

He felt for the photo in his shirt pocket.

Hussain was with Millie and Amara.

Hari vomited again. This time he retched till his stomach was empty. He slumped back against the wall, the exertions opening up his cuts again. Fresh blood ran, only some of it absorbed by the cotton of his shirt. Hari resolved to stay as still as possible. He breathed as deeply as his cuts allowed.

The sound of an engine drifted through the broken windows. It stopped outside. Everyone stood. Collins walked away. Hari hauled himself to his feet.

Oh Christ.

Ready for battle.

76

7.59 a.m.

ROBERTS CLAMBERED THROUGH the broken window of number 26. He stood briefly, feet crunching the broken glass, eyes adjusting to the room's curtained near-darkness. An ordered room. Quiet suburbia. Sofa, small wooden table, a pile of coasters, two worn armchairs. There was an empty bookshelf, a candlewax-covered gin bottle positioned nearest the window. An unused bookend. The smell of the room was musty, stale. The odour of decomposition was in the air, but less pronounced than it had been by the porch. Whatever the source, it wasn't in this room. He pulled open the door to the hall and retched. Definitely closer. Shutting the door he went and took a breath by the window and tried again.

Two bolts, a chain, and Talbot was in, the broiling street air still a welcome, freshening breeze.

Behind him, a small crowd lined the low garden wall. Water bottles in hand, pointing. If the police were breaking into houses on their street, they sure wanted to watch. Roberts closed the front door.

'Whatever it is, we're right on top of it. Right here.'

'Unless the whole house is the same,' said Talbot. 'Who knows what went on.'

Gloved hand over his mouth, he walked through to the kitchen. Tentative, cautious steps. Hotter here, the contents of the waste bin adding to the noxious air they breathed. Used and half-empty glasses of water stood on the counter. Roberts, following behind, counted five of them.

'Visitors,' he said. 'Don't touch them.' He tried the door to the courtyard. It swung open. 'Who left this way presumably.'

Both officers stepped outside. Two chairs had been placed by the far fence, another empty glass on its side between them. Talbot climbed on to a chair, peered over the fence. The parallel terrace offered a choice of alleys to escape down.

'And then over here,' he said. 'Two gardens and you're out.'

He stepped down, and both men looked up at the back windows. All shut, all curtained. More deep breaths.

'Right then,' said Roberts.

He led the way back inside, a single route through the house. The kitchen, the lounge, the hallway. There was no doubt where the stench was coming from. Roberts sat on the bottom step, lifted a corner of the hall's matting. There was about three metres of it, a thick, coarse weave of dirty brown nylon, running from the foot of the stairs to the front door. He revealed about a metre of the cheap, worn floorboards beneath. Ran a finger along a deep, battered groove that had been gouged in the wood, cutting across the grain. Talbot walked to the other end. Back to the door, he lifted what he could. It was enough.

'Jesus Christ,' he said.

Together, they folded the matting back on itself, the underside encrusted with congealed and dried blood. A new intensity to the rotting smell caused both men to turn their heads. Roberts closed his eyes briefly. Exhaled.

'Better do this.'

They exposed only what they needed to. Five lines of ill-fitting floorboards ran the length of it, most of their surface area now smeared in blood. Where the knots in the wood butted up against a join, most had fallen through. Disappeared long ago. Most of the holes were dark, empty, but towards the door a run of three showed a distinct lining of blue. A fabric of some kind, pushed up against the underside. Roberts and Talbot caught it at the same time, exchanged a glance. Stepping forward, the boards shifted beneath their feet. Left and right. Loose, like there was no glue, no nails keeping them in place.

'Someone has been very careless,' said Talbot.

'Or someone didn't care very much one way or the other,' said Roberts.

He stepped to the edge of the hall, lounge-side, to the one board that appeared solid. He nodded Talbot towards the kitchen end, and together they lifted the middle floorboard. It left a hole one metre long by nine centimetres wide, and revealed a shoulder, an arm and a neck that had been sliced to the grey cartilage of the trachea.

Roberts reached for his radio.

77

8.20 a.m.

IT WAS ANOTHER dazzling morning and Hardin was sweating already. The city's pavements and manicured green spaces were steaming, the high-rise, all-glass offices reflected the sun straight back at him. He adjusted his sunglasses, pushing them further up his nose. He crossed the street, the suitcase rattling in front of him. Four wheels and an upright handle made it more of a walking stick than luggage. It was his routine. The glad rags were pressed and packed. He would change at the cathedral, help the bishop with his service, then grab a taxi to get to the university on time. Maybe the bus if he could cope with the stares. And the heat.

He'd left his daughter sleeping, his wife a note. In it, he explained that the night had been reasonable considering the temperature, that he had last changed and fed their baby at seven. He had added that he was a little apprehensive about the 'demo' and hoped that he was doing the right thing. He asked for her prayers. And as a PS, that he loved them both more than he was capable of saying.

Hardin walked his route. He walked it with purpose to avoid looking like a lost tourist. Or a hungover delegate looking for his conference. He had been accused of both. Twenty-five minutes from house to cathedral. New town to old town. Modern city to ancient city. Coffee shops to cobbled streets. The shopping precinct was quiet, very few of the charity shops and estate agents that lined his way were open yet. Here and there rough-sleepers lay together in groups, sleeping bags and cardboard strewn in doorways. None of them looked up. He was grateful. He pushed on.

Earbuds in place, he listened to the local news station reporting from the campus three miles up the road. Their reporter had started to explain what she was expecting to happen on the protest – she had police crowd estimates, student and university quotes – but then broke off. Hardin could hear shouts, and the reporter explained that a large group of demonstrators had arrived. She described them as masked and purposeful. They were, she said, standing in front of the Senate Building, shouting at whoever might be inside. Then the tone of her voice changed – there was a new urgency to her words. The chants sounded closer to her microphone. She said that the demonstrators had seen her and that a number were walking straight towards her. She stumbled over some words and the studio host asked if she was safe. Hardin stopped walking to wait for her answer. He caught the reassuring click as she activated her vehicle's central locking, closely followed by a fusillade of banging. Shouting now, she said her radio car was surrounded and that the demonstrators were hammering on the roof and windows. The studio host said to keep talking. He asked if she had seen any police. She said she hadn't. He said his producer was dialling 999.

Hardin lowered his head. A brief street-corner prayer and

he pushed on. The steady, low rumble of the suitcase's wheels became an urgent, machine-gun clatter. The concrete slabs of the shopping centre had become the cobbled streets of the old city, and the sanctuary of the cathedral was only a hundred metres away.

78

8.40 a.m.

SAM AND SOPHIE sat on a high bank of stone steps. Sophie leant against a metal railing, Sam the next step up. In front of them, and rising high into a columned sandstone porch, was the vast glass wall which formed the entrance to the cathedral. Lines of saints and flying angels were etched into the glass, and in spaces in between, the reflection of the ruined old bombed-out cathedral. It ran behind them at right angles to the new, a hollowed-out Gothic space.

The porch had eight slender pillars, four clustered at each end, the outside pair connected with a wooden cross. Lines of workers, tourists and worshippers walked around them, a few for the cathedral, most passing through. Sophie had a water bottle in one hand, her burner phone in the other. She watched the thoroughfare in front of her, a meeting of the old and new, secular and sacred.

'Busier than expected,' she said.

Sam didn't respond. Glanced at his watch. 'Twenty minutes before the service. We should be doing something.'

'We are doing something,' said Sophie. 'Cathedral then

university. That's it. Until we hear from Famie, that's what we do.'

In front of them, a woman in grey shorts and long-sleeved white shirt with a shoulder bag kissed a farewell to a similarly dressed man, then turned into the cathedral. The man watched her go, then jogged down some steps towards the fountains that were playing in a wide piazza. Sophie glanced round at Sam – he was watching the man too.

'Christ, we're suspicious of everyone,' she said.

'So we should be,' said Sam. 'How many is that we've seen go in?'

'Eighty or so,' said Sophie. 'Didn't like any of them.'

Sam frowned. 'Meaning?'

'Meaning when you're pregnant and paranoid, everyone looks like they could blow your brains out.'

Sam shrugged. 'I think that, without even being pregnant,' he said.

She checked her phone. Full signal. No text. 'You wanna go in?'

Sam shook his head. 'Perfect view from here. We get to see everyone who goes in.'

A small party, maybe a dozen soberly dressed men and women, climbed the steps from the piazza and fountains, then disappeared inside.

'I think they're safe,' he said.

'But why?' said Sophie. 'What the hell are we looking for?' She could see the new arrivals the other side of the glass wall, huddled around what looked like a book stall.

'I just think we'll know,' said Sam. 'When the time comes. Maybe that's stupid.'

'Well they won't walk in and buy tickets, that's for sure,' said Sophie, pointing at the queue inside. 'But when you see the CCTV of terrorists arriving at, or on their way to, some atrocity, they don't stand out. They look normal. That's the whole point. You can't tell by looking.'

Some shouts from the piazza. A crowd of students, presumably, came running up the steps and for the briefest moment Sophie clasped Sam's arm. But they ran through the porch and out the other side, weaving their way through the people and around the columns.

'This is different,' said Sam. 'We might be in the wrong place. But if Hari Roy arrives, we'll know. I'm sure of it.'

Sophie looked doubtful. 'A round British Indian face isn't much to work with . . .' she said.

Sam nodded. 'But a terrified round British Indian face is,' he said. 'And he won't be on his own. And he'll be here in the next twenty minutes. So . . .'

'So what do we do, Sam?' said Sophie. 'If that happens. What do we do then?'

A rattling clatter from the cobbled approach to the cathedral. Sam and Sophie glanced left to the paths that ran through the old graveyard. A tall man with a dog collar, stooped and steering a suitcase with difficulty, was bustling towards the porch.

'Priest,' said Sam.

'Or dressed like a priest,' said Sophie.

They watched him negotiate his way into the porch. He paused, mopped his brow with a handkerchief. A passerby stopped and started talking to him. The passerby seemed happy to see him. The man in the dog collar put his hand on the passerby's shoulder and the passerby dropped his head as if in prayer.

'OK, priest,' said Sophie. 'Let's talk to him.'

She put a hand on the railings, pulled herself up. By the end of the priest's blessing, she was in front of him.

'Excuse me,' she said. 'Are you involved with the next service?'

Don Hardin frowned, then smiled. 'Yes, and I'm afraid I'm

late. If you don't mind, I'll need to press on.' He moved as if to pass her.

'What sort of service is it?' Sophie forced a smile. An innocent enquiry.

'One of forgiveness, peace and reconciliation,' said Hardin, patiently. 'There are many such services here, as I'm sure you know. But today is special. We have many foreign visitors and faith leaders.' Sweat beaded on his forehead. 'So I really do need to get on. If you'll forgive me.' He sidestepped Sophie, pushed at the glass door and disappeared inside.

Sam appeared at her shoulder.

'He's doing the service,' she said. 'Peace and so on.'

They stood in the cathedral's high porch under a glass-engraved, two-metre-high Thomas à Becket. Sam and Sophie stared at each other, both agitated, both visibly anxious. Sam's eyes began darting everywhere; Sophie spun one-eighty degrees then back again. Just over Sam's shoulder, she caught sight of an elderly man approaching. Grey-haired, black-suited and wearing an ornately patterned skull cap. He walked with four other men, two on either side. They too wore skull caps, these in a plain black fabric. They walked with deliberation and solemnity, as though behind a flag. She nudged Sam and they both watched the new arrivals as they approached them. She caught the eye of the grey-haired man.

'Good morning,' he said with a slight nod of the head.

'Good morning, rabbi. Are you here for the peace service?'

'Of course.' He smiled his reply as he passed. 'Aren't you?'

He was inside before Sophie had thought of a response. 'I suppose we are,' she said to herself.

The other side of the glass, a man in grey robes was greeting visitors. Warm handshakes, pats on shoulders. Old friends.

'So, do we go in now, Sam?' she said. 'Is that what we do? Give it five minutes then catch a bus to the university?'

Sam checked his watch.

'Ten more minutes on the steps,' he said.

'Really?'

'This service seems slightly more significant than its humble billing suggests. Maybe we should have paid more attention to it.'

'OK,' said Sophie. 'Watch for ten. Inside for five.'

'Deal,' he said. 'And there's a bus in fifteen.'

They scrambled back up the steps. Resumed their watch. Sophie leant against the railing, Sam sat on a step.

79

8.45 a.m.

THEY HAD BEEN told the journey was ten minutes. Maybe fifteen if the traffic was bad and the diversions were still in force. The van was silent. There was nothing left to say. Hari sat on the floor, pressed against Kamran and Binici. Collins was opposite. If the van hit a bump in the road or braked suddenly, their feet touched. Gregor drove. The radio was off, the windows were closed.

Hari's eyes were shut, his hands clasped. He felt the hilt of his knife pressed hard into his stomach. He felt the length of Binici's knife against his thigh.

The van slowed to a stop. Hari didn't open his eyes. It would be traffic – they'd only been travelling a few minutes. His breath came in short bursts, his heart beating so hard he was sure it was visible through his T-shirt. He took a deep breath, felt his scabbed wounds stretch, his ribs push up against a restless, fidgety Binici. Maybe the man was excited. The revolution he'd longed for was here at last and he would get to play the butcher after all.

His finger traced again the raised outline of the photo in his pocket. Millie and Amara had been a surprise to him. He'd been used to life being just him, his mother and grandmother. There was a rhythm and pattern to everything. The absence of his father tackled with order and routine. His grandmother had seen to that. If she could no longer be a revolutionary in India, she could at least be a revolutionary in her own household. His father had been 'weak' and 'reactionary'. If he was ever discussed, he was usually dismissed as a class enemy.

The van was moving again.

So when two sisters appeared, Hari's world shifted dramatically. The order of the old life disappeared. As his mother and grandmother were enveloped in the twenty-four-hour-a-day struggle with the twins, Hari felt liberated. His sisters were a gift. He had held Millie first. Sitting in the hospital chair, his grandmother had passed the tightly wrapped bundle to him, barking instructions about how to hold her. A squished and frowning face stared out of the towelling. Hari smiled, Millie frowned some more. Amara had been asleep when passed to him but Hari had blown on her face to wake her up. His mother was annoyed but Hari was captivated. His last year of primary school had been his favourite. He was a brother.

High revs, second gear.

Millie was the wilder of the two, Amara the more thoughtful. Millie was the louder of the two, Amara the more wily. Millie was the singer, Amara the story teller. They dressed identically, always. Their hair was cut identically, always. If you looked hard enough, you would notice that Millie's eyes were wider and that she still frowned a lot. That Amara's shoulders were slightly rounded and her front teeth were larger and slightly irregular. But most people were just happy to declare that they could never tell one from the other. And then that they were the most beautiful princesses they had ever seen. Hari was happy to agree.

Low revs, fourth gear. Moving faster now.

In Hari's secondary school, his sisters were better known than he was. Hari was just the boy with twin sisters. It was, he had decided, what some people thought was the most interesting thing about him and he didn't care. On a school open day, his grandmother had brought Millie and Amara along with her. Hari had shown them round, Millie holding on to one hand, Amara the other. He'd felt like a king. On the day before he left for university, they both had brought him some torn clothes to be repaired. Millie's elephant T-shirt and Amara's jeans both, miraculously, needed some of his fabled needlework skills at the same time. He had worked, they had watched transfixed, as though he was performing some mystical spell, using an ancient long-lost skill. He had handed back the patched-up clothes and received a fierce, prolonged double-hug for his labours.

Stationary traffic, engine idling.

He left the photo where Amal had put it. Removing it now would serve no purpose. He knew every millimetre of its surface. Millie on the left, Amara on the right. Frown, shoulders.

Slowing. Stopping. Reversing. Parking.

'Three minutes,' said Gregor.

Hari opened his eyes, peered through the darkened rear window. Ahead, through a piazza, the steps to the cathedral. The old on the left, the new to the right. Mounted on the cathedral wall was a huge bronze sculpture. It showed a triumphant, three-metre-tall angel, wings unfurled, a large spear in his hand. At his feet, a humbled, chained, supine devil. Good versus evil. Good triumphing over evil. A religious fantasy.

He watched a rabbi enter the cathedral. Hari started to shake. Binici placed a hand firmly on Hari's leg.

'Breathe,' he whispered.

Hari heard a powerful car pull alongside. He saw Gregor glance at it briefly, then look away. Doors slammed. Children's voices.

Voices he recognized.

80

8.55 a.m.

SAM AND SOPHIE saw them at the same time. Sam reached for Sophie's arm before he realized they were watching the same thing. From the car park in the piazza, just beyond the fountains, a girl, no more than twelve, was walking at a funeral pace. She was apparently on her own, her arms stuck to her sides. Oblivious to anything that was happening around her. She had long, shoulder-length black hair, brown skin, and was wearing a pink T-shirt and denim shorts. A few metres behind her walked an identical girl. Same hair, T-shirt and shorts.

'Twins!' said Sam. 'It's them. It has to be!'

Sam and Sophie stood up from the steps, then immediately sat down again. They peered beyond the girls, eyes searching the piazza.

'There,' said Sophie without pointing. A sharp intake of breath. 'Sweet Jesus.'

A grey-haired woman in a black and gold sari, wearing gold wire-frame glasses, with a squat, round-shouldered man in a suit and dark glasses. The man was only a few centimetres behind the woman. His arm appeared to be pressed against her back. They too walked slowly, as though all four were linked together.

'Amal Hussain,' whispered Sophie. 'Without question. Shit.'

'And the girls' grandmother,' said Sam. 'With a knife at her back. Or something.'

The first girl had reached the foot of the piazza steps. Her posture was ramrod-straight, walking as though she had a book on her head. She was chewing her bottom lip. As she reached the middle steps, her sister reached the foot. Hussain and their grandmother were a few metres further back.

Sophie scrambled behind Sam.

'Might he recognize you?' he said.

A pause. 'Definitely.'

Sam sat taller.

'They'll be inside in sixty seconds,' whispered Sophie.

Sam was hitting keys on his phone, found what he was looking for. 'It's a terrible camera,' he said, 'but it's a camera.' He pointed his phone at the two girls, then Hussain and the grandmother. A heavy, old-fashioned shutter noise came from the phone. 'Jesus,' he muttered, then, to Sophie, 'Text Famie, I'll call the police.'

Sam hunched down, covered his mouth with a hand. 'Police,' he said. A pause, then, 'My name is Sam Carter. I'm a journalist at IPS.' His tone was businesslike, urgent, hushed. 'I'm on the steps outside Coventry Cathedral and I'm sure I'm looking at Amal Hussain. Wanted for the May attacks in London. He appears to have hostages including two girls. We think there's an attack planned.' Another pause. 'Yes, I can still see him, he's getting closer. Walking up the steps.'

Sophie texted Famie, then glanced between the two girls. There was no doubt now: Hari's twin sisters were in front of her. The first was level with her, the second near the middle step. Eyes down, they both seemed to be talking to themselves. No one paid them any attention. At the entrance, the first girl glanced around. Seeing her sister close behind, she walked straight into the cathedral.

'No, this is not a hoax,' said Sam. 'I'm Sam Carter, IPS. International Press Service. Just get your people here.' He hung up.

The second girl, clearly distressed, stumbled slightly at the top, before regaining her balance. Step by careful step, she followed her sister inside. Now ten metres behind them, Hussain and the grandmother shuffled closer. The old woman looked straight ahead, Hussain, like some dutiful bodyguard on the move, looked everywhere. Into the cathedral, through the porch.

Up the stairs.

'Looking straight at us,' said Sam in the direction of his shoes. 'Stay small, Sophe.'

Sophie pushed herself tighter into Sam's back. She texted Famie again. Sam sent Famie the photos.

Hussain and the grandmother stopped outside the entrance. Keeping a firm hand on her shoulder, he took one more look around. Short, jerky movements of his head that took in all angles. Apparently satisfied, he steered the woman inside.

'All clear,' said Sam.

Sophie uncoiled. 'So what's it to be?' she said. She didn't need to explain.

'The official advice is "run, hide and tell",' he said, 'but I've already done the telling.'

'You want to run and hide?' she said.

'Yes, actually,' said Sam.

'But you're not going to, are you?'

He turned to look at her. 'Of course I'm not. But you are. Hussain knows you. You can't go in there.'

Sophie gave Sam a brief smile. 'Not arguing.' She kissed

him on the cheek. 'Let's hope the coppers are fast. Take care. Hussain is a psycho.'

'Agreed,' he said. 'I'll come with you now, make sure you're safe. But then I need to come back here.'

Sam scrambled to his feet, started to climb down the steps. Sophie stood too. Hussain had stopped just the other side of the glass, the folds of the woman's sari twisted tightly in his fingers. Sam hesitated. Hussain glanced round.

81

8.57 a.m.

HUNTER'S BMW HIT the Kenilworth Road to the university and topped ninety. Espie drove, Charlie behind her, Hunter the front passenger, Famie behind her. Hunter was on her radio, Espie on hers. Two separate, shouted conversations, a howler siren. Hunter identifying herself as a Met officer, Espie talking to Control.

Famie felt her phone vibrate, pulled it from her pocket. She read the text twice. 'Oh sweet Jesus,' she said. She handed the phone to Hunter. 'It's from Sophie Arnold. It's happening right now and we're heading to the wrong place!'

Hunter read the text out loud: 'Amal Hussain is here with twins and grandmother. Coventry Cathedral steps from car park. Sending photos.'

Hunter turned to Espie but she'd started the manoeuvre already. 'Hold on!' she shouted.

A brief, stabbed brake, then a screeched U-turn across both carriageways. Famie leant into Charlie. Charlie pushed back against her door. Tyres spinning, the tail end of the BMW swung into the cycle lane, then straightened as Espie floored it. Hunter was yelling into her radio, Famie rang Sophie. Who didn't pick up. It rang without answerphone and Famie hung up. Texted.

Get out of there now.

Hunter's BMW topped one hundred but it still didn't seem fast enough. Famie sat forward, willing the miles away. If Amal Hussain was in the cathedral, Hari and the others must be there already. Or on their way. And the twins and the grandmother must be hostages.

Famie spoke to the car, her head between Espie and Hunter. 'Hussain might not know that Sophie is pregnant with Seth's child. But if he does, Sophie is in serious danger. It's clear that for Hussain, this is personal. Whatever else is going on, his "honour" or some bollocks like that has been offended. He'll target her, I'm sure of it.'

'Send me those photos,' said Hunter.

Famie Bluetoothed them.

'Got it.'

Two photos. The first showed the crowd under the cathedral's high porch. The twins were tiny figures, almost lost in the hubbub and the architecture. She enlarged the image but the quality wasn't good enough to see much detail. Two brown-skinned girls in pink was all she got. In the second, the camera had swung right, to the pillars at the top of the cathedral steps. Hussain and the grandmother were framed between the sandstone columns. She enlarged again, filling her screen with Hussain's face.

'That's him. And it's enough,' she said. 'Even if it's only him, we need the ARVs. And the Level Ones. If Amal Hussain is in the cathedral, we need everyone we can get.' She forwarded the photos, got back on the radio.

'Am I still under arrest?' said Famie.

'Technically,' said Hunter.

'What does that mean?'

They flew past the station, braking hard at the ring road roundabout, then dipping and accelerating straight on towards the old city.

'I have effectively told my boss to shove it,' said Hunter. 'Back at the hotel. DC Milne said to take you in. I said we needed to get to the protest at the university first. Then I'd take you in.'

'He never liked me, did he?' said Famie.

'He did not, and does not,' said Hunter. 'An unreliable, hysterical fantasist is the gist of it.'

'What a bastard.'

They took two more red lights then a roundabout without dropping below sixty. The seatbelt locking mechanisms were working hard.

'If Hussain has come from the car park by the steps,' shouted Espie, 'we need to be on the other side.' She waved with her left hand. 'The Slug and Lettuce side. The Cuckoo Lane side. He might have men there too of course. We need to evacuate the whole bloody area.'

'No time,' said Hunter. 'And really no time for the Level Ones to get here either. A ten-minute deployment time is too long. This is happening now. We need to be in there now.'

They tore through narrow, deserted streets, ignoring the one-way system. They hit the cobbles and Espie killed the siren. She parked across the lane, blocking it completely. Their lights flashed around the bricks and windows of coffee shops and high-end cafés. Curious faces peered out. A couple at an outdoor table stood up, menus in hand, as if to complain about the noise. Espie was out of the car already, popped the boot. Hunter spun in her seat.

'Is there any point in asking you to stay here?' she said, her head flicking between Famie and Charlie.

'None at all,' said Famie. 'Even if I am under arrest. Technically.'

Espie threw a heavy jacket at Hunter and they ran from the car. Famie and Charlie fell in behind them.

'Lockdown around the cathedral,' said Hunter into her radio. She held the microphone tight to her mouth. 'Nothing out or in.'

Famie felt Charlie tug at her sleeve. She looked drawn, haggard. Charlie shook her head. Famie understood, indicated a pizza restaurant they'd just passed. Lights on, door open.

'Wait in there.'

She squeezed her daughter's arm, let go. Charlie pulled up, waved them on. Famie glanced back once. She lip-read her daughter perfectly: 'Just get the fuckers,' she said.

The three women ran till they reached the graveyard of the old cathedral, vaulted the low wall and crashed against the spire's ornate wooden doors. Famie had seen glimpses of the old spire from a mile out, reckoned it to be a hundred metres high at least. She wasn't sure being at its foot made her safer or a target. Back flat to the door, she was under a bevelled sandstone arch. Five rows of slabbing led to the grassy graveyard, a few ancient tombs preserved under the trees.

Espie caught her breath. 'The ruins of the old cathedral are the other side of this.' She jerked a thumb over her shoulder. 'The steps the photos were taken from are on the left, about fifty metres along from here. They lead to the new cathedral. Via that covered area with the columns. Where the girls were.'

Hunter took over, speaking fast. 'Procedure here is clear. We wait for the armed response teams to arrive. I'm told they're three minutes away. We don't have three minutes.' To Espie she said, 'So show me.'

Espie ran right, looping through an old Gothic arch, into the ruins – an open shell of old walls, chapels and empty windows. The three women ran tight up against the bricks, heads low, sidestepping statues and wandering tourists. Through the spaces where the old stained-glass windows had been, Famie could see that they were approaching the new cathedral. They were running parallel with the path that led to the columns and the etched glass.

Oh my God, Hari, stay safe.

The steps Sophie and Sam had been on when they took the photos were just ahead, beyond one more broken, restored, weathered, centuries-old column. The shadows were good to them, swallowing their figures in the massive gloom cast by the sandstone.

Espie stopped, listened to her radio. 'ARVs are two minutes away, sirens off. Orders are to wait.'

'We're not waiting,' said Hunter, and eased her way around the corner.

She recoiled immediately, startled eyes, bloodless lips. Famie saw the fear and shock, then, from below, heard running footsteps. Heavy, percussive, echoing around the ruins. Hunter slid to the ground, reached for her radio.

'This is DC Hunter in the old cathedral. Looking at . . .'

'Saint Michael's Avenue,' said Espie.

'Saint Michael's Avenue.'

Famie's stomach lurched. She retreated a few steps, peered through a small space where a holy window had once stood. She was just in time to see a crowd of men pushing, jostling their way through the glass door.

'Six maybe seven men are approaching from the car park.'

'Eight,' Famie called.

Hunter made the correction.

One of the men – green T-shirt, tattooed arms – reached for the back of his waistband. He pulled out what looked like a piece of black tubing. He pressed a button. A steel blade snapped into position. Famie gasped.

'I suspect these are the men from Boxer Street.' Hunter's words were coming in short, staccato bursts. 'And maybe the May twenty-two attacks also.'

The men were now inside the cathedral and, momentarily, lined up by the glass wall. Famie scanned what she could see. Six white skins, two brown. One was tall and sinewy, the other shorter, maybe rounder. Spiky black hair. Powerful arms held at his side.

Hari.

And he too held a knife.

82

9.08 a.m.

HARI, BREATHING HARD, put himself at the end of the line. He wasn't sure why. He pressed back against the glass wall, an engraved angel at his shoulder. The screen felt cool, the cathedral cooler. A young woman at the book stall looked up, frowned, looked away. Standing with her, a tall white-haired man in ecclesiastical grey robes studied the arrivals. His gaze was steady. He shifted his balance as he eyed the line. Hari thought the man sensed trouble. Damn right there's trouble. He held his knife at his side. If you've got a panic button, now would be good. The white-haired man flinched, steadied himself on a shelf. Didn't move.

Hari had never been in a cathedral – he'd had an opt-out from all RE lessons and expeditions – but he scanned this one, fast. It was a vast, open space. An aircraft hangar of a building. At first glance it appeared almost empty of adornment, the space dominated by a tennis court-sized tapestry. Hung behind the altar, floor to ceiling, it showed Christ sitting, dressed in white vestments, hands held up in benediction. A gold aura surrounded him, various winged figures

Hari didn't recognize attended to him. Everything else was a rich green. The white, green and gold shimmered down the length of the nave. Light seemed to pour from its zigzag walls, angling the sun on to the tapestry, like spotlights at a theatre.

Hari felt filthy and exposed.

A priest had started the service. He was dressed in robes of rich blues and reds, his arms held wide in welcome. From behind the altar – a raised platform with a bus-length slab of concrete on top – he addressed his congregation. Worshippers. Targets. Victims. About two hundred of them, Hari guessed, seated in neat rows on wooden chairs. A modest crowd, he thought, disappearing among the tapered pillars, the massive candlesticks and the thorn-like canopies above the choir stalls.

He had heard his sisters' voices. They were here, brought by that bastard Hussain. If he shouted for them, they would come. Hussain would kill them first of course. But they were close. As he studied each row, seat by seat, he gripped the handle of the Böhler even tighter.

Hari spotted the rabbi he had seen earlier, seated next to a bearded man in a blue kurta. An imam presumably. Other clergy wore vestments, robes or dog collars. A round man with a gold chain around his neck was studying his phone. Millie. Amara. Hussain. All here somewhere. How was it possible to hide in such a small crowd? How could he protect them if he didn't know where they were? He sensed Kamran next to him getting impatient. Hari didn't know what they were waiting for.

The priest was still talking. His head was down, he appeared to be reading. 'So, since the terrible attacks on this city in 1940, working for tolerance, forgiveness and understanding has been at the heart of everything that happens here.' His voice was strong, carried through the cathedral by discreet pillar-mounted loudspeakers. 'This month is the anniversary of the Allies taking formal control of Germany in June 1945. The Berlin Declaration brought peace and reconstruction.'

Hari glanced left. The citizens were restless, agitated.

The priest looked up, smiled. 'Today we welcome our American and German friends. Our Jewish and Muslim friends. Together we declare our resolute commitment to each other, and our communities.'

Then, in a priestly silence, a tiny cough. And Hari had them. Second pillar from the front. The other side of the second pillar from the front. It was a wheezy cough, an asthmatic cough. It was Amara's cough, and it was all he could do not to sprint the length of the nave and grab them both. He tapped the knife against his leg, wiped his face with his T-shirt. A five-second sprint. That was all it would take. He stared at the pillar, leant left and right to try and catch a glimpse. Confirmation came from half of Hussain's face as he peered slowly around the upright, inspecting the line. He was checking on Hari. Hari was checking on him.

It was also the cue. The waiting was over. Binici crouched, tied his laces, bounced back up. There was the muffled rattle of Böhler knives extending. The white-haired man at the book stall found a phone. Gregor started walking down the line, instructing, pointing. Each of them had a target. He leant in to Hari.

'The man in the blue suit, front row. He's the American. He's next to the Jew. Both would be good.'

Hari nodded.

Binici moved first. He walked straight down the centre of the nave, following a line of sand-coloured marble, crossed with stripes of obsidian black. Each stripe was a stride, thirty strides to the altar. Hari stepped forward a few paces. The others, like sprinters waiting on the gun, agitated, bounced and muttered. But they stayed against the glass wall.

Now was the moment. There were fractions of seconds in play and Hari needed every one of them. He matched Binici's steps, cutting right behind the fifth pillar. The bookseller and the white-haired man were crouched behind the bookshelves. They looked up, then quickly looked at the floor.

And straight ahead, he saw them. Thirty metres and three pillars away, Millie and Amara sat hunched, holding hands. Backs to Hari. They wore their pink ASOS tops. They had only cost Hari ten pounds, but they loved them like they were spun from gold thread.

The priest was speaking, reading from a book, his voice amplified by small speakers on each of the pillars. It was a prayer.

'All have sinned and fallen short of the glory of God.'

His head was down, Binici was at the choir stalls. Hari was at the fourth pillar.

'The hatred which divides nation from nation . . .'

Binici was at the altar rail. Hari had reached the third pillar.

'The covetous desires of people and nations . . .'

Some in the congregation shifted uneasily, eyes narrowing. Troubled faces. This was wrong.

Binici stepped up to the altar. Don Hardin looked up, startled. He managed another line. 'Our envy of the happiness of others—' Then he broke away. His firm 'Can I help you?' was heard by all. The few in the congregation who had their heads bowed, looked up.

Hari edged his way along the east side, past a kaleidoscopic wall of stained glass and a boulder-like font, framed in colour. He stopped a few metres from the twins, praying they wouldn't turn round. That, for these few seconds at least, they would be too scared to move. He stepped into one of the narrow spaces created by the angles of the zigzag walls. A floor-to-ceiling, green-to-gold window cast a shadow which no one saw. From here Hari could watch Binici, the priest and his sisters.

At the altar, Binici said nothing, Hardin said nothing. Between them, a cross of nails. Silence in the cathedral. Millie and Amara huddled closer. He saw Binici say his words. They were lost to the microphone, but Hari could guess what they were. He held his breath.

The cat toyed with the bird a few seconds more, then Binici lunged, stabbing Hardin under his ribs. The priest's shocked, agonized inhalation played across the cathedral's speakers. Screams from the congregation, many of whom stood. As the priest staggered back, Binici caught him, held him with one hand, stabbed his jugular with the other. The backward flourish of the knife threw blood in an arc across the tapestry, Christ's feet and vestments now stained crimson.

There was a brief, shocked silence, followed by scattered, guttural howls. Then came the scraping, the pushing back of a hundred chairs, and Hari lurched forward. For this moment only, the advantage was his.

He rounded the pillar.

He ignored his sisters.

He pushed his grandmother out of the way.

He stabbed Amal Hussain in the neck.

83

EVERYTHING HAPPENED AT ONCE.

Horror. Joy. Terror. Hussain fell against the pillar, his knife clattering to the marble. One hand clawed at the concrete, the other his neck. Deep-red arterial blood seeped between his fingers. Hari kicked his feet away and he slid to the floor.

'Guess what,' said Hari in his ear. 'It *was* a trick.'

Hari assumed Hussain's ferocious stare represented rage and humiliation but he didn't ask. And Hussain couldn't speak anyway.

His grandmother had scrambled into a crouch where she put arms around her girls. One under each. They looked from Hari to Hussain and back, their gaze unsure where it was safe to rest. The looks of anguish, confusion and surprise played on repeat. Hari dropped to his knees, threw his arms around all three. His head clear, his mind racing, he barely registered the familiar smells of Pears soap and strawberry shampoo. He hadn't known what he was going to do, didn't have a plan. But since the glass wall line-up, it had all seemed clear. The real danger was now. If the other citizens saw what he had done, he wouldn't make it outside. And neither would his family. Somewhere at the back of his thinking he was aware that he'd probably killed a man. But a man who had said he'd kill his sisters. Now, a new clock was ticking.

'Stay close, Nana, stay close, girls. I'll get us out.'

Their terrified faces held a thousand questions, but they asked none of them. Three swift nods.

The cathedral rang with screams. A man and a woman on the front row took a few steps forward to help the stricken priest but were pulled back by others. Their sleeves were tugged back with frantic gestures. The priest was dead, his killer wiping the knife on his vestments. So they turned and joined the surge for the exit. Those in the middle of the rows began pushing those on either side to move faster. Some tried to clamber over the chairs, forcing themselves forward. Most fell on top of the people already there, a few fell into gaps. A young woman in a denim skirt shrieked as a flailing man in a bright yellow T-shirt collapsed on top of her, both of them crashing to the ground. A snapping and splintering sound. Wood or bone, it was impossible to tell. The man hauled himself up, the woman curled, arms held over her head, expecting to be crushed. An elderly man with medals pinned to his blazer stooped to help her up but she didn't respond.

As the crowd surged towards the glass wall, they were confronted with six citizens, arms wide, knives held like swords. The back two rows of the congregation realized the danger first, pushing back against the advancing front rows. The middle rows were crushed. A reddening man in a khaki shirt, head high in the scrum, battered and pushed the shoulders of the man in front, trying to relieve the pressure on his chest. Pushed forwards and backwards, many more lost their footing.

The screams and shouts, magnified by the cathedral's cavernous walls, reached a new intensity. They all knew now there was a killer behind them and six more in front. On what had become the front line, the mayor, white-faced, had stepped in front of his wife, lifting his chair as a shield against the advancing Kamran. He made a few stabbing gestures with it, like a lion-tamer keeping his beast at bay. But his grip was weak. Kamran kicked the chair from his grasp, hauled him closer by his chain of office, then drove the Böhler into his heart. The mayor fell. Collins took his wife.

The front line stepped back again, regardless of who or what was behind them. Hands and shoulders were grabbed. Shouts of 'Jesus help us'. Gregor, grinning broadly, slashed at a tall blonde woman. She leant back, pivoting fast. The cut across her chest wasn't deep but her white blouse flooded red. Before he could follow up, Gregor was floored, crashing to the ground. The white-haired man in the grey robes from the book stall had rugby-tackled Gregor at speed, then followed up with a flurry of punches to his face and neck, the knife spinning away under the chairs. Red Head stepped over, stabbed the cleric three times in the back, then hauled him away. Gregor scrambled to his feet, a nod of thanks to his rescuer.

The old man's gesture of defiance ignited a fire in some. The American in the blue suit had fought his way to the front of the line. He wore a Stars and Stripes badge in his lapel, held a one-metre brass candlestick in his hand. It had a broad base, an elegant stem and a sharp metal point for securing a candle. He swung hard at Gregor on the forehand, then at Red Head on the return. Both men stepped back then rushed him. The American had to choose: the terrorist who had been tackled by the cleric or the one that had killed him. He managed a savage upward thrust at Red Head, piercing him behind his jawbone, fixing his tongue to the roof of his mouth, before Gregor stuck his Böhler in the American's gut.

The citizens advanced towards the altar, attacking anyone

they found in front of them. Each had their given targets but, in the melee, execution had become an imprecise science. The congregation now broke into three sections; one group of worshippers spilled left, another right. Small groups gathered fleetingly behind each pillar, judging distances, reaching, clasping. As the citizens passed, ones and twos peeled away, sprinting and stumbling for the glass wall and the exit. The third group had to retreat. Faced with four advancing attackers, they walked backwards into the choir stalls. The rabbi, his helpers and the man in the blue kurta were all in this group. Some shouted at their attackers, some cried, most were silent. Gauging the odds, glancing at the flanks, watching the others escape.

Hari hadn't moved. One arm around his grandmother, the other around his sisters, they held on to the column like a ship's mast in a storm. He had told them to pray. Their heads were down, his nana was singing quietly. He watched the advancing citizens, and if he leant left, he could watch the posturing Binici. He glanced at Amal Hussain, bleeding out. Gone soon.

There were no rules. Binici had his butcher's shop and, as he was closest, he worried Hari the most. As soon as he left the altar and walked forward to the choir stalls, he would see the dying Hussain. Second pillar on the left. Just by the little Indian family. The clock was ticking. He looked to the exit, to the glass wall and the now empty steps beyond. An empty thoroughfare. No one moving. Lockdown. Maybe the police were nearby. Maybe they weren't. He would assume nothing, he would do everything himself if he needed to.

From one of the middle rows, two men and a woman, suits and dungaree shorts, had reached the column in front of Hari. They looked at him, he waved them out. They crawled their way along the aisle. Past the font. Past the kaleidoscope window. Past the book stall. At the last column they dropped flat and moved, commando-style, along the polished marble to the door. They reached it together. They scrambled through. They turned left to the steps and the triumphant angel.

'We can do that,' Hari said.

He leant left. Binici wasn't there.

'OK, get up,' he said. Millie looked up a fraction of a second before Amara. Hari managed a smile. 'We're going to walk out. Stay close.' She nodded. The sisters helped their grandmother to her feet.

The old woman took Hari's hand. Hers were trembling. 'Take the girls, Hari. I'm too slow.' Her voice barely a whisper.

Hari shook his head. 'We're walking out, Nana. You're CPI-M. Remember? You're coming with us.'

He saw some steel return to his grandmother's eyes. She squeezed his hand, then suddenly pulled it hard. Her eyes, magnified by her glasses, were bright circles of fear.

'That man,' she managed.

Hari spun round. Binici had run round the back of the altar and choir stalls. To the east wall. Where he caught sight of Hussain, then Hari, then the girls. Where he changed course. Knife in hand. He pointed it at Hari, his face twisted.

'So you're the fascist!' he yelled. He marched closer. 'Traitor and fascist!' His strides got longer. Each step fuelled his rage.

Hari pushed the girls and his grandmother behind him, reversing into the pillar. The girls were backs to the concrete, his grandmother was back to the girls, Hari was back to his grandmother. He held his knife in both hands. A knife with Hussain's blood on it. He said nothing. He hoped that dying or dead Hussain, three metres away and lying in his own lake of blood, would speak for him. Give Binici a reason to hesitate. It seemed to work. Binici stared at a glassy-eyed Hussain then turned his head to Hari. His countenance changed again. He lowered his knife.

'I should kill you for this,' he said. 'Gut you like a pig. But, actually?' He looked again between Hussain and Hari, then nodded slowly, as though impressed by his own reasoning. 'The boy who killed Amal Hussain? He will have a haunted, terrified and terrible life. So many will want to kill him. There will not be a moment of peace.' He gestured with his knife. 'For him, or his family.'

Hari felt his grandmother shaking behind him.

Saw shadows at the glass wall.

84

FAMIE WATCHED FROM the ruins. Hunter and Espie, backs against the cathedral wall, had hesitated. Probably, guessed Famie, at Espie's suggestion. A few centimetres from the door, they had stopped, their sharply defined shadows falling just shy of the glass wall. Armed response was surely no more than sixty seconds away. There were heavy door slams coming from everywhere, the sounds bouncing around the walls making it impossible to judge numbers or direction. All they had to do was wait. But inside, the screaming continued, and when the glass door crashed open and three people escaped, Famie saw Hunter say some words to Espie. Espie nodded. They went in.

Famie had promised she'd not follow Hunter inside. Both women had known she wouldn't keep her word. As soon as Hunter threw the glass door open, Famie ran to the top of the steps where Sophie and Sam had been. Jumped down four and crouched.

'Armed police! Armed police!' Hunter and Espie's voices rang out together. Full-throttle, urgent, commanding. Even from outside, up on the steps, theirs were two voices echoing sharply above the fury. They weren't armed of course, Famie knew that. They had tasers and cuffs, not Heckler & Koch MP5s. But they were disrupters. They would change the story. Famie wondered if she'd met braver women in her life.

Three more terrified escapees ran out. Two had head wounds, the other bled from the thigh. They too ran down the angel steps. Famie wondered if she should direct them some other way – the terrorists had all arrived from there, maybe there were more lying in wait. But what did she know? And why should they trust a stranger outside, when so many were killing inside? She kept quiet.

Hunter and Espie stepped out of Famie's eye-line and she inched down to the bottom step. The repeated shouts of 'Armed police!' seemed to have encouraged those near enough or fast enough to make for the door. Four more now, running, almost tripping. They ran past Famie.

'How many injured?' she called after them. They ignored her. Kept running.

Inside, the screams continued. Through the open door she saw three men run towards Hunter and Espie. Both women crouched, fired their tasers. Famie heard the rattle, saw two men fall. The third slowed, dipped, picked up one of the dropped Böhlers. A knife now in each hand, he held his arms wide and advanced on the officers.

From her left, the old graveyard side, Famie at last heard the boots. Heavy steps. Running fast. Three men, black caps, body armour, submachine guns held at the ready. They pulled up just short of the glass wall. They saw Famie together, swung their guns together. She raised her hands, and spoke fast.

'Famie Madden from IPS! Two officers just went in. They're under attack. Eight men, all with knives, didn't see any guns. I'll back off.' She stood and ran up the steps.

When she was at the top, she turned. The police were inside. Advancing as a unit, guns raised, more shouts, then they stepped out of her view. A single shot, then two more. Staccato, metallic thuds magnified into small explosions by the extravagant proportions of concrete. More escapees. Sirens. Cars arriving fast now. Three police vans screeched into the car park, two Range Rovers behind. Three more armed officers sprinted to the cathedral door. They took a beat outside the glass door, then ducked inside. More shots.

Famie followed. As she knew she would.

Inside was chaos. Smoky, acrid chaos. Hunter was down, stomach wound, Espie cradling her. Shouting in her radio. The tasered men had been shot in the head. Knocked-over chairs, bodies sprawled over and under them. Famie counted five. Some moving and crying, others silent. The first armed police group edged their way along the right-hand pillars, the second pushed from the left. Fallen orders of service served as stepping stones through the blood.

Beyond the chairs, in front of the choir stalls, the congregation. Corralled. Cowering. Retreating behind the knifemen, who were retreating behind the police. And above them all, a huge tapestry of Christ, now with an arc of blood splatter.

Where are you, Hari?

85

AT THE FIRST police shout, Binici had flinched, ducked. A final look to Hari. 'This is your doing,' he snarled.

'I hope so,' said Hari.

Binici ran towards the glass wall; Kamran joined him, to his left, Teeth to his right. Two officers, one black, plainclothes, the other white and uniformed, had run to the centre of the nave, lit by the blues and greens of the kaleidoscope window. Seeing the onrushing knifemen, they crouched, then pointed yellow tasers.

Hari's heart sank. That's not armed, he thought. That's pretending to be armed.

The two officers jerked their weapons between the assailants but the gap between them kept closing.

Is that all you have?

The black officer fired first, quickly followed by her uniformed white colleague. The electrodes hit. Kamran and Teeth fell, Binici lunged. The black officer took a knife to her side and fell, the white officer smashed her baton on to Binici's arm.

She was moving in for a second strike when a man pulled Hari away from the pillar, grabbing his shoulders. The man in the kurta. Fifty, maybe older. Shaved head, light brown skin, a trimmed, short white beard. Pained eyes. He stepped back, wary of the Böhler. He took in the twins, the old woman and the dead man.

'Who are you with?' he said. A hoarse, urgent whisper.

'I'm with my family,' said Hari. 'And I'm with you.'

Another look at the girls. The despairing eyes of the old woman. 'Then come with me. All of you.' And he ran, looping back around the choir stalls.

Hari stuck the knife in his belt, grabbed his grandmother's hand, then Millie's. Amara took her grandmother's other hand. One more look at Binici fighting the white policewoman and they followed the man in the kurta. They dropped a step. They were beyond the altar, at the foot of the tapestry. A small chapel had been constructed behind three-metre-high black steel bars. Another altar, lower, smaller, more humble. Twenty chairs and piles of kneelers. A bronze statue of Mary. A sign in a wooden frame that said 'Lady Chapel'. A small gate to allow access. And behind the bars, at least fifty terrified, silent souls.

Those that could, sat or lay on the floor. Standing, you could look over the high altar, through the nave and out to the glass wall and steps. See and be seen. Sitting, you saw bars. You disappeared.

Three women instantly recognized Hari. Pointing. Stage whispers. 'He's one of them! Keep him out!' They pushed back from the bars. 'He still has a knife!'

Hari raised his hands. 'I came with them, but I am not with them. I am here to protect my family.'

The man in the kurta pushed the gate open, ushered them all inside, then turned a large brass key. 'He killed one of them. Maybe he can protect us.'

'Or maybe he'll kill us all!' said a woman, her voice straining.

'I am with you!' Hari urged again. Then, to a sceptical-looking couple in his path, 'You must believe me!'

They held on to each other, kept their distance as well as they could.

The rabbi and his helpers were there, sitting on the embroidered cushions, praying. Around them, agitated men and women listened. Any silence managed to be both encouraging and ominous. Cries and crashes were all greeted with fear and flinching. Others were on phones, whispering teary messages. One of the women who had hissed at Hari was now saying goodbye on hers. All of them looked at him with troubled, fearful faces. Millie, Amara and the old woman were pushed straight to the back. Here the tapestry reached the floor, its thick weave in blocks of green and yellow, divided by a crucified Christ in greys and blacks. There was a small gap between tapestry wall and the altar. They sat with their backs to the tapestry, their feet against the concrete altar.

Hari glanced at the bars. They were wider at the base, tapering to an elegant, flattened top. Decorative certainly but strong. Bolted together. A surprising sanctuary. They were climbable but the assailants, when they came, would have to work together. He knew Kamran and Teeth were down, Hussain obviously, Binici possibly. They all knew he had a Böhler. Maybe they wouldn't bother with these people in their cage.

He found the man in the kurta. 'Thank you,' he said. 'When we're out of here, I'll tell you what happened.'

The man almost smiled. 'One day then,' he said.

There were shots. Deafening in the confined space.

Not a taser, thought Hari. Not this time. Come and get us.

But the running steps and shouted instructions that followed did not belong to the police. Hari gripped the knife again, stepped back from the bars. He knew he should drop to the floor or hide behind the altar but for a crazy second he thought it cowardly, and then it was too late. The voice he recognized was Gregor's, and seconds later he and Collins ran in front of the bars. They pulled up fast, saw Hari immediately. Gregor looked momentarily confused but Collins got it straight away. Her eyes narrowed, her blood-splattered face turned predatory.

'So it was you,' she said.

Hari couldn't hear what she said next over the rolling accumulation of echoing gunfire and shouting, but he didn't need to. Collins leapt for the bars, hauled her way to the top in seconds. The tapering gave her all the space she needed to squeeze through and she dropped into the cage. She landed legs apart, balanced, glowering. She pulled her Böhler from the back of her waistband and grabbed the nearest body to her, backing against the bars. Collins now held her knife against the neck of a freckled girl in a jumpsuit.

'I want your knife and then I want you, Hari Roy,' said Collins. 'You fucking traitorous piece of shit.'

86

THE SECOND POLICE unit hesitated between the west-side fourth and third pillars, Famie hung on to the fifth. She was close, but not so close they'd turn on her. In a war zone, accidents happened. She'd seen it before. The MP5s were aimed at the altar and choir stalls, occasionally snapping to new positions. The acoustics of the cathedral were confusing. Echo and reverberation hampered any ability to locate the source of any sound. A cry, a shout or a crash – any sudden noise – could appear to be coming from three places at once.

Also, Famie thought, how do they know who to protect and who to kill? If you had a knife, you were guilty, but there was nothing to stop the attackers dropping or hiding their weapons, then running for it. Joining the congregational exodus. Three gun barrels tracked a long line of escapers bolting for the door, a few running hunched and low to the ground, the rest just running for freedom. They couldn't see any active attackers, neither could the police. At the glass wall, more police hustled them away, frantic arms waving them to safety.

When they were out, the guns tracked back to the front. Espie still cradled Hunter.

Famie tried to count. She'd seen eight attackers, including Hari. So make that seven. Plus Hussain. Eight then. She could only see two dead, plus another one taken out. Five to find? She'd seen maybe a hundred of the congregation escape which still left many unaccounted for. Another eighty, possibly more.

To her left, there were a few steps to a small chapel. Circular, intricate flooring. More stained glass, more chairs. A sign said 'Chapel of Unity'. She wasn't good on cathedral architecture but that might be the answer to the missing congregants. Or hostages, as she should think of them. Eighty or so missing hostages, maybe five terrorists with knives, six police with guns. It was a question of who would find who first.

Espie appeared at her side, pointed at the chapel. 'Same thought as you. It's empty. Been watching since we came in.'

Famie nodded at the prone Hunter, her head now propped up, Espie's uniform jacket tied tightly around her midriff. 'Will she be OK?'

'Think so. But the medics will need to get to her soon, she's lost a lot of blood. We tasered two but the third got to her.'

The armed unit was moving again, this time with a sudden burst of speed. Famie and Espie followed. Now they saw it. Movement behind the altar, a head turning behind bars. Bars that she hadn't noticed before. She had seen the tapestry, the high altar, the cross and the candlesticks. The bars she had missed, their vertical lines blending with the markings and design of the weavers.

Outside there were sirens, a multitude of them, closing fast. Inside, just shoe leather on marble. Rapid, short steps. The two police units were coordinating now, the three men on the east side mirroring the movements of those on the west. Pillar to pillar.

This felt to Famie like it would be the end of things. She had been there at the beginning of this story, she needed to be at its conclusion. When the police unit turned behind the last pillar and swivelled right, Famie followed.

87

IN THE CHAPEL, Collins held the jumpsuit girl with one arm, the knife with the other. Back to the bars. Outside the chapel, Gregor, on watch, head tracking from side to side.

'Everyone kneel,' ordered Collins.

Everyone but Hari knelt. There wasn't room. Some crouched. Collins didn't notice.

'First your knife,' she said. 'One hand only.'

Hari held up his left hand, took the knife from his waistband with his right. He held it up, his eyes only on Collins.

'Quickly. To the bars, hand it to Gregor.' She pushed the knife against jumpsuit girl's neck, its tip snagging her skin. 'You know I will, Hari, don't you,' she said. 'And after her, I'm sure I'd find your little sisters in here somewhere.'

Hari flinched in spite of himself.

Collins grinned. 'Thought so. Get a move on.'

He stepped to the bars, held the knife for Gregor to take. He felt it being snatched from his fingers, heard Gregor say 'You're so fucked', and stepped back.

'Let him in,' said Collins, nodding at the gate. 'Open it. Do it now.'

Hari hesitated and Collins pushed the Böhler in again. A small cut. Only a nick but it bled, and it was enough.

'OK! OK! I'm doing it.' Hari's voice was raised.

Around him, his fellow captives pushed back, scrambling on their knees. Someone took the small cross of nails from the altar, began reciting the Lord's prayer.

He stepped to the gate. Reached for the key. Gregor bouncing on his feet. 'You're so fucked, Indian boy,' he said, his face deformed with a grotesque expectation.

Hari turned the key.

Stepped away.

Gregor raised both hands, a knife in each.

Stepped forward.

Three 9×19 Parabellum bullets took the top of his head off.

In the chapel, the percussive force of the shots was traumatic. Everyone yelled or screamed. Gregor's body disappeared. Collins released the girl, dropped to the floor, forced her way to the small altar. Hari, wedged between the hissing woman and one of the rabbi's helpers, felt metal pushed into his hand. He recognized the feel immediately. The rivets, the steel bolster, textured handle. Someone in the chapel had given him a Böhler knife. He didn't have time to see who it was. Collins was heading for Millie and Amara. As she said she would.

He knew he couldn't stand. He had a knife. The police wouldn't hesitate. Hari squirmed round one-eighty degrees, then dived between the terrified hostages, clawing his way to the altar step. Knife in his right hand, he hooked the fingers of his left around the altar corner and gripped hard. He dragged himself to the narrow space between the altar and the tapestry. The safe space. Behind him at the bars, six voices yelled in a chaotic chorus of warning: 'Armed police! Stay down! Armed police! No one move!'

Hari would stay down, but he had one more move. Collins was stretched out in front of him, reaching for Amara, her hands in the girl's hair. With all his remaining strength, Hari drove the Böhler through the back of Collins' knee. The blade sliced her hamstring, quadriceps and cartilage, the force of the blow detaching her tibia and shattering her knee-cap. As she convulsed in pain, Hari threw himself on top of her. Collins had passed out almost instantaneously, lay motionless beneath him. Her knife at Millie's feet. She kicked it to Hari.

From no more than three metres away, a clear command, shouted into the chapel: 'Everyone behind the altar stand up. No one else move. If you are behind the altar, stand slowly. Arms high where we can see them.'

Hari was now a brown-skinned man with two blood-ied knives at the scene of a terrorist attack. Six armed police officers who could easily take his head off the way they had Gregor's were three metres away. His sisters looked at him.

'Don't stand, Hari!' whispered Amara. Pleading. 'They'll shoot you too!'

Everyone behind the altar was moving now. They scram-bled to their feet using the altar table to support them, then raised their hands. Some glanced back down at Hari as they stood. His grandmother stood. The girls stood.

Hari was the only one left.

'You behind the altar! Stand! Now! Arms high!' The police-man's voice was piercing enough to reverberate around the cathedral.

Hunched against the cold concrete, kneeling on Collins' insensible shoulders, he heard the police repositioning them-selves along the bars. He placed both knives heavily on the altar. One on top of the other, out of Collins' reach.

'High! Put them high!'

Millie and Amara started to cry.

Hari raised his hands. He had saved his sisters. He had saved his grandmother. He didn't really care what happened next.

88

WHAT FAMIE SAW as she rounded the last pillar and approached the Lady Chapel was this: all six armed police officers side-on to the bars, their MP5s pointing through the gaps. A man lying face up at their feet, his frontal bone crushed, the top right quarter of his head missing. A chapel with ornamental bars, crammed with terrified hostages all with their arms raised. And in the middle of a small, concrete altar, hands above his head, a round-faced man of Indian heritage. Short black hair. Blood-soaked shirt. Blood-splattered arms. Twin girls at his side.

Hari Roy.

This time, she did shout.

'His name is Hari Roy, twenty-six Boxer Street, Coventry, and he's a journalist!'

Hari stared at Famie. His mouth dropped open, then he shut it again. Pressed his lips together. If his arms weren't held so high, he'd have wiped the tears that rolled down his face.

Espie called out too. 'PC Jean Espie. Roy was undercover. He's safe!' She pulled Famie back. They'd done their work.

The police, realizing the gate to the chapel wasn't locked, pushed it open. One by one the hostages were waved out. The rabbi, his helpers, the hissing woman, the man in the kurta, the phone-callers, the twins, the grandmother and the jump-suit girl, a handkerchief held to her neck. One by one they filed past Famie and Espie, then hurried from the cathedral past a score of heavily armed, newly arrived police. Hari and the still-prone Collins were last. Six police guns still pointed at his head.

'There's a woman here, she needs a medic,' said Hari. 'I put a knife in her knee.'

The commands from the police were still urgent, shouted. The operation was ongoing. 'Walk slowly. Arms up. Come towards the gate.' The barrels of the MP5s followed him all the way. 'Smaller steps,' demanded the officer nearest the gate, then 'stop', when Hari was a metre away. 'Espie,' he called. 'And the other woman.' He beckoned them over.

Espie led. Famie walked past the first three officers – still feet apart, still one hand supporting the gun just forward of the trigger guard, still fingers curled around the trigger. She stood in front of the gate. She smiled at Hari, and he, slowly, reluctantly, smiled back.

'Hi,' she mouthed.

'Hi,' he mouthed back.

The officer glanced at Famie. 'I'm Sergeant Tom Winstanley. Did you say you were IPS back there?'

'Yes.' There seemed no point in complicating matters with her recent retirement.

'So talk to me,' he said. 'You've got twenty seconds.' He lowered his weapon.

'I don't know everything,' said Famie. She took a beat to condense her thoughts. She spoke fast. She spoke only to Sergeant Winstanley. The first witness for the defence. 'All I know is that Hari was undercover, hired by IPS. He's a student at Warwick. That was his twin sisters and grandmother next to him. The woman who hired him was killed in the May twenty-two attacks. I think today was the May twenty-two gang with local extras. He contacted me, tried to tell me what was happening. There'd be a lot more dead without him. That's it in a nutshell.'

Winstanley nodded. 'Understood.'

'Can I speak?' said Hari.

'No,' said Winstanley.

'That's Amal Hussain,' Hari said anyway. He pointed at the east-side first pillar, and the sprawled man, face down in a pool of blood.

Famie recoiled, hands in front of her mouth.

'He was about to kill my sisters.' Hari's voice trailed off.

'You killed Amal Hussain?' she said.

Hari nodded, his eyes locked on Famie's. 'You'd have done the same,' he said. 'I know it.'

Winstanley to his officers: 'Stand down.' The MP5s all lowered. To Hari: 'Hands down. Step out. But don't go anywhere.'

Hari walked from the chapel. Famie embraced him briefly. She with both hands, he with one.

'You're a brave man, Hari,' she said.

'But too many died,' he said.

His voice was weak and he slumped against her. Famie eased him to the floor. He leant back against the bars, closed his eyes.

'We'll get you to hospital,' she said, and leant against the bars next to him.

'I never thought this would happen, Famie Madden,' he whispered, his words sticky in his mouth.

'I doubted it too, Hari Roy,' she said. 'We need to talk. When they've sorted you out.'

He nodded, eyes still closed.

Famie pulled herself up. Armed police were searching the building. Small pockets of bewildered people were emerging from side rooms. The 'empty' Chapel of Unity had actually hidden at least ten of the congregation. Others had played dead under chairs and now scrambled for the door.

Espie reappeared, Sam Carter in her wake, his IPS press ID swinging very obviously from his neck. He was white-faced and shaking, eyes everywhere. Famie walked over to meet him.

'Is Charlie OK? Where's Sophie?'

'They're fine, Famie,' he said. 'Charlie's OK, Sophie's OK. In the pizza place back on Cuckoo Lane. I was there too, but in the end . . .' His eyes filled. 'Jesus, Famie, it's good to see you. We heard the shooting, saw the ambulances and, well . . . Charlie was going crazy – as you would if your mother was in extreme danger. Hunter was being taken to an ambulance but she and Espie here got me in.' He looked up. 'So that's Hari Roy. Is he OK?'

'He's OK,' said Famie, 'and he killed Amal Hussain too. That's him over by the pillar.'

And suddenly Famie stopped. 'Wait,' she said, holding on to Sam's arm.

'Wait for what?' said Sam.

Famie was counting. Lines. Attackers. Bodies. Then the faces of 22 May.

'Hari can't leave,' she said.

'What?'

'Hari can't leave,' she said again.

And from somewhere in the cathedral, echoing, reverberating and difficult to place, the sound of a mobile phone ringing. Could be coming from anywhere.

89

THE RINGING STOPPED. Winstanley was with Hari, helping him to his feet. Famie ran over.

'Wait, wait. Shut the doors. Hari can't leave.'

The sergeant didn't look up. 'He's leaving now. He needs to be in hospital. Two of my men will go with him. He's safe.'

Famie stepped closer. 'No, he's not,' she said. 'And I can tell you why. Give me another twenty seconds.'

Winstanley looked up now. 'OK. Go. You've got twenty.'

She took a deep breath. She hoped her thinking was sound. 'How many attackers have you got? Dead or accounted for?'

'We have seven. Six dead, one in cuffs. Hari here makes it eight.'

'That's wrong,' she said.

'I was told eight came in. That was from DC Hunter's call.'

'And from my counting,' said Famie. 'But Hussain arrived separately. With the twins and the grandmother. So that's nine.'

'Nine is right,' said Hari.

'So,' said Famie. 'Talk fast, Hari. Who were you investigating?'

'I was recruited by Mary Lawson to go undercover with a small cell of far-left revolutionaries. Radicalized by jihadists but secular. They were planning extreme violence. They think Britain is ready for revolution. They're totally off-grid. No emails, websites or messaging. May twenty-two was part of it. This is – was – part of it.'

'So if one of them has escaped, Hari's role will be exposed and he and his family are right back in danger. You need all nine. Hari can't leave until then.'

Winstanley got it. 'Come on,' he said to Hari. 'We got 'em all lined up. Tell us who we haven't got.' He beckoned a colleague who came running. 'No one in or out till I say.' The man nodded, ran off.

Somewhere a phone rang again. Six rings and stopped.

Hari, Famie, Sam and Winstanley walked to the font under the kaleidoscope window. Six bodies. Hari walked the line. He identified Hussain, Teeth, Kamran, Binici, Gregor and Red Head. All dead. A cuffed and sedated Collins was on a stretcher with medics who were keen to leave. So that left Tattoos.

'The guy who isn't here is heavily tattooed,' said Hari. 'Six two. Muscular, white. Didn't speak much. I'd guess eastern European. Fast. Dangerous. Best I can do, sorry.'

Winstanley nodded. 'It'll do.' He reached for his radio, snapped out the orders. Within seconds, a line of police ran in front of the glass wall. The cathedral was sealed.

The mobile phone again, closer now. Winstanley was annoyed. 'Whose bloody phone is that?' he snapped. The sound was still bouncing around but it was obvious to Famie now that it was just metres away.

Hari, closer to the bodies, pointed at one. 'It's here,' he called. 'It's Gregor's.'

All the bodies were lying in spectacular pools of light. The kaleidoscope window was throwing its blues and greens directly on to the dead. Gregory's three-quarters head had turned a vivid mauve. Winstanley crouched in front of Gregor. He felt in the dead man's trouser pocket. Combat-style, single button. Winstanley opened the pocket, removed the vibrating phone.

The screen identified the caller with the letter 'I'. Winstanley hit the green button, then speaker. Stood back. Famie, Hari and Sam stepped closer. Sam crouched. The phone's speaker hummed with life and background noise. The caller was waiting for the receiver to speak. The phone waited for the cathedral. The cathedral waited for the phone. Winstanley, Hari, Famie and Sam all stared at it. Eventually some words. Echoey, spoken at distance into a speakerphone.

'You need to tell me what's happening. It's on the wires.'

Famie got it in a second. Then Sam's horrified expression confirmed the evidence of her own ears. Famie blanched, hands in front of her mouth.

'Well?' said the voice.

Sam stepped forward, ended the call. He stared at Famie. 'Holy fuck,' he said.

'I take it you know the voice,' said Winstanley.

Famie swallowed twice. 'That,' she said, 'was Andrew Lewis. The IPS bureau chief.'

90

THE TATTOOED MAN was Tomas Beres, a thirty-one-year-old former policeman from Miskolc, Hungary. When he had been dismissed from the service for excessive violence, his brother Gregor had recruited him to the Hungarian Workers Party. He was a willing convert, convinced his country had been captured by capitalism and Jews, then destroyed by the recession, capitalism and Jews. The Beres brothers had campaigned briefly to push the party to a more revolutionary stance but, quickly disillusioned, had quit both the party and the country. Gregor and Tomas had drifted around the fringes of European far-left politics, occasionally taking jobs as hired muscle. A succession of robberies, then the assassination of a troublesome Catholic, centre-right mayor in Poland, brought them to the attention of Russia's FSB. There was some work, they were told, that it was better for Russia to stay out of. They had stayed as their low-rent hitmen and agitators for eighteen months before meeting Amal Hussain. They had no truck with Islamist terror groups, repulsed by their religiosity and grandstanding, but they were still impressed by their methods and their commitment. When Hussain told them he had work in England, the brothers made themselves available.

Hussain was their recruiter but he had made Gregor the contact for the FSB. Hussain had made it clear to them that he had no dealings with technology. It was, he explained, what had kept him safe and what would keep them safe. He had put together a team. He had promised revolutionary, sectarian work, and 22 May had been precisely that. The brothers had loved it and wanted more. The country had been convulsed by what they had achieved. Money and resources were available. They were in it for part two.

But Coventry had gone wrong almost from the start and now his brother was dead. He had been told to get the rabbi but he never got close. He had seen Hussain slump to the floor, then, distracted, had only stuck two. When the police arrived, so much earlier than they should have, he was working his way to the front fighting an idiot woman who had slashed his hand with scissors. He had stuck her in the end but was too late to help repulse the black woman with her taser. Soon after that, the attack was over. When the shots were fired, he'd played dead, falling near toppled and broken chairs. A discarded jacket, draped over his shoulders, had covered his tattoos. He'd waited for his moment, listening to the chaos around him. He had heard much. In spite of the crazy tattooing of ETB, Hari Roy had been a traitor after all. He had been communicating with a journalist. And now that journalist's daughter was in a pizza restaurant a hundred metres away. A pizza restaurant they had driven past in the van. Triple windows, a picture of a dancing chilli in the middle. He would go there.

Newly acquired jacket over his shoulders and knife stashed carefully in its newly ripped lining, he had rushed from the cathedral with some of the last of the escaping congregation.

They had been herded down the steps, past the angel and devil statue and towards a fleet of ambulances. Their back doors were open, crews ready. Flashing blue lights strobed the piazza. Beres took a proffered bottle of water, waited for his moment, then slid between the ambulances.

He took a hard right along a paved path which looped back past the ruins of the old cathedral. Three retractable yellow-striped bollards had failed to retract, so police and fire trucks were backed up along the path, their lights also flashing. Beres walked fast, hitting the cobblestones within a minute. The sign said Bayley Lane. It rose steeply past the ruined nave on his right, and was lined with some sagging Tudor buildings on his left. Beres kept left. He needed a speed that said he was happy to be moving away from chaos but not so fast that he looked suspicious.

The air filled with sirens. When six uniformed police officers ran in from a side street, he slowed, leant against one of the locked, ancient doors. Like he was taking a breather. Each of them stared as they passed, only the last peeled away, prompting his partner to join him. A few glances back from the others and they were gone. Beres let his hand drift to the lining of his jacket.

'You need to be out of here, now,' said the first to stop.

Beres stood up straight. 'I am sorry,' he said. 'I am lost.' Heavy accent, sing-song phrasing.

The policeman pointed at the street they'd just emerged from. 'Hay Lane. Turn left into it, don't stop till you're out of it. Go. Now.'

Beres mumbled his thanks.

He walked as fast as the police would expect. He could act like a tourist if he needed to, he'd done it many times before. But now he ignored the Gothic tower, the historic graveyard and the quaint pubs; he had been given his orders. The approaching sign, black letters on white enamel, said 'Hay

Lane'. He turned left. Cobbled street and cobbled pavements. More sandstone, more leaning Tudor beams. High-end cafés, tables and chairs in the street. Linen, white towels, perfume. And at the end, the grey sign with the red chilli. The pizza restaurant.

Behind Beres, the sudden appearance of blue and white police tape, rolled out by two policewomen. It stretched across Hay Lane. The cordon was up. He had just made it in time. The pizza restaurant was less than a minute away. A few curious shoppers drifted to the tape to see what was happening. Beres stepped out of their way, head down. Conciliatory. Respectful. Humble. He put his right hand into his jacket, found the Böhler's handle and gripped it. He winced as the cut in his hand from the idiot woman's scissors opened again. He gripped it tighter.

At the first of the pizza restaurant's windows, Beres stopped, peered in. Neat rows of circular stone tables were set out in a tidy rectangle. Only one had two women together. They were both white, both had curly hair, the younger's wilder, less cared for. The older one had her hands resting on her stomach. He looked from one to the other, then shrugged. The other tables contained four customers in total. Three sat together near the door, one sat near the open kitchen. Four chefs, three waiters.

He walked to the door, pulled out the knife, stepped inside. Sophie looked up immediately. Saw the knife. She stood up and screamed at him. Charlie stood too. Beres ran at them. The two women began tipping tables in his path as they retreated towards the kitchen. Stone, metal, cutlery, crockery and glass all hurtled to the floor in great waves of noise. The other customers stood, the waiters and chefs froze. Charlie hurled a Coke bottle which hit Beres on the ear, then a pizza cutter which missed. Sophie picked up a knife, handed another one to Charlie. They stood a metre apart, crouched, arms out. Furious.

Beres hesitated.

'Call the police!' yelled Sophie.

'Then grab a knife!' pleaded Charlie. 'This is one of the fuckers from May twenty-two!'

The three who were sitting by the door bolted. Disappeared up Hay Street. The lone diner ran into the open kitchen. Beres switched knife hands, stepped closer. Sophie landed a tall glass on his head, lip-side first. The shower of shards left a trail of tiny lacerations down both sides of his face. A few dropped into his open mouth and he spat, the force of the expulsion cutting into his upper lip. Still he advanced, still they retreated. As they passed the open kitchen, a sinewy woman with a chef's cap caught Sophie's eye. She held up a steaming saucepan. Sophie nodded.

It was clear to all that the man had miscalculated. The man seemed to sense it too. An enraged Beres launched himself at Charlie, knife high. She ducked the knife but the force of him knocked her to the floor. She twisted and rolled, locking her legs around his feet. Lying on her side, she snapped her legs up. Fast and high, calf to thigh. Beres tottered, grabbing a table for balance. Sophie lunged. Her knife wasn't sharp, its serrated edge dulled by months of continual use, but the strength of her attack, the ferocity of her strike, forced it through the tightly packed bones and muscles of his left hand. The capitate bone splintered, tendons severed. Sophie jumped back as he lashed out, the Böhler's flailing tip finding her temple. It cut from hairline to cheek bone. Losing her balance, tripping over iron table legs, she tumbled to the floor. Crabbed her way backwards. Beres staggered forward.

The sinewy chef appeared next to Charlie. The steaming saucepan had become a steaming two-litre jug and she handed it over. Charlie had less than a second to balance. Some water slopped over her hand, but she ignored the burn. As Beres shaped to strike, Charlie hurled the boiling water. It caught Beres side on. Neck, jaw, cheek, nose, eye, forehead and scalp. He pirouetted one-eighty degrees and dropped the knife, hands held to his rapidly reddening and peeling face.

Two tables landed on his legs.

A waiter locked the door.

91

5.20 p.m.

BRITISH POLICE REPORT FATALITIES IN SUSPECTED TERRORIST ATTACK IN CATHEDRAL

THE HOSPITAL, PROMPTED by Winstanley, had provided Channing Hunter with a private room. It had the unshiftable hospital smell of other people's sickness mixed with bleach. A framed picture of a summer meadow hung opposite the door, a small oval mirror above the metal headboard. Five refectory-style plastic chairs had been arranged in a horseshoe around the foot of the bed. Famie sat with Charlie, then Sam, a patched-up Sophie and Hari. The DC, in hospital gown, was propped up with pillows, monitors and a drip on one side, Jean Espie on the other.

'Status update,' said Espie. 'She's lost a lot of blood and her doctors are very unhappy we're here at all. So if there's any way this can be brief, they'd appreciate it.'

Hunter raised her right hand, the one without the tubes attached. 'I'm not a basket case yet,' she said. Her voice was reedy and weak but she forced a smile. 'I'll be fine. And anyway, this meeting isn't happening. It's unofficial. You're just friends wishing me well. Remember that.'

Sam took charge. 'So one part of the shit storm is over, the other starts now. We don't know how many cells there are. We know London, we know Coventry. We know nothing else unless Hari can help.'

Hari shook his head. 'Can't help. Sorry. I never knew much about the London cell till they turned up. Coventry was it for me. Might be others, might be none.'

'What did Mary say when she pitched all this to you?' Famie asked.

Hari frowned, recalling. 'She only contacted me because I'd contacted her. This is a year back, pretty much. I was desperately keen to be a proper journalist. I wrote to loads of reporters I liked. No one replied. Then, out of the blue, Mary got in touch. Actually rang me. Said she'd kept me on file, and now she had a job. And an offer. She said that there was an organization involved in revolutionary activity. That there was a cell in Coventry and she wanted me to infiltrate it. Report back to her. I wondered about other cells but May twenty-two was the first proof that they existed. No other contacts, as far as I know.'

Famie leant in. She placed a hand on Hunter's bed frame. 'Did Andrew Lewis come up at any time? In any context?'

'No,' said Hari. 'I knew his name because I knew about IPS. Mary never mentioned him. But when Hussain turned up, he was obsessed with finding a traitor. Maybe Lewis suspected Mary had hired someone. Binici saved me, to be honest. Said he'd already killed the traitor.'

'The guy found at Boxer Street,' said Famie.

Hari nodded. Spoke quietly. 'Zak BJ,' he said. 'I need to tell you more about him. When we're done with this. But Hussain mentioned someone called Toby Howells who they'd executed after they found him sending messages to Mary Lawson.'

Sam hung his head, Sophie blanched. 'Jesus Christ,' she muttered.

'And, by the way, it was the same guy who killed Howells and Lawson. Name of Kamran. Came from Karachi originally.'

'Saw him in the church,' said Famie. 'Bullet in the head?'

'Bullet in the head,' confirmed Hari.

'Fair,' said Charlie.

Sam's turn again. 'So why was Lewis on that phone? Why is he calling Gregor? If anyone has an innocent explanation, please shout it now.'

A few seconds of silence.

'Occam's razor,' said Hari. 'Simplest solution wins. The one with the fewest assumptions. I don't know this guy. But if he's on the phone to Gregor, wanting updates, either it wasn't him and you identified the wrong person, or Lewis runs the cells. No other options.'

Famie nodded. 'Hari's right, isn't he?' Her voice was exhausted, dredging the words up from somewhere. 'No other options.'

'And you're sure it was him?' said Sophie.

Famie nodded again. 'I am.'

'Me too,' said Sam.

Hunter shifted slowly under her blankets. 'So this is where it gets tricky. And I'm assuming all of this is off the record.'

Nods around the horseshoe.

'DC Milne is my superior. One of the investigators on this case at the Met. He's knocking around the hospital somewhere. He told me to ignore Famie's theories. Said they were "the ravings of a menopausal lunatic".'

'To be fair, he's not wrong on that,' said Charlie.

'Actually, agreed,' said Famie.

Brief laughter in the room.

'Which explains the total lack of interest from the police,' Famie added. 'With the notable exception of DC Hunter here.'

Hunter nodded her acknowledgement.

'But my theories are right,' Famie continued, 'and it means we're the only ones who know about Lewis. What do we do with it?'

Hunter deflected. 'So what did Lewis hear back when he called? Anything?'

'Nothing,' said Sam. 'No one spoke. I cut the line.'

'So he knows someone heard him,' said Hunter. 'And the official statement out there is that all the cell are dead or in custody.'

'So he knows he's in trouble,' said Sam. 'At the very least. Which makes Hari's position tricky again.'

Hari laughed. A brief, humourless outburst. 'And makes Andrew Lewis a traitor. Yes?'

Reluctant nods from all in the room.

'And makes your boss complicit,' said Sophie to Hunter. 'Or an arse.'

'Or both,' said Hunter.

Charlie raised a hand. 'I don't know Andrew Lewis like you guys do,' she said, 'but this makes no sense. Your top man. In charge. Journalism is his life. Why would he have anything to do with killing journalists? Sounds crazy.'

'Same old reasons,' said Sam. 'Always the same. Money, sex, power, religion. Maybe all four, maybe just one or two. Who knows.'

'I think we can discount religion in Andrew's case,' said Famie. 'I really don't see him as an undercover Islamist. But the others?' She looked sceptical. 'I mean, he's worked everywhere. China, the States, Japan. You name it. Last foreign posting I think was Chechnya. Which would finish anyone off. Desk job and management beckoned. He seemed OK with it.'

'But all of this is academic,' said Sam. 'If Lewis is behind this, it's over to you, DC Hunter.'

'Channing, please.'

'OK, Channing. But you, or someone, needs to act fast. Hari needs protection. His family need protection. And Lewis needs taking down.'

Hunter closed her eyes. Took a breath. 'OK, well, like I said, this is tricky. But I'll be off work for a few weeks with this.' She tapped her left side. 'I'll have to go high. I can get you protection, Hari. Pass it off as press harassment or something. It'll do for now.'

Sophie fished a small card from her bag. 'And this might do after that,' she said. 'Picked it up when the Assistant Commissioner called.' She placed it at the foot of Hunter's bed. 'It's got an email and a phone number. High enough?'

92

Friday, 15 June, 10.55 a.m.

BRITISH POLICE SAY SIX DEAD IN CATHEDRAL ATTACK, INCLUDING PRIEST, WITH A DOZEN MORE SAID TO BE CRITICALLY INJURED

POLICE CONFIRM TERROR INCIDENT LINKED TO MAY 22 ATTACKS – STATEMENT

FAMIE ARRIVED FIRST, headphones on. Sophie and Sam arrived together, left her alone. They knew how this worked. When her music finished, she'd be back. Until then, they could whistle.

They all stood in the Peterson-IPS marbled entrance lobby without speaking. Their silence said it all. Famie was nervous. She glanced at the television screens above the reception desk out of habit, took no notice of the news show that was running. She realized she hadn't even checked the huge scrolling news ticker outside. It was a different time.

She took off her headphones, hugged Sophie then Sam. 'Ready?' she said.

'We just need to get this over,' said Sophie.

Eleven o'clock. It was time. On cue, the main entrance door spun round and the Metropolitan Police Assistant Commissioner stepped through. She was followed by two armed officers, carbines held ready. Left hand on the barrel, right index finger curled around the trigger. Then came DC Hunter, leaning on crutches having swiftly discharged herself from the hospital, and two senior plainclothes officers from the West Midlands force. The Assistant Commissioner nodded at Famie as she passed, leading the way up the polished staircase. Famie, Sam and Sophie followed at a respectful distance. No one spoke. Everything had already been said.

Four floors to climb. Their small group made a big noise. Hard leather and hard rubber-soled shoes clicked and squeaked on the marble.

As she climbed the stairs, Famie thought of Tommi Dara. How they had, all of them, reported on 22 May. The terrible rush-hour deaths and images. The growing realization they were reporting the murder of their colleagues. The row of empty desks next to her. And Seth. Sweet, loving, unfaithful, catastrophically abusive Seth Hussain. One Bastard Prick Womanizer to beat them all. She touched Sophie's hand as they reached the fourth-floor landing. Same thoughts, she guessed. With added baby.

Into the newsroom. Cavernous, quietly buzzing. A room lit by neon and screen. Two hundred stories being written and all of them about to be forgotten. The Assistant Commissioner strode down the lines of desks, reporters standing in a wave as she passed. Famie spotted Jane Hilton moving in for a better view. Ghosting towards the story. She tried to ask the AC a question but it fell on deaf ears. Famie smiled as she drew level, leant in. 'Shocked and devastated,' she said. 'Interview me later.' She didn't wait for a response.

Ahead, the glass office of the bureau chief. Andrew Lewis

was at his desk. Computer screen, bowl of mints. His head was down, typing. Someone tapped on his door and he looked up. Famie leant left to catch everything now. She saw smiles for the Assistant Commissioner. Puzzlement and worry for the armed officers and Hunter. Then Lewis saw her. Understanding began to flower. A quick glance to Sam and Sophie, then back to her. And Famie saw a quiet look of horror pass across his face. A career-ending, life-changing, family-destroying horror.

Guilty as fuck.

Lewis rose and stood behind his desk, one hand holding his chair for support. The AC opened his door, left it wide. The armed police stayed outside, Hunter and the West Midlands officers followed the Assistant Commissioner inside. Famie stood in the doorway, Sophie and Sam at her shoulder. Behind them, a whole newsroom listened.

'Assistant Commissioner?' began Lewis. That was all he managed.

The AC read from a card. She spoke loudly, her audience stretched all the way back to the stairs. There were a lot of names. 'Andrew Lewis. I am arresting you for the murder of Mary Lawson, Seth Hussain, Harry Thomas, Sarah Thompson, Brian Hall, Sathnam Stanley, Anita Cross, Tommi Dara, the Reverend Don Hardin, John Carney, Arnold Hall, Gill Gallagher, Tobias Smith and Paul Shilling. For carrying out acts of terror, and for attempted murder. And for being in the pay of a foreign country. You do not have to say anything, but it may harm your defence if you do not mention, when questioned, something which you later rely on in court. Anything you do say may be given in evidence. Do you understand?'

Famie thought she would remember each word, every name. It was only a very short time since she had been accused of some of those murders. In the twenty-four hours since Coventry, she had learnt from Hunter that the inquiry was focusing on Lewis's reporting in Chechnya, the possibility of faked stories and his subsequent recruitment by the FSB. The arrest was possibly premature but they feared his disappearance. His defection. It had to be now.

Lewis stayed standing, eyes glassy, unfocused. Said nothing. When the Assistant Commissioner was finished, she nodded at one of her officers. The ratchet and snap of her handcuffs played loud in the room. She steered Lewis to the door. He looked at the path that had opened in front of him. The route to the lifts was now lined on both sides by shocked, disbelieving staff. The line between the UK and City desks, one he had trod a million times before, had just become a gauntlet he had to run.

The AC went first, then Lewis. She set the pace. It was conspicuously slower than her arrival and just the right speed for every journalist present to eyeball their departing, traitorous bureau chief.

93

9 p.m.

LONDON POLICE ARREST INTERNATIONAL PRESS SERVICE BUREAU CHIEF

POLICE CONFIRM SUSPECT HELD IN WAKE OF UK TERROR ATTACKS

LONDON, June 15 (IPS) – London Police said arrest of IPS bureau chief Andrew Lewis was in connection with their enquiries into the British capital's May 22 attacks and Thursday's murders in Coventry.

Six people were killed and twelve seriously wounded in Coventry Cathedral, England.

After the pub, after the toasts to their departed friends, Famie cabbed it home. The driver recognized her, waived the fare. As soon as he drove away, she heard some of Max Richter's music playing. She smiled. Charlie might not get her music taste but she tolerated some of the newer composers. The slow repetition of the ambient piano drifting from the flat was a sign that her daughter was home and had probably sorted food. Something she needed badly.

'Chinese and Thai,' called Charlie as Famie hauled herself up the stairs.

'All of it,' she said.

'And a guest,' said Charlie.

'Oh God, no guests,' said Famie. 'I hate fucking guests.'

Laughter from the kitchen. 'You'll like this one.'

The food had arrived with Hari. Plastic containers of rice, green and red curry, shrimp soup, spring rolls and crispy duck filled the kitchen table. Pinot Grigio had been poured into tumblers. Famie embraced Charlie then Hari. She ate two spring rolls before speaking.

'I think I might cry,' she said.

Famie did cry. Afterwards, relief and alcohol worked their way through her self-control. She wanted to talk, they wanted to listen. Wanted to hear every extraordinary, speculative, prejudicial word that she had to offer.

'They couldn't tell me all the details in the debrief earlier, but they think he was turned in Grozny,' she said. 'That Lewis filed fabricated reports about a massacre in 2003. It made his name but turns out he just made figures and quotes up. The Russians got to him first. He became their agent. Paid to undermine the UK. All of his work is being re-examined.'

Charlie and Hari wanted her to keep talking. They let her eat. They kept silent. They served more duck.

'Lewis hired Amal Hussain to run his cells. He was up for some mercenary work. The timing was perfect. He had discovered that his brother had been shagging his wife and nanny. As well as half of IPS. So he killed Seth himself. On that zebra crossing. That knife was his. While we all obsessed over Islamic terrorism, it was good old-fashioned fratricide. Family honour and all that shit. Once it was clear I'd been one of Seth's partners, he came after me. Us.' She waggled the fork between her and Charlie. 'It was, they think, probably Amal who ordered the attack in Exeter, then the one that would have been on me, here. A moral crusade, you see. If he'd found Sophie in Coventry, he'd have killed her and her baby too. Niece or nephew. Whatever.' She raised a glass to Hari. 'Here's to justifiable homicide,' she said.

Hari sipped, stayed quiet.

'The money thing, Seth's borrowing, was probably a red herring. Seems he was a gambling addict who was just shit with money.' Famie shook her head. Disbelieving still. 'Two totally separate lives. And I only saw the compassionate journalist side. What an idiot.'

Her shoulders slumped, her fork held mid-air. A silence. Charlie was about to ask a question when Famie started up again.

'Having set up the cells, he then set about exposing them. The whole point was to undermine the UK. Make it look stupid and weak.'

'Like we need help with that,' said Hari.

Famie acknowledged the point with her fork. 'So he tells Mary Lawson that he thinks there are no-tech, off-the-grid revolutionary cells working in the UK and she takes it as her next project for the Investigating team.'

The Richter playlist finished. Charlie selected some Chopin.

'So set up the chaos,' said Hari, 'then report it. So it looks like everything is totally messed up.'

'The first doubly incontinent country in Europe,' said Famie. 'Correct. They think Lewis knew about poor Toby Howells but not you, Hari. You must have been Mary's idea. Maybe she suspected Lewis by this time. Who knows? Certainly Lewis told the police not to trust me. That I was some bat-shit crazy reporter who'd lost her marbles. That's why the police did nothing and why Milne was such an insufferable prick.' Famie's grip on the fork tightened. 'And then there's Tommi,' she said, her voice quieter. 'They think his search for Toby's name on the IPS computers triggered an alert. Lewis had time to get one of his thugs on it.'

She pushed her plate away, dropped her cutlery together. 'That might be enough for now,' she said.

'And we're assuming there are just the two cells,' said Charlie. 'Otherwise Hari is most definitely not safe.'

Famie felt sleep coming up fast. 'Probably. Not sure. They think they got everyone.'

'Think?' said Hari.

'Maybe Lewis had help?' said Charlie.

'They don't think so,' said Famie.

'Think?' said Hari again.

A final drop of Pinot. 'You should stay here tonight anyway, Hari,' said Famie. 'It's not safe out there. The couch is quite comfy.'

'Charlie has already offered it,' he said. 'I hope that's OK.'

Charlie began to clear the plates.

'Oh right,' said Famie. 'Fine. I'll say goodnight then. And leave the piano tunes, it'll help me sleep.'

She closed her bedroom door, sat on the bed and listened. She held the moment while she could. She knew she was drunk, she knew she was safe. She knew Charlie was safe. And she knew it was the Nocturne No. 8 in D Major. Vladimir Ashkenazy, she thought. Delicate, exquisite playing. So many ornaments in such a short time. When it finished, she was aware that the sotto voce, through-the-wall conversation had finished too.

She wondered if she was missing something.

Acknowledgements

A few words before we go . . .

Knife Edge is dedicated to the memory of Sophie Christopher, a senior publicity manager at Transworld. She died of a pulmonary embolism in 2019 at the age of twenty-eight. Sophie was an inspirational woman, mourned and missed deeply by everyone who knew her. I read her the opening chapter of this book (it actually made her laugh, but the names of the victims have changed since then!).

The character of Famie was inspired, at least in part, by Nyta Mann, a former BBC and *New Statesman* journalist I worked with at 5 Live, described by Nick Cohen in his *Observer* obituary of her as 'spiky and arch'. She was tough, uncompromising and, to quote the BBC's Chris Mason, 'waspish, funny and super bright'. The blessing used by Reverend Don for his daughter comes from 'Beannacht: A Blessing for the New Year', part of the collection *Benedictus: A Book of Blessings* by John O'Donohue. The 'Embrace the butcher' quote is from Brecht's *The Decision* (*Die Maßnahme* in German) and referenced in Howard Brenton's *Magnificence*.

I feel I should add that Coventry Cathedral has been a centre of Christian worship and prayer for over a thousand years and has a noble tradition of working for peace and reconciliation. It was also where I received my degree from the then-chancellor Lord Scarman! You can find out more about their work from www.coventrycathedral.org.uk

Some thanks . . .

To Bill Scott-Kerr and Eloisa Clegg at Transworld. Bill is editor supreme. The Emperor. The Governor. The guru. Eloisa is the sage. The wise councillor. The author's satnav. A great team. None better.

To Sam Copeland at RCW. He tells me he's agent of the year and I'm inclined to agree. To Gordon Corera, the BBC's security correspondent, to former police commander John Sutherland, author of *Crossing The Line* and *Blue*, to author and broadcaster Anita Anand and Reuters journalist Robin Pomeroy for their expertise and advice in shaping this book. And to the unsurpassable Lee Child who shows us how it should be done.

Any mistakes are, of course, all mine.

About the Author

Simon Mayo is a writer and broadcaster. He is the presenter of the podcast *Simon Mayo's Books of the Year*, a daily host on Scala Radio and co-presenter of *Kermode and Mayo's Film Review* for the BBC. His previous books include *Mad Blood Stirring*, *Blume* and the *Itch* trilogy, filmed for TV by ABC.

Knife Edge is his debut contemporary thriller.

MAD BLOOD STIRRING

Simon Mayo

On the eve of the year 1815, the captured sailors of the Eagle arrive at Dartmoor prison; bedraggled, exhausted, sustained only by a rumour heard along the way. As Joe Hill announces the news of the end of the war, the guards bristle and the inmates stir. The powder keg was fixed to blow and Joe has just lit the fuse.

Elizabeth Shortland, the Governor's wife, looks out at the unsettled crowd. The peace means the end is near, that she needn't be here for ever. But suddenly, she cannot bear the thought of leaving.

Inspired by true events, *Mad Blood Stirring* is a story about how sometimes, in our darkest hour, it can be the most unlikely of things – or people – that see us through.

'Bristling with energy, written with passion . . . a joy to read'
John Boyne

'Fascinating . . . it has genuine energy and drive'
Sunday Times

'Well researched and full of action, Mayo brings a forgotten moment in history to life'
Sun